A SECOND SELF

ELIZABETH I, MY MOST REMARKABLE FRIEND

Lori Callan

Printed in the United States of America

First Printing, 2020

ISBN 9798604437704

Spring I – A Daughter's Loss

If there is anything good in nobility, I think it is only this: that there is a necessary condition imposed upon the noble not to fall short of the virtue of their ancestors.   --Boethius

22nd April, 1558

I hover, my head bowed, in their presence. How I wish for an end to the turmoil. Her Majesty and Sir William Cecil circle each other in the Withdrawing Chamber, tossing accusations to and fro. Their tone mimics a controlled debate. A humming monotone lulls my senses. But the content of their exchange troubles me. Each argues with a bristling intensity. Until one or the other tires and withdraws. Or more often, my Majesty's rage so fills the room, Sir Cecil finds no space for himself. And then he flees, gasping for a quiet breath.

"Do not presume me a fool, Sir William. It will be at your peril. Like my father, I see all but say nothing."

"Well then, hear me Majesty, and reply in all honesty. The entire country whispers of your attachment to Lord Dudley. There is a general alarm. Does your liking for Dudley mean you will not consider a favourable marriage?"

"Sir William, my affection for Robert says nothing about my opinion of marriage. As I…"

"But the succession, Madam…"

"Do not interrupt your Queen. As I have declared so many times before, my fondness for the wedded state is well-known. I do not like it."

"But Your Majesty, think of the realm. It requires an heir. England's security depends on it."

"The realm? I think only of the realm. Do you accuse me of placing my own interests before those of my beloved people?"

"No, Your Majesty. I beg forgiveness ..."

"Do you understand what I sacrifice for you? Do you, of all my people, not know?" Her Majesty twirls the sapphire on her pointer finger. Then she thrusts it on and off her knuckle with a ferocity I fear will lead to the chafing of her skin.

"I think not. Leave me alone, so I may contemplate my pitiable fate. A Prince's cares are never free from uncertainty. I care only for my beloved people."

"Your Majesty, if I might just..."

"Go." Her Majesty's slender fingers wave Sir William Cecil away as though he was an errant chambermaid, arrived with the wrong ointment to rub on Her Majesty's ulcerated thigh.

"Your Grace. I apologize for causing you distress ..." Sir Cecil bows as low as his middle-aged bones permit, withdrawing backward toward the Chamber door.

"Leave." Her Majesty addresses Sir Cecil. Her jaw clenched tight, she stares with the implacable force inherited from her illustrious father. Sir Cecil uprights himself, turns, and flees the Chamber, and his Queen's ire too.

***

After Sir Cecil's departure, Her Majesty glances to her left and up, behind her shoulder. She searches the life-sized Hans Holbein portrait of her father, our late King Henry VIII.

Our King remains an enigmatic father figure, gone from us, his English subjects, for over a decade now. It is 1558, and his reign is only a glorious memory for some. Our King peruses his daughter's every action from his station on history's wall. Still especially mindful of his second daughter. For it is Elizabeth who seeks to fill the enormous breach in England. A void made wider with the loss of all her dear siblings before her.

If I were to guess at our King's musings, I'd hazard a wry fatalism brings about King Henry's smirk. An unceasing certainty of his guilt. He has been punished for having carnal knowledge of his own brother's wife. Never should he have wed his devout sister-in-law, Queen Catherine of Aragon. The hefty price? God's wrath, and untold years of fruitless yearning for a male heir. Thanks be to God, King Henry did not live to witness his own Edward's death at the tender age of sixteen years. Surely this, if nothing else, would convince our King of his poor esteem in the eyes of God.

This portrait of His Highness, Holbein painted nearer the end. From the artist's aesthetic standpoint, a mature monarch surveys his legacy. King Henry personifies imperial vigour. Though his beard grows grey streaked, his stout limbs remain firm-planted, slightly apart, toes pointed out. His enormous girth, faced front with hands on his hips suggests a King who fears no opponent. This monarch relishes the challenge a confrontation provides.

He wears, with confidence, the colours of royalty – purple, gold, silver, crimson. All the shades forbidden to us of lesser fortune. And he dons his brocade waistcoat, close-fitting breeches, a mantle trimmed with ermine fur, with a surly humour.

His fingers dazzle with jewels putting a healthy-sized apricot to shame. All speaks to his position as fortress for his people. His jeweled livery collar, like his country's necessity, weighs upon the breast of a king who rejects the very notion of burden.

I wonder what fascination our new Queen finds in the gilt-framed masterpiece. What does she search for that she was forbidden to know while her father lived? Written over our youthful Queen Bess's features as she studies him is a layered tableau of emotion. Each new expression betrays the previous one: pride, respect, kinship, and dare I say? Just a little blame.

Most of her faithful subjects fail to notice a curled lip or a furrowed brow. Not a hint of disrespect crosses the features of our Queen when she casts her eye upon her father's likeness in company. Contrary to Her Grace's ambivalence, she poses by her father's portrait in the Presence Chamber at Whitehall whenever an occasion offers itself. I believe Her Majesty does it for her detractors. Many deem our monarch unfit to govern England. Some blame her weak feminine disposition, some her mother's tainted Boleyn lineage. For these enemies, Her Majesty claims her throne with her father's fierce authority at her back.

Our Queen conceals her innermost turmoil beneath voluminous layers of lace-trimmed petticoats, velvet and silk-trimmed taffeta gowns. Her blame stays buried under the weight of the diamond-shaped sapphire pendant hanging above her square neckline. Tangled ropes of pearls, wound round her neck, hide her many hurts. The trappings of her royal privilege demand her silence, prohibiting any display of filial disloyalty.

Though my Queen strives to mask womanly emotion, I know her too well. I bear unobserved witness to the stalking tirades she performs while gazing up at the beloved portrait of her father. Just days ago, Her Majesty raged. She muttered under her breath the most shocking pronouncements. She hastened to and fro in her flowing gowns, like one of her favourite mares. Galloping with such vigour, I wondered she didn't trip herself up, and send herself sprawling in a manner unbecoming a monarch. But our Queen did not fall. Her Majesty does not stumble so easily as that.

Instead, she quiets her frenzied pace. She approaches the portrait with a graceful ease, as though Henry himself stands before her. His authoritative pose elicits not a bit of apprehension in Her Majesty.

More striking yet is Her Majesty's calm demeanour as she levels her hideous accusation. Her composure more persuasive than any raging might suggest. For her words do not sound unrehearsed, or of an irrational womanly nature. Hers are the thoughts of a seasoned Prince. Our new Queen addresses His Majesty as his determined equal.

"My Dear Father. You know how much I love and honour your cherished memory. Yet, I demand the impossible from you. That you should forgive the unforgivable. Know this, Father. For my reign's legacy, I desire one thing above all…"

Her Majesty glides closer to the portrait, adopting her own threatening stance. Such an unwomanly display.

"That I, with all my feminine infirmities, and though a weak substitute for your princely example… will reverse the memory of my father. I will not choose to whisper while violence rages amongst my people. I will maintain peace at all costs, dear Sir. I will not stand by and witness their slaying by my own hand, nor by each other's. No reason shall be reason enough. I will not condone a murderous kingdom. My people will know better from me."

Is it the shortness of the breaths I draw? Or the diligence with which I tightened the straps of my bodice this morning? Perhaps the stillness I maintain in order to remain unseen? I glance up at King Henry's portrait, and I swear, he lifts an eyebrow. Our great King tilts his attention toward the wayward daughter of Anne Boleyn as if to reply: *You criticize my means? A woman ruler of England. You berate my reign? Who will supplant me? Who will do better? Mary and Edward, before you, are taken from us. And you, our little Elizabeth, will trump your own father's accomplishments? The hubris coursing through your veins might only be Tudor in its origin.*

I await the King's laughter. That which I witnessed so often while he lived. Whether he be playing at cards with Suffolk, or taunting the Parliament about his latest taxation scheme, he did roar. But as I crouch silent in my little nook, hidden from this awful familial drama, I realize King Henry's chuckle will not follow.

My Queen pauses. She shudders, as though the dampness of the room defeats her. Her Majesty only tolerates Whitehall Palace, with its cavernous galleries and formal decoration. More suited to the entertainment of royal ambassadors than the Spartan lifestyle she prefers.

Her Grace moves her accusing eye off her father's portrait. To my horror she whirls around, searching the chamber as though sensing the presence of unwelcome company. In the ponderous silence I stifle my breath. Crouching, my hands fidget. With index fingers, I tap my knees as I remain huddled behind a Turkish tapestry; a magnificent crimson and gold rendition of a lioness, frolicking with her cubs only moments after a successful hunt. I fear my Queen will notice my presence. But my dread of disclosure proves baseless. Her Majesty's cares preoccupy all her senses. I allow myself a shallow breath.

The dutiful daughter acknowledges her father. "For the privileges you so kindly bestowed I am forever in your debt, Father. I reflect upon my robust health, my strong will, and the ease with which I command intimidating opponents. They kneel in my presence with the deepest respect. I find my demeanour, though inferior to your princely wisdom, still in your image. My crown I will wear with dignity, and with a true appreciation of the privileges of kingship, until my death."

Then my Queen pauses, gathering her breath. In the silence that ensues, Her Majesty prepares for the launch of her next lethal assault. What brutal hostility she hurls at our beloved King. The tide of filial gratitude withdraws. My Queen resumes her haphazard pacing to and fro, with a wringing of her fine hands. Linking her fingers together, Her Majesty draws her clenched arms in toward her torso.

She rushes to her father's portrait, and then shies away as though she might capture and contain her unwanted message. She scrapes at the backs of her hands, causing them to grow reddened, her skin aflame with angry welts. Her Majesty punishes herself for allowing her wrath to escape.

I hesitate to dip my quill to record the condemnation my Queen offers. If any other were heard speaking of our King in this manner her head would soon be separated from her dainty shoulders. I must stifle my dismay, in the interests of duty.

"Father, I do not speak of my Boleyn blood before our people. No good will come of it, and there is no purpose. However, I do not forget my mother. My Boleyn relatives I favour well enough, with all the honest privilege I can bestow. You have left me more than any daughter dares to request. I am a Queen. And yet..." Again my new monarch hesitates, unsure. So infrequently do I witness uncertainty in my Queen, I nearly intrude on the moment with my muted gasp. Her silence grows in volume.

Her Majesty's tone, when she resumes, is subdued. The intelligent phrasing so familiar to my Queen. So eloquent in her deliberate choice of rhetoric. If only she might maintain her graceful demeanour.

"...yet you stole Her from me when I was barely known to Her, and She to me. Father, I dare not tarnish your beloved memory...but growing to womanhood motherless as I have...I fear it will have its eventual consequence." These last few accusations she hurries. They suggest a malice our Queen prefers not to acknowledge.

"I am surrounded by my ladies-in-waiting. And for all my twenty-five years, I have not experienced a lonely existence. Yet I do not know what it is to love, or to be loved by a woman of my own, except for my faithful governesses, who are required to do so by their duty. Granted, I have loved and been loved by my Lady Margaret Bryan, Kat Ashley and Blanche Parry..."

She names me. Her Majesty names me.

"...but Father. My dear Mother... unknown to me." Our Queen opts for silence once more. She tosses her head as though throwing off an unwanted bridle. Her tone adopts an unpracticed compromise.

"I consider complaint to be a distasteful scourge. Nor do I wish to express ingratitude. This is not my intent. You have proffered to me by my birth, a kingdom, a country and a people I love more than anything I shall ever know. However, I am inclined to believe this princely love will be all there is..."

Her Majesty draws away from her father's portrait, turning her head from her own unwelcome words. An ungodly quiet descends on the Presence Chamber, as though judgment will follow. What daughter confronts her cherished Father with such an accusation? I clutch my hands together in quiet protest, but dare not wring them for fear of alerting Her Majesty to my presence.

I have not overheard our Queen mention her mother's name in all the years I have served Her Grace. My service now totals twenty-three years, since she was but a toddling princess. How my Majesty laments a daughter's loss.

"I beg you will not take offense my dear, dear Father, but I fear...you have riven me from my natural feeling...and though I know my duty to my beloved people well, my ability to give of myself to another, I fear, is absent."

Unlacing her fingers, Her Majesty drops her hands to her skirts, fussing with the pleated fabric. Her curls, once a delightful sign of her youthful energy, unfurl. My Queen turns from her beloved, abused portrait and strides from the Chamber.

Her Majesty wastes no effort in searching her father's conscience. Nor does she peer close at his portrait, looking for hints of Anne Boleyn's blood on Henry's jewel-laden fingers.

No hint of regret weighs on his vast breadth. No suggestion of doubt burdens his bold stance. As unremorseful in death as he once proved while still our great English Lord. The unrepentant Father of England, France and Ireland.

***

Friday 19th May, 1536
  "Good Christian people, I am come hither to die, for according to the law, and by the law I am judged to die, and therefore I speak nothing against it. I am come hither to accuse no man, nor to speak anything of that, whereof I am accused and condemned to die, but I pray God save the king and send him long to reign over you, for a gentler nor a more merciful prince was there never: and to me he was ever a good, a gentle and sovereign lord. And if any person will meddle of my cause, I require them to judge the best. And thus I take my leave of the world and of you all, and I heartily desire you all to pray for me. O Lord have mercy on me, to God I commend my soul." --Anne Boleyn

***

"Word arrived from Court; Queen Anne appeared joyful upon her death this morning. She smiled with as gay an outlook as though she were going out to ride." Lady Margaret Bryan whispers behind Lady Constance's tilted head. She muffles her words as she glances down on the tiny Elizabeth's red-blonde curls.

"What if Queen Anne's conscience is as blameless as she has professed?" The muted question emerges from behind a cupped hand.

"To that I have no answer. Our Queen was reported to have told Lord Kingston as he led her from the Tower she had but a "little neck" for severing, and she clasped her hands around it, chuckling with excellent good nature at her own jest."

"Our King places his Queen on the block. And will wed Lady Jane Seymour tomorrow. What next, pray tell?"

"My poor little princess. No Mama's breast to weep on. No Queen to speak on her little daughter's behalf." Lady Bryan murmurs her observation as the ladies accompany Elizabeth in the fields of Hatfield Palace. The governess holds tight to Princess Elizabeth's hand, suffering with the knowledge it is she alone who will provide the little girl her maternal ease.

A three-year-old Princess Elizabeth clutches Lady Bryan's hand in return, secure in the familiarity of her entourage. Confident in her daily routine, Elizabeth wanders with her ladies on the peaceful grounds of Hatfield Palace. Daily, the ladies escort their charge, guiding her out of doors for an early stroll.

Nature's abundance claims all Elizabeth's attention. Vast heavens hover, offering a gift of nurturing ease. Tiny conies, the plentiful charcoal-coloured rabbits Elizabeth loves so much, mercifully distract her from her impending fall from grace.

The toddler marvels at the warmth of the early morning sun on her upturned face. She plunges her free hand through her auburn curls to examine whether they too absorb the sun's goodwill. Nurturing beams reach through the canopy of the ancient oak tree, dappling Elizabeth's gown with a pattern of gleaming diamonds and pearls, accented by shadowy onyx jewels.

The little girl, unaware of her mother's ill-fortune and her own change in circumstance, takes notice of, and greets with delight a family of three white-tailed deer. The animals graze on flowers resembling pristine parchment stars.

"Queen Anne pampered her precious girl so, insisting on feeding her little princess at her own breast. Imagine. A Queen forsaking her wet nurse to suckle her own babe? It's a wonder the King stood for it."

"I have heard the same. People have spoken of our Queen's unnatural proclivities. Queen Anne often challenged his Majesty on more than one topic. Their daughter being the main one. Well, we have the result today. We tend a motherless princess. And we shall have a new Queen tomorrow."

"For all her supposed faults, I swear Queen Anne adored her Elizabeth. How she must have suffered at the thought of parting this world so soon."

"Queen Anne's attentions were directed elsewhere lately, I dare say. Elizabeth has not visited with her mother in many months. And now, nevermore. Poor little Princess." Lady Margaret casts a sidelong glance at the pink-skinned youngster and clutches her hand. Princess Elizabeth's locks bounce in unison with each step the women take.

"Muggie, look! I'll join the party!"

As Lady Margaret turns her attention to the child, Elizabeth breaks free of her hand. The princess gallops across the grassy meadow, abandoning her ladies. She skips toward the clearing. Her skirts of creamy taffeta, a pale green sash at her waist, Elizabeth crunches up into an unwieldy ball. She lifts the fabric to her chubby knees as she frolics, cutting a swathe through the parting grasses. The deer, startled, interrupt their feeding and bound into the forested area beyond.

Charmed by her sighting, the toddler reaches the edge of the forest. She stands motionless, staring into shadowy trees, awaiting the deer family's return. Her skirts, lifted before her in a fluffy cloud, and rooted as she is, Elizabeth resembles the humble milkweed, offering the contents of its pod. Like the nourishing plant, she anticipates the passing butterfly. Only occasionally does Elizabeth glance back over her shoulder. She smiles at her Muggie, and places a finger on puckered lips to request the ladies' silence.

Her caretakers hesitate for a moment, observing Princess Elizabeth. The child's deep grey eyes cast a concentrated gaze on the place she expects the deer to emerge. Both ladies know they must put an end to the Princess's patient anticipation of that which is not to pass. Yet neither wishes to break the spell the child's hope inspires.

"Queen Anne did not speak ill of His Majesty upon her death. Imagine it. Our King asks for her very life, yet his Queen defends his honour. Well, at least the cries of 'whore' and 'wench' that followed everywhere she walked, will now be silenced."

"Shush, Lady Constance. Do not forget who you watch over. His Majesty's daughter, our Princess Elizabeth." The ladies cast their glances once more to the toddler in their charge. Now grown tired of awaiting her deer family, Elizabeth bends on her knees in the long grasses, exploring the variety of wildflowers in her midst.

Plucking a buttercup, Elizabeth raises it to her cheek. She draws its velvety petals along her jaw, and it leaves behind a trail of golden pollen. Charmed with the pretty flower, the princess scrambles to her feet, gathers several more, adds some Queen Anne's lace, and returns to her governess with a bouquet held before her.

"Have you not been informed of the child's changed circumstance, Lady Margaret?" Lady Constance lowers her voice so her companion must lean her ear closer, straining to hear more.

"What change?"

"Our Elizabeth has been stripped of her title. She is no longer Princess, but must be addressed as Lady Elizabeth. I fear our resources will be sorely reduced in the near future. Lady Elizabeth has been declared by the King, a bastard."

The words, though whispered, feel to Lady Margaret like a hard slap on her cheek. "Our poor dear. Motherless, and now without a name." Lady Margaret raises her hand to the side of her face where Lady Constance aims her cruel blow. She rests it there as though to protect herself from further assault.

"Our young Lady grows so very quickly. Yet no provisions have been made to support her many needs. No gowns or petticoats. Not even a night shirt. I do not know what will become of her."

"The Lady Elizabeth will not want for anything under my care, Constance. I promise you. I will write to Master Cromwell immediately, and request an allowance. Bastard, indeed. Our Elizabeth may have lost a mother's love and a crown today, but she will not be without my comfort." Lady Margaret strolls toward Elizabeth, forces a smile onto her lips, and marvels at the bedraggled bouquet of buttercups Elizabeth offers. The delicate buttercups already stoop. Bending downward in a graceful arc, they lean on the hardier Queen Anne's lace.

Her expression fixed, Lady Margaret smiles with a feigned ease. She too has been known to play actress when circumstance dictates. Behind her mask of maternal calm, she composes her letter to Cromwell. The women accompany the former princess back to her quarters.

My Dear Mr. Cromwell,

I write to you this day on behalf of our Lady Elizabeth, as toward a child and as gentle of conditions as ever I knew any in my life. As you know, our lady has suffered a great change in circumstance of late, and a reduction in her household is most understandable. Yet, I implore you to have pity upon our young charge, to acknowledge the child's household must yet be maintained. At the moment our needs are most desperate, for she hath neither gown, nor kirtle, nor petticoat, nor no manner of linen nor smocks, nor kerchiefs, nor rails, nor body-stitchets, nor handkerchiefs, nor sleeves, nor mufflers, nor biggens. I have driven off as long as I can, that by my troth I can drive it off no longer: beseeching you, my Lord, that ye will see that her Grace may have that which is needful for her...I do implore you, my Lord, have pity.

With Warm Regards,
Lady Margaret Bryan,
Governess to Her Ladyship, Elizabeth

"Come now, my Lady Elizabeth. Let us leave our fellow creatures to their natural home, and go inside for some pudding, shall we?" Lady Margaret, grasping her precious buttercups in one hand, reaches for her favoured jewel with the other. Elizabeth's outstretched hand finds her governess's. She skips beside her caregivers, two steps for each one her ladies take.

"Muggie?"

"Yes, my lady?"

"Why, just this morning, was I Lady Princess, and such a little while later am I only Lady Elizabeth?"

Lady Margaret hesitates, taken aback by the swiftness with which she must face Elizabeth's inquiry. Lady Constance draws in a breath and looks askance. The governess recovers herself, offering the little girl a careful reply.

"Well my Dearest, there is one thing a young lady as fortunate as yourself, daughter to a great king, should always prepare herself for. The mighty waves will shift beneath your dainty feet. And just as the unknowable tides rock your father's ships to sleep, sometimes with gentle prods, sometimes with savage thrashings, your world will be one of uncertainty."

Elizabeth stares hard at Lady Margaret, nodding with an eerie comprehension as her governess portrays the royal navy with her hands. With fluid, graceful motions she rocks an imaginary fleet, gradually building to a violent storm at sea. Now her arms swing to and fro. The elements rage against Elizabeth.

"Change holds fast to your hand, just as I do. She will become your closest companion. You must embrace her, and welcome her always. From today forward, we shall address you as Lady Elizabeth, and we shall mean it with all our hearts." Lady Margaret grasps Elizabeth's tiny fingers in her own, holding tight with reassurance.

"I believe I favour the change you speak of, Muggie." The little girl revels in her new title, its meaning escaping her. "Lady Elizabeth sounds just lovely."

The two women, high above the little girl's sing-song voice, study one another's expressions. The devoted servants wonder if they too might survive the blasts emanating from the turbulent court of King Henry.

***

"Sir William, I do not live in a corner. A thousand eyes see all I do, and slander will not follow after me forever." As I write, our Queen forgives her Sir William Cecil, as she is wont to do for her favourites. She has beckoned him to her Presence Chamber. Will she discuss, in all seriousness, the prospect of her impending marriage?

Her Majesty condescends to explain her behaviour with Lord Dudley. Shocking, really. That our monarch should feel the need to defend her dignity to her Secretary of State, a mere advisor on her council. Though Sir William Cecil, with all sincerity, is no mere anything. More doting parent to our Queen than King Henry ever was, I think.

"Your Majesty, I mean no impertinence. Nor do I require an account of your Majesty's privileged emotions. Please believe me. But the matter of the succession. This rejection of the married state? Our people might begin to regard it as..." Sir Cecil declines his Queen's invitation to discuss Robert Dudley, Earl of Leicester, and proceeds to his own concern. Again with this talk of the succession. No wonder my lady grows weary.

"Do not hesitate then. Speak, by God's Death, speak Sir Cecil."

"Your Majesty, living a solitary existence such as you have so far chosen...it is not viewed as an altogether natural, womanly inclination." Sir William Cecil glances up at Her Majesty, gauging her response. Sensing he treads on volatile ground, he attempts another winning joust.

"It is my sincerest hope God will send Your Majesty a husband, and by and by a son, so that England's throne may have a successor. His head bowed, Lord Cecil pours his demands into our Majesty's waiting cup. He speaks quickly, and with such meekness, I can hardly decipher his whispers.

"Of course, my Lord. There is a strong idea in the world that a woman cannot thrive unless she is married." Her Majesty sighs. The matter of Lord Dudley - a thorny one – both choose to skirt for the moment. He will not stray from my Queen's consideration for long. Of this I am certain.

"Who should your monarch accept, Sir William? France? Spain? Or is it the Habsburg Empire this time? What Popish Prince have you unearthed for my perusal?"

"Your Majesty..."

"Why do you refuse to understand, Sir? You, the first of my trusted advisors? I love the people of England as no other monarch has or shall. God save them all. But observe..." At this, Her Majesty approaches Sir William Cecil. She raises his chin before her, forcing him to meet her eye. "I am already bound unto a husband, which is the kingdom of England..." Our Queen raises her hand before Sir Cecil's astonished countenance. She displays her coronation ring directly under his nose, so close his breath lands up it as though to ready it for polishing. "Every one of you, and as many as are Englishmen, are children and kinsmen to me. Is this not enough? Why cannot this be enough?"

***

"I see all but say nothing." Her Majesty's phrase. She remains true to it. And so the task falls upon myself, her faithful servant. To unfurl the tapestry. The front side? A work of artful promise. And underneath? A tangle of threads, unseen by most. A Monarch's life. Here I pledge an oath to upend the gilded textile. I will lay bare each sparkling thread. Will you raise your forearm to shield your eyes from the luminous fabric that is a Queen's soul?

Most prefer the official transcript. The historical record, as prescribed by our Queen herself. To them, I say: "God bless you." I bear no ill will. Nor do I require any credit. I do not proclaim my truths more genuine than our Queen's. That might suggest disloyalty. Almost sounding treasonous in nature, and I love my monarch too dearly to commit such a disservice.

Though my facts might sometimes contradict Her Majesty's, my intent is wholesome. Our Queen must convince her people she is a Prince. Her Majesty chooses her own counsel first and foremost. In the interests of governance, for the betterment of England, well she should.

I, conversely, declare no such obligation to the State. My only duty is to Her Majesty. In my humble opinion - which some label hubris unbefitting a lady - I have one duty to Her Majesty: to bear witness. To transform a Queen, the stuff of mere legend, into something else. While a legend may amaze, an authentic monarch establishes genuine bonds to her people. And that union may only be properly understood when my intricate woven details are displayed in the light. Even if our Queen chooses to draw the curtain, dimming the very light I wish to shed.

Though many a meal she enjoys alone in her Privy Chamber, sometimes I perch at Her Majesty's side. In silence we dwell. Until the delicate tearing sounds she makes splitting her stone ground bread, the rhythmic ease of her jaw, the swallow of her watered-down wine, interrupt the quiet.

When our Queen composes her correspondence, I attend. It is I who arrange her quill and ink. It is I who fetch her finest paper. And it is I who dab at the stray blots of ink with my silky linen cloth. When Her Majesty rides out with Lord Dudley, I lag behind, seated side-saddle on my old pony, just far enough to provide the appropriate decorum. My mistress insists I offer her a semblance of privacy. She favours the traitor's son, Lord Dudley. Our Queen does not deny doting on the upstart.

When Her Majesty dances her galliards and her saltarellas, I too leap high, following in her every step, attempting to match her graceful posture. When Robert Dudley - a pox on him - Sir William Cecil or Lord Norfolk beg for her ear, it is I who hover, invisible by her side.

My Queen insists on my presence, regardless of the gentlemen's sideways glances, their obvious displeasure. It is as though one lady in their illustrious company is already too much to bear.

When Robert Dudley, her "Eyes" she likes to call him, slips out of her Presence Chamber and into Her Majesty's inner rooms, my own blue eyes accompany him there. My Virgin Queen. Who am I to question my lady's characterization of the title? I adore her. And so does he. And so I provide her with whatever veil of ignorance she requires me to wear.

Who is so bold as to whisper her Queen's secrets for all to hear? I should offer my assurances these revelations can with confidence, be accepted as true. My Christian name is Blanche. Blanche Parry my full name. But my name is not the one in question. It is of no account. Like my Queen, I was educated at Cambridge, by Ascham. A brilliant man. We, my Queen and I, could not have asked for better.

Our Virgin Queen's title I defend without a sneer or a snicker. If Her Majesty is today Astraea, tomorrow Cynthia and the day after that, Diana, I concur. My loyalty I offer freely. My oath and my allegiance guarantee her Majesty's acceptance by her people, given her delicate situation. Though none profess it, many doubt my Queen's ability on the throne. I have no doubt.

I guard her Majesty with jealous zeal, like a tenacious, loyal terrier. She nicknames me "Letters" for all my scholarly service and for my formal duty as Keeper of the Queen's Books, and I accept her naming with honour.

Only her favourites receive such playful nicknames from Her Majesty. "Letters", not to be confused with Lettice Knowles, another of our Queen's ladies who does not receive a nickname.

Her Majesty's public face, long and slim, fair-skinned and freckled, her deep grey eyes and long, slightly hooked nose, our Queen offers, with little pride. Her gentlemen will criticize Her Majesty for her meandering among her subjects. Especially in perilous times such as these. Assassins abound. England's enemies lurk behind each corner of each palace wall. Yet in my presence, our Queen offers something of singular value. A part of herself known to few. This I will share, and with her permission.

My monarch. My protectress. My mother. My friend. I owe Her Majesty everything, and yet nothing. Truly, I give all I have. My Queen thanks me with her boundless trust, which I in turn, cherish.

Her Majesty knows of my reckless scribbling. She thumbs through these pages on occasion, indicating a grammatical inconsistency, a peculiarity in my phrasing. She giggles at my scornful description of her "creature", Robert Dudley. She questions passages I cannot with any integrity report on. I cannot always be by her side. To answer her, I explain. I do not possess the gift of omniscience. Nor would I claim it. I will sometimes turn to others for their watchful reports. I do vouch for the strict reliability of my information. And so Her Grace permits me my humble diary, and continues to encourage all my careful efforts.

No doubt, I will reveal myself to you as I write. Did I say myself? My first error. It is our Queen whom we seek, in all her complexity: simple woman, yet infinitely complicated; carnal virgin; childless mother; flirtatious tyrant; loving executioner.

Her Majesty proves herself the unafraid monarch. And I? I, the cringing confidante, duck behind skirts of imperial metal. My Queen does not flinch at her task. I, too often, falter in her shadow. Thanks be to God she throws such a protective shade, providing me the needed obscurity for my task at hand.

As I go on my progress through the winding words, will I arrive at my desired destination? Will the Lord's guidance and Lady Fortune's good grace assist me in my journey? Perhaps, if I open myself to the suggestion of Her Majesty's humanity, I may alight on more than the tip of a barbed crown. Perhaps, through this hopeful act of scribbling, I will discover my unknowable Queen.

Spring II – A Search for a Mother Who Stays

Whoever wants to wield high power
Must tame his passions fierce;
His heart to evil must not cower
Or bow to lust's fell yoke.
                              --Boethius

26th September, 1559

For the moment, Sir William Cecil appears satisfied. Her Majesty agrees to entertain the idea of a match with one of Cecil's European Princes. So numerous they are: Spain, Habsburg, Sweden, France, not to mention our own English hopefuls: Arundel and Pickering.

I believe Her Majesty mocks Sir Cecil privately. Not with unkind jests, but with the language her eyes speak when she turns to her real favourite: the one who materializes in our Queen's presence when Sir Cecil fades away. When found together in a room with Her Majesty, Sir Cecil and Robert Dudley revolve around each other. Not like planets encircling a nurturing sun, but like hostile stars, flaring with a brilliance intended to blight the other. Both are so volatile, so luminous in their hatred, they risk their own extinction by the blaze they ignite.

Lord Robert Dudley, our Earl of Leicester. I speak the name as little as possible. I can hardly utter it without a retch rising in my throat. What does Her Majesty find pleasing in him? I only pretend to tolerate the obsequious, slavering toady. Try as I might for my beloved Queen's sake, I do not like him.

Lady Olivia, Lady Catherine and especially Lady Lettice Knowles favour Lord Robert with smiles and fond greetings when he bounds into Her Majesty's private quarters. I grow more impervious to his flattering charms as his frequency in my Queen's company increases. Why cannot I, her most loyal of allies, understand that which captivates my beloved Queen?

I do admit his Lordship displays certain qualities Her Majesty and her ladies might admire. Tall of stature, dark of complexion, a master of athletics. How he dances the La Volta! Her Majesty greets him with delight, nicknaming him her *Eyes*. We who know him better say *Gypsy*. Gypsy indeed. His groveling at Her Majesty's slipper earns him Gypsy more than his outwardly appearance, swarthy and pleasing though it may be.

Admittedly, her knee-bending Master of the Horse shares many a common passion with his Queen. As my duty to Her Majesty, I saddle up and ride out with the pair each day. I admire the spirited couple attired in full riding apparel, their whips at hand, crossbows strapped to their mount's flanks. They canter from the palace gardens into the forested parts of Her Majesty's Whitehall Palace grounds. A challenge it is to rein my little horse back with all Her Majesty's attendants. My Queen requests twenty-four paces so that I remain out of earshot. I must steer away from her Gypsy's tender lovemaking.

Urging their horses on, they trot ahead of prying confidantes. How do I guess at the content of their exchange, when not a word reaches my ear? By the inclination of Her Majesty's person. I know her too well.

Her Majesty rides with Lord Robert as she does with no other. Their horses, magnificent grays, canter in perfect unison. They share an accord so synchronized as to suggest a practiced one. Yet the pair goes forth with a natural ease, requiring no rehearsal. So tight apace their horses trot, a single misstep and all might tumble.

I imagine, as I ride out behind them, an awful heap of splayed legs, reins wound round ruined horse flesh. Most heartbreaking of all, broken crowns lying side by side in the devastating tranquility of the meadow.

Then there is the inclination of our Queen's gracious neck. Her Majesty turns toward Lord Robert. As though if she were to glance away, he, as an apparition dissolves, might vanish from her sight. Her Grace inclines her entire form toward him, setting her slightly askew on her mount. It is fortunate her Pool, a tolerant gray, has accustomed himself to her awkward stance. Otherwise our Queen might take a dangerous spill.

Lord Dudley offers Her Majesty great deference. As a Master Horseman, he could be expected to doubt his Queen's equestrian ability. He does not. Or should I say, he dare not? His Queen will have none of it. If Lord Robert appears to ride with an ease Her Majesty considers condescending, she positions herself straight on her saddle, calls, and beats at her Pool's flanks until her other "creature" comes to heal. Always, Her Majesty sets the pace.

More commonly, rather than a spirited pursuit of Lord Dudley into the woods, our Queen chooses a leisurely gait. Without whirling to meet my eye, Her Majesty raises aloft her arm. She knows my gaze, as is my duty, follows her. Her leather-gloved hand, bold against the morning sky, means "Stay". I tug on the reins of my dappled Captain, and with the others dismount. I nourish my pony on tender greens found outside the canopy of the woodland. Much laughter and sharing of jests carries on within the trees.

On occasion, I wander with my pony amongst the wildflowers of the meadow. My skirts dip into spreading pools of lily of the valley. Spear-like leaves, pristine bells wind across the expanse of the fields.

A deathly quiet now lurks within the foliage, in place of laughter. The others do not, will not, notice. But the stillness causes me unease.

Which should I fear more? Her Majesty's wrath, if I interrupt her few moments of solitude with her creature? Or worse, I approach Her Majesty and her paramour unnoticed, and discover them united in a pose our Queen claims to have no knowledge of?

This morning, daisied meadows are not my concern. Today my Queen remains indoors. Her Majesty commands my presence outside her Privy Chamber door, where she entertains the presumptuous Lord Dudley. The door stands slightly ajar. Is this purposeful on the part of My Queen? I do not know.

I seat myself at my Queen's threshold in silent repose. And then my heart quickens. The purpose of my presence dawns upon me. Even so, I bend to my fine paper, my quill in irresolute grip to record the date of my diary entry: 26th September, 1559. I will scribble my terrible intelligence. My judgment will be written large on my Lady's record.

Her Majesty claims to permit no gentleman to embrace her. And yet, I fear Lord Robert wanders where no other treads. I wince at my Queen's fate should she offer herself to her Gypsy. I only pray my accusations find no facts to render them an indelible blot on my Majesty's honour.

Our Queen forgets her oaths to Sir Cecil. Instead, she lavishes the warmest affectionate glances on Lord Dudley's upturned face. Her Gypsy returns to our Queen's side, just as the persistent moss clings to the manicured lawns surrounding Whitehall Palace. And as the generous earth nourishes the wretched weed, our Queen reaches across the table to place her fingertips on the villain.

Her Majesty traces Lord Robert's unbearded cheek. She strokes first one side of his smooth jaw line and then the other until he leans forward, pressing moistened lips to her palm. Her Grace, unaccustomed to another's handling, stifles an intake of breath. My Queen swallows hard, and fumbles with her blousy skirts beneath the table.

Though Her Majesty names me "Letters", and grants me much favour for transforming pretty scenes into elegant script, I question her faith in me. I damn myself with accusations of treachery. My tactless prose suggests indignities, unbecoming to Her Majesty. I do not seek to transform our Queen into a monarch undeserving of her title. Yet my fickle hand belies my honest intent.

Something about Lord Dudley animates our Queen in a stirring fashion. Each of her humble subjects: ladies, gentlemen and children, concur. None compares with Her Majesty's vibrant spirit. A single nod of her head in appreciation of a recent performance of *The Faerie Queene* moved its lead actors to weep. My Queen placed audience and performers in opposing roles, as the players bent to their knees and applauded their beloved sovereign.

Yet Her Majesty's allure in company cannot match that which she exudes in one man's presence. Her public charm is like the poorly cut, palest diamond chip compared to a fulsome blood-red ruby. This is the luster she radiates in Lord Dudley's company. In the scoundrel's attendance our Queen's very essence issues forth.

Enough wayward talk. I return to my faithless task.

"I will never marry, Robert. I am certain of it. For my part, I hate the idea of marriage more each day. The reasons I would not divulge to a twin soul, if I had one, much less to a living creature. Even to you, my cherished companion. I cannot tell."

My Queen offers her hand for Lord Dudley to caress. She watches as he brushes each tiny knuckle with his insistent lips. He only interrupts his treacherous wooing to heap on Her Majesty more scandalous flattery. Today I fear my Queen's appetite might match her greedy companion's.

"Your Majesty made this proclamation once before. This threat of yours to live a chaste life. If I were a more tentative suitor, uncertain of Your Grace's devotion, I might believe you would reject my pursuit of your gracious hand."

The gentleman drags his parted lips from my Queen's knuckles to the back of her hand. He slides his cheek, his mouth open, along her forearm. When he reaches the flesh opposing her elbow, he kisses the silken indentation where Her Majesty's pulse beats. He burrows his face into her sheltered vein until our monarch's arm glistens with damp. My Queen does not appear to mind Lord Dudley's trespass on her person. Instead, Her Majesty smiles on his encroachment.

"My delightful...and wedded Bonny Sweet Robin. You understand your Queen better than any other. I find your pursuit the most detestable to decline. Yet your offer I cannot consider, because it is no offer. Your beloved, ailing wife awaits you in Abingdon as you and I frolic here at Whitehall." To her credit, Her Majesty reclaims her arm from his grasp, returning the fabric of her sleeve to her wrist. But her Majesty plays, I fear. Forever smiling on the rascal, Her Grace allows him altogether too much wandering on her person.

"Do you recall Majesty, that moment many years ago? We were children together when you first uttered these same promises. You swore you would remain chaste. Never to be had, in law, by any man."

The gypsy persists in his chase, refusing to acknowledge mention of his lawful wife. Again he makes claims on our Queen, taking hold of her hand within his own fawning one.

"Of course I remember, Robin. The very day. I was a girl, no longer a Princess by name, but an impressionable young Lady of eight years. It was the evening of the same day I lost my Catherine Howard. She was both stepmother and cousin to me. I will not ever forget it. Though many years have passed since I made the oath, nothing alters my thinking on the matter. A husband, while comforting to the bosom in the privacy of the bedchamber, sticks a dagger into the heart of a Queen's rule."

Lord Dudley pauses in his pursuit. Finally, my Queen reins in her Gypsy. Releasing his Queen's hand, Dudley rests it on the table between them. Her Majesty remains perched by his side and yet she leaves him. Gone back in search of yet another mother who would not stay.

***

Lord William Kingston, Keeper of the Tower, squanders little time pondering the moral righteousness of his position. And then King Henry's young wife, Queen Catherine Howard arrives in his custody. King Henry's fifth chosen wife, and unlikely to be his last.

"Lord Kingston, I request one favour of you, though I know I am in no position to claim any privilege."

Kingston studies the delicate Queen Catherine. Barely a woman, at twenty-one years. A beauty within and without, by the most exacting standards. Yet, destined for the block tomorrow morning. He swallows the treasonous urge to wonder at King Henry's ruling. Then, his self-preservation trumping perilous empathy, Kingston hardens his judgment.

The Keeper of the Tower wills himself to think of his monarch's pitiable state. Though King Henry denies he has been cuckolded, the unwished for title wears heavily on His Majesty's failing health. Word has it from Hampton Court, since being informed of his young Catherine's adulterous liaisons, King Henry appears gravely ill. He distances himself from his closest advisors. He declines the company of any who might lift his spirits. His Majesty's beloved friend, Charles Brandon, Duke of Suffolk, paces outside the King's Chamber whispering words of condolence that are heaved back at him in the ugliest of echoing curses.

Shutting himself within his rooms, the King rants and moans with devastating injury. So sorrowfully does our monarch complain of his young wife, Suffolk dares to interrupt His Majesty's pathetic lament. Forcing open the door to the King's self-imposed retreat, Suffolk intrudes on the Privy Chamber. Casting weary eyes on his monarch, Suffolk witnesses little more than a hovering spirit. Suffolk does not risk throwing his arm around his King's broad shoulder, for fear the shoulder would not hold the weight of his embrace. Nothing of substance remains to support his comforting hand.

Lord Kingston considers the state of affairs a familiar one. He concludes the King's sorry tale a commonplace. Far from the first time or the last, a monarch will be brought to his knees by a harloting wench. The Keeper of the Tower, determined to pursue his duty with required zeal, rehearses the evidence against Queen Catherine: three lovers of note, including Thomas Culpepper whom she still claims to adore. Francis Dereham and Henry Mannox, past-lovers all. And all sent to their untimely deaths before Her Majesty.

Despite Queen Catherine's grievous offences, Kingston hopes his young Queen was unmindful enough to hold her gaze down as she approached Traitor's Gate and entered the Tower.

He hopes, with a generosity he can ill afford,she failed to notice her foul welcome to her temporary home. For the traitors' severed heads, Culpepper's most prominently displayed, greet the fallen Queen. Still dripping their woeful contents, expressions more like discarded masquerade disguises, they remain perched on their wooden poles. High on Tower Bridge, open eyes stare down on the young Queen's plodding form.

Kingston's compassion provides little comfort to his young Queen Catherine. Her broken expression, the palsy afflicting her childish hand, suggests she has seen all.

"Your Majesty, as Keeper of the Tower it is my duty and my honour to assist. In what manner may I serve you?"

"You will think me little more than an absurd girl, my Lord, but my throat aches from calling for King Henry. I believe if he were to hear me, His Majesty might reconsider his wife's desperate case. I cry out his name and still he does not answer his Catherine..."

"The King resides at Hampton Court, Your Majesty."

"Yes. Of course he does." Queen Catherine blinks, hesitates. She swallows the gathering panic rising within. "I called to him there also. From my lodgings, before I was transported to this dismal cellar. Yet he did not answer. Perhaps, a salve for my aching throat, Sir?"

"Certainly, Madam. I'll have the guard fetch it."

"Also..." Queen Catherine hesitates; aware her next request defies all common practice. "As you know, I have little experience with what is to happen when the sun rises tomorrow. I believe it is important to take my leave of this world in a dignified manner, as befits the Queen of England, France and Ireland. Yet I do not know what to expect..."

"Forgive me Your Majesty. Would your apprehension find ease in prayer? Surely the good Lord will hear your plea, and grant mercy on your soul. Shall I fetch Lord Cranmer to you?"

"No...not Lord Cranmer." Queen Catherine shudders, and waves off Kingston's offer.

"I have already prepared my soul for my heavenward journey, Lord Kingston. It is a worldly concern I trouble you with. Would you bring to me a block? Similar to that which I will put my neck on tomorrow? I will put my head on it, just as I shall in the morning. I must prepare myself to leave our blessed kingdom with a semblance of the dignity owing His Majesty. Perhaps in death I will provide for His Grace what I could not while alive."

Lord Kingston, priding himself on remaining the detached servant of the King, can only nod. He wonders at the courage his young Queen musters. He hopes the young woman will hold some fearlessness in reserve for the ordeal she has yet to endure.

"Of course, Madam. At once."

True to his word, Lord Kingston returns, gripping his onerous burden. Though the cumbersome block of wood stains his uniform, smearing ashen particles on the woolen fabric, tarnishing the brass buttons of his waistcoat, he attempts to rid himself of his inconsequential concerns.

Queen Catherine has but a few hours remaining to rehearse her execution. Lord Kingston promises to provide what little ease he can for the doomed girl. With a meticulousness, verging on ceremonial aplomb, he places the block of cedar timber before her on the earthen floor. He steps back, his blackened hands laced together behind him in deference to his unfortunate Queen.

To his amazement Queen Catherine hurries to the block, the symbol of her death, as though her little remaining time demands she rush. She rests one expectant cheek on the rough-hewn log, then raises herself up. With the back of her hand, she rubs at slivers of cedar before attempting the second cheek. His Queen proceeds with her practice as though her life depends on her choosing the correct position. Queen Catherine forgets Lord Kingston's presence in the cell, her solemn attention remains so focused on her wooden platform.

"I will leave you, Your Majesty."

Her Majesty does not reply. Instead, she returns to the original cheek. Laying it down on the block, she attempts to find comfort where none exists.

Kingston bows slightly. Refusing to search his Queen's expression for that which he does not care to know, he reels around and strides from the dismal Tower. As the weight of the padlocked door clangs behind him, Kingston hears only the muted, childish sobs he sought with such haste to escape.

***

"Come along, Sweetheart. We're leaving Hatfield Palace for Hampton Court. Your Father waits." Kat Champernowne, a favourite governess of Elizabeth's, readies the eight year old Lady for her journey to visit King Henry at his official residence.

His Majesty declares Elizabeth a bastard on record, but still he enjoys his daughter's company on occasion. Elizabeth's presence lightens our King's burdened heart.

Though Hampton Court is not Elizabeth's favourite home, she does not complain of its haunting gloom. Elizabeth thinks more of the cheer she will bring to King Henry's heavy eye. Of the distance she will leap to reach her perch on his gartered knee. Of the scratch of his prickly beard. She giggles as she remembers his coarse cheek. And how the brilliant red stones on his sleeve poke into her shoulder blade when her father folds her into his massive embrace. Elizabeth cavorts before him with the energy of a young pup. Arms raised high above her shoulders; she spins her favourite galliard before his throne. All to earn a pat on her uncovered head.

"Does our brother, Edward, go to Hampton Court with us, Kat?" Elizabeth watches as her governess folds the last of her linens. Kat ensures her charge will be well provided with adequate petticoats, crinolines, skirts and shawls for the visit, which may linger a fortnight or more.

"Yes, of course, my Lady. As will your esteemed sister, Mary. And of course, Lady Margaret will attend Edward, as she once did Your Ladyship."

"My Muggie too? How wonderful. My entire family reunited at once. How I look forward to visiting with Cousin Catherine. I am so fortunate my father wedded one so close to our hearts. We are blessed to have a cousin who is yet our mother, and so youthful and pretty too." Elizabeth's complexion, so faint the little girl appears almost transparent, pinkens. My Princess turned Lady, grins at her imagined reunion with her beloved father and siblings. She dips and turns as she practices the curtsey she will offer her much-loved stepmother.

"My Lady, I must speak with you..." Kat Champernowne trains her eye on her labours. Her hands, occupied with a nervous energy, fold and unfold the dainty articles of clothing.

Elizabeth, oblivious to her governess's discomfort, dances over to stare out the tiny leaded panes of her window. Divided and beveled glass distorts her view so she squirms, searching for a vantage point. Elizabeth attempts to study the grooms, bent low to tether skittish horses to the parade of carriages below. Cocking her head this way and that, she prattles on to Kat.

"My father names Catherine his 'Rose without a thorn', Lady Kat. I cannot disagree with his affectionate praise. She is lovely. And she smells of field flowers. And of honeysuckle and lemon thyme too, I dare say. How I anticipate visiting with our dear mother, Queen Catherine."

"I am not certain you will find Queen Catherine at home, my Lady. I am afraid she has incurred the disfavour of your father, our King."

"Disfavour? But how? Whenever we enjoy the privilege of her company, our Queen Catherine remains full of entertainments. She does not care at all about my Greek or Latin lesson books. Of these ..." Elizabeth taps the pouch at her waist where she carries her readers "...she says, 'Oh pretty Papa's girl, put those away. You may recite and translate with your tutors another time. When we meet one another, we shall play at dress-up.'

"And then my newest mother leads me to her Chamber, where we rustle through her gowns, and she reveals to me her latest and her favourites. And she unfastens every compartment of her jewel chests, and allows me to place her pretty pearls around my own neck. Once, I beheld an emerald so large, I mistook it for a tropical lime from Turkish kingdoms. And it was all surrounded with diamonds of the clearest bluish hue...."

"Pardon me, my Lady, but I must…"

"…why if I did not know she was a lady of twenty-one years, I believe I might mistake her for a schoolgirl such as I am myself. Kat, I do believe Catherine enjoys her Lady Elizabeth almost as much as I yearn to share my new Mother's company."

"Lady Elizabeth…I fear you will not find Queen Catherine at Court. We go abroad on this occasion to cheer your father alone."

Elizabeth, with the limitless optimism of all eight years, fails to notice Kat's growing discomfort. Elizabeth will not seize the hint, as her governess ducks behind the stack of layered and folded skirts.

"Cheer my father? I always attempt to do that. But, what ails His Majesty? Is it our Catherine's absence? Where does our Queen travel then? Kat, I do not fully understand the purpose of our voyage." Elizabeth withdraws her attention from the window, turning to address her governess.

"I am sorry, Lady Elizabeth…" Kat interrupts her task, grasps Elizabeth by her bolstered shoulder, and seats her on the bedstead. The governess lowers herself beside the little girl. She manages a few deep breaths in an effort to steady her composure, and continues.

"…I am sorry, but I must bear news of a significant weight. Queen Catherine no longer lives…"

"No longer at Hampton Court with my father? Well, where then, pray tell?" Elizabeth's raised eyebrows, her innocent inquiries, threaten to unhinge her governess.

Kat Champernowne, unable to skirt the issue with partial truths any longer, concedes defeat. "Queen Catherine has died. I am so very sorry, Lady Elizabeth." The governess's arm encircles the girl, squeezing her shoulder. Kat rests her chin on Elizabeth's curls.

"She has taken ill then? And has died without my knowledge? Why was I not told of this earlier? Queen Catherine is my cousin…and also now my Mother." Elizabeth persists. She continues to speak of her beloved Queen, her youthful, beautiful stepmother, in the present tense. The enormity of Kat's announcement mystifies the little girl. Her gleeful proclamations of moments before altered to raspy whispers.

"My Lady, it was not the smallpox, nor the plague. Queen Catherine died on the block…at the sad behest of His Majesty. It seems she incurred his disfavour…"

"Disfavour? Is that a reason for a Queen to die? My father's disfavour means death?" Lady Elizabeth attempts to puzzle out the impossible. She wrinkles her eight year old brow as she considers Kat's revelation. Elizabeth rises from the comfort of the feather duvet. She returns to her place before the window. Below, preparations go forth. But Elizabeth's wonder at the ceremonial pomp dissolves, replaced by a disheartened confusion.

The Chamber grows dim. A passing cloud, all shadow, erects yet another barrier to Lady Elizabeth's view. A tentative breeze stirs the cloud mass, but does not prove powerful enough to move it. The stubborn mist hovers, like a newly-built ceiling. It floats high above the palace, shuttering the brilliant sunshine. An ominous dusk hovers over Elizabeth's window to the world, altering her mood yet further in the direction her governess has already lead her.

"Must we go abroad today, Kat? Perhaps another day would be brighter…more fit for travel?" A sturdy vessel meant for sailing turbulent waves requires cheerful winds on its sails. Lady Elizabeth's momentum declines as gusts blow against her upcoming voyage.

"Your father expects you, my Lady. Edward and Mary wait. Come now. Little Edward says his Sweet Sister Temperance adjusts to every untoward event. Do not disappoint your brother. We really must go. The entourage awaits us."

"Kat, do all Kings treat their Queens in this manner? What has our sweet Catherine done to deserve this sentence on her?" Still Elizabeth stands rooted in her Chamber, determined to solve this new puzzle before setting out on her journey.

"I cannot answer for our King, Lady Elizabeth. But this I know: He is your beloved father and the King, God's chosen, and you must not forget it. Come." Kat extends her hand, knowing everything awaits the little girl's compliance.

Elizabeth persists. "Perhaps I should be grateful I am my Father's Lady and not his Queen?"

"Yes, my Lady, be pleased you are the great King Henry's Lady Elizabeth."

"Kat?"

"Yes, my Love?"

"I will forever obey and love my father, the King, with all my heart…"

"Excellent, my Lady."

"…but I believe I shall never marry."

***

Her Majesty's refusal of her Gypsy's offer of marriage makes for only the briefest pause in her heedless march toward ruin. My impetuous Queen rises from her cushioned seat. She circles round behind Lord Dudley. Resting her small bosom on his shoulder, she whispers muffled commands into his eager hearing. Hold Madam. Do you comprehend what you risk?

Lord Dudley offers his reply. Unlike Her Majesty's hushed discretion, the Gypsy shows little regard for who might hear. "Your Grace claims possession of all of me. My very breath, you own. And yet, I may only worship you privately. In the world at large I am nothing more than Master of the Horse."

"Do not forget your Queen's recent gift, Robin. You are a Knight of the Garter also."

"I am not ungrateful, Majesty. For the Knight of the Garter, I humbly thank you. As I thank God for your kind attentions. Within doors, I wander as though in a sheltered woodland, graced by the tenderest of forest awnings, which is your favour..."

The scribbling of my quill on my tablet cannot express the horror with which my ear receives Lord Robert's seductive prose. The liberties Her Majesty condones. I raise my palms to my ears to shield my injured hearing. One of us will escape his tempting snare.

Lord Dudley reaches round for our Queen's elbow, bringing her before him. His shrewd hand, knowing no bounds, lifts the hem of Her Majesty's gown. He raises the fabric, in tumbling layered pleats, to the height of her thigh.

My Queen, forgetting my perpetual presence, forgetting *all* it would seem, stands rooted before him. Her Grace stares hard at her Gypsy. Her Majesty's eye, usually so comprehending in its gaze, wanders far from her throne. Lord Dudley's hand forages. The pale lace at his wrist combines with pristine silken petticoats. All disappears beneath layers of regal dress.

"...while out on the grounds of the palace, your Robin only replaces the shoes on the hooves of his Queen's favourite stallion, or polishes the arrows for her crossbow, or rubs the leather of her saddle until it glistens..."

Her Majesty lifts her chin and stretches her graceful neck backward. She arches her back, curving her jewel-encumbered torso toward his Lordship. My Queen offers all. Her Grace's elegant form bends as she laughs at her Gypsy's crude advances. In her pleasure, Her Majesty encourages the gentleman's willful search of her person. While he disrobes my Queen beneath the jeweled bell of her gown, still the Gypsy's fawning issues forth.

"I so enjoy the brilliant illumination within your Chamber, My Grace. Your cheeks alight. The meaningful silence. Unwelcome eyes may go elsewhere." In one act of disreputable grace, Her Majesty's Gypsy leans over her. He presses himself against Her Majesty. The scoundrel advances without ceremony. Now he hoists his Queen's gown, so it crowds between them, a resisting bundle of fabric separating them at their waists. The ropes of pearls at Her Majesty's throat clatter in wanton applause, encouraging a Gypsy's onslaught.

Well-practiced in his seductive maneuvers, he retreats. I cover my brow. A wash of colour paints my cheek as the pristine flesh above the tops of Her Majesty's hose finds my reluctant eye. I would sooner crack my quill across my knee than record Her Majesty's ruin. Yet, I pledged my oath. I vowed to my Majesty that by my hand the unabridged truth will make itself known.

A Gypsy fondles Her Grace beneath billowing layers of dress. He unfastens, with the finest precision, her silken hose from her garter. Lord Robert rolls the fine silk down Her Majesty's thigh, his hands meandering in their descent. Still my Queen remains perfectly still, as though depicted in portrait. Her person so rooted in certainty, I dare not question the reasoning with which she proceeds. I fear no amount of reason guides this drama. Only our lady's pitiable want.

Her Grace's favourite tugs at the fastenings on his waistcoat. Metal clasps, formerly shut tight with some semblance of propriety, open, exposing his bared torso. My Queen and I study a Gypsy's form. So wondrous in its sturdy shape, and yet a repugnant reminder of Her Majesty's imminent ruin.

Only Lord Dudley's breeches remain. The flimsiest layer of cloth separates Her Majesty's honour and England's demise. As the Gypsy disrobes, all the while holding Her Highness rapt, our Queen only stares. Her eyes wonder about the exotic flavour of a Gypsy's flesh. Yet he proves a tainted feast. All fatal with the threat of Her Majesty's dishonour. I fear for our Grace. Her reputation teeters on the verge of extinction. And I? A helpless witness to its demise.

"Hold, Sir. I cannot. Have mercy, Robert. You know I cannot." Her Majesty awakens, extending her arm in a half-hearted push. Her Grace's plea proves enough to remove Lord Dudley to a safe distance. He steps backward, little surprised by her reluctance. Her Majesty lowers her skirts with due haste.

To his credit, Lord Robert desists. Her Gypsy refastens his breeches. His head bowed, her suitor wraps his tunic about himself. The top buttons of his waistcoat hang open, revealing a chest more exposed in its disappointment, than preparing for Her Majesty's disgrace.

"Forgive me, Majesty. I behave in an imprudent manner. So stirred is your servant by your cherished companionship. I should leave Court. My departure might allow mischievous envy to cool, and controversy to stall." Lord Robert grasps hold of and fastens the buttons of his ruffled collar. Still I do not trust his attempt at honour.

"If I were to find my way back to Abingdon, and become a constant husband to Amy, wagging tongues would surely cease. More ease might follow both Your Majesty and her humble servant. I see my duty lies in my displacement. Thereby permitting you, Majesty, to fulfill your own obligation..."

"Robin, do not speak of marital burdens, husbands and wives in my presence." A sigh escapes Her Majesty before she hardens her countenance. "Do you learn nothing from our shared conversation? The marital bed is but a secure port for those unable to steer their lustful cravings upon the open sea. I will not offer up my entire person in the name of mere fleshly weakness."

Encumbered with a different sort of passion, Her Majesty advances on her Gypsy. She studies his beleaguered expression. "Do you know what your Queen endures in the name of this damnable institution? It is not enough that Sir Cecil and my Lords in the Parliament bite at my heels, choosing husbands to mate me as they would their brood mare. You, of all my gentlemen, would not spare me this torturous sermon? Even as we embrace...my own creature."

Disappointment wets my Queen's cheek as she snatches at her pearls. Strung tight round her throat, the opaline beads trail downward at Her Majesty's back. Her Grace gathers the precious ropes and drags them forward. She rearranges the lengths, and with them her familiar seemliness returns. Her gown, a shambles beneath the belled form, she smoothes with the heel of her hand. Over and over Her Majesty swipes at the creased fabric. Still the unwanted folds return to unnerve her.

The Gypsy, witnessing Her Majesty's distress, falls silent.

"Robin, my good Mother forfeited her life for her title. As did all my beloved mothers after that....If my father's perpetual anger did not carry them off, then a son's ravaging birth brought about the same result. You mock an eight year old girl's certainty, Robin. But I meant it. I will never marry."

***

Here lieth a Phoenix, by whose death
Another Phoenix life gave breath:
It is to be lamented much
The world at once ne'er knew two such

Queen Jane Seymour, so recently delivered, misses her little son's presence inside her womb. Wracked by childbed fever, she contemplates the powerful surge of Grief. Such command. To eclipse a Joy so recently felt.

"Lady Margaret, I beckon you to my childbed and my deathbed both, to discuss Prince Edward's future. As it appears I will not survive to nurture my son in his infancy, I bequeath his careful tending to you."

"Your Majesty, I beg you. Retain your strength. You will rise from your childbed and attend to His Highness Prince Edward for many years to come." Lady Margaret Bryan chafes at her helplessness. Her faithful Queen Jane so soon to be dispatched, after providing the King with his sought-after son at last. The infant prince bawls in the royal nursery, unaware his mother prepares to leave him.

"Do not flatter me with untruths, Lady Margaret. I have no time to debate fanciful pleasantries with you. I will not demand more than is my son's due. Nor that which you cannot furnish him. I believe the least said is the soonest mended, and so I hasten to my point."

"Yes, Your Grace."

"I am not a Queen of many words as my predecessor, the Boleyn woman proved to be….Oh, my skin tingles as though a flame lights it from within…." The Queen places her palms on her blazing cheeks, and still she does not find any relief from her feverish state.

"Allow me to press a cooling cloth to your temples, Your Majesty." Lady Bryan reaches for the ceramic bowl at her Queen's bedside, dips her handkerchief in the tepid liquid and holds the dampened linen to Her Majesty's forehead. The intense heat radiating beneath her palm nearly causes Lady Bryan to withdraw her hand.

"I have made my motto *Bound to Obey and Serve*. Though I reigned as Queen consort for only one short year, I have given our King what he most desired. In this, if nothing else, I take pride. I accept my ordained fate, and have prepared my soul to go from this world in peace. But before I meet our Lord God, I must arrange for my son's welfare. You have proved an excellent nursemaid to our Lady Elizabeth."

"Thank you, Your Majesty."

The Queen, weakened by her effort at speech, allows her lids to hover over her eyes for a moment. Lady Bryan wonders if her Queen has spoken her last. But with a determination garnered from maternal concern, Queen Jane continues.

"Elizabeth excels at so much already, even at the tender age of four years. She has robust health, and she succeeds with her early education, which appears to be having an excellent effect on her learning. I credit Lady Elizabeth's success to her patrilineage, but you too deserve credit, Lady Margaret."

"You flatter, Your Majesty. I beg you; please conserve your strength for your recovery…"

"Lady Margaret, have pity. Do not test my patience. I must see to my son's needs." Queen Jane flushes a brilliant crimson as she challenges Lady Bryan's attempt at accepted decorum. Lady Bryan reaches toward the bowl and bathes her Queen's forehead with cool water once more.

"Your kindness to Lady Elizabeth has not gone unnoticed. Your service proves exemplary. Elizabeth loves you as her own Mother....I know your attachment to her is great. Yet, I must ask you to release our Lady Elizabeth, and direct your loving attention to my son Edward, the future King of England. We have arranged for Katherine Champernowne to relieve you of the Lady Elizabeth's care. I beg of you to find it in your heart to transfer your fond attachment, Lady Margaret. My son depends on you managing this shift in your affection."

Her Majesty reaches for Lady Bryan's hand, appealing to the woman's sympathy. Lady Bryan clutches the Queen's fingers in her own. With her free hand, she places the dampened handkerchief on the Queen's forehead once more.

"Your Majesty, I beg you. Do not be troubled. I consider it my humble duty to serve my Prince's needs. He is a fine, fulsome babe. And of a delicate pink hue, with his father's auburn locks already. And though my attachment to Lady Elizabeth is a mighty one, my Lady reaches four years, and must embark on her formal learning. The moment to release Lady Elizabeth arrives." Lady Bryan's eye, at first focused on her Queen, shifts to her own slipper.

"You love her, Margaret." The Queen whispers her acknowledgement, smiling on Lady Margaret's goodwill.

"With all my whole heart Your Majesty. Did you witness Lady Elizabeth's happy countenance at Prince Edward's christening? Though the tapers lit Hampton Court Chapel, Lady Elizabeth sparkled also, and with a true enthusiasm. Such felicity greeted Edward's birth that we could have doused all torchlight. I dare say our Lady Elizabeth's heart lit the procession for her new baby brother."

"I am told it was a beautiful ceremony. With much joyful celebration..."

"And with such pride Lady Elizabeth carried aloft Edward's gown. She is so small herself that Lord Beauchamp had to hoist her high on his shoulder to the altar. Lady Elizabeth sighs at the mere mention of her new brother, our future king. He will have not one, but two little mothers to attend him, the Lady Mary and her sister, the little Lady Elizabeth. They love him so."

"Yes, two mothers..." Queen Jane appears confused by Lady Bryan's story, yet she smiles in agreement. "I am certain my son, the future King of England shall be reared by the finest, nurturing mothers." Her Majesty holds Lady Bryan's hand and squeezes. "Please send forth to me Lady Mary and His Majesty after that. I believe I take my leave soon." The Queen retreats into her pillow, turning her face from the woman who will replace her in her son's heart.

"Yes Madam, I will fetch them immediately. May I give a message to the Lady Elizabeth, Your Grace?"

"Tell my darling Lady Elizabeth she must remain strong for her father and for her little brother too. Tell my Lady, her Queen Jane relies on her kindly disposition toward her beloved brother, our future King..." The Queen's whisper falters and goes silent. She waves Lady Bryan away, her fingers barely lifting from the silken duvet.

I permit myself a bit of relief, but that proves reckless. My Queen punishes me for it with more impropriety. If I did not trust my senses, I would deny the mischief reaching my ear. Her Majesty adopts the role of courtier herself. Heedless of her royal dignity, my Queen pleads with the naughty Gypsy.

"Bonny Sweet Robin, do not speak of leaving me. I cannot do without you at Court. Your brilliant statesmanship, your managing of affairs is not to be parted with because of a husband's obligation. Nor will a foolish passion divide us. I will not accept your leaving. I cannot." My Queen approaches her ruin as the child reaches to the poisoned berry vine. And with the same exuberance. Her Majesty embraces her honour at one moment and at the next pitches it to the breezy gusts.

And what of the shameless Gypsy's hands? Empty of shame, they journey once again beneath silken layers. Lord Dudley roams on our Queen, I do not know where. Again Her Grace poses before him, rooted as an artist's rendition of her faithful self. Without that graceful motion so familiar to her public person, Her Majesty appears bereft of the dignity she bestows on her people. Her promise of purity a shameful deceit, Her Majesty's cheek stains a livid pink. Her lips tremble with the knowledge of Lord Dudley's wandering touch. Her Grace shuts her eyes so they blind her to her own betrayal. A Queen's sacred oath? All forgotten.

A simple shudder and all is over.

Then a faint swish outside her chamber awakens Her Majesty. Whether a swallow's hushed wing beneath her window ledge, the rustle of her skirts, or the tinkling of my quill within its pot of ink, awareness tears the blindfold from her pleasure.

Our Queen remembers at last. She pulls away from her Gypsy, who always dutiful, releases his hold. As she retreats, Her Majesty's hands continue to brush at the fabric of her dress. Sweeping at the layers, Her Grace denies her Gypsy's roamed there at all.

"You grow over-familiar with your loving Queen, Robin. Perhaps your restless energies are better spent elsewhere at Court. Though I warn you, turn your attentions away from my ladies. I do not care to watch them smile at your approach. Respect and decorum shelter my Court. Your Queen insists on it, and she will have it."

Her Majesty reaches for her Gypsy's broad-brimmed hat and tosses it on his head. Before he can turn from her, she grabs hold and removes his extravagant plume. She waves the feather before his eye in the most teasing manner. Finally, Her Grace fluffs the flattened lace at his collar, chastising his unkempt appearance. In farewell, Her Majesty kisses her Gypsy hard on his ever-watering mouth. He leaves at last.

Spring III – Too Great an Expense

In all adversity of fortune, the most wretched kind is once to have been happy.

--Boethius

29th August, 1560

I do not presume to know what dwells within my Queen's soul. Yet I would consider this summer of 1560 one of my Majesty's happiest. At a tender twenty-six years of age, our Queen's renown soars. Her Majesty occupies the centre of heaven, while those around her revolve in wonder. Her Grace displays a brilliant Prince's intellect. Her womanly care for her people combines with the advantage of a great kingdom. Still she attracts an abundance of suitors. Sir Cecil seethes at Lord Dudley's interference in the Queen's affairs, but he does so from afar.

Regretfully, no sun, even that possessing the most nurturing rays, maintains an infinite radiance. Ruthless Time intrudes. A cruel expiration hovers over my Queen's joyful attitude. By this same year's end, I fear Her Majesty's naïve confidence could fade. She will be tested by the vagaries of her cherished throne.

August draws her curtain shut on temperate evenings. September soon visits us. I shiver in the chill air. With the season's shift, I fear rustlings at Court. New whispers, not heard in the warm weather, make themselves known to my ear.

I thank Lady Fortune for her goodwill. The two opposing forces, who seek to alter Her Majesty's position, remained at a safe distance from one another throughout our Queen's blissful summer. Lord Dudley, close by Her Majesty's side, at my Queen's insistence and by the gentleman's inclination, stands to gain all.

Sir William Cecil, less fortunate soul, languished in far-off blustery Scotland, negotiating the Edinburgh Treaty. At the request of his Queen, Sir William also sought to reclaim from the French Her Majesty's beloved island of Calais. I celebrate his late return, for Sir Cecil alone appears to possess the mature judgment our neglected land seeks. Our radiant Queen, with each new dawn, only brings more damage on her virtuous reputation.

"What of Scotland, Sir William?" Her Majesty displays ease in her stature, stretching her entire length on her throne. All unperturbed in her regal dress, Her Majesty expresses an indifference to Sir Cecil's return to Court. Aloof in her observation of her Secretary, Her Grace does not offer her hand. Nor does she smile on her faithful councilor. Though her "Sir Spirit" has been absent these many months negotiating a peaceful Protestant border for northern England, Her Majesty does not acknowledge his accomplishment with any warmth. I do not like it.

"We are glad you return unharmed. And the Scots Treaty all but ratified. Though this past Spring Leith stood with force against us, we are pleased to hear our brave soldiers prevailed. What are the losses to be counted in Grey's artillery?"

"Your Majesty, if I may..."

"Sir William, we do not relish it when the failures of our Admiralty sink the fortunes of our honest men. We fear without the assistance of the French warring amongst themselves, without God's will and the wayward Fates dispatching Leith's Regent to his death, we might not meet this day with such glad tidings."

"Your Grace, our forces suffered some five hundred casualties in the assault on the Scottish fortress. Our wooing with expert negotiation accomplished more."

"Should your Queen express astonishment at this, Sir? Why can't we write our peaceable words *before* arrows puncture the hearts of our people? Why must our soldiers' blood provide the ink our wretched document gets drawn with?" Her Majesty sighs, and glances down on Sir William Cecil's bowed head.

Though accustomed to his Queen's unpredictable manner, Sir Cecil appears startled by his reception. He draws back from Her Majesty's throne, wincing at the impatient harangues meeting his declaration of success. But Sir Cecil continues. He does not rise to Her Majesty's goading, or allow it to silence him.

"....As I have written you from abroad, Your Majesty, The Treaty of Edinburgh was proclaimed on July Sixth, and is to be ratified this month. Our northern border is well within our command, and Protestant Lords prevail."

His Queen persists in her interrogation. "What of Calais? When will it be returned to England? I nearly forfeited myself to a French King in order to regain her cherished shores. What have you done in order to assure our re-acquaintance with our favourite Isle, Sir William?"

"Majesty, while the French agreed to Scotland in the north, yet they stand entrenched upon Calais, and will retain their claim to the island."

Her Majesty's slender fingers begin a rhythmic drumming on her throne's arm. Petulance overlays our Queen's understanding. "Sir William, you know well of my greatest desire, yet you fail to delight me in my cause. Must your Queen turn elsewhere for the answers she seeks? Must we find ourselves a swordsman to equal our scribes?" First our Queen prevails on Sir Cecil to favour diplomacy. Now she seeks a resolute military stand.

Sir William Cecil bends lower at his thick waist, so Her Majesty looks on the black of his skull cap. His fellow councilors linger in small clusters of two and three. They avert their eyes and clasp their hands behind their backs. A few clear their throats and shift their feet.

"I will not surrender Calais, Your Majesty. My sole care is to serve Your Grace and the kingdom, which is why I beg of you, to consider carefully where you choose to find your own recreation."

As though Sir Cecil has not earned enough of our Queen's ire, he saunters out onto a plank that might only provide for him a refreshing and salty dunk. Amazement, mixed with gasps of grudging respect greets the Secretary of State's reckless speech. The council, as a unit, shifts from foot to foot, creating a scuffling sound Her Majesty snaps her fingers at.

"You toy with your Queen, Sir Spirit?" Her Grace averts her eye, moving it instead to her Gypsy, Sir Cecil's evident target. Robert Dudley maintains his envied position, not far from her throne's side. The Gypsy returns Her Majesty's sideward glance with a smirk, setting his Queen into an unladylike chortle. As Her Majesty, strewn across her throne, shakes with laughter, she transforms in my mind's eye. Henry VIII roams the Court again, if only in my roving imagination.

"Surely you do not suggest you know better than your Queen where she should enjoy her leisure? Do not inform us, Sir William, you harp on the damnable succession again. We will not have it."

"I only propose you step carefully, Majesty. Much is at stake. The realm whispers..." As Cecil speaks of gossip at Court, he lowers his voice accordingly.

The Presence Chamber echoes a chilly silence. Her Majesty's shout breaks through it. Her sharp assault on Sir Cecil boxes the unprotected ears of all. "I will not whisper. I will raise my voice above the entire kingdom to declare a Prince's will. My small pleasures, infrequent as they are, will be enjoyed at my discretion alone. No interference. No dispute. Leave my presence at once, Sir. Such a saucy rebuke for your Prince. God's Death! You return from abroad, and within minutes grumble about my reign's demise. Sir Cecil, and all present, listen well. So long as I live, I shall be Queen of England."

No longer does Her Majesty recline within her throne. No longer does its protective authority envelop her. Our Queen's willowy form leans toward Sir Cecil's cowering one. Then, bereft of the little patience she began with, she leaps to her feet and strides from the Chamber. Her councilors remain, but only to wonder at what might next prod Her Majesty's temper to its easily reached limits. Her Majesty cares little what Sir Cecil, Lord Dudley, or her Council advises on her marital status. Ill-timed Sir Cecil and his vigilant attitude. It is said her Sir Spirit considers resigning his post. His Queen disparages his sage counsel so often.

Each evening I kneel by my bedside, but tranquility escapes me. I pray Her Majesty will rethink her hasty judgment on Sir Cecil. Though she chooses not to know it, our Queen treads in perilous territory. Why does Her Grace disparage the one who assists her most in the face of such ardent opposition?

Parliament squawks with unceasing concern about an heir. The gentlemen in both Houses fear for England's future. Yet, while suitors from all ends of the continent pursue our Queen, Her Majesty plays. She toys with her Gypsy alone. Her Majesty persists in bestowing such favour on Lord Dudley, the entire realm and beyond into far-reaching European hamlets chatter at Her Majesty's flirtations. At Court today, I overhead His Lordship, the Spanish Ambassador Signor de Faria muttering about our Majesty. I believe the Ambassador, in his carefully spoken English, declared: *"She is determined to be governed by no one!"*

***

"Your Majesty, may I speak freely?"

If any dare, surely the sweet-tempered Kat Ashley can approach the subject without attracting the worst of our Queen's threadbare temper. Kat, of any of Her Majesty's ladies, has formed a comradery with her Queen, uncommon to Her Majesty's general custom. While the voices of Lord Dudley, Sir William Cecil and the two Nicholas's, Lord Keeper of the Great Seal, and Chamberlain of the Exchequer reach Her Majesty's waiting ear, few of her Ladies will find Her Majesty so inclined.

Our Queen has even been known to strike those of her ladies who dare to contradict her judgment. Recently, Her Majesty addressed Lady Blythe with the utmost severity for agreeing to wed Thomas, son of the Privy Councilor without Her Majesty's express permission. The young Lady Blythe's head was turned, both left and right, by the punishing force of our Queen's blows.

"Damnable folly. What is it you do not comprehend, Lady Blythe? Your duty to your Queen and to your realm requires all of you. If you must take yourself a husband, you require your sovereign's sanction to proceed. Your absence will be sorely felt, and must be replaced at a great disturbance to the realm."

"Your Majesty, I beg your pardon, I do grasp your meaning, though..."

This is where the slapping ensues. Our Queen does not tolerate any argument. Before Lady Blythe can raise an arm to shield her cheek, the flat of our Queen's palm lands with a sharp smack on her left ear. Next, the back of Her Majesty's hand thrashes Lady Blythe's right cheek.

Fortunate for Lady Blythe, Her Grace wears an oval ring of mother-of-pearl. The flat gold setting contains no sharp edges. The stone is polished smooth to the touch. The Lady's handsome face is spared, except for an astonishing pink disc-shaped patch Lady Blythe shelters under a tentative hand.

Amazement fails to materialize in the room, as our Queen's ladies have more than once witnessed this scene. Each of us has learned when Her Majesty's temper reigns we best carry on as though we do not notice it. We gather in our tight-knit circles of threes or fours as though unaware of the violence. As though our own ears have been, on some previous occasion, slapped into a similar deafness. Bold chatter envelops our growing unease.

"Lady Blythe, allow your Queen to complete her thought. If you must take yourself a husband, it is at your own peril. Are you certain this decision is yours, and in your best interest? Do not answer that.... We observe by your deportment you intend to move forward with your ruinous intent. Leave our sight, Madam. Before you find yourself bound for the Tower. Go."

Lady Blythe trembles in the face of her Queen's disapproval. To our horror, the young woman remains, her terror rooting her in place.

Her Majesty cannot comprehend Lady Blythe's ill-advised attitude. She raises her arm to shoulder level once more. Her ladies' heads bow lower in our circles, concealing any involuntary flinch. But this time Her Majesty only points with one finger toward the chamber door. Cowering beneath the weight of their anxiety, her ladies fail to observe the quiver in our Queen's hand, or the tremor in a voice accustomed to command. Their heads tipped in deference; her ladies do not notice Her Majesty's unbidden emotion. But Her Grace's fear makes itself apparent to my appraising gaze.

Our Queen, buried deep within the unwanted pull of childish memory, inhales the sharpest of breaths. And with her small breast's increase, her generous spirit succeeds in returning to us. A wave of an impatient arm coupled with Her Majesty's hard eye, awakens Lady Blythe. Our Queen sends the frightened lady bustling from her position at Court. Lady Blythe turns to the bidding of another Lord and Master. Her Majesty cannot fathom Lady Blythe's fond desire.

As Lady Blythe scurries to escape Her Majesty, we occupy ourselves with our duties. I attend to Her Majesty's reading materials, replacing Castiglione with some Latin translations she toils over. On top, I place Ariosto and Ovid, should my Queen require readings more befitting her mood of late. With all sincerity I hope Her Majesty think me not too forward in guessing at her inclinations.

Her Grace, somewhat returned to herself, paces the chamber. She whispers under her breath all manner of insult and rebuke, a variety of broken phrases, all scattered and incoherent.

"Lady Blythe leaves us... Can she not find fulfillment here with us?...Why do they all persist in the pursuit of...Hideous..." Her Majesty circles her chamber. We bend our heads to our tasks, affecting the deafness so necessary to those of us in our Queen's service.

"Why subject herself to?... Is lust really so powerful?...Why do they leave me?... Willingly to... To subject herself to ... God's Death! Do they not know I attempt to preserve them? Yet, they abandon their Queen..."

Exhausted by her questioning of another's unknowable heart, Her Grace stops her tormented pacing. She lifts her chin, as if just noticing our undesired presence. With a simple wave, Her Majesty dismisses us. A Queen's disappointment in Lady Blythe spreads, as a deadly plague, over all of us together.

***

I quarrel with my scruples once more. Do I violate Her Majesty's abiding trust? I linger in my Queen's library. With the finest ostrich feathers I brush dust from Her Grace's sacred volumes. I re-shelve her leather-bound beauties on handsome lemon-oiled walnut bookcases. I arrange Her Majesty's correspondence so she might read a letter from a faithful subject; or put her hand on a parliamentary statute; or update a draft of a speech she will deliver to the Lords of the Privy Council; or rewrite a stirring prayer to her Clergy.

Though I fulfill my tasks with adequate attention, and though I handle her beloved books with care, my conscience accuses me.

I put my hand on the packet of letters. A ribbon of amber encircles the bundle. I have read and reread the yellowed documents on many an occasion. As the letters are addressed to me, my reading them does not offend any sense of moral propriety. It is not what I *read* causing my anguish, but what I write.

I consider it my duty to transcribe Her Majesty's character. And so I illustrate, in the dog-eared leaves of my diary, a portrait of her person. I seek a way to dignify Her Majesty's conduct respecting her unkindness to Sir William Cecil and her slapping of poor Lady Blythe. Can I wipe these blemishes from my Queen's character? Can I make understood My Majesty's many burdens? I will attempt it.

An adolescent Lady Elizabeth composed these, my treasured letters, from her happiest of homes. And all within a scarce few months. She was just a girl of fourteen years at the time. My future Queen shared with me the few meager instances of familial warmth she would experience within the complex bonds of kinship.

Our Lady Elizabeth had only recently lost her father, our mighty King Henry. Her young brother, Edward, then reigned. Lady Elizabeth was fortunate to find herself living with her last great mother. Our dowager, Queen Catherine Parr, resided in Chelsea. Lady Elizabeth writes with an innocent gratitude. How precarious is such naiveté? How long can this idyllic state of grace persist for a future Queen?

***

10th May, 1547

My Dearest Blanche,

I write from Chelsea, where I have lived these last weeks. It is four months since my dear father's death, and so I dress in my mourning clothes. Their heavy weight and oppressive charcoal tint oppresses my spirit. Yet, for an orphan child I deem myself most fortunate. You see, at last I have found the love of a mother. My Catherine Parr dotes on me, her late husband's child, as though I have always been her very own daughter.

Blanche, perhaps I will at last know what it is to be lavished with a mother's warm endearments. Catherine enters my Chamber each morning with a jolly greeting, and shares with me a light breakfast of lemon tea and biscuits with my favourite orange marmalade.

We share our meal together in her back garden. We stroll arm-in-arm under the blossoming cherries, laughing and speaking of silly things, such as why the creek trickles in one direction rather than another, or how a hapless he-wren twitters his ardent love songs, while his proposed mate replies with harrowing alarm. Perhaps she does not welcome his serenade of courtship. We laugh together at the nonsensical possibility.

Lady Catherine appears to enjoy our revelries very much, and so she dwells with me in the garden until Master Ascham arrives to carry me inside to my Latin and Italian verses. Ah, this prompts my poor memory. I must prepare a translation of John Calvin's *Institution de la Religion Chrestienne* for Master Ascham. He requests the first chapter tomorrow.

Wishing you good health, I apologize for the stingy length of my letter, and will certainly make it up to you soon. Awaiting your reply.

Your Assured Friend in Word and Deed,
Lady Elizabeth

***

9th June, 1547

Dearest Blanche,

I have received your recent letter, and humbly thank you for thinking of your friend with such kindness. I also thank you for your sympathies in the loss of my father, and for the charming way you comfort your poor friend.

I especially enjoyed your thoughtful metaphor comparing a mother's love to "sustenance without which our hearts might with parched thirst wilt within our very breasts, wasting in a barren world of callous want". Though I wholeheartedly comprehend the sentiment, I hope it was written with respect to my orphaned state, and that it does not in any way reflect your own heart's cares. In that case, I would say, "There, there, dear Blanche. I would not wish such an affliction on a friend so true.

Shall we move on to lighter subjects? It is with joy I write to you from my dear mother's house in Chelsea once again. Though there is little knowledge of it, and I must ask you to keep quiet with the news, my stepmother is to marry Lord Thomas Seymour, the High Admiral of England.

He is a fine gentleman. His manners are so elegant, and yet he entertains us with his wit as we dine, forever smiling on us both.

His Lordship especially excels in oratory, regaling us with harrowing stories of his adventures at sea. He speaks of uninhabited lands across the ocean I hardly dare imagine. His Lordship never issues a harsh command to my dear mother, or to me, only lovely words of praise and encouragement. He compliments us both on our beauty. And he makes much of my pretty hands, occasionally patting my dainty fingers. I blush as I write this.

I believe I have not witnessed such happiness and ease in my stepmother before. Truly, she loves our Lord Admiral with all her heart, and though nothing can replace my father's care, I believe I will love His Lordship mightily too.

Your Assured Friend,
Lady Elizabeth

***

17th July, 1547

Dearest Blanche,

Though I do not wish to cause you distress, I must insist this letter, on pain of death, you keep concealed. I am not writing of my dear Catherine Parr's secret marriage. As you know, that news is all about the Court. My brother, King Edward, though perplexed at the haste of my stepmother's marriage, has with his typical good nature, conceded his blessing and relieved our family of any objections he might have to his stepmother's hasty nuptials.

We have moved our residence to my stepfather, Lord Thomas Seymour's home at Sudeley Castle, in Gloucestershire. I have no complaints about my new home. I am happily surrounded by loving step-parents, Kat Ashley, who forever attends me and gives me comfort, and still I do tutelage under Master Ascham from Cambridge. He polishes my pronunciations to the best of his ability.

What, you may enquire, is of such a furtive nature? Wait, dear Blanche. I will guide you there without haste, as I fear you will receive a little shock at what has transpired. As did I, I assure you.

It first happened in the Lord Admiral's rose garden two mornings ago, when I bent to enjoy the aroma of some fulsome red blooms. The gentleman approached without my knowledge, bent with me to the identical rose I inhaled, until the very bristle of his beard rubbed my cheek. With haste I withdrew, and the Lord Admiral laughed so, I thought he might injure himself with it.

If that were all, dearest Blanche, I would not trouble you with the paltry nature of my claim. But the morning after that, the Lord Admiral visited me within my Bedchamber. He approached, and seated himself on my bedstead while I, still unaware of his presence, slumbered on.

When I awakened, my Lord tickled me about the shoulders and arms, causing me to giggle with much mirth. Though our Lord Admiral jests with a pleasant affability, I fear he conveniently forgets the proprieties. I do not breathe a word to Catherine, as I do not believe her inclined to approve of my stepfather's familiar pranks.

I share with you my confidence, as I feel I must relieve my mind of compromising thoughts, for you see, though Lord Thomas behaves too familiarly, I quite enjoy the fun and frolic of it all.

Your Assured Friend in Word and Deed,
Covertly So,
Lady Elizabeth

***

12th August, 1547

Dearest Blanche,

The amusements continue at Sudeley Castle. I am sorry I have shocked you so you spilled raspberry cordial on my recent letter, but dear Blanche, you are the only friend I can trust with my confidence. Dare I share some more? Set down your goblet before proceeding further, my dear friend.

He kissed me on the mouth. My Lord entered my Chamber in the morning, as he is wont to do, and pressed his bearded lips on mine. Many amongst the servants observe my Lord Admiral's unusual manner, and I believe there is some chatter afloat; however Blanche, I assure you, all is in jest. They do not know his true nature as I do. He adores his Lady Elizabeth, and only provides special attention, as a loving stepfather will. I appreciate and heartily enjoy His Lordship's tendency to play. And so His Lordship's kiss I allowed, and responded with warmth.

The Lord Admiral stroked my small shoulder in the most delicate manner as he embraced his Lady Elizabeth. Shivers ran up and down my spine with the delight of it. Then he began his tickling again, and I lashed out with my bare foot, until he placed his hand around my ankle and held tight. I shrieked as he ran his hands down my sides in an unforgiving manner. How I laughed. Such joy I find here at Sudeley.

Your Assured Friend in Word and Deed,
Lady Elizabeth

***

28th August, 1547

Dearest Blanche,

I fear our antics may have gone beyond that which might be deemed strictly supportable. This morning I strolled with my loving step-parents under the bowers, when our Lord Admiral noted the time had arrived for Lady Elizabeth to shed her mourning dress. Catherine agreed, insisting I return to my habitual manner of clothing.

As I hesitated, in consideration of their proposal, the Lord Admiral drew his sword, and cut the dress from me, leaving me standing on the cobbled path before my Lord and my dowager Queen in only my petticoat. My Lord Thomas and Catherine expressed great amusement at the escapade, chuckling, as did I, while I scurried indoors to discover for myself a suitable dress. The event evoked hilarity, though I hope the servants did not observe for they might misinterpret the good fun in it.

Your Assured Friend in Word and Deed,
Lady Elizabeth

Postscript,
The servants have taken an unnatural notice, or should I say the servant who dwells most in my heart. Kat Ashley approached His Lordship, and requested he cease his morning visits to my Chamber. She advises our Lord Admiral the servants will make much of the matter if he does not immediately alter his behaviour with respect to Lady Elizabeth. To which Lord Thomas replied: "By God's precious soul, I mean no evil, and I will not leave it."

***

21st November, 1547

Dearest Blanche,

Glad tidings. My Lady Catherine Parr is blessed with the expectation she will bear Lord Thomas's child. My new mother expresses much joy. When now we amble through the garden together she hums the sweetest melody, then breaks off from her song to speak of layettes, and christening gowns, and naming, and my place in the ceremony. What a happy family we are. Oh,

Blanche, how Lady Fortune smiles on your faithful friend....

Your Assured Friend in Word and Deed,
Lady Elizabeth

***

20th February, 1548

Dearest Blanche,

Lady Fortune does not smile on your friend any longer. My Lord's supposed liberties have carried me from my family to the home of Lord Denny in Hertfordshire.

How did my banishment come about? The Lord Admiral entered my Chamber, and embraced me as so often he does. Though your concern for my well-being was duly read with close attention, and duly appreciated, I preferred to welcome His Lordship's innocent antics, sometimes returning his tickling and fondling. I now wish I had taken a friend's sage advice.

On this particular occasion, our Lord Admiral slapped his Lady Elizabeth on my buttocks with a direction to "Rise from my bed at once, upon God's death." Unhappily for the Lord Admiral, his hand found too great a liking for my undressed buttocks, and kneaded there somewhat before leaving it. My Catherine, heavy with child, entered the Chamber as His Lordship laid his hand on me. The good lady demanded, in her quiet way, I should leave Sudeley for Hertfordshire. So here I dwell. Bereft and alone once again if not for my Kat Ashley, and my studious Roger Ascham.

I thank you for your continued correspondence dear Blanche, as it is your written company and yours alone I enjoy in this time of my dreadful banishment.

Your Woeful Friend in Word and Deed,
Lady Elizabeth

Postscript
My mother Catherine does not forsake me entirely. She continues to correspond with her woeful step-daughter. But it is now from afar. Afar is a wretched locale. The only place I seem to receive any mothering from. I took delivery of a short letter from her today, advising me of her healthy condition. Her infant within grows at a miraculous speed, she advises. Catherine tells me she misses my company desperately, but that for my protection, I must remain in Hertfordshire until further notice.

***

2nd October, 1548

Dearest Blanche,

Many months have passed since I last corresponded. I beseech you to please forgive me for my thoughtless lapse. I fear I impose on your sympathetic ear. I hardly know how to unburden myself on your honest friendship. It feels once more like your Lady Elizabeth has lost all. Our dearest Catherine, mother in both word and deed, gave birth in joyousness to a baby girl named Mary at Sudeley Castle last month. The little girl thrives with remarkable good health, however, true to my maligned destiny; another mother occupies an early grave.

Only days after her little Mary's birth, my beloved stepmother contracted a fever, carrying her away from me, as each has gone before her. Yet again, I don the charcoal tint of mourning, the weight of black taffeta on my soul. This is not the end of my concerns, for the Lord Admiral's heart yearns so at the loss of one wife, he would have another. He suggests his Lady Elizabeth would make a fine replacement.

Blanche, though I feel some affection for our Lord Admiral, and though I dare not cause offence to his Lordship after all he has given me, I shy away from such harnessing of my freedom. Unlike my dear, lost stepmother I do not care for hidden rendezvous, and impromptu nuptials.

The Lord Admiral persists in offering various incentives to me, including the unlimited use of Seymour Place, however each new offer I have assiduously declined. I do not appreciate the Lord Admiral's new persistence. It has lost its previous luster. I shall appeal to my new acquaintance, Sir William Cecil for his sage advice. Perhaps Sir Cecil will provide for an orphaned Lady, that which the Lord Admiral cannot.

With Sincere Good Wishes,
Your Assured Friend in Word and Deed,
Lady Elizabeth

It is with misgiving I wait as another trusted friend appeals to our Queen's discretion. I fear for Kat Ashley. Though a longtime favourite of Her Majesty's, and our Queen's governess and teacher for many years, Kat dares to raise a subject which could determine her fate in the unhappiest of ways.

"Speak to us, Kat. I believe every subject in this realm knows better than his Queen how to proceed in the best interest of our kingdom." Her Majesty leafs through Ariosto's *Orlando Furioso*, skimming to the folded down page where Angelica arrives at Charlemagne's court. It is here, within one of Her Majesty's favourite passages, Orlando first notices the woman who will captivate him entirely.

Kat Ashley, determined to occupy her Queen's whole attention, advances closer to Her Majesty. As Kat's skirts bustle with purpose, I pray her cheek does not suffer Lady Blythe's same fate.

"Your Majesty, I speak only of *your* best interest, which is my own. Nor do I, in any way, detract from your gracious and ever-loving rule…"

"Of course you do not. Proceed." Our Queen's impatience simmers, but does not over boil. The delicate leaves of her book she thumbs, page after page, searching for the Canto she studies more than any other: Rinaldo and Angelica each drink of the magical fountain, attempting to unite their two fates. However with each attempt, one lover becomes more smitten while the other suffers more disdain.

Her Majesty finds pleasure translating Ariosto's verse from the original Italian. She takes pride in her linguistic skill, often toiling for hours over a particularly intricate passage.

Does the scholarly task appeal to our Queen's intellect? Or does Ariosto's poetry captivate Her Majesty's own smitten heart? If our Queen finds her place within the text, Kat's moment will be lost. With the subtlest of looks, I urge Lady Kat to hasten to her point.

"Your Majesty, I say this only because I honour and love you as my Queen, and as the true friend to my entire family you have shown yourself to be..."

"Get to it, Kat. I do not know for certain how long my reign will endure. Best hurry to your point, before your next sovereign ascends the throne."

Her Majesty, in her restlessness, flips too many pages, wading too far into her text. She locates Orlando's madness and Angelica's sad plight. With a sigh of disappointment, she slams the book shut on Angelica as the princess finds herself exposed, tethered to a rock in the sea, offered to Orc in sacrifice. The weight of Angelica's cares only serves to further burden Her Majesty today.

"Your Grace, the attentions you offer the Master of the Horse have occasioned a great deal of malicious talk. If you continue to favour Lord Dudley, you will encounter great mischief at court. I fear Your Majesty risks what you value above all...the love of your subjects."

"Ah, the rumours. The evil speaking, yet again. I must ask, Kat. Has your Queen ever had the will, or found pleasure in living a dishonourable life? May God preserve me, I do not know of anyone who could forbid me, but I trust in God that nobody would ever live to see me so commit myself." Her Majesty places a muzzle on Kat's understanding. She leads her lady through a veritable maze of pretty, poetical forays.

"No, Your Majesty, it is not your behaviour I question, nor do I presume...however, others wonder at your attachment to Lord Robert..." Do not falter Kat. The realm, and I most of all, support you.

"Kat, it is true. I value Lord Dudley's attentions. In this world, your Queen has so much sorrow and tribulation, and so little joy. Would you deny me so little? Would *they*?" Her Majesty lifts and spreads her arms wide. The ample sleeves of our Queen's velvet gown billow in a magnificent display of authority. Her Majesty sweeps the air so Kat feels a breeze drift by her flustered countenance. Hopefully that little breeze is all Kat feels on her cheek. Whether Her Majesty aims her dramatic gesture at her ladies-in-waiting, bent to their labours in her adjoining chamber, or to her beloved England, I am not certain.

"No one seeks to deny Your Majesty. However, Lord Robert occupies his rooms so near yours at Whitehall. And now at all Your Majesty's residences - Greenwich and Richmond too. It sets tongues to waging war against Your Majesty's good name. It is said Your Grace dances only with Lord Robert, embracing only him. It is also said Lord Dudley garners all Your Majesty's favour. Any remaining preference you might bestow is but a single drop in the bottom of what was once considered the deepest of wells." Though Kat's initial approach is hesitant, like an armed regiment without its charge, her finish erupts like Her Majesty's trumpeters signaling their Queen's entrance.

"Kat, I thank you for your considered words, and for the care with which you speak. How gently you offer your Queen this sobering notice of the gossip wending through our kingdom. Those who publicly ridicule their Queen will soon hear their monarch's reply. I assure you. It is a Prince's duty to mete out punishment....To be a King and wear a crown is more glorious to them that see it than it is a pleasure to them that bear it." Her Majesty stares as though she forgets Kat's presence.

"I cannot smother altogether the wandering imaginations of our subjects. Dear God. Your Queen will not stop up England's creative fount with regal authority, even if it is she who drowns in their torrent of criticism. Their careless gossip, though regretful, and hurtful to my person, is but a reflection of their own fearful dispositions."

"It is Lord Dudley's relentless proximity they question, Your Grace…"

"Lord Dudley found his previous rooms, located so near the river, plagued by dampness and cold. To protect my friend from rheumy symptoms, I merely moved his lodging where he might find comfort. My favourites will be protected by their doting sovereign. This includes you, Kat Ashley." Her Majesty embraces her former governess. As our Queen holds onto Kat, she redirects her friend and confidante toward the chamber door.

"No one cares as much as your sovereign for the safety and quietness of you all. I thank you for your love, Kat. You may go."

Our Queen watches as Kat leaves her chamber. I follow close behind. I believe Her Majesty's smile, and her abundance of ornamental words camouflage her heart's real inclination. But I say nothing.

***

9th September, 1560

Whitehall Palace cannot contain a Gypsy's ambition. Now at Windsor Castle, in another sun-washed chamber, Lord Dudley works in tandem with the waning summer. Determined shafts of sunlight, allied with the gentleman's embrace, reach for their Queen. The rays probe our sovereign's protected heart. Penetrating the diamond shaped, leaded windows of Her Majesty's Privy Chamber, sunlit arcs dissolve our Queen's detachment. The beveled glass panes retract and redirect the glow in a spectacular manner on the upholstered window seat. Sunlit rainbows paint Her Majesty's cheek. And she wears it well. The regal violets, azures, and glorious crimsons decorate our Queen with a splendour almost ceremonial in its design.

Her Gypsy pretends to brush exotic jewels from Her Majesty's smiling countenance. Will he tarnish our Queen? Will he claim another piece of her priceless reputation? As Lord Robert strokes one cheek, and then another, our Queen smiles on him. Her Majesty places her hands on his, declaring her permission for the liberties he takes. I cannot with certainty report if the Gypsy's proximity to Her Majesty heats her cheek, or if sunbeams do their own mischief on our Queen's fair complexion. Her Majesty warms to him.

"My Eyes, your embrace provides more comfort than any your Queen receives. Yet those who claim to hold their Majesty in the highest regard wish to remove from their Queen my one sweet diversion." Her Majesty sighs and removes her Gypsy's hand from her sun-patterned cheek.

"He who loves you best remains next to you, Your Majesty. It is I who offer you everything." Lord Dudley leans forward. Always forward. Her Majesty, adrift in her reverie, fails to hear her Gypsy's declaration. My Queen studies the dancing squares of sunlight as she follows the thread of her own wandering musings.

"...my Bonny Sweet Robin's darling hand on my cheek reminds me of a gentleman I knew in my youth. I first received his amiability with delight. Then, with no liking at all. You see, the cost was too dear. Am I forever to be reprimanded for wanting so little? Are you, Robin, too great an expense for the destitute Queen of England?"

"Your Majesty, I give you all of myself, freely, and with no expectation in return." Forever he offers an answer to a question that does not look for his opinion.

"You mistake what it is to love a Queen, Robin. With each breath I take of my realm's sweet air, my own existence mocks my free will. My people's expectation guides everything. Providing them with a monarch whom they can love, and a realm that is both peaceful and prosperous, requires me to sacrifice my very self. I must decline what my own beloved people consider their earthly right and privilege. I cannot love with my heart. All of my decisions must be made with a head that balances a crown on it."

"Your Majesty, if my inability to be the dignified companion you require brings you discredit I will leave, and with pleasure. Then I will know I have given you my greatest gift." The Gypsy offers a sacrifice that he knows will be refused. It is no offer at all.

"No, Robert. I have dismissed the question of you leaving. You are too valuable for me to forfeit your service. If only I could transport you with me, invisible to all but my own eye. I need your gentle encouragement in everything."

"You have my kind sentiments, Your Majesty. My doting attachment, every aspect of my person accompanies you always. I marvel at your beauty as I linger under this rainbow's arc. And when only memory must serve to mimic your presence in my restless mind, I think about you still." Her Majesty hesitates, willing herself to believe in her Gypsy's devotion.

"Majesty, after many years of knowing you as no other man has, you continue to surprise and delight your dedicated servant. So vast is the understanding your soul occupies. So varied the gifts you offer your Robin."

"You only flatter your Queen. I have many faithful subjects who offer that sort of tedious chatter." Her Majesty vacillates. First she encourages her Gypsy's wanton lovemaking, smiling on his whispered confessions. Then she deplores the liberties he takes. I fear in the end his tactics will overpower our Queen's peaceful resistance. Already she wavers in the grasp of his seduction.

"I have no reason to flatter my Queen. Her luminous qualities are such that no exaggeration need be required. Your Majesty, you encompass all; my entire universe. There is nothing to fabricate which you do not provide. No gift you do not possess. We would need an eternity to think of it. And so the solution to our dilemma presents itself. Should we agree to remain together forever?"

The Gypsy's lavish praise imperils Her Majesty's resolve, and maybe my own too. Have I relied too long on opinions bandied about the Court?

"*Forever?* Robin, do not force me to mourn our time together before it is over. You know, as I do, Father Time's disposition ensures limits are on us. Time cannot resist his own finite nature, as I cannot turn away my Bonny Sweet Robin. I do not wish to think about Time or its lack. These past months of riding out together, our joining in genuine friendship, have brought an elation which I did not know existed. Yet it cannot hold forever, no matter how a Queen wishes it might."

"Do not think of the unhappy clock, then. I have a gift to offer Your Majesty which will toss from our twin minds all desperate thoughts." Lord Dudley rises, gathers his offering in his embrace, and places the beautiful instrument into the arms of Her Majesty, who cradles it with the same care.

Though I do not claim much knowledge of these objects, the gittern appears to be of a superior quality. The crafted body glistens with hand-rubbed brilliance. Lovely woodland creatures, carved in intricate detail, prance all around the neck. A deer bounds along its side, a fox lurks nearby, and several hunters on their stallions, slavering dogs surrounding them, chase after. The delicate carving inscribes the entire gracious neck of the musical instrument.

Our Queen examines her gift. She rolls it over in her hands, running her fingertips along the elaborate carvings. Finally, she holds it to her bosom. Her embrace and silent gratitude, her only reply. Her Majesty's answer pleases her Gypsy. He casts his eye on her as though Her Grace holds their cherished offspring.

"Your Majesty, I offer you this gittern for my own selfish reasons. It is my solemn wish when you play and sing - whether it is of Tallis's merciful God or of Byrd's joyful dance, I will forget Time exists at all. Your fingers strumming the pliant strings dictate my breast's rise and fall. Your melodic voice fills the cup that is your Robin's spirit. You, Your Majesty, direct all my soul's senses."

My Queen smiles on her Gypsy. She arranges the bell of her dress on the window seat, positioning the instrument so she might indulge her Bonny Sweet Robin with a happy melody. But as Her Grace places her fingers on the pliant strings, preparing to tune her newest gift, an interruption arises.

Lord Robert's servant, a certain Thomas Bowes from Cumnor Place, requests entrance. The stricken look on the man's countenance speaks of his message before he delivers it. I do not know what reserves Bowes calls on to hold himself upright in place; he trembles so with his heavy intelligence.

"My humblest apologies for my intrusion Your Majesty, but I deliver news to Master Dudley. A tragedy of the gravest consequence." As Bowes inclines forward in his posture of obeisance, I fear he may not find the wherewithal to upright himself again. His Queen abandons her cherished gittern on the upholstered window seat and approaches the man servant.

"You are forgiven your intrusion, Sir. Speak to your master, our Lord Dudley. Tell him of your concern."

His Queen's forbearance enchants Bowes, alleviating the man's uneasy disposition. Bowes finds the courage, and a voice with which to offer his news. "It is with regret I must inform Lord Dudley, his wife Amy Dudley has, by possible foul means, met her death. She is dead by a broken neck; a fall from a pair of stairs."

Bowes searches Lord Dudley's countenance, then Her Majesty's, returning to his master's expression. No reply greets his dreadful message. The Gypsy and his Queen, only a moment before joined in kindred harmony, disengage from one another. Bowes' few words unleash a force dismantling all their mutual affection. Each stares ashen, askance, disappearing into separate spheres.

When Lord Robert and Her Majesty refuse to acknowledge his presence any longer, Bowes offers a final bow and steps backward, into the uninhabited reaches of the room. The sun-drenched rays will not follow him there.

The hush following Bowes' unwelcome message echoes with the magnitude of its weight. Silence redefines itself. An absence of sound fractures the chamber's tranquility. A false serenity reverberates within Her Majesty's agitated spirit. Behind her veil of regal composure, a blood-curdling howl hurls itself at our Queen. Realization devours calm. All this the aftermath of one trembled utterance.

Still the Gypsy and my Queen make no gesture toward the wretched messenger, nor toward one another. They pose in the stillness, paralyzed by the loss laid on them.

"Thank you Bowes. You may go." Robert Dudley's voice interrupts the absence of sound.

Her Majesty offers the man no reply. The impact of the servant's words unravels her composure. As a drifting moon, having lost its attraction to its home planet, careens untethered in a wordless galaxy, Her Majesty's calm melts away. My Queen's former gladness explodes into fragments as Her Majesty comprehends her loss.

"My wife...dead." Lord Dudley bends forward, head bowed. Separated from his Amy by death, the rupture Dudley fears is from his Queen. The revelatory power of Bowes' few words may prove more devastating than all of Sir Cecil's and the Council's months of blustering about illicit activities at Court.

"I am sorry, Robin." As is her inclination, Her Majesty's response in times of crisis proves reticent. A blanket of stoic restraint replaces painted rainbows on my Queen's cheek. If her Gypsy were not so preoccupied with his own loss, he might recognize Her Majesty retreats within.

My Queen meditates on her foremost concern. Always, her dear people. What will her subjects conclude when presented with Amy Dudley's untimely death? For months her intimate counselors, Parliament, and her people have harangued Her Majesty with slanderous accusation about the nature of her relationship with Lord Dudley: "He poisons his wife, while doting on his Queen."; "The Gypsy secretly betroths himself to Her Majesty."; "The Queen does not go out on progress without delivering her Gypsy of another son."

While heedful of the rumours and their potential harm, Her Majesty believed she was immune to all the gross fabrications. She tossed her jubilant curls, and giggled at the crude and ridiculous slanders. And now? Her Majesty's blissful months of infatuation take a sinister turn.

My Queen will not deliberate on her personal loss until later, when fickle Time permits. When an unreasonable universe returns to a semblance of equilibrium, and planets circle one another in their former easeful way, Her Majesty will consider Robert Dudley's newfound viability as suitor.

Her Grace will withdraw, alone within her Privy Chamber and reflect on a Gypsy's courtship: his gloved hand holding Her Majesty close around her waist as he assists her to her mount; his open smile as he tosses her high in a spirited galliard. Her Majesty will ponder the way her Robin's collar bone rests on her shoulder, when he fondles her beneath blousy skirts. And his cradling of her gittern, as he places his gift into her arms. And then Her Majesty will curse Bowes and his wretched news. The servant delivers her Bonny Sweet Robin to her, and snatches him away at the very same moment.

Still the Gypsy prattles on.

"Your Grace, we must launch an inquiry at once. We must demand to know what evil has befallen my household. My wife....we must determine the manner of her death. If we do not, infamy will lay waste to my reputation. We must obtain answers...or my name will be ruined..." In contrast to my Queen's silence Lord Robert talks and talks.

Finally, Her Majesty ends his panicky tirade. "I fear, Robin, my people will adopt their own dreadful conclusions no matter what resources we apply to our probing of this evil. You must leave for Kew at once. Your Queen will make public the news, and advise the Court investigators of their task. Your reputation will be restored Robin. Your Queen shall see to it."

"Father Time takes offence at our recent banter, and intrudes on us if only to remind us of his omnipresence." Lord Dudley readies himself for a hasty departure as our Queen looks on.

Her Majesty's entire form deflates. Time levels its vengeful wrath at more than just her joyful excess. "Goodbye, Bonny Sweet Robin. I will send by messenger with news of the investigation. Your Queen will not stand for any tarnishing of your name."

"Do not doubt me, Your Majesty. I am no murderer." Dudley covers Her Grace's hands with his gloved ones.

"I do not doubt you, Robin." Her Majesty bends at her waist, dispatching him with a formal kiss, one on each cheek. Our Queen withdraws her graceful form from Lord Dudley, only brushing his face with her constant lips. The kiss, now a demonstration of loyalty alone. Before her Gypsy approaches the chamber door, our Queen has hastened from him.

No sooner does Lord Dudley leave our Queen's presence, Her Majesty beckons to her ladies. "Kat, seek out Sir William Cecil. Advise him his Queen requires his attendance at once."

***

The chamber stands empty. Glaring rays, recently more temperate, adopt a brutal insistence. Waves of stifling heat penetrate delicate window panes. They enter a barren room. Once beckoning, playful, the sun blazes with summer's thick intensity. I fear springtime dashes headlong into an inviting flame, giving in to summer's balmy welcome. Her Majesty's youthful spirit, prepared or not, must learn to welcome summer's seasoned wisdom.

Summer I – Governed by No One

And wherever the power that makes men happy comes to an end, lack of power enters and makes them wretched. So that there necessarily exists among kings a larger share of misery.

-- Boethius

I attempt to weave a tapestry that is my Queen. To make her understood. I fear my efforts, though well-intentioned, fail to uncover what Her Majesty hides beneath all her finery. I roam too far forward. And now essential stitches in time will not hold. I must retrieve all the broken threads and knit them together so that more than my Queen's self-portrait can emerge.

It is October, 1562, and Her Majesty, a half-grown Queen of twenty-nine years, suffers great disappointments for one so young. Her physical well-being staggers under the strain. This sets the cawing ravens of Parliament squawking. Unmercifully, they demand she name a successor. It is my duty to report on her ailing condition, but first I will retreat to an earlier place in time. A place where many who were considered stronger than my fragile Lady Elizabeth met their own untimely disasters.

***

The death of Catherine Parr did not hinder the Lord Admiral Thomas Seymour's pursuit of my young mistress. Indeed, the Lord Admiral displayed no grace in his acceptance of the fifteen year old Elizabeth's rejection. My Lady Elizabeth learned a valuable lesson from Lord Seymour's unchecked ambition.

"My Lady, are you not betrothed to the Lord Admiral Thomas Seymour, now residing in the Tower on heinous charges of treason?" Sir Robert Tyrwhit and his delegation pounce on Hatfield Palace in an egregious manner. The gentlemen confront our adolescent Lady Elizabeth. They spare no one in their effort to protect her brother, our King Edward.

My young Lady suffered a terrifying episode this morning. Kat Ashley and my own cousin, Thomas Parry were taken from Elizabeth by the palace guards. They were led away to the Tower, where they now reside. Their stories will be unearthed. Under what duress I do not know. So many tears were shed by the two young ladies; I do not know which were regal in nature, and which were the caregiver's.

My fellow servants leave my Lady Elizabeth without that womanly care she seeks. Sir Tyrwhit, on behalf of His Majesty King Edward, isolates our young Elizabeth. His intent? To harry my Lady until her own damning words carry her to accompany Kat Ashley in the Tower.

"No my Lord. I am not, nor have I ever considered a betrothal to the Lord Admiral." The adolescent Elizabeth's tranquil demeanour conceals her devastation at the loss of Kat Ashley. I praise our young Lady's spirit. Elizabeth sits before Master Tyrwhit, respectable and unadorned, unrecognizable even to myself, her faithful servant.

After Kat Ashley and Thomas Parry's removal, Lady Elizabeth retreated to her chamber, emerging in attire unknown to the household since her great father's death. Her skirts of modest black muslin, adorned with white collar and cuffs. No jewel adorns her person in any manner or form. Her delicate skin she has scrubbed pristine, as though with a brush employed by the stable servants. Her complexion at first appeared all flushed and scratched after all the brushing. Now her cheek fades with this gentleman's badgering, imitating more the pearly paper on which I record her story.

Who is this plain, Protestant girl returning her questioner's scrutiny with composure, all gracious? Master Tyrwhit must contain within his breast a glacial heart if he is not moved by her humbling modesty.

"Why then does the Lord Admiral insist you are betrothed?" Tyrwhit persists with his prodding, his duty to King Edward foremost in his mind.

"Lord Seymour regretfully mistakes my intent, perhaps due to his own aspirations, my Lord. I do not now, nor never have considered a proposal of marriage from his Lordship." Our Lady offers her version with aplomb. She raises her chin, not with defiance, but with a prim knowledge of her moral fortitude. A mischievous part of me delights in my Lady's excellent performance.

Master Tyrwhit displays less pleasure in her artfulness. He cocks his head from side to side, peering at Elizabeth as though to penetrate our young Lady's reason. "But you will confess to having an inclination to accept Lord Seymour's suit? Several have testified to this." Master Tyrwhit scours a ledger on the table before him, indicating with a tap of his gnarled finger where others have reported on Lady Elizabeth's delight in the Admiral's attentions.

"The Lord Admiral was step-father to me when I lived at Sudeley with Lady Catherine Parr, my father's widow. He provided for us a genuine and loving place to reside. But I lived there only months, when Catherine delivered her child, Mary. The dowager Queen's subsequent death from childbed fever has meant my separation from Lord Seymour for a considerable time." Elizabeth's agile fingers go to her collar, adjusting and flattening it. Her attention turns to the pristine cuffs of her dress, which she pleats in perfect order. With each gesture, Lady Elizabeth directs Master Tyrwhit's attention toward her aesthetic semblance of modesty. A careful self-discipline moderates all she speaks.

"Yet he proposes marriage." The gentleman persists.

"What Lord Seymour proposes, does not a marriage make, Sir. Though the Lord Admiral suggested a betrothal, I referred him to the Council. I am Lady Elizabeth, the daughter of King Henry, Sir. I know well my duty to my brother, King Edward. I will not consider any offer of marriage without the Council's prior knowledge and permission."

Our young Lady whispers her reply with patience. Both she and her interrogator share an identical respect for the proprieties. 'Why', our Lady asks, 'do Tyrwhit and she confront one another with antagonism, when both share an abiding desire to please her brother, King Edward?'

"What of the Lord Admiral's behaviour when you dwelt at Sudeley Castle, then? Your servants, namely Lady Kat Ashley, have indicated improprieties ensued."

"My life at Sudeley was without tarnish, Sir. I enjoyed a happy and sedate relation both with my dear step-mother, Catherine Parr and with the Lord Admiral. Though we frolicked some, no barrier was breached that would put to question my strict wholesomeness. I am innocent of the detestable gossip that litters the countryside, and I wish to have a proclamation made to refute such infamy... Of Kat Ashley, I will need to know when she returns to us. We cannot do without our governess and friend." The tables turn. My Lady makes her own requests known.

"I cannot comment on Lady Ashley's fate. All will depend on her testimony, taken within the Tower walls. If she remains blameless in the Lord Admiral's affairs, she will be returned to your side. If, however, she plays a part in the machinations of Lord Seymour to unseat His Majesty, King Edward, I cannot vouch for her secure return. Shall we resume, Madam? Though you claim to have lived comfortably and without blame in the house of the Lord Admiral, you were sent to live away, with Lord Denny in Hertfordshire." Again Master Tyrwhit refers to his bulky ledger, his pointer finger landing on our Lady's home with the Denny's.

"As I stated previously Sir, my stepmother found herself with child, and was inclined to direct her attentions to her own, and her dear child's well-being." Lady Elizabeth does not allow impatience to intrude. Yet she indicates to Master Tyrwhit the tiresome nature of his questions.

"Did you not resent the implication? Your secondary significance to the dowager Queen?" The gentleman plays on. His spectacles slide down his lengthy nose, as melting wax along a spent taper. Distracted, he removes them altogether, peers harder into my Lady Elizabeth's flushed countenance. But she, dear Lady, does not acknowledge his chagrin. Her fair eyebrows she lifts. Her grey eyes she opens wide in surprise.

"Resent? I have no resentment. My Lady Catherine was nothing but an attentive mother and friend to me always. I miss her yet." With this admission of loss, Elizabeth wrinkles her brow. Her eyes cloud as she studies her own chafed hands. Genuine tears threaten, deepening the grey to a mournful shade, though Lady Elizabeth allows no unbidden grief to sink her chosen demeanour.

I understand Lady Elizabeth's authentic affection for Queen Catherine and I pity my dear girl her suffering. But her Tudor pride will staunch any salty flow well before Master Tyrwhit has the opportunity to look on her tears.

"And the Admiral? How do you regard Lord Seymour?" Tyrwhit remains oblivious to my lady's unbidden emotion, his head tilted down into his massive ledger still.

"Though I risk sounding heartless..." Lady Elizabeth masters her sadness in the few seconds it takes Master Tyrwhit to formulate his next query. How she leads the gentleman by his snout. I half expect Lady Elizabeth to reach beneath her seat and draw from it a leather harness and lead to place on Master Tyrwhit's starched collar.

"What say you, Madam?" He, poor ignorant man, joins her in the chase. Leaning forward, the gentleman remains certain he will triumph over my young Lady's wit. If asked, our Lady's tutor, Master Ascham, would instruct him otherwise.

"...I might appear ungrateful to His Lordship the Admiral, but my sentiments remain quite empty of sorrow at his loss of companionship. It has been many months since I dwelt in his presence. In that time I find enjoyment and satisfaction in the company of my ladies, and in the scholarly instruction of Sir Roger Ascham. Again, I must plead with you to release Kat Ashley. She has done no wrong, Sir."

"Lady Elizabeth, I have advised you, she will be questioned, and if found..."

"I must be allowed to write to Protector Somerset of my innocence. He must hear from my own pen, all my intention toward my brother, our King Edward, is of a loving, and reverent nature." Lady Elizabeth loses patience with the ordeal. She attempts an ending to the farce, drawing the curtain closed on Master Tyrwhit's interview.

"Alright, Madam. Argue your innocence in writing to the Protector. Would you then tolerate my questioning of your feelings toward your brother, our King?" He, unconscious of Her Majesty's gamesmanship, mutters beneath his breath "*...she hath a very good wit and nothing is gotten of her but by great policy.*"

"I have only love for our King Edward, my dear little brother. This he well knows. Are we quite finished, Master Tyrwhit? To my pen, I must turn." Lady Elizabeth rises from the carved table. Her attention now rests on the message she will compose for the Lord Protector in her own interest.

"As you wish, my Lady." Master Tyrwhit concedes the round to Lady Elizabeth. A sublime tournament indeed. Our Lady manages the gentleman with such deft attention to his dignity; he does not suffer the discomfort of surrender, nor bend to the humiliating awareness of his defeat.

***

28th January, 1549
To Edward Seymour, Lord Protector Somerset

My Lord:

Your great gentleness and goodwill toward me, in this thing as in other things, I do understand. I do give you most humble thanks. And whereas your lordship wills and counsels me as an earnest friend to declare what I know in this matter and also to write what I have declared to Master Tyrwhit, I shall most willingly do it.

I declared that the Lord Admiral offered me his house for my time being with the King's Majesty. He further asked me if the Council did consent that I should have my Lord Admiral, whether I would consent to it or no. I answered that I would not tell him what my mind was, and I inquired further of him what he meant to ask me that question or who bade him say so.

As concerning Kat Ashley, she said always (when any talked of my marriage) that she would never have me marry – neither in England nor out of England – without the consent of the King's Majesty, Your Grace's, and the Council's.

These be the things which I both declared to Master Tyrwhit and also whereof my conscience beareth me witness. I would not for all earthly things offend in anything, for I know I have a soul to save as well as other folks have.

Master Tyrwhit and others have told me that there go rumours abroad which be both against my honour and honesty, which be these: that I am in the Tower and with child by my Lord Admiral. My lord, these are shameful slanders. I shall most heartily desire your lordship that I may come to the court after your first determination, that I may show myself there as I am. Written in haste from Hatfield this 28 of January, the year of the lord, 1549.

Your assured friend to my little power, Elizabeth

My Lady scribbles her message in a flurry. She folds the paper, attaches her waxen seal for closure, and places it into my open hand. As the lightness of the paper rests there, belying its weighty contents, Lady Elizabeth beckons my eye with her hooded one. One hand remains on the crucial message, her fingers alighting on it as though she dare not release it to its burdensome task. Her other hand, Elizabeth links within mine so we stand forehead pressed to devoted forehead, united in contemplation of one another's cares.

Though our brows lean one on the other, offering physical proof of our friendship, a gap lies between the concerns milling within each. Parallel paths we travel. Arm-in-arm, onward to a shared horizon. Each of us clings to an enduring devotion. My Lady's passion, when not preoccupied with her survival, burns for her beloved England. And mine, in turn, for the beloved Lady.

We voyage to diverse destinations, she and I. Though my Lady's journey will offer her a throne and an adoring kingdom, I prefer my humble road. All littered with tattered pages. My narrative: chosen by my recall, transcribed by my quill, and cherished for its fidelity to my solemn purpose. I pray Lady Elizabeth finds this same enduring comfort in her more privileged condition.

Her interrogator leaves her with a nod of his graying head. A tasseled curtain closes on the final scene of the third act. My Lady exhales. Lady Elizabeth abandons her actor's disguise, bows her head, and sobs on my shoulder like the fifteen year old woman-child she is.

***

"Kat." My Lady hesitates, afraid to believe what her eye insists to be true. "You return to your Elizabeth? I cannot express how I have missed your faithful company these last months. Lady Elizabeth's springtime arrives." Elizabeth's cheek, recently dulled with tears and hemp-rubbed harshness, sparkles.

The capacity of our animated girl to revel in the moment contrasts with the artifice she practices on Master Tyrwhit. I marvel at the Lady's multiplicity of character, so natural to her.

"My sweet Lady Elizabeth. I am relieved to see you so hearty, so well, under these dire circumstances." Lady Kat Ashley takes Elizabeth into her embrace, then holds her Lady at arm's length for further consideration. An approving smile lifts Elizabeth's spirits higher yet.

"What dire happenings, Kat?" Elizabeth dare not release her servant's hand, as though to do so might mean another painful separation.

"Have you not heard? The Lord Admiral Thomas Seymour was executed on the block at the Tower this very morning. It is said he died unrepentant, unwilling to confess his plotting against your brother, our King Edward. Many stand in agreement on his evil nature, and bid him a hearty Adieu!"

"Though I would not think to attribute malice to our Lord Admiral's unruly character, I fear this day died a man with much wit, and very little judgment, Kat."

Lady Elizabeth finally lets go Kat Ashley's hand and links her arm through her governess's. She leads Kat into her Privy Chamber. Kat Ashley fails to escape her charge's watchful eye for the next few days. If I understand my Lady Elizabeth's heart as well as I think, she will not allow Kat's estrangement from her for a long while. The Lord Admiral, conversely, flies from my Lady's concern with the same ease the sharpened axe dislocates the cords holding his traitorous neck on his broad shoulders.

***

Countless hazards accompany Her Majesty's romantic liaisons. Peril litters my Queen's path just as teeming magnolia petals rain down on a cobbled walk after a few days of blossoming.

A once admired fixture, the Lord Admiral Thomas Seymour departs Her Majesty's girlhood, unlike the way he entered. His foolish head the price he forfeits.

Yet today, some thirteen years later, Her Majesty's dalliances threaten our sovereign's reign more. All of England's promise rests on her Gypsy's awkward fate. Lord Dudley, threatened with an infamy as disastrous as the Lord Admiral's, still captures my Queen's attention.

"You cannot know how I have missed you, Robert." Disdainful of her monarchical dignity, Her Majesty hastens into the Gypsy's embrace. Lord Robert receives his Queen as though years have elapsed, rather than the few short months it takes Sir Cecil to complete his inquiry into Amy Dudley's death.

"I have felt like a prisoner in my own home, Your Grace. Divided from my Queen, I am but a suggestion of a man. Only your abiding goodwill, your faithful support of my innocence, has returned me whole to your side."

"Let us leave this odious subject, Robin. The preceding months have caused me great distress. I tire of gossip....scandal and complaint. The constant battering of my poor ears wears at my nerves. Only the silencing of the mob's innuendo quiets my anxious mind. Our worthy Sir Cecil has put the affair to rest with his tribunal. That is all."

The Gypsy flinches when his nemesis's name passes Her Majesty's lips with this honourable mention. "I do not wish to appear ungrateful, Majesty. Surely the ruling on Amy's death proves enough to lift suspicion from my name. However, doubt remains amongst the people until a culprit is apprehended. Perhaps a second inquest will uncover something further to eradicate all concern..."

"What would you have me do, my Eyes? Should I fabricate a murdering intruder, when none exists? When your unfortunate wife simply fell on some stairs and severed her fragile neck? I forbid it. Have you not heard for yourself the indignities attributed to your Queen? The ceaseless provocation? My subjects question whether their sovereign commits murder. It is done, Robert. I will not venture forth into the murky details again. Leave it, and let us proceed as we have."

"I cannot court you with the dignity you deserve, Majesty, when my infamy continues to haunt our every endeavour."

"Bonny Sweet Robin", Her Majesty sighs, shuts her eyes, inhales the deepest of breaths. Our Queen holds to Lord Robert's arm, at once gladdened at his proximity, and chagrined with his lack of political prowess.

"Do not question me, Robin. If your Queen were ever to wed, you must know the only man she would consider. Yet, under the suspicions we presently endure, with tongues insistent on stirring Court gossip, I cannot consider such a liaison."

"Your Majesty..." A delicate leather glove raises itself in response.

"Take heart, Robin. Let us carry on as we always have. Inseparable companions, friendly lovers in all aspects, if not written in the binding ink of Kings and Queens. I cherish you, and always will." If I did not know my Queen and her independent mind so well, I might attribute her soothing tone to her consummate politician, Sir Cecil, himself.

Our Gypsy, once so assured of his lofty position, dare not offend his Queen. He mustn't taint their heartfelt reunion. Lord Robert accompanies Her Majesty back to her Chamber. He fondles the auburn curls coiled just beneath her lifted jaw line with a tentativeness I have yet to observe in him, and retreats to his rooms.

As he departs the chamber, Lord Dudley casts a sideward glance at my hovering form. I avert my eye to avoid provoking him. Lord Robert walks with his usual energetic grace, though there appears a subtle change in his confidence. As though the cobbled stone floor beneath his elegant form might crack and shift at a moment's notice.

We both comprehend, the gentleman with resigned certainty, I with some relief, the magnitude of his fall. Though Her Majesty esteems her Gypsy as no other, and grants to him more of her devoted affection than any other, her elegant hand remains our Queen's guarded possession. And hers alone.

***

10th October, 1562

The Gypsy's wheel, no longer favoured by changeable Fate, spirals downward. If not in the heart of our Queen, then in his drive for royal ascent. Yet, on occasion a circumstance arises when Lord Dudley's presence does oblige.

Do not misunderstand me. My distrust of the Gypsy persists. Yet, Father Time reveals Lord Dudley's motives more complicated than my pen has previously recorded. I must concede the Gypsy retains some capacity within his flawed soul for Her Majesty's own interests. Even within the Tudor Court, ambition cannot be all. Sometimes, tenderness blooms like a newborn shoot on a meandering vine, blanketing the stone wall of ruthless drive. Sometimes, genuine affection overcomes a reaching Gypsy's resolve.

"Are you well, Your Majesty? Your cheek appears flushed."

Searching for a reason to handle his monarch, Dudley lays his palm on the warmth of Her Majesty's pinkened cheek. He strokes its hot surface with his resting thumb.

Her Majesty does not object. Instead, she grasps Lord Robert's other willing hand, and cradles it within her own. My Queen invites her Gypsy's wanton touch.

The innocent talk of the pair, their careful conversation, suggests oncoming illness, healing caresses. But the Gypsy's searching of his Queen's every feature acknowledges a warmth quite apart from Her Majesty's flushed cheek. This watchfulness speaks of other things. Topics known better to themselves.

"Robin, you persist in doting on your Queen. I enjoy excellent health. Only a trifling warmth denies me access to my terrace and my daily stroll." Our Queen pats both his hands with her own. Dismissing her Gypsy's concern, Her Majesty, with uncharacteristic confusion, withdraws from her Gypsy's embrace and dabs with her silk handkerchief at tiny beads of perspiration on her temple.

"I will bathe away my discomfort, and enjoy a vigorous walk through my father's Hampton garden. No infectious blight can withstand all God's elements. Water and air will cool the fire on me as I stroll amongst our earth's happiest locale."

"Take care, Your Grace. You should seek your bed, where rest heals a host of maladies. The smallpox stalks our nation in all its virulence. Though it prefers to set upon the aged folk, reports have it ladies make up its second most favoured host. Many a vigourous lady has submitted to an untimely and permanent rest, Your Majesty. I fear this disease will not trouble to recognize your Tudor name, nor our dependence on our Queen's well-being."

"My Eyes, you cluck at your Queen as though an old hen wags your tongue on your behalf. Do you consort with Parliament? Not only does the Commons chase at my heels with their succession fever, the House of Lords would wed their Queen to any European Prince. Desist Robert, or the warmth of your Queen's anger will match that in her steamy cheeks."

"Your Majesty, I do not wish to press the issue of the succession. You, above all others know I wish to wed…"

"Hold, Robin. I am well enough. And in no need of physicians and their questionable ministrations and concoctions, or their mounds of bedclothes and darkened rooms. A little air and I will regain my healthy spirit. Accompany me to my father's favourite garden. Let the honeysuckle restore me with its glorious aroma."

As Her Majesty hastens toward her chamber door smiling, all the while reassuring her Gypsy of her excellent health, she stumbles, nearly falling to the tiled floor. Lord Dudley hurries to her side. He wraps his arms around her, supporting the full weight of her by her elbows.

"Perhaps my Eyes comprehends something his Queen does not. But remember," Her Grace wags a playful finger at her favourite. "… only this once." Her Majesty leans on Lord Dudley's arm, appearing less the young monarch she is, and more the stricken patient her Gypsy fears she will soon become.

I struggle to transcribe the transformation my Queen undergoes within a mere day and night together. My heart pains me, witnessing our sovereign's beleaguered aspect. Yet Her Majesty will not be persuaded she has contracted the dreaded illness. Her porcelain complexion, ripened by fever, fails to erupt in cankerous sores, so telling of the disease.

When Her Majesty's physician asserts smallpox's dreaded presence, our Queen discharges him, declaring him a fool and a charlatan. Her Majesty's fever climbs higher. Dr. Burcot returns, and with courageous certainty, repeats his unwished for diagnosis.

It is several days and nights before Her Majesty, in a voice almost unrecognizable so tinged with weakness is its whisper, beckons me to her bedside. She displays to me her hand. I draw a quick breath and hold it. Blistering pustules emerge on Her Grace's knuckles. Ignoring my Queen's pleas that I remain by her side, I hurry to Dr. Burcot, and reveal to him the new and ominous symptom.

"The Fool's diagnosis proves worthy of some attention then?"

I do not contradict him, nor do I care to discuss Dr. Burcot's vindication. Only one care consumes me: the dreadful countenance of my Queen, blasted with fever, her breath a shallow pool. Sores erupt on her skin, blighting our Majesty's parched frame with an oozing rash.

"Please go to Her Majesty at once, Sir. Her Grace requires your entire attention."

"Of course, Madam. Follow along with these provisions...I shall apply an Arab remedy, of general success in such cases. Hasten, young lady." He rushes past me, thrusting a crumpled bundle into my arms, assuming I wait on our Queen as a chambermaid.

Without care for my place or position as Keeper of the Queen's books – my calf-skin wrapped histories, and doting diaries prove of little use to my Majesty - I accept the flannel cloth and vials of potions without question. I fling the leather strap of his medicinal pouch over my head so it crosses my chest, its weight resting with comfort on my hip. Together, we hurry to our Queen's bedside, where all England's hope writhes in a fitful, feverish torment.

***

For six days England cowers at the prospect of a monarch's loss. A full two days and nights pass with no wakefulness knocking on Her Majesty's shuttered consciousness. Within palace walls where more is known of our Queen's ailing condition, the fear does not simmer, but threatens to over boil. Her Majesty's councilors try to suppress the awful knowledge that no heir awaits should our Majesty succumb to her dreaded disease.

Fortunately for England, Dr. Burcot's medical skill matches his considerable pride. When Her Majesty awakens, her physician nurses her with relentless attention. He wraps our Queen tight within his ancient Persian red flannel cloth, and stretches her fever-wracked form on a pallet before the hearth. He administers his curious potions night and day though Her Majesty barely swallows, and often gags due to their horrendous taste and odour. *An Arab remedy*, he states in his all-knowing manner. No one dares contradict his assertions, for fear we of lesser knowledge might offer a hand in the slaying of our dear lioness.

On the seventh day, Her Majesty speaks. After declaring, *Death possessed almost every part of me;* our Queen summons Sir William Cecil, her protector in all emergent cases. Her Majesty makes some of the most peculiar proclamations I've heard issue from her usually measured lips.

"Sir Spirit, listen well. Time may be short before my failing health once again places me within a nightmarish slumber. Two particular matters of State play on my ailing mind. You must dispatch these troublesome affairs so your Queen may rest, and with God's will, recover from this vicious malady."

Her Majesty's voice takes on a hoarseness with the effort of her appeal to her trusted councilor. By its end, she half-whispers her earnest directive. Though her person reels with the effort of the command, still our Queen's spirit radiates, enveloping Sir Cecil, and the entire chamber in its aspect of absolute authority.

"I will carry out your every ruling, as always, Your Grace."

"I know, Sir Spirit. I know you will. First then, Lord Robert Dudley must be declared Lord Protector of England." The Gypsy's wheel ascends once more.

"He, of all others, loves his Queen with a devotion beyond his own Self. If I should not recover, Lord Dudley will oversee our nation's interests, and ensure the throne's next worthy sovereign. He will, on my behalf, secure our people's future. As for my second decree, it is of a more personal nature, Sir William. I must address Lord Robert himself."

Her Majesty, propped on an elbow in an effort to gain close proximity to Sir Cecil's listening ear, releases the lock on it and slumps, wholly spent, into her bedclothes. I fear Her Grace may lose consciousness again before Lord Dudley can be beckoned to her side.

Our pitiable Sir William Cecil. With utmost diligence he seeks to mask his disappointment. But his brow betrays him. Deep chasms of vexation divide it in two halves. His bearded lips hold to one another pressed tight.

"Sir Spirit, hasten to fulfill my wishes. It is of utmost import to the realm. Robin, Robin!" Already his sovereign turns her attention away from the bereft Sir Cecil. Sir Cecil, overcome by his Queen's elevation of her Gypsy, shuffles from her bedside.

Through the Chamber door Robert Dudley enters. The two gentlemen pass next to one another so close their shoulders rub, yet neither cares to notice the other.

Though wholly dedicated to his Queen's service, in this her latest request, I fear her Sir Spirit might not readily oblige Her Majesty.

"My Bonny Sweet Robin, I have instructed you be made Lord Protector of our realm while my illness prevents me from my duty." Dudley claims his place at his Queen's side, while the Chamber still warms with Sir Cecil's ire.

"I am grateful, Your Majesty. Your Grace does me more honour than I..."

"Hold, Robert. With great privilege, so too enters the weight of accountability. I must elicit an oath from you which I fear will be difficult for each one of us to endure. But the realm requires it."

"My allegiance is yours, Majesty. I would claim your illness as mine if it meant your health and your return to the throne."

"My Eyes, I fear when you know what I ask of you, you will not so eagerly wish to submit to your Queen's will."

"Do not doubt my fidelity, Majesty. I am yours, in every aspect."

"Very well, Robin. I ask that you wed my esteemed cousin, Mary Stuart, Queen of Scotland. The match will ensure your high placement, and our kingdom will have, with your progeny, its successor..."

"Your Majesty, forgive me, but..." Lord Dudley cannot conceal his dismay. So appalled is he with Her Majesty's suggestion, her Gypsy reels. His revulsion twists his handsome features into a ghastly death mask. Her Majesty's favourite steps backward from our Queen's sickbed, and stumbles toward the doorway. So filled with confusion does Her Majesty's Master of the Horse appear, I fear he will take himself from her chamber without leave to do so. Her Gypsy behaves as though our Queen requests he betroth Medusa, herself.

"Your Grace, forgive me, but I cannot consider such a match. The Catholic, French-loving Queen Mary Stuart? The barrens of Scotland? So far from my beautiful Bess? If your Robin's death is your wish Majesty, you should place my neck on the block at once. This match would surely mean my end."

"Robin..." Her Majesty raises her weakened hand in an effort to reach for her Gypsy's.

But the gentleman, too vexed to take notice of her enjoinder, steps further away. Out of his Queen's reach, he stares with wild-eyed wonder at his newfound prospects. "My heart would shrivel within its sheltering chest. It would not withstand such torment..." Lord Robert, transformed from attentive suitor to humbled subject with one royal request, persists in shifting backward, away from his Queen's demand. Its threat alarms him even as the smallpox does not.

Her Majesty returns her unnoticed hand to her silken sheet. Unfazed by a Gypsy's distress, she directs a stony gaze into England's future, concentrating with special care not to acknowledge her Gypsy's affliction. I do not know whether it is the strain of the smallpox our Queen labours under, or the loss of her Gypsy, but Her Majesty continues as though Dudley does not speak.

"...the match ensures your future Robin. And with your progeny, England will have her high-born sovereign. Leave me. I tire."

***

I do not doubt the suffering Her Majesty endures while writhing with the fever the smallpox produces. But Her Majesty's hurt encompasses more than physical discomfort. As our Queen's illness finally loosens its hold on her person, she beckons me to her side. We smile together, a dimple appearing on her flushed cheek for the first time in a fortnight. Her Majesty shrugs, all good-humoured, as we listen to her bevy of councilors outside her chamber door. Cecil and Dudley amongst them, fret about their Queen's imminent death.

My own Elizabeth's loss of life considered insignificant when measured against the death of England's cherished sovereign. Do they suppose the smallpox deafens, as well as disfigures? How I long to fling open the chamber door, and thrust the entirety of my authority - though all I might claim is my Majesty's fond affection - into their presence. Like my Queen in one of her fiery moments, I long to slap their flapping mouths wholly shut. But I do not. My Majesty's frail health would not withstand such a dramatic gesture. Nor do I wish to imitate my Queen's combative nature. These animated moments, and I pray to God there will be many more, I will leave for Her Majesty to perform.

My only intention in disturbing this pristine page with insistent ink, is to illuminate my Queen's suffering. While wracked with fever, that which caused two days of unconscious delirium, Her Majesty found herself awash in a troubling vision. Torment, for which I cannot name a physical equal, haunted her restless slumber.

Her Grace, now upright within her bed, reveals an eagerness to share in a friendship sorely missed while she lay writhing in her feverish illness. She whispers to me of the spirits who haunted her fugue-induced state. I will transcribe Her Majesty's nightmare with no unwelcome intrusion:

I wander out of doors, swaddled in ermine furs and adorned in roped pearls. I wrap my arms around myself. A lone and hooded figure, I hover in the perfect centre of my father's hemlock maze, deep in the gardens of Hampton Court.

Above the burdensome weight of my crown, sweeping bowers reach. The foliage fills me with heady odours of Nature's presence. It is just after dawn, and droplets of dew cling to hemlock clusters, releasing an earthy, after-rainfall musk. Though I strain to hear the harmonious song of the meadowlark, I am disappointed. Silence greets my ear. I turn within my confined space. Hemlock branches brush against my cheek, as though to wash it.

I vow to escape the confines of my father's natural prison. But the foliage grows denser than any thicket I have known. Shadowy avenues beckon, and I realize I am not alone within the confines of the maze. Each corridor leads to someone I have loved: my poor mother summons me from a far-reaching corner of the maze; my revered father, our Henry VIII, from another; Lord Robert, My Eyes, stands at the furthest reaches of the circuitous route; Sir William Cecil, My Sir Spirit, occupies the opposing corner to Lord Dudley. Sir Cecil's expression offers no feeling. I search his countenance for evidence of his compassionate nature. But I do not find it. My beloved stepmothers, all lost to me, and therefore shrouded in black taffeta of mourning, occupy their own separate avenues.

I enter the labyrinth. Securing my gaze on my mother's, I wrap my furs tightly around my shivering form and prepare to reunite with my beloved Anne Boleyn. But each time I approach, I hear, like the tinkling of Tallis's cathedral bells, my mother's hysteric laughter, the rustling of her skirts in the grasses. And silence.

Returning to my original place in the centre of the intricate maze, I glance back. My blessed mother's gaze does not leave me. She poses where she'd stood all along. A welcoming smile plays on her painted lips. She gestures for me to approach. But I do not.

When I fail to return to her grassy pathway, Mother grows desperate to convince me of her maternal promise. Her entreating arms stretch toward me. If only I would yield to my mother's welcoming embrace.

And then she speaks. But only to defend my cruel father. "Do not cast blame on him, my Sweet. Our King failed to understand the enduring bond between a mother and her daughter. He cannot know the forever nature of our affection. Stay my child. Do not leave me bereft of my tiny Bess."

I cannot bear her complicity. I alter course, to attempt my Robin. But now the maze stretches and yawns. Lord Robert pleads for his Elizabeth. He struggles within the nettles of the monstrous hedge. And he remains far beyond my reach. He will go from me too. Spirited from England, into the arms of bonny Scotland. Where of course, I have sent him myself.

Not one to surrender with ease, I alter my course yet again. In search of another mother. But Jane Seymour, Anne of Cleves, and my two Catherines, shrouded in their mourning dress, blend with the bleak underbrush.

The path to my distinguished father I do not attempt. Not for lack of devotion. I simply cannot bear it if the rejection is complete.

As I hesitate, pondering my next step, the undergrowth closes in. Walkways converge. One hemlock hedge joins with another. The paths disappear within the shrubbery. Tightly webbed vines weave an overhead bower.

A dispassionate Mother Earth approaches. She holds before me a crown of gold. Behind her straight back, my loved ones crouch.

***

My Queen's interpretation of her feverish vision splits my heart wide. Her Majesty recognizes but one message in the dream. Still weakened by ill health, Her Grace tilts her aching head from her pillows and whispers with hoarse resignation in my waiting ear.

"Scepter in hand, my peoples' love and gratitude abundant, I shall live and reign alone in this world. Isolated from those I love by that which entangles my heart in duty. England claims me entirely. She will reject all suitors for my friendless heart."

"But Majesty..." Rarely have I witnessed this sorrowful resignation from Her Grace.

"Do not interrupt. You listen with your ear, intent on the words, while refusing to hear the message I convey from my heart. Do not liken yourself to those outside my chamber door, who do not comprehend their Queen. For in the end, this shall be for me sufficient. A marble stone shall declare that a Queen, having reigned such a time, lived and died a Virgin." A smile of satisfaction plays on Her Majesty's mouth, and she reaches for my hand as though her singular touch transmits what her words cannot.

Still, a chattering Council predicts Her Majesty's death. Competing voices harangue one another about England's catastrophic demise. The doomsayers outside her chamber door fail to comprehend the determined healing within. Behind the thickness of the oak boards in my Queen's chamber doorway, a miracle takes place. Her Majesty laughs.

My Queen's smile transforms a room shrouded in illness into one of quiet celebration. Her Grace revels in her victory over the smallpox. As though she'd considered no other outcome, Her Majesty recovers, held close within my sympathetic embrace.

***

My Queen's healing only serves to raise to a higher pitch the bleating of those in the House of Commons. Her Majesty's miraculous renewal, with hardly a blemish on her milky complexion from the horrid pox, fails to silence their rabid cries for a successor.

Without regard for their Queen's dignity or for their own self-respect, the gentlemen in Parliament debate Her Majesty's marriage and birthing, as though our Queen were their own prized livestock.

I speak where I should not. Their harping on the succession needs no more repeating than it already receives on a daily basis in the Commons, and now too in the House of Lords. How they wear at Her Majesty's fraught nerves with their insistence on her imminent betrothal. I do not blame her for seeking an end to their insolence. Her Majesty has hatched a plan to take them in hand, and I wholly support her endeavour.

Of one mind, my Queen and I prepare an address to those Lords who show their sovereign little of the deference she deserves. Together within Her Grace's Privy Chamber our temples lean heavily against each other's. My Queen's jeweled ear brushes the tiny pearl earring at my own lobe. We huddle behind Her Majesty's desk, giggling like errant schoolgirls in Master Ascham's Latin lessons. With saucy aplomb I dip my quill into ink that will spill all of my Queen's chagrin onto the deserving heads of those wagging their tongues against her judicious leadership.

The parliamentary representatives – brutes all – do not guess at the delight we share in their scolding. I choose one condemning phrase, while my Queen takes another, more chiding yet. We stage mock quarrels to figure out who provides the more fulsome argument. Whose phrasing contains the more persuasive rhetoric to move an elected government in a direction more conducive to their loving monarch?

I should report shame at this gladness I feel during my Majesty's trying time. But we do laugh and make merry as the arguments tumble from my scribbling quill. Her Majesty insists she begin in the interrogative, a tactic she gleaned from Castiglione's *Courtier*. I agree with her strategy, scribbling her every command. My Queen dictates her finished argument, and I transcribe it on our unabashed document.

November 5, 1566

Was I not born in the realm? Were my parents born in any foreign country? Is there any cause I should alienate myself from being careful over this country? Is not my kingdom here? Whom have I oppressed? Whom have I enriched to others' harm? What turmoil have I made in this commonwealth, that I should be suspected to have no regard to the same? How have I governed since my reign? I will be tried by envy itself. I need not to use many words, for my deeds do try me...

***

"Your Majesty, gratitude overwhelms my inadequate tongue. Your generosity in the giving of Kenilworth Castle, and in my elevation to the peerage, represents a gift I will never be fortunate enough to repay." Her Majesty's Gypsy bows and scrapes. Obsequious Sir. My Queen pushes aside our important matters of State to attend to a Gypsy's song and dance. Her Majesty names Lord Robert Dudley the Earl of Leicester, and master of glorious Kenilworth Castle. Still he grovels at our Queen's generous foot.

"It is unnecessary to thank your Queen, Robin. Your loyalty to our crown will be recompense enough. These gifts reward you with the respectable living my cousin, Mary of Scots, expects a worthy suitor to possess."

Though I and Parliament await, and our speech goes half written, Her Majesty turns to her favourite once more.

"I would sooner die for Your Majesty, but I beg of you. I cannot wed the Popish Queen of Scots." The Gypsy, in a fit of unbridled distraction, prostrates himself at Her Majesty's ankle. His forehead presses uncomfortably on the domed pearls and sharpened gems in her satin slipper.

My Queen glances down on the top of the new Earl's beleaguered head, then around the empty chamber. So uncomfortable does she appear I dare say Her Majesty combs palace walls and entryways, in quest of an opportunity to take her leave. After an awkward silence, Her Grace disturbs his prone position with a shaking of her foot. A quick scuffling of her dainty shoe at his shoulder. When the Earl of Leicester raises himself in response to her rousing, Her Majesty addresses him. Her fractious tongue completes what her impatient foot begins.

"Robin, rise from there. It does not befit an Earl of Leicester to swoon on his Queen's slipper. Of what earthly purpose is your demise to me? That would not address the Commons or the Lords. God's death! Have you no investment in the success of our realm? Do you not recognize we must appease the ravenous vultures within the Commons? Unnatural sons of their loving mother, they force an unwanted marriage on their monarch. Do not think with your head, this once. But think with your heart, for your Queen's sake, Robin!"

***

I sent them answer by my Council I would marry, although of mine own disposition I was not inclined thereunto. But that was not accepted nor credited, although spoken by their prince. And yet I used so many words that I could say no more. I will never break the word of a prince spoken in public place for my honor sake. And therefore I say again I will marry as soon as I can conveniently, if God take not him away with whom I mind to marry, or myself, or else some other great hindrance happen. I can say no more except the party were present. And I hope to have children; otherwise I would never marry. A strange order of petitioners that will make a request and cannot be otherwise ascertained but by the prince's word, and yet will not believe it when it is spoken!

***

"Your Grace, your capacity for sacrifice outweighs my own. As does your virtue and your tolerance too." The new Earl of Leicester rises. His head remains bowed with the shame of his womanly outburst.

"Robin. Do you so soon forget who tickled you on your chin when laying the ermine mantle of Earldom on your shoulder? And before the eyes of my subjects, too? My own hands do not prove faithful to their sovereign's wishes." At this admission, Her Majesty stares down at her wayward fingers as though they might have a separate, more knowledgeable will than their owner.

"Your Queen does not sacrifice with perfect ease. You, of all others, know where my passion lies. But we speak of the realm. My Lord. Am I the only one who understands the requirements of a throne? Parliament demands a successor to the English sovereignty. These considerations must outweigh our own. Do you not care to write your name on our blessed country's history? We offer you a kingdom, Robin. Does your love for Elizabeth trump the honoured position of father to a King of England? Perhaps I undervalue my Bonny Sweet Robin. Perhaps you are the most loyal subject I will ever cast my royal eye upon."

***

But they, I think, that ask it of their monarch will be as ready to mislike him with whom I shall marry as they are now to move it. And then it will appear they nothing meant it. I thought they would have been rather ready to have given me thanks than to have made any new request for the same. There hath been some that have, ere this, said unto me they never required more than that they might once hear me say I would marry. Well, there was never so great a treason but might be covered under as fair a pretense.

The second point was the limitation of the succession of the crown, wherein was nothing said for my safety, but only for themselves. A strange thing that the foot should direct the head in so weighty a cause, which cause hath been so diligently weighed by us for that it toucheth us more than them....

***

As Her Majesty scolds her Earl of Leicester and then casts a condemning eye on him, her expressive hands make known her true feeling. Our Queen cradles a small package in her cupped grasp. Though of insignificant size - a miniature depiction - the tiny portrait, wrapped in plain brown paper reflects a Queen's furtive attachment.

Her Gypsy Earl of Leicester wished to know secrets concealed within a Queen's bosom. But he will not. Her Grace presses his tiny portrait to her heart as she tosses the genuine gentleman to Scotland's cold borders. Within the brown paper, labeled in her own careful script "My Lord's Picture", she clings to a Gypsy's likeness.

Just yesterday the Scottish Ambassador, James Melville, pleaded with Her Grace. Might he take the tiny memento to employ it in persuading the Queen of Scots of the Earl's physical charms? The ambassador's petitioning was in vain. My Queen, though she might wish to, could not let go of her precious treasure.

I wonder. If a Queen clings so fervently to a painted likeness, how on God's earth might Her Majesty find the will to let go of the portrait's dear subject?

"You underestimate your cousin Mary of Scotland's strong will, Your Majesty. It competes with your own steely resolve. The Queen of Scots speaks with boldness of her refusal to wed such as myself. She even goes so far as to refer to me as your castoff Master of the Horse. The Scots Queen views your gift of the Earl of Leicester as rebuke and insult all wound together. She will not bend to your wishes. I, too, doubt this farcical marriage reflects your preference."

Still her Gypsy prattles on. Making his case. Her Majesty puts on a brave show of pretending otherwise, but I, for one, believe the Gypsy will have his wish fulfilled.

"Robin, must you make this a more thorny endeavour for your Queen than she already endures? Do you not know how our parting will weigh on my heart?"

Her Majesty persists in her charade. Does Her Grace believe she will part with her Earl of Leicester? Or has the whimsy of having to let go her Gypsy become a sort of melancholy romance? An entertainment, so our lonesome Queen might fantasize the fond notion of unrequited love?

"Your Majesty, why can you not join me in my staunchest hope, and become my Queen? And I your doting husband, in all respects. Let us reply to the people of England with our happy marriage and with our own charming babes." Our new Earl of Leicester refuses to join our Queen in her romantic fantasy. The Gypsy, true to his nature, will have all.

"Robin, still your understanding does not unite with mine. The people will not approve it. They will reject our love, just as you do Scotland's throne. Neither your low birth, your Protestant faith nor your ill-repute lends you suitability. How I tire of this same argument. It seems I have it repeatedly, and with all I meet. Leave your Queen to her duty. Though Elizabeth would like to rest, Her Majesty tends to England's relentless cries for a mother's nurturing."

Summer II - "We Differed on Religion"

You know there is no constancy in human affairs, when a single swift hour can often bring a man to nothing.

--Boethius

17th October, 1571

Father Time wears at a Gypsy's desire. It seems unlikely an English crown or Her Majesty's pretty hand will be Lord Dudley's fate. Still, her Earl of Leicester hovers by her side. Still he dares to enter into spirited debate with Her Majesty on matters tempting her ire: Her Grace's refusal to marry; the English throne's lack of successor. No one excites our Queen's anxious nature like her charming Gypsy does.

Thankfully, the Earl's reaching does not resemble a lover's attentions, as it once did. Her Gypsy presses only his unwanted counsel on Her Majesty lately. Lord Dudley treats his sovereign with a kind deference, and with due respect for Her Majesty's throne. To my relief, the remainder of himself he keeps at a tolerable distance.

Perhaps his marriage proposal, now six long years ago, and again declined by his Queen, finally means the dying embers of a Gypsy's enthusiasm? Her Majesty, though it is little spoken of by those at Court, and I hesitate to record it, approaches her middling years. Our Queen celebrates her thirty-eighth birthday. Does the Gypsy recognize what all of Europe whispers? Perhaps

Her Majesty, not inclined by temperament for marriage and motherhood, does not make such a tempting match.

No such decline in passion affects the antagonism between the Gypsy Earl of Leicester and Sir William Cecil, now our Baron Burghley. I applaud her favourites' efforts. They hide their antipathy well before Her Majesty. And provide for their beloved Queen; if not absolute ease in their goodwill, at least a dignified pretense.

If it is hatred of which we speak, the reckless Earl of Leicester should glance away from Sir Cecil, our Baron Burghley, and cast a wary eye toward the Duke of Norfolk. I attend my Queen and listen as Norfolk casts the darkest of aspersions on her Gypsy. Her Majesty does not accept Norfolk's slander of her Bonny Sweet Robin. But the Duke, given his title, his general popularity among the nobility and his vast wealth, might yet succeed in scraping the golden dust from Leicester's pretty façade.

And yet. In all my years in my Queen's service, I have failed to witness good fortune so closely follow a man as Her Majesty's Gypsy. Lord Dudley alone makes his way down the Wheel, only to climb heavenward once again. The agile gentleman plunges to the very depths in our Queen's good graces for the sole pleasure of making the treacherous and daring ascent once more.

His resentful enemy, the Duke of Norfolk, tiring of an Earl of Leicester's constant company with our Queen, will try his luck at a different game. Rather than joust with a fortunate Gypsy, Norfolk makes his way toward the opposing Queen's side.

Her Majesty's ladies, and I too in my spare time, whisper of the latest scandal at Court. We bend our heads, wishing to avoid undue notice. Her Majesty's ladies keep wary eyes on the mosaic tiled floor in their Queen's presence. I too, humbly admit to fearing Her Majesty's honestly inherited, if vile temper.

What is the dreadful rumour sending all of us scurrying from our Queen's presence? The Duke of Norfolk proposes to wed the Catholic Mary, Queen of Scots himself. We fear the two together, King and Queen of Scots united, will join as one to grab at Her Majesty's throne.

***

The telltale wringing of Her Majesty's hands, the frantic to and fro pacing of her silken slipper, her skirts rustling like scurrying royal ghosts against the cobbled floor, should alert Lord Robert to Her Majesty's vexation. But the Earl of Leicester luxuriates in his supposed favour, no matter how his Queen's foul mood seeks to rouse him from his slumber.

The Gypsy lounges in Her Grace's anxious presence. His white-stockinged legs stretch out before him. His woven fingers rest behind his reclined head of curls. Will Lord Dudley maintain his ease after Her Majesty has her say? Her rage this morning when she learned of the Duke of Norfolk's marriage plans resembled a she-bear's charge in defense of her cherished cub. Rouse yourself, Gypsy. If you do not waken of your own accord, a sovereign's wrath will move you for certain.

She speaks. Her Majesty presents an outward calm, but her new composure contradicts the unrest enclosed within. "Perhaps it is *your* beloved head we should seek Robin."

Her Majesty approaches her too comfortable Earl. She lifts his girlish locks at the back of his neck, pretending to scrutinize the exact place along his hairline where the executioner's axe might fall. Now she draws a line with the point of her finger. She traces a place across the nape of his neck where the blade might sever his cocky self in two disparate pieces.

When this none-too-subtle warning does not rouse her Gypsy from his nap, Her Majesty changes tact. Drawing the heel of her hand against his exposed nape, she playfully chops now and again where she imagines an executioner's blade might land.

"Your refusal to wed the Queen of Scots has thrown us into this new and abominable affair, Robin."

Her Majesty issues her threat with the same self-possessed precision she employs on the hunt. Her honeyed tone, all cloaked in teasing smiles, soothes with its quietude. Our Queen's angry intent she coats in a sweet disguise of pleasantries. Her thought, spoken aloud and with an awful serenity, at last alerts her Gypsy to his peril.

"But Your Majesty, the Queen of Scots would not have your faithful servant. It is not my refusal, but my dejected resignation I offer you. How can you hold me to account? To gain a French speaking, popish Scots Queen would mean the loss of my Gloriana." The flattering Earl of Leicester glances up, hoping to move his steely-eyed Queen to sympathy.

Her Majesty leaves off her teasing appearance. She scoffs at his attempt to placate. Her good humour has long since evaporated in the heat of this morning's news at Court. Lighthearted flattery will not move Her Majesty from her belligerent stance.

And yet Lord Robert presses his argument. "I offered to the Scots Queen my title as the new Earl of Leicester, all my acquired wealth, my very self, so that your throne would be secured." The Gypsy lounges no more. He lifts his lithe form to attention. Lord Dudley bolts to his feet, his previous calm a happy memory. Sheltering Her Majesty's jeweled hands within his own; he joins his dark-eyed gaze to her fair one. Only a Gypsy dare embrace his Queen.

But Her Majesty's brow, weighed down under an entire kingdom, will not lift for her Bonny Sweet Robin this time. The Earl's flattery does not provide the same diversion as when Her Majesty's younger, mirthful self sought his stealthy touch.

"Yes, yes." Her Grace waves the Gypsy away like a gadfly who has invaded her riverside picnic. "We have heard all of this before. The Queen of Scots senses your lack of enthusiasm. She seeks a more willing companion to her throne..."

Her Majesty withdraws her hand, returning her accusing finger to the Gypsy's jaw line. She draws her fingertip from ear to chin along one cheek, then changes to the other side and traces his face yet again, imagining how pride might display itself when life ceases to animate her Gypsy's fine features.

Still our Queen refuses to meet his eye. She turns from the allure of Lord Dudley's countenance, and sighs. Whether Her Majesty's displeasure lies with herself and her attraction to her Earl, or with his inability to forward her political aims, only our Queen knows for certain.

"Your Majesty, your cousin made most clear her distaste toward your proposed match. She flaunted her refusal, insisting a Queen of Scots might not consider an English Queen's Master of the Horse. Then she chose Darnley."

"And yet she rid herself of Darnley with haste when it suited her...when he no longer appealed to my cousin's fickle liking in such matters. With more wooing, with greater effort on your part, we might have succeeded in our wishes, Robin."

Her Majesty, more the anxious sovereign than the raging lioness, offers the Earl her trembling back. She shudders as she stares through the beveled glass before her.

The pane, imperfect in its construction, distorts her view of Whitehall's garden, causing her to squint. I wonder what inclination prompts her to argue for a match that her own heart forbids her to condone.

Mourning a sunnier time past, Her Grace turns from the window casing, her head bent. Her Majesty considers leaving the chamber and her Earl's presence altogether. An action not in her Gypsy's best interest, I dare say.

"I do beg pardon, Your Grace, but all respectful attempts were made to succeed…"

The Gypsy contradicts his Queen. And true to her disposition, Her Majesty drops any suggestion of the puckish lover or the beleaguered monarch, and turns on him with the force of her raging supremacy.

"And now we have a Scottish Queen, our own cousin, under house arrest and suspected of murdering her husband, Darnley; a Duke of Norfolk, also my beloved cousin, in the Tower with clamouring demands for his head; and a full-fledged popish plot against our throne. Ridolfi and his cohorts want England for the Pope. I have witnessed too much bloodshed over matters concerning the Church. While I reign on my throne, I will not have it. Did your Queen not promise my subjects that in matters of religion, neither fire nor sword would be used? Was this not my oath to my people, Robin?"

"Your Majesty, you have always looked with kindness and temperance on the citizenry of England. But perhaps these perilous times require you to alter slightly your honourable intent. Your father attempted a similar approach. Recall, King Henry stated: 'Let man conform outwardly to the state religion, and keep their beliefs, if any, to themselves.' Though, in the end our King, by necessity, found his role a more active one in the people's choice of worship."

"You invoke my father in this matter? My father's approach to popish sympathies you would condone?" Our Queen stares at her Gypsy with something resembling awe. It is as though her childhood paramour, by some ungodly miracle, has been snatched away by fairies, leaving in his stead a befuddled imposter.

"While my father spoke his cozying words of peace and civility to the Catholics, his foot soldiers sacked our gracious people's modest dwellings. They plundered the popish citizens' charitable and holy houses of worship. By my father's command, His Majesty's faithful, pope-loving subjects were strung from the bows of England's elm trees. I vow to you Robert, this barbarous force will not be practiced under my rule. Do not dare to suggest I emulate my father's butchery. While I am Queen, the sword will not answer my people's cries for their Clergy."

Her Majesty's hands, previously occupied with their wringing, hang at her sides. A tremor, born of Her Grace's frustration, causes her to press both silken palms hard against her skirts. Our fretful Queen turns to and fro. Her eyes search palace chamber ways for a means of escape from her impossible predicament. Yet she remains posed in place, unwilling to give way to the urge to flee.

"But Your Majesty, I have heard you name Catholic priests fools. And also deem the greatest of Puritan clerics, 'not the wisest of men'?"

"Hold, Robin."

"...I believe you have gone so far as to refer to the 'darkness and filth of popery', while disparaging our Protestant Reformers as too fundamentalist in their preaching. And still you speak unhappily of King Henry, your great father, who in his wisdom and regard for England, endeavoured with his armies to rid us of the very popery plaguing his reign. What pray tell, as our sovereign, do you propose?"

Raw and vicious impudence. Her Gypsy throws his lacey cuffs into the air, exasperation his closest ally. Surely, the rogue has gone too far. Perhaps Her Grace will give serious consideration to her previous empty threat, and the Earl of Leicester will join his nemesis, Lord Norfolk, in the Tower.

Our Queen trembles with the effort of mastering her excessive fury. "And you, Robin, would with such confidence speak my own words against me? How dare you tempt my wrath on the delicate matter of Church and Stately rule? Have I not in all ways attempted to thwart religious zealotry? Have I not spurned the notion of becoming the flagrant tyrant I swore never to be?

"Have I not adopted, myself, the title Supreme Governor of the Church of England, though I hold no interest in this honour? Only grief and dismay accompany this so-called sacred position, yet your Queen must fill it to ensure the throne remains free of clerical meddling."

Her Majesty labours to contain her temper as she acts as solicitor on her own behalf. Her tremulous voice wavering, she clasps her hands together before her. "Is it too great an expectation, Robin, for our loving subjects to behave with the probity, the dignified example I have set, rather than this fanatical worship they seek?"

"Your Majesty, perhaps your careful leadership, your tolerance of variation in religious practice, does not suit your people's will. Do your subjects seek a more literal path to follow in the worship of their Lord God?"

Aware they tread precarious terrain, a route which might draw them to a precipice neither wishes to approach, Her Majesty and the Earl retreat. A stillness, steeped in conciliation, replaces the previous blow and bluster within the chamber. Her Majesty's voice lowers to such dulcet tones; it more resembles a hoarse whisper, a sated growl, than the roaring once heard.

"And you Robert? You would defend this ignorance? This unconsidered fervor? Do I know this man?"

Her Majesty glances away from her inquisitor. She speaks the final query aloud, though she speaks it to herself alone. The emotional turmoil accompanying the news of Norfolk's plotting against her weighs on Her Grace's well-being more than her Gypsy realizes. I fear for my Queen's tranquility.

"Are you the trusted friend I have known since my unhappy childhood? The same condemned prisoner who shared with your Elizabeth, an unreasonable blame? You and I, a boy and a girl - barely twenty-one years old. That wretched period of months within the Tower while my Catholic sister Mary sharpened her blade in the interests of her beloved Church of Rome." Her Majesty wonders aloud at her Gypsy's poor memory. Her Earl of Leicester offers only silence. His tendency to interrupt stopped by quiet amazement.

"Who is this imposter within my Chamber? He cannot be the same one who knew, together with his Lady Elizabeth, what it is to suffer the ill-will of religious intolerance. This cannot be he. For if the genuine companion, he would join with me in understanding the evil of fervent belief."

***

That dreadful time in the Tower. I accompanied my Lady Elizabeth there. I try to dull the horrific memories with a cushion of years, and happier experiences since, but I too recall that awful time my Queen alludes to. Almost two decades ago, I likewise feared for my Lady's rationality. Then too, I considered the dreaded possibility Lady Elizabeth's exceptional wits might forsake her altogether.

The parting water made hardly a sound as the palace guards rowed us toward Traitor's Gate, beneath St. Thomas's Tower. As we negotiated our watery path into the Tower's yawning entry, I wondered whether my Lady's tender understanding would also enter. Or would her harried sensibility remain locked outside the clanging jailhouse gate? Might my Lady's senses leave her altogether? Feasting on a freedom she and her loyal companions no longer enjoyed?

Queen Mary's summons of her sister, Lady Elizabeth to Whitehall Palace arrives at a most inopportune time. Elizabeth has felt unwell these last weeks, especially since we received word of unrest, led by the reckless Andrew Wyatt. If I know my Lady Elizabeth, it is the Wyatt affair responsible for her poorly condition. Her English countrymen cross swords on behalf of their Protestant and Catholic deities. They pit one book of devotion against another. One group decries the others' idols and crucifixes. Jesuits spill the blood of Puritans. All of it raises the bile, and provokes a retch in our Lady's throat.

Lady Elizabeth's countenance, usually a pinkish hue, fades into a deathly pallor. Though never a hungry girl, she eats barely a morsel of broiled perch, some lightly steamed greens, and a few mouthfuls of coarse bread for her supper. Elizabeth's dark ale she hardly touches. The almond macaroons our Lady once craved, her favourite aniseed candy, she declines. Her auburn curls hang limp to her slumping shoulders. Fear transforms the healthy cub into a cowering whelp.

The somber black gown Lady Elizabeth wears hides her shapeless, almost boyish form. Not a single ornament - no button, no lace, no pearl or jewel - relieves the eye of its uninspired design.

Though her simple dress serves as testimony to her Protestant faith, her garment inflames the distrust Elizabeth's Catholic sister, Queen Mary, already holds for my young Lady. The dreary silks pour an elixir of melancholy on Elizabeth's fragile temper. I fret so for her well-being.

"Perhaps my sister Mary will respond with God's grace to my ill health. She might allow a postponement of our visit. Conditions dictate I should remain safe at Hatfield, away from the unrest rattling the Court at London."

Naiveté courts my Lady's frantic hope. But Queen Mary's reply douses all lingering fancies Elizabeth holds onto. Queen Mary does not concern herself with her younger sister's humble interests. Our devoutly Catholic Queen sends her personal physicians to advise on Elizabeth's health. The Queen's healers, acknowledging some watery humours, and mild inflammation of her kidneys, permit Elizabeth to travel immediately to Whitehall.

We journey the thirty long miles from Lady Elizabeth's beloved Hatfield to Whitehall Palace by litter, all arranged for by our loving Queen Mary. We arrived last evening, accompanied by Lords Hastings, Howard and Cornwallis, all of Queen Mary's Privy Council.

A protective shock buttresses my otherwise stable mind against the horrific scene. We are afforded an astonishing greeting in London. Though I make sincere efforts to erase the atrocity, I cannot thoroughly scratch from my poor mind's eye the dreadful spectacle.

How does a proper lady record this depravity? Certainly my dainty quill, hand-crafted of mother-of-pearl, was not devised for these filthy exploits.

Surely this instrument, made to portray feats of human dignity – my Lady Elizabeth's, among others - has done nothing to deserve the infamy it must endure upon its loyal and efficient tip.

But I prevaricate in my attempt to avoid the inevitable foulness. There is a stain human hatred splashes on us all. I fear my stubborn ink, like my ghastly memories, might prove to be of the indelible and everlasting variety. Nevertheless, I will not recoil from my duty. I must hold to my oath, and write of the odious tableau.

Death greets us at London's doorstep. His hooded cloak, scythe and crooked finger need not parade themselves. For all about us, his vile handiwork announces his attendance. Mutilated and decomposing corpses - men, women and children alike - declare his presence. Elizabeth's countrymen gather to meet her. Each dangling by his pitiable severed neck. Palace walls, hung with fraying ropes, display her citizens' bodies. Others lie down together, stacked on one another in reeking pyres of charred flesh.

Limbs, bent in prayer to an unfavoured Protestant God, appear as frayed as the ropes holding the bodies aloft. Ruined arms and legs bend in awkward and unnatural positions. Their persecutors ensure their victims will not kneel before the offending deity, even in death.

Forever-blinded eyes stare. They seek ours in return. They do not search for forgiveness I think, but rather look to probe our poor judgment. What earthly reason might we have to approach this bubbling cauldron? Why do we not turn at once, and find immediate shelter away from this popish Queen's sacrificial altar?

The horror that I, a mere servant suffers, cannot compare to the misery my Lady endures. Elizabeth studies each unfortunate soul with a searching concentration. The agreeable Lords, who accompany our retinue, and even the servants at the helm, grow weary. The gentlemen chafe at our delay, as Elizabeth requests that our carriage slow, and then stop, so we might approach each new victim of her sister's pious devotion.

Her ladies cower. We press gloved hands and lacey handkerchiefs before eyes squeezed-tight. We attempt with little success to shield our senses from the unthinkable sights and putrid smells surrounding us. I glance at Kat Ashley, who presses her entire form backward into the corner of the upholstered seat. Lady Kat retches involuntarily, though she turns her head from us with discretion, in an effort to protect Elizabeth.

Lady Elizabeth does not share Kat Ashley's discomfort. Elizabeth refuses to look away, insisting on setting an example for us all. Our young Lady will recognize this slaughter of her English people. With a deliberate and solemn attentiveness, she accepts the weight of each body. My Lady shoulders each one upon her desolate conscience.

If not on her devout sister's behalf, then from her own need to atone, our young Lady absorbs every detail of the Protestant families ruined by belief: a lifeless mother's torn and soiled petticoat; the differing shades of blue on a father's bruised and broken neck; each caked-up sore on the blackened flesh of their tiny son's cracked skull, his knees miraculously free of the usual childhood bruising.

I peek from behind my linen handkerchief, which shields little more than my own cowardice, to wonder at my Lady. Elizabeth observes their suffering. Our Lady will bear witness to the charred remains of her fellow citizens.

"Is this the fate I too must prepare to accept? If so, I should turn to my Lord God. None other than the heavenly Father will provide comfort enough to shield an innocent from her unearned punishment." So forlorn does our Lady Elizabeth seem, I know of no better consolation than that which she suggests herself.

We arrive at Whitehall Palace later than expected, and more dejected than any of us imagined. Lady Elizabeth does not speak. In response to our inquiring glances, she turns away, her lips moving, as though still in Holy Communion with the dead. Neither Kat Ashley nor I can comfort Elizabeth, as our Lady disappears into her chamber. Hunched at her table, Elizabeth scribbles a long and rambling letter to her pious sister, Mary.

March 17, 1554

From Whitehall Palace

To My well-beloved sister, Mary

If any ever did try this old saying – that a king's word was more than another man's oath – I most humbly beseech your majesty to verify it in me, and to remember your last promise and my last demand: that I be not condemned without answer and due proof. Which it seems that now I am, for that, without cause proved, I am by your Council from you commanded to go unto the Tower, a place more wonted for a false traitor than a true subject. Which though I know I deserve it not, yet in the face of all this realm appears that it is proved. Which I pray God I may die the shamefullest death that ever any died afore I may mean any such thing. And to this present hour I protest afore God (who shall judge my truth, whatsoever malice shall devise) that I never practiced, counseled, nor consented to anything that might be prejudicial to your person any way or dangerous to the state by any mean. And therefore I humbly beseech your majesty to let me answer afore yourself and not suffer me to trust your councilors – yea, and that afore I go to the Tower (if it be possible); if not, afore I be further condemned. Howbeit I trust assuredly your highness will give me leave to do it afore I go, for that thus shamefully I may not be cried out on as now I shall be – yea, and without cause. Let conscience move your highness to take some better way with me than to make me be condemned in all men's sight afore my desert known.

Therefore once again kneeling with humbleness of my heart because I am not suffered to bow the knees of my body, I humbly crave to speak with your highness. Which I would not be so bold as to desire if I knew not myself most clear, as I know myself most true. And as for the traitor Wyatt, he might peradventure write me a letter, but on my faith I never received any from him. And as for the copy of my letter sent to the French king, I pray God confound me eternally if ever I sent him word, message, token, or letter by any means, and to this my truth I will stand in to my death.

I humbly crave but only one word of answer from yourself.

> *Your highness' most faithful subject*
> *that hath been from the beginning and*
> *will be to my end, Elizabeth*

Our Queen Mary, daughter to the compassionate Catherine of Aragon, does not spring from the same mold as her mother. Elizabeth's pitiful plea to her sister does not succeed in softening an impassioned monarch. Instead, Queen Mary hides herself behind her shield of Catholic principle.

I fear our Lady Elizabeth's letter hastens our dreaded journey into the Tower. We find ourselves afloat on the Thames once more, silent waves lapping against our vessel with a sinister understanding of our plight.

As if the great river's sympathy is not enough, the ever-present clouds over London release a watery remorse for a young Lady, who destined to be Queen instead finds herself imprisoned. And in God's own name.

Hushed rainfall above us and reaching waves beneath us whisper to one another. With every drop that seeps into our drenched clothing, countless others commune with the river underneath our vessel. One negligible drop after another falls into the welcoming Thames, leaving in its wake silent, spreading rings. And like the ripples of a promise unfulfilled, my disappointment expands, until hope sinks down beneath the river's murky surface.

My Lady, determined to reject our miserable plight, sees all in a different light. For Elizabeth, who smiles into the depths below us, the rainfall is companionable comfort. On landing at Traitor's Gate, the guards assist us in disembarking. Lady Elizabeth, her ladies in attendance, steps out of our small vessel and onto the wooden slatted landing. With a sort of enchantment, Elizabeth transforms herself. A weepy, bedraggled woman-child fades into London's foggy alleyways, and in her place poses a dignified heir to the throne of England.

Lady Elizabeth harnesses her two magnificent strengths: her well-earned place within her people's hearts, and her claim to royalty. Our Lady will remain the daughter of King Henry VIII. Though Queen Mary's passion for her Pope guides her every decision, our Catholic Queen best consider whom she imprisons within her Tower's walls.

The palace sentries bow with reverence before our remarkable young Lady. Their Queen Mary would be incensed to learn of it, but her guards do not forget Lady Elizabeth's esteemed place on the heights of our English landscape. Our Lady takes ample notice of their bowed heads, and speaks to her advantage when offered an opportunity to defend her honour.

"Here landeth as true a subject, being prisoner, as ever landed at these stairs. Before Thee, O God, do I speak it, having no other friend but Thee alone. Oh Lord, I never thought to have come in here as a prisoner, and I pray you all bear me witness that I come in as no traitor but as true a woman to the Queen's Majesty as any as is now living."

Queen Mary's Palace Guard bend further at their belted waists. They hesitate in their awful duty for a moment, eventually giving way to it. The guards escort our Lady Elizabeth and her small retinue to the Bell Tower, where we will now reside.

***

A month and more passes. Temperate May approaches and still we find ourselves locked within the despised Bell Tower's walls. Lady Elizabeth whispers to herself more with each day. Sometimes she hums tunes I could mistake as jovial if it weren't for our dire circumstance. On occasion I stumble on my Lady sharing conversation with an article of clothing: a knitted shawl, a corset, even a feathered hat, as if it contained God's gift of speech.

I despair for Lady Elizabeth's indomitable spirit. If by some miraculous turn of fortune, Queen Mary decides to free her younger sister, I fear the Elizabeth who emerges from her stay within the Tower will not resemble the same girl who entered six short weeks ago.

Our lodgings, due to their paltry size, oppress our spirits, but I cannot mark them as altogether uncomfortable. Lady Elizabeth, Kat Ashley, and I find ourselves together on the first floor of the Bell Tower, one storey away from where our honorable Sir Thomas More did stay. I do not remind Lady Elizabeth of this particular honour. Sir Thomas's untimely death at the hands of King Henry might fail to put Elizabeth's frame of mind in the hopeful place Kat Ashley and I endeavour to maintain it.

The Tower walls, forged of the unforgiving stone blocks all the Tower wears, wrap around us, so our lodging is circular in form. It is almost as though the structure itself colludes with our unforgiving Queen, as it offers no corner of escape. No nook for private contemplation. I consider myself fortunate to find diversion. A little wooden desk with matching stool squats beneath one of our three windows. I consume much of my day scribbling in my faithful diaries.

Though Kat Ashley and I hover close by her side, Lady Elizabeth does not fare well. Like one of her magnificent mares, Elizabeth fails to thrive without her much needed physical exercise. My young Lady chafes at our close quarters. She stalks about the room each morning after tea, until the guards arrive to escort her out of our tiny vestibule and into the courtyard. Here, Elizabeth mingles with the children of the guards. This small privilege provides our Lady with some small comfort.

Just the day before yesterday, I paused, quill in hand. I glanced out my window as I filled my companionable pages. There I witnessed a small boy of four or five years approach Lady Elizabeth and place into her open palm a carefully arranged trio of wilted daisies.

Elizabeth received the wild flowers as though they were a magnificent bouquet of finely bred tea roses. She laid them on her forearm for all to admire, and bent to one knee to speak to the lad.

Whatever sweet gratitude she whispered into his ear formed the widest of grins on his face. My Lady, all encouragement, offered an open hand to the child. He in turn took sturdy hold, and the unlikely couple managed several turns about the courtyard walls, like suitor and his beloved. This strolling continued until the Bell Tower's resounding peals signaled an end to the daily exercise. Kat and I smiled together, grateful for the smallest of God's mercies.

But yesterday our Lady's privilege was with characteristic cruelty and swiftness revoked. The Privy Council monitors our every movement within the Tower walls. Finding Elizabeth had become a favourite of the children - and by extension a favourite of the palace guards - our Lady is ordered to remain within quarters. All contact with others denied.

We fear Lady Elizabeth drives herself to distraction in her anxious boredom. Our Lady alternates between lying prone on her bed, the back of her hand on her forehead, staring at the ruined stony ceiling of our cell, to a seated position on her same bed. Her torso bent into two thin wafers, she clutches and groans at muscle cramps plaguing her intestines. If Queen Mary does not see to the end of our Elizabeth with a swift execution, our Lady's anxiety will wrack all life from her wasting form.

If Elizabeth appeared pale and drawn when we entered the Tower, six weeks later she more resembles a starved apparition. Our Catholic Queen Mary removes from Elizabeth her lusty health. She denies her own sister the smallest privilege that might nourish Elizabeth's sensitive soul.

I fear it falls to Kat Ashley and me to forage for Elizabeth some paltry suggestion of hope. Surely, within this wretched Tower of death and decline, hides a spark to reignite my Lady's restless spirit.

"Lady Jane! We shall soon be sisters by law. And both Dudleys we will be. Your marriage to Guildford and mine to Lord Robert will tie us by the bond of wedlock. Perhaps not a likely proposition for me... Wait. Do not leave so soon. You only just arrive, and we have not yet had our tea...." Elizabeth reaches into the empty cell before her, beckoning to I know not what. I must interrupt this nonsensical parlay. I will ply our Lady with rational, wholesome talk to distract her from forays into imaginary worlds.

"To whom do you speak, Lady Elizabeth? May we accompany you?" Kat and I, locked arm in arm, approach Elizabeth's bedside, determined to ease her distress.

"Blanche, Kat. How lovely. Please join our party, for we are about to have our refreshment. Today we enjoy buttered scones with orange marmalade, and some pretty apricot tarts with curdled cream. I will ensure the servants strain our tea with utmost care, just as my Catherine Parr prepared it. Do come and join us." Elizabeth beckons us to her. Seated at her tiny wooden table, our Lady waves her arms in a flourish as though she offers a sumptuous banquet. The table remains bare, except for a lone earthenware cup.

"My Lady, we are not certain the palace guards can gather such delicacies, but we will gladly sit by you. Shall we read together, then?" Kat reaches to Elizabeth's bedside table, where her prayer book resides. Of course, it is the popish version, the only edition condoned by Queen Mary. Elizabeth takes no interest in Kat's offer.

"Kat, Blanche. Have your manners abandoned you? We cannot be so rude as to ignore our guest. Lady Jane Grey visits. She will, of course, take tea with us."

"Lady Elizabeth, Lady Jane does not join us today." Kat casts a sharp eye in my direction as I correct Elizabeth. I determine to offer our young Lady the woeful reality that will keep her with us.

"But of course she does…Jane sits right here, next to me." Elizabeth's smile betrays no confusion. Still our Lady plays the confident host at her imagined tea.

"Do you recall what happened to Lady Jane some months ago? Lady Jane and her husband Guildford were summoned to the block before we arrived here. Though they once resided in the Tower, no longer do they walk among the living."

I reach out and stroke Elizabeth's cheek, turning her chin toward our eastward window. With any good fortune, I might reawaken her sore spirit. "Lord Robert has behaved as a true Dudley. He joins the rebel, Wyatt, and the rest of his unfortunate family in the Tower. Lord Dudley resides in the Beauchamp Tower, just across the courtyard. You might catch sight of him if you keep watch a while."

"But Lady Jane is a friend. Just a girl of sixteen. What harm can she do to my sister, that she might deserve a beheading? Only a girl of sixteen…"

"…and a lovely Protestant girl, in line for the throne. Your sister protects her envied seat in the most insistent way."

"Then why have I not been summoned to the block? With patience, I await my fate each day. Every morning, I rise and stare toward the chamber door. But no guards enter. No fatal summons for Elizabeth. And so I vow to wait until the next morning. And the next morning, though I know in my heart I should not look, should instead turn toward the window, I direct my gaze at that door, where Death might enter to claim me."

Elizabeth glances from Kat to me. She pleads with us to explain Queen Mary's reasoning. But we offer no reply. We do not know Queen Mary's mind. I seat myself next to Elizabeth and hold her trembling hand in my own.

Our Lady snatches her hand back, leaping from the bed as a new energy takes hold. "Perhaps I should pen my sister another letter. Why will she not grant me an attendance so I may speak to her of my innocence? I have done nothing to deserve this unjust treatment, and yet here we dwell, with the rodents of the Tower." Elizabeth's gaze turns to where block wall meets earthen floor. A favoured place for the creatures' nocturnal antics. The image, imprinted on my Lady's slumbering eye, makes her shudder.

"Look eastward, my Lady. Look where the sun eases us from our broken slumber." Again I direct Elizabeth toward the Beauchamp Tower, toward her fellow prisoner. Behind the barred window, a barely visible shadow wanders to and fro.

"Blanche. Our friend, Robert, passes at his window. Instead of squandering ink on my unmovable sister, I will offer a rekindling of my friendship to Lord Robert. Do you think it a wise idea?"

"Yes, my Lady. Write to Lord Dudley. I am certain he would appreciate a kind word from your Ladyship." I am equally certain the letter will never acquaint itself with Lord Robert's eye; however we welcome the diversion for Elizabeth. I hasten to clear my desktop, so my Lady might replace me at its helm.

The excitement of her discovery – a childhood friend, only a few steps from her threshold - sharpens the pangs in our Lady's abdomen.

Elizabeth wraps her wiry arms around her torso and clutches her skeletal form, bending at her waist in an attempt to ease the muscular spasms. So far do my Lady's reaching hands stretch round her tiny waist, I swear they seek to come round to her front again in a double embrace. With several deep breaths, she stems the painful muscle contractions.

"I wonder if I can engage Lord Dudley's attention at his window instead? We should probably avoid a record of our correspondence, or that privilege too will be removed from us." Elizabeth scrambles up on the face of my desk to reach the barred window.

"I will show my forlorn countenance at this opening until Lord Robert catches a glimpse of his friend, Elizabeth. Together we might devise a way to share the companionship we knew when studying under our brilliant Master Ascham. If I recall well my friend Robin, he possessed striking features, all lit from within with a genuine warmth of character."

Lady Elizabeth perches on the desk. Three long hours pass. Leaning her elbows on the stone windowsill, she awaits Lord Robert's notice. Though she shifts occasionally from one foot to the other, my Lady's patience endures. When no recognition takes place, when the shadow disappears from sight altogether, our Lady Elizabeth refuses to mourn her misfortune.

"Lord Robert does not yet glance our way. But surely, soon. And when he casts his glimpse outside his narrow cell, I will be the first to greet him."

Shadows gather in the courtyard, casting doubt on Lady Elizabeth's new endeavour. Kat and I share worried glances. Lord Dudley's window grows dark. Elizabeth climbs down from her little desk, and returns to her bed to study her earthen ceiling above.

Each day, after that first glimpse of her childhood friend, when stomach cramps do not bend her frame in two, Lady Elizabeth climbs to her place on top of her desk. She stares from her window toward Lord Robert Dudley's cell. On each occasion, disappointment eventually replaces hope. But youthful belief endures.

I will not soon forget the poignant scene. Dusk follows each interminable day. As the days converge into weeks, our beautiful young Lady clambers onto a broken down desk, leans tender elbows on a windowsill of chiseled stone, and places her chin on a tangle of expectant fingers. But what remains most memorable? The resolve fixed in our Lady's eye as she awaits the pacing shadow of her lone friend in the kingdom.

Kat Ashley and I share gratitude for our Lady's diversion. Though she searches for a phantom Lord Dudley, a spectral outline of a man slices less deeply into Elizabeth's sensibility than the daily expectation of burnished steel on her slender neck.

***

At last, the grim morning Lady Elizabeth expects, arrives. It is May 19, 1554 and two awful months pass as we languish in the Tower. The endless turn of an iron key in its lock, would ordinarily suggest release. A joyous occasion even. But when we hear the awful sound, all within our tiny cell fall silent.

Kat and I cast glances toward the twenty year old Elizabeth, then we hasten to her bedside. We sit, Lady Kat at her left, I pressed next to her right. So close do we huddle together, my Lady's heat spreads, until the warmth of her cheek flushes my own.

Her entire form shudders with a frantic pulse. Terror envelops her in a blushing fever, tingeing even the roots at her hairline, where pretty curls spring. While frantic heat spills forth, an ominous chill consumes our woman-child. Lady Elizabeth quivers like a newly hatched sparrow.

Still she perches, otherwise motionless on her bedstead. Her hands grip tight the sodden mattress beneath her. Elizabeth's grey eyes, at home in the charcoal stone of our dismal surroundings, lock on the minutest movement of her cell door. The massive weight of it swings in toward us.

"Lady Elizabeth."

Elizabeth draws a deep breath. She rises with her ladies beside her to meet Sir John Brydges, the Lieutenant of the Tower. I take hold of her hand and squeeze it within mine. A feeble assurance. A friend's ineffectual presence.

"It is I, Sir. Do speak."

I hang on tight to Elizabeth's rigid fingers. She holds them out straight, taut with alarm. Still I hold on, willing her emaciated form to steady itself. She inhales once again and lifts her chin. A tranquil exhalation and calm reasserts itself. Elizabeth returns my squeeze as though it is I who need reassurance.

With an ominous correctness, the Lieutenant reaches down, unhooks his satchel, and draws from it a decree. He removes the ribbon from his scroll, unrolls the fine paper, and recites. Sir Brydges offers his pronouncement in one long extended breath. "Her Majesty Queen Mary, orders you, Elizabeth Tudor, daughter to His Majesty King Henry VIII, remove from the Tower, with your servants and belongings. You shall hereby be placed under house arrest at the palace at Woodstock, where you shall remain until a further decree follows."

It is done. My Lady lives.

***

With a certain whimsy, I now consider Lady Elizabeth's saviour. For he who ensures Elizabeth's release from the Tower will soon become her greatest adversary. Queen Mary's husband, King Philip of Spain, persuades his Queen to free her own sister. 'More a Catholic than a sovereign', our Lady Elizabeth says of him. More a brother-in-law than a husband, I suggest.

I cannot attest to Philip's sympathies for Lady Elizabeth's Protestant faith. But his wisdom and cunning in political matters and his understanding of Queen Mary's doting heart, he does grasp well. Philip, aware of his unpopularity as a Spanish King of England, too keenly understands our Lady Elizabeth's high esteem with her people.

While his Catholic wife remains ensconced within the seductive doctrine of her holy bible, enraptured with the clacking of her rosary beads, Philip's understanding of the English people opens the door of the Tower, ensuring a future Queen's escape from the executioner's block.

And what does my Lady say of her ordeal within the Tower of London? Of her ill-treatment at the hands of her sister? It is well and good my mistress leaves her memoir to me, her Keeper of the Books, for Her Majesty is known to speak little of the affair. And of her sister, Mary? What does my Queen offer? Only this: *"We differed on religion."*

***

Though Her Majesty mutters nonsense: issuing threats of death, pretending to cast doubt on her Gypsy's identity, in truth, Lord Dudley may be one subject our Queen need not suspect. When ravenous Death stalked both young people in the Tower, her Gypsy-to-be remained devoted to his Lady Elizabeth and to her Protestant faith.

Our playful Queen at last accomplishes her goal. She awakens her lounging Robin. The baffled Earl of Leicester no longer offers insolent replies. Comprehending his precarious standing, the Gypsy Earl of Leicester attempts a change of subject. I fear Her Majesty's favourite chooses a path more perilous than the last one he travelled.

"Your Grace, the marriage of the Queen of Scots to the ambitious Duke of Norfolk may not represent the calamity you foresee. Would it not satisfy the majority? Those who grumble about an heir to England's throne? Might it not console both Protestant and Popish interests?"

The Earl's aim to please reinvigorates Her Majesty's agitated state. Her Grace approaches him as though studying a specimen of sudden new interest. A man her astute faculties may have misjudged.

"Robert. You attend with us our civic duties, accompany us about the countryside on our progresses, witness our people bending at prayer within our cathedrals….and yet you persist in adopting dissimilar conclusions to your Queen. Will you not comprehend anything? Though our people love and honour me as their monarch of the moment, still they wonder what promise awaits them in their next sovereign."

Her Majesty's circuitous route, as she marches round her Earl's unmoving form mimics her questioning of him. I fear the Gypsy grows dizzied with the effort of conjecturing Her Majesty's meaning.

"If a knowing heir must wait for the death of a sitting Queen, how might the waiting be felt? With patience? Or with the resentment so often witnessed in such successors? I will not allow this harm to overshadow the realm."

"What harm do you refer to, Majesty? And to the Clergy or the Kingdom?"

"It is one and the same Robin. All woven into our realm's fabric. God ordains His Queen. By His Grace, and His alone I reign. In so doing, He provides whatever means I require to maintain the social order. I, in turn, must provide the opportunity for our citizens to flourish. If prayer aids in my peoples' well-being, they may worship as they choose." Her Majesty pauses and the Earl makes as if to speak, but Her Grace rounds on her Gypsy before he can attempt another contradictory rally.

"Yet, neither in His name, nor in my own, will I allow fanaticism to interfere with good governance. The Clerics must stay to their purpose, enriching the citizenry's souls. They must refrain from the political realm. England will not be ruled from a pulpit. Nor on any account do I confuse my religious tolerance with treasonous pairings such as Norfolk's and the Scots Queen's."

"But Your Majesty, the Duke of Norfolk claims his innocence. He attests to both his Protestant faith and his allegiance to his Queen Bess. Is it not the Queen of Scots whose head should be placed on the block, and not the hapless Duke's?"

"Robert, I fail to understand your sudden thirst for blood. First, you suggest my father's routing of his popish citizenry, and now you would have me place an anointed Queen, a woman whom I consider kin, on the block. If I condone this blood-letting, this primitive execution of she who ascended to her throne, and with every right to it, when shall it stop? Perhaps on a day when Elizabeth's light gleams less brilliantly over her kingdom, another Queen's head will be lopped to the ground."

Her Majesty, returning to her previous rollicking spirit, cocks her head to the side, tilting her golden curls on one shoulder. But the lusty Earl cannot share her good humour. "Your Majesty, no. I do not suggest such a thing..."

Our Queen smiles and sighs. But Her Majesty's time to debate is not limitless, and her patience with her Gypsy wanes.

"No, you do not Robin. I merely allude to the end of the avenue you wish us to stroll along. If my sister, Queen Mary, had paid heed to your counsel instead of her husband, King Philip's, you and I would have hastened hand in hand to the block ourselves. And the merciful executioner would have saved both of us the suffering of this absurd dispute. Leave your Queen, and have my ladies seek out Sir William Cecil. I must see my Sir Spirit."

***

Her Majesty paces to and fro before her throne in anticipation of Cecil's arrival. Her hands, like the wings of vigilant doves, flutter a rhythm on the bell of her gown. Though she remains alone within her Presence Chamber, Her Majesty's lips move, as if in conversation. Surely she deliberates on Norfolk and the Queen of Scots.

When Sir Cecil enters, bows low, and apologizes for his tardy arrival, Her Majesty waves away his fussing with her customary impatience.

Her humble Cecil offers Her Majesty his honest appraisal. "Though the Earl of Leicester and I do not agree on many a topic, I fear, in this we concur, Your Majesty." Cecil balks at having to support the Gypsy's advice.

"The Duke of Norfolk and your cousin, the Queen of Scots, intend to wed and they will indeed seek to overthrow you and sit on the throne of England. The Duke alone has no strong claim. However, his authority with the nobility, coupled with a Queen of Scotland's bloodline, makes the pairing a sharp needle in the spine of Your Majesty's reign."

"Surely together we might discover a means to divide the incendiary pair, and thereby douse the risk? Separated by distance and a Queen of England's decree, the two might remain innocent?" Her Majesty seeks an alternative resolution to relieve her of her odious duty.

"The Duke, were he to remain unwed, remains unobjectionable, Your Majesty. But his intent proves otherwise. The Scots Queen rattles her saber of traitorous action everywhere about the realm. The French-bred, popish Queen of Scots *will* unseat Your Majesty if concise action is not taken. With all respect Your Majesty, heed my careful advice. The Queen of Scots cannot be offered freedom to roam about your kingdom, for it is your kingdom she seeks to reign over herself. Do not fret about Norfolk. The Duke inflicts a mere pinprick next to that envious Queen of Scots, who thrusts her sword of ambition into Your Majesty's dear person. The popish Scots Queen gives not a thought for any royal blood that would stain the throne on which she seeks to perch herself."

Cecil reasserts his authority with the gravity of his disquieting message. It is now the turn of Her Majesty to shift within uncomfortable robes, as she searches for an ever-elusive security.

"Sir Spirit, no nuptials can take place when Norfolk trembles within our Tower walls and my cousin Mary remains cloistered with our guards in her Scottish Palace. And yet... this perilous threat cannot be endured for an endless time. My people clamour for the traitors' heads."

Her Majesty grips the ornately carved arms of her throne until her knuckles turn a paler shade of white.

"Your Majesty, on behalf of England we must advance our aim. Both the Duke of Norfolk and his proposed wife, the Queen of Scots, must go to the block."

"We cannot proceed in this bloodthirsty manner. What of our vow to spare our subjects such vile kingship, Sir Spirit? God save them all. This is not how we attend to our people."

"Your Majesty, it is your own decree that states your very permissible expectations for your subjects' conduct. Shall I place it before you for your perusal?" Sir Cecil, certain of his cause, parleys his violent intent into saucy confidence.

"No. I know it well enough." Her Majesty rarely tolerates such boldness.

Her Grace stares hard at her counselor, daring him to challenge her further. But Sir Cecil, well-versed in Her Majesty's character, plies her instead with thoughtful reason. "Your requirement of your people remains at all times fair, Your Grace. But if you do not proceed against this traitorous activity, you will be viewed as inconsistent. A feeble woman with a feeble woman's will."

"Tread carefully, Sir. Although I may not be a lioness, I am a lion's cub, and I do inherit many of his qualities." As though prompted to do so, Her Majesty swivels her head toward the portrait of her father on the facing wall. Sir Cecil's attention follows his Queen's. King Henry stares back at the pair, the picture of defiance. His little Elizabeth will know what it means to be King.

"I beg your pardon, Your Majesty. However, the situation worsens to where caution alone no longer buoys England's good fortune. Decisive action must be taken."

"Leave me, Cecil. Leave me so I may consider this torment that is forced on your sovereign. I will have a writ for you presently."

Her Majesty studies Sir Cecil's hunched form as he turns to leave her, then stares up to her father once more. King Henry only smiles his soundless reply.

***

April 11, 1572 (2:00 a.m.)
William Cecil, Lord Burghley
My Lord,
Methinks that I am more beholding to the hinder part of my head than well dare trust the forwards side of the same, and therefore sent to the lieutenant and the sergeant, as you know best, the order to defer this execution till they hear further. The causes that move me to this are not now to be expressed, lest an irrevocable deed be in meanwhile committed. If they will needs a warrant, let this suffice, all written with mine own hand.

Your most loving sovereign, Elizabeth R

***

Her Majesty's councilors test her lofty ideals with their pushing of her cousins toward the block. Her Grace's principles, though they stand against tyranny and create a happy conscience, leave our Queen in mortal danger. Her Majesty will not know sleep as she once did. Insomnia wracks Her Majesty's person, until our Queen paces her bedchamber floor as though imprisoned within the Tower herself. And so Her Grace's councilors receive a nocturnal answer they do not seek. An answer that will not put to rest England's misgivings.

Her Majesty's pen, coupled with her noble intention, provides the traitorous Duke of Norfolk one more springtime within the Tower's jealous walls. But summer approaches. And Mother Nature knows only ruthless progress. Eventually, the succulent crop must be plucked from the branch.

Our judicious Majesty, though consumed by her conscience, will provide the decree for Norfolk's beheading. Her Majesty finally sacrifices the luxury she has enjoyed in deviating from her father's rule. No longer can she so easily distinguish the cub from the pride's despotic head. Youthful promise will give way to prudent necessity. The Duke of Norfolk, the lesser half of Her Majesty's traitorous couple, is plucked from the branch of the burdened state on June 2, 1572. God bless his traitorous soul.

Summer III – Waging Peace As If It Were War

Alas for the man, whoever he was,
Who first dug heaps of buried gold
And diamonds content to hide,
And gave us perils of such price!

--Boethius

26th September, 1580

"I stand before you again, Father. How you must tire of this cub padding to your weary side, forever in search of what you cannot give." Her Majesty pauses as if awaiting a reply. The Holbein portrait of King Henry offers none. Our Queen paces to and fro before his life-sized depiction. She hesitates and meets his steady, self-possessed gaze.

King Henry's celebrated memory looms over Her Majesty. Like a too-doting parent, his shadowy presence intrudes on our Queen's quest for mastery of her throne. Will he always eclipse his Elizabeth's brilliance with the weight of his renown? With the too-tight grasp of a father's well-meaning hand? Does he offer to our Queen a model she would rather spurn or imitate?

Her Majesty occupies Richmond Palace. It was her grandfather, Henry VII's, favourite dwelling, and it is Her Highness's too. And yet, I fear she does not know a home. So solitary does Her Majesty reside within the pressing walls of a sovereign's duty.

How will a renowned King's velvet-draped shoulder, depicted only in portrait, provide comfort to a Queen in her perpetual loneliness? I see how she yearns to enfold herself, for just a moment, in a father's devoted embrace. Or does Her Majesty endure a further source of anguish? Perhaps our King's likeness represents for our Queen all the harsh and bitter recrimination she suffers.

Our much-admired, unattainable Queen. No competent King by her side. No husband or children to nurture as her own. A mere woman. She is taunted and cajoled by her councilors, her parliament, her people, all whom she has mothered with unceasing concern. Still, she neglects her instinctive duty. Unnatural woman. Does our King's portrait speak for this larger community? Does a whole constituency await Her Majesty's surrender?

Or do I err? Do I judge too rashly my Queen's distress? Surely Her Majesty only seeks from King Henry the authority he represents. An authority our Queen wishes to enjoy, just as she embodies his imperious will, his long, slightly hooked nose, his curled and golden locks of hair.

Once, long ago, under an ancient oak tree on the grounds of Hatfield Palace, our Elizabeth, when told she was Queen of England, buried her knees in the high grasses and declared: *"This is the Lord's doing: it is marvelous in our eyes."* Today, more than twenty years later, I fear my Queen suffers the keenest sorrow that the weight of a kingdom brings. The entire realm rests on her fine-boned shoulders, bolstered as they may be by a pearl-encrusted gown's unyielding sleeve.

I record today's date, 26th September, the year 1580 and bend to my daily task. No longer do I make myself scarce when Her Majesty summons King Henry for his wisdom. I feel no need to crouch behind Turkish tapestries, drawing half breaths. Nor do I scratch lightly on my tablet with my silent quill, fearing discovery. My

Queen no longer concerns herself with my humble attendance. Her Majesty accepts my company in the same way she invites ever-lurking doubt to interrupt her occasional certainty. I seat myself in plain view of the pair; the father confident in his mastery, though death overtakes him; the daughter alive with a misgiving only felt by the breathing flesh.

I scribble in my beloved journal, ignored by my masters.

I fear a stranger could happen on my Queen like this. Any person could emerge from the complex labyrinth of palace chambers. Any person might behold our Monarch in earnest conversation with her deceased father. And any would wonder at the fragility of Her Majesty's restless wits.

Her Grace leans her entire self into the conversation, as though her whole Privy Council was present. Her hands gesticulating, Her Majesty wages battle. She argues with her father as though he lives. As though at any moment he might bellow a raucous answer to her persistent questioning of his judgment.

The beloved portrait shows only patience. A patience, I dare say, King Henry did not possess in life. And a patience he failed to bequeath our Queen. It is a wonder she persists in her tirade before him. The reply Her Majesty seeks seems to elude her. King Henry, an imposing though passive bystander, reminds Her Majesty of her gifted lineage.

Stay to your course, child. A full twenty years and more have passed under your reign. With cautious counsel, with regard for the realm's security, you emerge a fine king. Do not fear your shadow, little Elizabeth. Step out from your favourite hiding nook. Embrace your destiny.

God's very death. The exact intrusion I worry about stumbles in. A bevy of unruly footsteps trample the hallway as the raucous group approaches our chamber door. Defiant shouts accompany the charge. The odd hoot of laughter too. The gentlemen engage in the pleasure of adamant debate. A determined rapping at the door ensues.

Her Majesty whirls round with customary grace, to meet her favourite councilors. All her motion deliberate, unhurried. With her unique transformational ease, our Queen greets her trusted Lords. Her smile radiates genuine pleasure.

The Gypsy Earl of Leicester, Walsingham and Baron Burghley, our Sir Cecil, cast lengthy shadows through the chamber doorway, belying the celebratory news they deliver. Each in his own distinctive manner endeavours to claim his sovereign's attention ahead of the other. Each devoted gentleman seeks to offer Her Majesty some new intelligence of importance to the realm.

In the end, all share the same concern. Their monarch secure in her throne; their kingdom sheltered in their Queen's doting care. Little they offer surprises Her Majesty. Only moments before, she discussed all their various concerns with her father on the wall.

As the gentlemen approach Her Majesty, Sir Cecil, now our Baron Burghley, steps aside. The elder statesman and consummate courtier laces his hands behind his dark robes and waits. In a competitive onslaught his gracious manner serves Burghley in poor stead.

Sir Francis Walsingham, recently returned from his ambassadorial work in France, impresses Her Majesty. He carries out the duties of Secretary of State – a role Her Majesty's Sir Cecil gladly retired from some years ago. Clothed eternally in somber black, and wearing a dour expression to match his attire, our Queen names Walsingham, with only a little affection, her Moor. Walsingham, in turn, offers Her Majesty his goodness. His integrity hides itself well in the shadows of a perpetual, sardonic sneer.

Too well-schooled in his diplomatic ways, Walsingham joins Cecil in the rear row. The gentlemen nod to one another, good-natured, accepting with a gracious ease, the Earl of Leicester's favoured place.

Only the Gypsy scrambles forward. His impetuous nature, so charming to his Queen twenty years before, still offers its own reward.

Will our cordial lady remain captivated by the Earl of Leicester's masculine energy, his audacious will? Lord Robert Dudley, the Earl of Leicester, initially squeezed betwixt and behind the shoulders of his two fellows, divides the others with one step forward, and bows low before his beloved Queen. Always the lover before the courtier. Forever appealing to Her Majesty's most visceral sensibility.

"Francis Drake returns triumphant, Your Grace. He brings with him an enormous cache of treasure. And all at the expense of King Philip's Spanish fleet. Prized spices, bars of gold, silver, and precious jewels too plentiful to enumerate. The popish Spaniards will rue the day *El Draco* set sail from Plymouth." Leicester turns, and directs his attention over his shoulder. With wide-eyed appeal he petitions Walsingham for the support his fellow councilor has pledged.

For the moment, Her Majesty's Moor simply nods, complacent, awaiting his Queen's reply.

"Francis Drake? An excellent seaman I am told. Though I know very little of his exploits. He commits this lawless plunder of his own accord, for he receives no formal commission from the Crown."

Walsingham stirs, and dares to glance at Sir Cecil, our Baron Burghley, who only raises his eyebrows, maintaining his attention on his Queen.

"Yes, Your Majesty, but what *El Draco* lacks in social grace and courtly know-how, he makes up for with the tremendous weight within the hold of his ship." The Earl of Leicester, ever Her Majesty's Gypsy, cavorts about the room. His masculine energy uncloaked, some joyful greed stirs his form. I believe he will soon request his Queen's hand to dance their favourite La Volta.

Walsingham and Cecil fail to share the Gypsy's fervour. Both gentlemen, their full beards masking downturned expressions of disdain, look askance as her favourite showers his Queen with glad tidings. Ever conscious of Her Majesty's changeability, their experience warns them to tread with care.

"But we have heard so little of our brave adventurer these three long years. I had begun to consider Drake perished at sea..." Her Majesty betrays increasing interest in Drake's success. The Gypsy's exuberance does catch.

Walsingham considers the moment advantageous to weigh in. "Drake returns and regales the Court of sailing about the entire globe, Your Grace. From Plymouth to the Spanish Americas, through the treacherous Straits of Magellan and into Pacific waters. Spanish ports from Panama to Peru felt the prick of Drake's sword at each landing. King Philip needn't fret about his heavy cargoes sinking his vessels. Drake has lightened Spain's plunder considerably."

Walsingham heaps his praise on Drake's navigational skill, ignoring Cecil's dismay. Beside him, Sir Cecil shuffles back and forth. Examining first the Earl of Leicester, then Walsingham, and finally his Queen's expressionless countenance, Baron Burghley senses his exclusion from the council meeting, though he stands planted firm within it.

"Walsingham, we have granted Francis Drake no permission for wayward activity on the Channel, nor on the world's great seas. Unless an express Letter of Reprisal is issued by our own hand, piracy is strictly forbidden. We have made an oath to Philip of Spain; such treachery must be outlawed..." Her Majesty looks toward Cecil with an exaggerated emphasis, inviting him into the debate. Cecil only nods in tacit agreement, though his posture suggests he senses his Queen's betrayal.

"...and with ardent energy, punished by us." Another glance Cecil's way.

Sir Cecil finds his entry into the deliberation. "Your Majesty, I heartily agree. Cordial relations with Spain must be maintained. The security of the realm relies on Your Majesty's fellowship with King Philip. Our coffers run dangerously low at Court, and the realm possesses no standing army to speak of. We have no readied fleet with which to protect the English coasts against marauding Spanish galleons."

"Why finance an entire battalion when we have the fire-breathing Dragon on our side?" The Gypsy Earl of Leicester, giddy with imagined treasure awaiting inspection within the holds of Drake's *Golden Hind*, pirouettes. He falls to one knee before his Queen. As always, he is rewarded with an indulgent burst of laughter from Her Grace.

Spotting his advantage, the Gypsy stares long into his Queen's hooded eye. Though ashen in colour, Dudley imagines it ignites as though imbued with Drake's golden ore. He approaches Her Majesty's throne, drawn there by an ancient sorcerer's fiendish command. Does he consider placing his wretched hands on our Queen, and in company?

Walsingham and Cecil bow their heads; glancing away from the Earl of Leicester's impropriety should he attempt it. But they need not. Her Majesty's dainty hand, with only the slightest act of rising up, stays her Gypsy's approach. Her smiling gaze hardens. A steely rebuff greets her Bonny Sweet Robin's eye, and with iron-willed certainty drives him backward to stand with his fellows. The Council resumes as though the little drama does not transpire.

Baron Burghley, our poor Sir Cecil, ever on the wrong side of the argument, remains without good humour. He feigns absolute unawareness of the Gypsy's interruption, furthering his petition to Her Majesty.

"...Our coinage has been unfortunately devalued, Your Grace. The English fleet is in desperate need of repair, while Philip's navy flourishes with monies gotten from the Americas and from the Pope himself. Still the Catholics doubt Your Majesty's claim to the throne. I must advise Your Grace, a fruitful match would serve to silence the European din. Your marriage to the French Duke of Alencon would ensure Catholic support on the Continent..."

I cannot comprehend Sir Cecil's desire for Her Majesty's punishing temper. Of all his Queen's cares, he raises the marriage question at this juncture.

Fortunate for Baron Burghley, our Queen's mood, like her Gypsy's, lightens. Burghley owes thanks to Francis Drake's generous filling of her yawning treasury. Her Majesty's brow knits itself together in a weave of disdain at the idea of a French Duke. But her expression, resplendent with mischief, portrays only good-natured disbelief. Sir Cecil's gaffe threatens nothing more than a further outburst of riotousness. Her Majesty contains her mirth, exchanging a sly smile with her Gypsy as Cecil drones on.

Walsingham, ever the stone-faced diplomat, buries his bearded chin in his collar of lace, sighs and awaits an end to Baron Burghley's hopeless plea.

"...Only the most diplomatic of measures should be employed with the King of Spain. His reserves contain galleons beyond anything our English fleet might muster. And he worships his popish God ardently..." Burghley draws breath, allowing Her Majesty to intercede.

"My Sir Spirit, I am informed unceasingly of the dreaded Spanish fleet. And of the omnipotent King Philip of Spain. I understand Philip is more Catholic than the Pope. Well, his popish God must consider him a worthy disciple. King Philip demonstrates the utmost charity in sharing his alms with *El Draco*, and England too. The generosity Spain exhibits. Blessing our impoverished England with all the golden riches of her well-equipped galleons."

I would expect Her Majesty to restrain her revelry, if only to honour Baron Burghley's serious concern. Our Queen owes much to Cecil's wise counsel. Surely her love for him will not permit her to squander his goodwill.

The muscles surrounding Her Majesty's upper lip twitch as she seeks to maintain some semblance of order over her high-spirited relief. Gladness too often succeeds in overtaking good judgment. Contrary to Her Majesty's honest intention, her mouth breaks free of restraint, stretching wide across her face in an ecstatic grin. Our Queen cannot conceal her excellent mood. Relief intoxicates Her Grace, as the weight of a kingdom falls from her stooped form. A carefree Lady Elizabeth returns to our midst, whirling about a Hatfield Palace garden. Her Majesty draws the deepest of delicious breaths from the well of respite. If only for a wondrous moment.

Within seconds, true to her chameleon-nature, Her Majesty's features reform. Her Grace returns from her frolic amongst daisied meadows of childhood, to her solemn place on the throne. I believe she succeeds in her deception. The gentlemen remain unaware of Her Majesty's recent flight from them. Most remain oblivious to our Queen's special gift of transfiguration.

"Your Majesty. Forgive me, but that pillaging pirate, that heedless corsair must be stopped. Drake commits acts of war against the Spanish fleet..."

I commend Baron Burghley's infinite courage. Though winds blow with alarming rigour directly into his bent frame, still he shouts his unwanted message into the gusts.

"I prefer, Sir Spirit, to name Francis Drake our *merchant adventurer*. A fine navigator I am told..." Our Queen lounges within the protection of the palace walls. Out of the blustering tempest, she shelters in the security of Drake's plunder.

"Stopped? You cannot be serious, Burghley. Drake is our best and rarest advantage. Why he is the very 'fox who would recognize the trap, and the lion who does frighten off the wolves'." The Earl of Leicester, adept at recognizing Her Majesty's goodwill, proposes Drake as saviour.

Though Machiavelli's *Prince* occupies our Queen's shelves, open comparison to his methods does not provoke the desired effect. The Gypsy's quoting of the notorious Italian does little to impress our Queen.

Her Majesty's indulgence for her Gypsy's antics begins to wane. The Earl of Leicester receives only a perfunctory nod before our Queen motions to her councilors for silence.

"Gentlemen, I will require detailed reports from all of you. Baron Burghley, my Sir Spirit, a full accounting of the realm's assets should be undertaken before Master Drake's bounty is inventoried and stored within the Tower. Include all ready monies, properties and sources of taxation. Lord Walsingham, secure England's coastlines from the Spanish. I suspect King Philip might be seeking retribution for our sudden good fortune. And my Earl of Leicester..."

"Your Majesty." The Gypsy bends before Her Grace's throne. So near does he approach her person, his saucy temple brushes her knee beneath her gown as he bows low. Walsingham and Burghley look on with distaste.

"Robin, send to our merchant adventurer, Drake. We must receive from the seaman himself a report of his dramatic success."

Baron Burghley, preparing to take his leave, turns back in protest. "Your Majesty, I beg of you, hear me. The Spanish ambassador insists on an audience."

"Insists, does he? He should consider carefully to whom he makes his persistent claims..."

"Mendoza complains bitterly of Drake's exploits, Your Majesty. The Spanish Admiral, the Marquis of Santa Cruz, already names Your Grace the *Pirate Queen*. If you receive the lowly corsair, this *El Draco*, before attending to Spain's ambassador, King Philip's ire will be hotly stirred."

"Sir Spirit, we do value your careful judgment. Like a devoted father you guide and protect your Queen. Your service will ever be remembered. However, first and foremost, consider the realm. Drake's splendid success allows us to wage peace as though it were war. Spain's complaint will wait. Let us send to Plymouth. We must hear from Drake."

***

It is rare to witness my aging Queen's face alight with the anticipation which shone from it when she first claimed her place on the throne. The burden of Catholic plotting against Her Majesty weighs on our Queen's expression. Anxiety transforms the playful smile once hovering on her pretty lips, leaving in its place a dejected stare of wistful unease. Or worse. Her Majesty's mouth shapes itself into a mocking, matronly sneer. Creases, resembling parched rivers of contempt, mark her once cheery disposition. It is said those unfortunate souls who once embraced the loftiest of ideals, with exposure to the world's multitude of disappointments, become the most hardened cynics. I cannot imagine a more hopeful monarch who did ascend the throne than my Queen.

But today Her Majesty brightens her Presence Chamber at Richmond with a radiant gladness. Like a late-August afternoon, where the sky glows auburn before tucking itself away in an autumnal haze, our Queen beams. Her Majesty adorns her gown with her finest lace collar. Pearls nestle within her jaunty curls and hang in teeming strings around her neck. The precious ropes encircle her hopeful mood. Her expression of gratitude lingers, turning her lips upward, as she awaits *El Draco*.

Our Queen's pleasure heats the Presence Chamber with a seductive vitality, as though Her Majesty waits on a clandestine visit from Bonny Sweet Robin himself. I return in my mind's eye to a day when her Gypsy lover courted our Queen's restless mind and her illicit want, as one. Within my Queen's Privy Chamber I stopped my ears, and forbade my pen from recording the rustlings of hands beneath protecting layers of silk. More than once I pretended not to hear the heartfelt promises of a shared future.

The same flushed anticipation sets Her Majesty aglow today. Her cheek does not tint for a gentleman this time, but for his ill-gotten bounty. Her Majesty's realm basks in the sunlit amiability of good fortune. Drake pinkens our Queen's fine complexion and stokes a kingdom's fiery pride with his treasure. All unearthed from a Spanish galleon's reeking timbers.

"Francis Drake. I trust you are well since returned from your exploits about the globe?" Her Majesty lounges on her throne. Her ease transforms recent frowns into girlish pleasure. Our Queen offers the pirate her draped hand, smiles and nods with satisfaction as Drake bends low before her.

"I have never felt more robust in all my life, Your Grace. It is an honour to be in your presence."

"You are most welcome, Sir. My council reports you have harvested magnificent fortune for England at the cost of King Philip of Spain's fleet. Have you succeeded in shifting Philip's Catholic aim at my throne onto his more pressing financial concerns? Have you singed the beard of the King of Spain, as you promised your hopeful Queen?"

"Your Majesty, forgive me. In due course, I will give and tell all. First I must present to you a token from our voyage. A gesture of my own and my crew's gratitude for your loyal support."

The stout seaman bows low before Her Majesty. On lifting himself up, he displays in his open palm a magnificent cross of gold. Measuring a full hand in length, the emblem hangs suspended from a linked chain. Engraved flourishes decorate the vertical and horizontal lengths of the religious artifact, so the precious metal appears differentiated in a variety of bright and shaded tones of yellow.

As Drake holds the cross for Her Majesty's closer inspection, five glorious emeralds the size of our Queen's discerning eye, cast verdant hues on her bared chest. There they reflect a spectacular rippling effect, resembling the seas Francis Drake sailed only days ago.

I wonder that Her Majesty does not detect the incongruity in Drake's gift. A cross. The cherished symbol of her Catholic enemies. I fear this interview, while hardly begun, might end in a seaman's disgrace. Perhaps, Francis Drake, the lauded sailor does not navigate as well the waters within his Queen's Court. Or within his Queen's temperament either.

Yet Her Majesty chooses to ignore the popish significance of the pirate's gift. Does gratitude cloud her judgment, rendering our Queen insensible to the Catholic idol? Perhaps Her Majesty's understanding travels beyond the article's usefulness as relic of popish idolatry.

Our Queen, accustomed to gifts of enormous beauty and worth combined, appears humbled by the elegance of the glittering cross. Her Grace bows her head to the lowly seaman, accepting his splendid offering. The hushed moment, so important to the realm, requires a respectful silence. Her Majesty and her adventurer acknowledge the gift as an article apart from its monetary worth. Even its spiritual emblem does not register. Instead, both Queen and buccaneer defer to the golden cross as a symbol of peace for England.

It is the mariner who breaks the wordless pause. "I must thank Your Grace for a gift which emboldened your servant on more than one occasion. A token from your own hand, which you may have since let pass from your memory, but which I have held in the highest of esteem throughout my arduous journey."

Drake, named *El Draco*, "Dragon" by the cowering Spanish, does not resemble the swarthy gallant I imagined. Rather, he is a stout and fair-headed sailor, sporting a wispy moustache, all speckled red-blonde. Her Majesty's Dragon resembles the commonest of Her Majesty's subjects.

Our Queen's corsair thrusts his powerful arm into his gunny sack, from which he pulls a disheveled article of graying fabric. Though once a fine piece of embroidered silk, it has travelled the world with the hardy Drake, weathering more abuse than most items of its fine quality.

Her Majesty shifts in her throne. Does she lose patience with Drake, and his avoidance of her queries? Our Queen appears curious as she leans forward, her hand grasping her jewel encrusted cross. Her Majesty's varied lengths of pearls scrape the floor at her feet, her exposed décolletage within the lusty seaman's view. But neither Queen nor sailing captain concern themselves with matters of the flesh. More urgent concerns of the realm's treasury press on them. Her Majesty examines the bedraggled items Drake grasps in his hand.

"It is the very cap and scarf I gave to you when you set sail in the *Pelican* three long years ago." Delight bathes Her Majesty's features in the warmest glow.

"Embroidered in your own hand, Your Majesty. *'The Lord guide and preserve thee until the end.'* I carried it on my person next to my copy of *Acts and Monuments*. While relieving the Spaniards of their treasure, always present in my waking thoughts were our Protestant martyrs. Those who fought with bravery against the tyranny of the Popish state." As Drake refers with evident pride to his religious fervour, Her Majesty looks askance, but only for a trifling instant. Her merchant adventurer fails to take notice of his Queen's hesitation.

"No matter how ill the winds blew in our little band's favour, never did I cease to feel your warm support of our mission. I give all my life's thanks to your constant care, Your Grace."

"Remember well, Sir, our agreement. I will champion your brilliant exploits, but you must recall my explicit commandment. Of all men, my Lord Treasurer, Baron Burghley must not know of our complicity."

"I do not neglect my oath, Your Majesty. Though Baron Burghley may happily come to understand our shared position when he looks on the vastness of the treasure we bring to England at King Philip's expense."

Her Majesty smiles on Drake's optimism, but her serenity wanes. A subtle fluttering of her pretty fingers thrusts her disagreeable Sir Cecil from the conversation. She pursues more pressing concerns. "Enough of Burghley. Much has come to pass while you sailed the globe. Our realm is in particular need of the bounty you bring us. On several fronts we face resolute opposition." Her Majesty pauses for a breath. Seeking to replace exasperation with calm, she exhales a prolonged sigh.

A common sailor's generous gifts pry open Her Majesty's spirit. She almost relaxes in the solace of Drake's company. Her Grace entrusts her misgivings to a pirate of the lowest order, motioning for him to seat himself at her foot. The seaman bows again, and lowers himself down on a satin pillow by her slipper.

"Our mutual enemy, King Philip of Spain, supports a papal mission to Ireland. The Pope's Jesuit priests, with Philip's active encouragement, form an uprising against England..."

"Surely, Your Majesty..." Drake interrupts and then hesitates.

Our Queen stays him with her outstretched hand. She has more to report. Her Majesty details the endless list of Catholic plots. "A new King of France bends to all Philip's darkest wishes, uniting the Spanish and French in popish collusion against our realm. King Philip claims the crown of Portugal for himself. It seems all Europe has its Catholic fangs set to tear into England's exposed flesh. Such a multitude of threats reveal themselves, we find it necessary to ally ourselves with Constantinople. The Turks will balance the scale somewhat in England's favour..."

As our Queen tallies for Drake the challenges to the security of England, her serenity departs. The expansion of Philip's control in Europe sounds more formidable to her ear when her own tongue recites Spain's growing number of allies. Her Majesty's prudently composed report, delivered in her controlled cadence, threatens to become an admission of weakness Her Majesty can ill afford.

Our Queen's anxious fingers, weighed down with the jewel-encrusted rings of which she has become so fond, travel forward and back along the reaches of her throne's arm. Drake notes Her Majesty's distress and attempts to distract his Queen with his own zealous arguments.

"Your Grace, Rome's far-reaching grip has attempted to strangle our nation since my earliest memory. Its efforts to inflict its popish sentiments set me on my present journey."

"We believed it was your loving Queen who motivated you to such vigorous defense of your country..." Her Majesty bestows a teasing smile on her pirate. Our Queen seeks to distract Francis Drake from his pious defense of his Protestant faith. To his discredit, the preoccupied seaman does not possess the Gypsy's sensitivity to Her Majesty's desire to leave religion to her clerics. He prattles on at his peril.

"Circumstances alter since I sailed three long years ago, yet much remains unchanged, Your Grace. Still it is the Popish princes who trespass on our Queen's waking thoughts and restless slumbers. Catholic mobs devastated my family home in Devon. My brothers and I vowed vengeance on the idolaters. It appears it is I who stand to wage the battle in my own little way."

When flirtation fails to redirect Drake's attention away from his Protestant God, Her Majesty turns with her usual dexterity to a more candid approach. If her womanish charm cannot shift the navigator from his brooding on Catholic misdeeds, his Queen's resolve will move him from it.

"Understand Drake. There is nothing little about your success. Your glory is all of England's. Your accomplishments alter our humble State's fortunes. Your achievements are laudable, and shall be acknowledged as such in due course."

I marvel at Her Majesty's success. She nudges her pirate away from those subjects closest to his heart and furthest from hers. She replaces creeping fear with coquettish teasing. Flirtation with flattering promise. The new tactic serves Her Majesty well. The mariner is silenced, and his Queen steers his attention once more.

"Let us leave this subject of our kingdom's woes. I must have knowledge of your voyage. A Queen's progresses are limited by her great responsibility within the realm and by the weakness of her sex. I may only venture as far a distance as my grand carriage can roam. As distant as England's tugging reins permit." Her Majesty indicates her desire for her *merchant adventurer* to extend his stay. His startled expression gives way to happy compliance.

"Find comfort by your Queen's side Drake, and speak to me of this vast world I cannot peruse with my own eyes. Of the various people I do not have the pleasure of encountering myself."

Fluidity informs Her Majesty's transformation. The regal monarch turns coquette. The flatterer shifts shape, leaving in her place a serious interrogator. And now our Majesty lapses into the curious child who stood with forehead pressed against tiny beveled panes at Hatfield Palace. Though she no longer awaits a carriage to speed her to Hampton Court and her beloved father's side, she remains eager for knowledge of worlds she cannot find her way to.

Drake complies, and with a growing ease in his Queen's company. "Your Grace, there is a variety of man I admire, and without whom I am certain we would not have achieved our tremendous success."

"What of these people? What assistance did they offer our English adventurers?"

"These brown-skinned, well-muscled men are named by the locals, "Cimarroons", Your Grace. We first encountered them in Cartagena, and then in Panama and Peru. Unfortunate souls, these honest men were bought and sold by the Spanish, but have since escaped their shackles, and become independent souls."

"How then did you come to know these native people, Drake?"

"I believe our English customs appealed more to their courageous natures than did the Spanish ones, for the Cimarroons sided with us, Your Majesty. The natives provided us with intelligence about Spanish settlements. They informed us of advantageous places to attack the Spaniards' villages. Thus, we took the popish Spaniards by surprise on several occasions..."

"I trust, Drake, you did use those Negroes well. If, as you say, they allied themselves to our cause with loyal exertion, they deserved no less."

"Your Majesty, though I do not wish to appear prideful, I have benefited from my travel of the globe. I have become a great observer of the natures of all men..."

"Well done, Drake. One might never comprehend too much of another's motives. Though we cannot know what it feels to inhabit another man's soul, it is the ability to grasp another man's suffering that separates our higher nature from those base instincts."

"Your Grace, I admit to knowing little of these people, and yet my understanding did grow somewhat as our friendship flourished..."

"But I refer to the *trade* in men, Sir. I have ordered its cessation in the realm. Did the Cimerroons offer their assistance of their own will, or have we supplanted the Spaniards as their new masters?"

"I do not seek to deceive Your Majesty. I admit these generous people served us in many ways. They tended to our sick and injured with medicines and herbal concoctions. Their elixirs healed beyond any I know of in our fair land."

"Not a particularly difficult task to outdo the medicine practiced in England, my dear man. Your Queen evades our respected practitioners and the perils they offer. We are glad your men benefitted from such able care. What other assistance did these faithful servants give you?"

"Your Grace, they crafted a shoe called a moccasin from the hides of the game they hunted. No finer slippers may be found in all of the Americas. And all this they did to serve us. Perhaps, Your Majesty, it is in their natures to assist..."

"And perhaps it is in their natures to survive, Drake. I repeat it. I hope you used those Negroes well. We cannot condone trading in the flesh of men. Our beloved people, our conscience cannot endure it."

"Your Majesty..." In his attempt to placate his Queen, Drake interrupts.

Her Majesty rises from her throne and spreads both hands before her, imposing silence on her merchant adventurer. She prevents his attempt to console her.

"False reports offered to soothe a Queen's ear only serve to transform the speaker of the untruth, Drake." Her Majesty steers her pirate toward a place in their conversation where they both can avoid objectionable realities. She would rather not hear. Her Majesty has learned to appreciate the refuge ignorance sometimes provides.

"We will choose to believe the loyalty these people have shown you, Drake, was well-earned. We cannot consider the alternative. Do you understand your Queen?"

"I do, Your Grace."

"Excellent. Now, to the treasure. We hear of its vastness, but nothing have we witnessed or assessed. Have you brought samples for your monarch to look on?"

"I have, Your Grace. The packhorses rest in your stables. I have brought with me all the precious jewels we appropriated, several tons of spice, including the cloves you so enjoy, and samples of the gold and silver coinage."

"Excellent, Drake. We have heartily enjoyed your visit. The hours have flown by too quickly." Her Majesty rises, indicating an end to the lengthy interview. Her pirate, caught unprepared, scrambles to his feet, bowing low before his Queen.

"You will be richly rewarded for your courage, Francis Drake. Magnificent achievement. I will speak to Baron Burghley about payment of your commission. Your monarch and your country are entirely indebted to your daring. We vow to you, you shall not be forgotten. Not by your Queen, nor by our good people of England."

***

1st April, 1581

Six months have passed since Francis Drake's exultant return. Spring beckons Her Majesty to her lush gardens early each morning. Every day, without fail, our aging Queen marches along her petal-strewn, cobbled paths at the briskest pace. Another of the Gypsy's suggestions. Her Majesty's waist remains slender. So inclined is Her Majesty to exercise, to *get up a heat*, as she terms it, the royal architects build a Long Terrace at Windsor. Now our Queen enjoys her daily stroll no matter what inclement weather storms without.

Windsor's enclosed terrace remains one of the few luxuries Her Majesty allows herself. Until Drake materialized and added weight to her sorely wanting treasury, even this modest addition was in doubt. Given my Queen's parsimony, or should I say poverty, it is fortunate her extravagant father built Nonsuch Palace before our Queen ascended her throne. Though Her Majesty appreciates King Henry's fairy-tale palace, and goes there often to hunt or ride, neither her purse nor her practical nature would allow our Queen to build a palace of such grandeur.

Her Majesty persists in her concern with her appearance, and strives to look youthful with her daily walkabouts. Yet, I believe our Queen also seeks to stave off the dreadful insomnia plaguing her nights. Often I awaken in the early hours to the rustling of pages, the sharp odour of paraffin's relentless burn.

Our Queen's graceful hand draws swirling calligraphy on the page. A translation exercise. A speech to parliament. A letter to Leicester, Hatton, or Walsingham. Or, when her delicate hand rushes with harried precision across the empty page? A clipped note to herself. Too frequently, Her Majesty shows herself the least amiability.

This fair day promises more exhilaration for Her Majesty than most. Betraying no sign of a restless night, Her Majesty strides with an especially purposeful air. On this perfect spring morning our Queen and her retinue travel to Deptford to view Francis Drake's infamous *Golden Hind* in dry dock.

Once, her Gypsy was the one who most enjoyed Her Majesty's favour. Now, Francis Drake, named "The Fortunate" by all who know him in the Queen's Court, maneuvers his way into Her Majesty's regard with his own navigational daring. Is there no end to our Queen's gratitude? On the pirate's return, I overheard Her Majesty order Sir Cecil, Baron Burghley to pay to Drake a full ten thousand pounds sterling for himself, and another fourteen thousand for his crew. Parsimonious indeed.

Drake's – or should I say Philip of Spain's – generosity has rubbed its golden dust onto Her Majesty's open palm. Untold sums of booty travel via horseback to the Tower. Baron Burghley, his pen poised, jaw agape, reports to Her smiling Majesty, England's treasury stands stocked for all of 1581. The *merchant adventurer* pays the realm's expenses for an entire year.

Our Queen unfastens her clenched fist. At last Her Majesty frees herself of the dreadful grip scarcity attaches to her scepter. She rests on her pillow with the knowledge unpopular taxes no longer need be inflicted on her people.

"God bless you all my good people." Our Queen steps with pointed toe onto Drake's *Golden Hind*, pausing to address her cheering subjects. All join in the celebration of England's excellent merchant adventurer.

At Her Majesty's side, hovering only slightly behind, Monsieur de Marchaumont, the French Ambassador to England, strolls toward the banner and ribbon-bedecked vessel. Wry bemusement hovers with some strain on his countenance. The French envoy can't help but wonder what the English Queen plays at, demanding his presence at the controversial pirate's gala.

Then the unthinkable. Her Majesty glances down with mock astonishment as her purple and gold silk garter slips from beneath her skirts, tumbling at the foot of the French diplomat. Monsieur de Marchaumont can hardly believe his misfortune when the all but elderly English Queen – surely she nears her fifth decade – stares with exaggerated expectation on him, as though to inquire: *"Qu'as- vous fait de ma jarretelle?"*

Her Majesty, an aged coquette in Monsieur de Marchaumont's learned opinion, expects the French Ambassador to fetch her errant undergarment and return it with some semblance of grace, to her hand. And all before a clamouring audience of Englishmen. Offered little choice in the matter – the island's most vocal occupants await his gallantry with an intake of breath – the unfortunate diplomat bends to the wooden planks. Monsieur de Marchaumont retrieves the object - reprehensible little dainty - and rises with straightened back, pressing the garter with firm, and he hopes, subtle disapproval into the English Queen's glove.

"Merci, Monsieur. We must return this naughty piece of lace to where it belongs." Ambassador de Marchaumont, taken aback at Her Majesty's use of the royal 'we', gapes open-mouthed. *"Qu'est-ce qui se passe? C'est horrible."*

The Ambassador wonders at the legendary status of the Virgin Queen as Her Majesty proceeds with undue haste to hoist skirts above her knee and return the garter to her shapely, stockinged calf. A tight smile hovers on his beleaguered countenance as Monsieur de Marchaumont attempts to anticipate the wicked English woman's next ploy. Our jovial Majesty remains, as usual, one maneuver ahead of her companion.

"I promise you Monsieur Ambassador, when its usefulness is done at the end of this prodigious day, I shall send to you the intimate object as a souvenir, and a memorial to a proud moment in the history of our realm."

The gathered crowd responds with an encouraging hurrah. Ambassador de Marchaumont, each muscle in his clenched jaw fraught with the effort of maintaining his sorely tried dignity, bows in stiff acknowledgement. Though de Marchaumont employs every modicum of his diplomatic will to maintain his composure, I detect a faint blush on his bedeviled cheek.

Her Majesty betrays no notice of Monsieur de Marchaumont's disapproval, beckoning him forward into *The Hind's* hold. Do I imagine it, or does the gentleman hesitate, unsure whether to proceed into Drake's waiting lair? If a retreat occupies the Ambassador's deliberations, he might listen to this wheedling voice of reason. If experience foretells it, Her Majesty has much in store for her French diplomat.

Guests, fortunate to receive our Queen's invitation to the feast enjoy a magnificent array of delicacies. Exquisite dishes, served at only the most splendid of occasions, fill gleaming silver serving trays. All lay stretched along white-linen covered tables the entire length of the ship's deck.

Roast partridge, freshly boiled lobster, baked lark, quail and curlew, porpoise, shrimp, oysters on the shell. All is marveled at and consumed in hearty measure.

An array of uniformed servants offer guests the impossible choice of drinking their wine from Venetian glass goblets inlaid with delicate diamond patterns, or edible sugar glasses, which guests are invited to feast on after drinking their fill.

Her Majesty's sated guests draw away from the table. Wine casks trickle with sediment-laden dregs. Our Queen rises and stands over Drake, who is ordered to kneel before her. Her Majesty ensures Monsieur de Marchaumont remains by her side throughout the celebration. She showers the French Ambassador with small attentions. She introduces him to her favourite courtiers, and offers him the finest meats, pies and pasties. Our Queen directs her servants to show her French visitor a hospitable English welcome. All washed down with her vintner's smoothest claret.

When the illustrious company pushes chairs aside, and stands surrounding their Queen and her saviour-adventurer, *El Draco,* Monsieur de Marchaumont stands shoulder to shoulder, to Her Majesty's right. Her Majesty holds before her, within two clasped hands, a beautiful gilded sword.

"My good people, should I strike this daring head from its shoulders for the shameless plundering of Spanish galleons on the high seas?"

The gathered crowd, in mock horror, responds in the negative. Monsieur de Marchaumont, too late, realizes his error in boarding the *Golden Hind.* Her Majesty stares straight into his eye. She offers to Monsieur de Marchaumont, the Ambassador of France, her gilded sword. France, represented by the distinguished Ambassador de Marchaumont bestows a knighthood on Sir Francis Drake. In so doing, the French break with Spain and join Elizabeth I's England.

***

2nd April, 1581 (3:00 a.m.)

Several hours later, when civilized folk occupy a dreamless slumber, I realize Her Majesty has not entered her Privy Chamber. I consider my Queen's enforced quiet within the carriage on the return journey from Deptford. Though we sat face to face on our hard leather benches, our knees only a hair's breadth from touching, my Queen remained locked behind a wall of tumultuous thought.

I climb from my bed, reach for my dressing gown, and drift out my chamber's door, into Windsor's winding halls. Common sense insists I should sound the alarm and cry out for assistance. My Queen's absence mystifies. And yet my slippered feet pad a familiar route. I meander through high-ceilinged corridors toward the ante chamber where King Henry's life-sized image hangs. Well before I enter the room, Her Majesty's frantic whispers reach my anxious ear.

"You do not hear my complaint. You *will* not hear it. With whom shall I speak if my own phantom father will not pay heed?" Her Majesty's lowered voice hisses with emotion. She stands posed before her father's image, pleading with the intelligent blue eye, painted by Holbein.

"*You have succeeded with more wit, and with more artistry than your father could have risked imagining, little Elizabeth. Well done. You have silenced Philip and his henchmen from Rome for quite a time.*"

"It is true. Drake fills the Spaniards with fear for their hulking galleons. They set sail and hasten back to the port of Madrid at the whisper of El Draco."

"*Yet you do not appear to rejoice, my darling daughter? Your treasury overflows. Your people bask in England's newfound wealth. They flock to the streets to meet and thank their Queen Elizabeth for her resilient leadership. What more do you seek? You have conquered the mighty Philip of Spain. Where else do a daughter's ambitions wander?*"

"At what price, Father? And at what cost to the realm? What of my reputation? My people trust in their Queen to keep a peaceful England. To ensure Spain's interests lie across the Atlantic in their golden Americas and not with England's vulnerable coastal villages. As you know, a war is easily begun but not so well ended. I fear Philip of Spain will offer a reply yet."

Her Majesty, considering the dreadful prospect of Spain's attack, paces. She turns her attention from her father, into the depths of the darkened hallway.

"With or without Drake, King Philip will deliver his message, my darling daughter. Is it not better to parlay with the Spanish King from a position of strength on the Channel, than from a position of want? And what is this of war? No war do we wage. Our mighty dragon takes care of the Spaniards single-handedly. It is only for you to spend Philip's gold with the wisdom a king possesses. I am confident in your shrewd judgment."

"Father, take heed. Sir Francis, while an able sea captain, does little to respect the laws governing our European allies. If Sir Cecil only knew of his Queen's involvement … I commend all Drake's exploits, while he and his men burn and pillage an English passage all through the Spanish Americas."

"Yes. It is excellent Spain comes to notice an English presence…"

"You will not hear me. While Drake denies brutal murder, claiming to leave the women of the Spanish American colonies inviolate, I fear his men commit crimes I would despise. Rampaging about the globe in our name. It chastens a Queen to forfeit her conscience on behalf of the realm…"

"Forfeit nothing daughter. You serve your God well when you look on the realm before all other cares. God first, then Monarch. No space remains for a woman's wheedling conscience."

"And the Cimarroons? Gentle people, who have shown us no harm..."

"No slave ships populate England's ports. Drake claims to have treated these men well. Do you not value your own pirate's word?"

"Father, do you attempt humour at my expense? Drake's honest pleas? I doubt my pirate's scruples trouble his evening slumber. His Queen carries that burden. Wandering drafty halls, I pour forth my own troubled conscience to portraits of ghosts. While gratitude warms me to Sir Francis Drake, it does not altogether wash from my awareness his dubious methods."

"Enough of your womanly complaint. I grow weary of such infirmity. Return to your bed, daughter. You must be rested to meet Philip's challenge with a king's mighty roar."

"Foolish, foolish daughter." Her Majesty exhales, and wraps her arms about herself. She grasps her delicate elbows. Disappointment causes her errant curls to shudder with their own vexation. "I seek a sympathetic response from Tyranny himself. Would I govern as He did? The blood of our English citizens on my hands? God save them all. Will Drake's success bring cherished peace to our people? Or only stoke Philip's vengeful Catholic fury?"

Her Majesty stands, head bowed, before King Henry. Her form bends too, folding in on itself. My Queen turns her palms up to meet her troubled gaze, as though she searches for traces of her subjects' coagulating wounds.

She speaks once more to her beloved portrait.

"Though your blood flows within my womanish veins, Father, you left your throne to Elizabeth. Your ferocious schemes died the brutal death they so deserved long ago. With sincere intent, I *will* mother my people. I will tend and watch over a peaceful, sleeping England. If that requires my roaming wakefulness, so be it. I will bear Drake's guilt, as you suggest. I will pretend. So my beloved people can celebrate the riches our pirate provides, and not the infamy. But Father, listen well. You, the dead, do not feel the prick of a burdened conscience. A tyrannical King dies another kind of death before his time. Your Elizabeth will remain awake to Virtue's complaint. I vow to you, upon my soul, all England will benefit."

Once more, I find myself pressed hard against a wall of unyielding stone, breath stopped. Her Majesty, at first eager to address her father's likeness, bounds from him with quickened step. My Queen's voluminous robes, caught within the swirling motion of her departure, reach behind, binding her to her father's will. But Her Majesty presses forward, her slipper advancing her purpose.

My Queen struggles to resist a father's influence. She will remove herself from King Henry's domineering presence. Armed with a well-forged sense of a mother's duty, Her Majesty cradles a sleeping kingdom in her embrace. Like the fanged mother of the woodland, she will defend her hushed offspring from their fathers' hunger.

Autumn I - Whether to Kiss a Frog?

How splendid, then, the blessing of mortal riches is! Once won, they never leave you carefree again.

--Boethius

I am a seamstress of a tale that unravels, and I mislead. With haste I sew the embroidered trim, while the seams underneath hold together with weak basting stitches. Drake's *Golden Hind,* swaggering pirates, magnificent treasure all offered to my anxious Queen. But close at home, Her Majesty's injured heart, like a threadbare tapestry, rips and shreds apart. I offer an inadequate telling of my Queen's tattered self. While I choose to reveal Her Majesty's princely concerns, her real suffering goes untold.

The Gypsy Earl of Leicester continues to influence Her Grace on matters concerning the realm. But my gracious Queen rejects her Robin, the attentive Gypsy lover. With upraised open palm, her fingers widespread, Her Majesty slows Bonny Sweet Robin's advance. He now hesitates with an awkward unease before her throne. With a monarch's resolve my Queen protects a heart no longer open to a Gypsy's flirtation. Her grey eye, once beckoning, hoods itself in loss. Her steely tongue she wields with scornful precision. Her Majesty resists a Gypsy's faithless disposition in order to preserve her own tender spirit.

I wrestle with my duty. Do I keep my oath to my beloved Queen? Do I serve Her Majesty with the loyal discretion she values, recalling always her desire to *see all and say nothing*? Or do I remain true to our mutual objective? The sharing of my Majesty's most intimate experience. What of value can result from the spilling of Her Majesty's deepest affections on the historical record?

I could alter Her Grace's reputation with unseemly reports of her friendships. Or with the lingering taint of enduring resentments. My hand grips my quill until my fingers ache. A brutal tension seizes my treacherous pen.

Countless passions simmer within Her Majesty's breast, but she reveals only those fitting a monarch. My mistress obscures all evidence of a smoldering hurt. Elizabeth's personal fancies, like the less-favoured sibling, grow accustomed to abandonment by our great mother. The realm alone needs all Her Majesty's doting attention.

But what of *my* truest purpose? Did I set out to report the official version of events that shape a finished Queen? Or to delve into the workings of a monarch's careworn heart? Perhaps my duty includes both of these narratives. I do not know. A host of different mistresses occupy England's throne, and I cannot explain all of them. So I perform my task as a fretful child might. Eager to please. Determined to do right. Yet, lacking all the heartfelt certainty with which to accomplish my task.

Once, my Queen confided to me her secret marriage plan. We settled ourselves within her Privy Chamber. Her Majesty dined on a light meal of roasted pheasant breast and greens, washed down with her short glass of newly-brewed ale. I was honoured my Queen sought out my humble company, as she usually takes her supper alone within her chamber. As Her Majesty toyed with her dessert, a rich cake of Corinth currants, she spoke with unusual candour.

"If I ever marry, Blanche, it will be as Queen of England, and not as Elizabeth." I heard even then the death knell of her love affair with her Gypsy.

Though he knows her best of all – Her Majesty declares this to be so - on this topic he fails to understand. Lord Dudley, whether to appease his own ego, or because he does not comprehend his Queen's particular needs, still courts his Lady Elizabeth. Perhaps the Gypsy remains caught in his own enchanted web of infatuation. And so he persists in denying the taxing want of a Queen's throne.

And what of the Lady, Elizabeth? What does she favour? Does she remain attracted to her Gypsy's sultry eye, his broad smile, his graceful turn on the dance floor? Elizabeth's heart, still intrigued with an enchanting Gypsy, differs much from that of a steadfast Queen's more discerning one.

***

28th April, 1578

Still within my silent bedchamber, I stare over the Thames, admiring spring's handiwork. This day at Whitehall Palace dawns like any other. I pray it sheds its evening shadow with the same ease. My Queen takes her regular turn about the Garden below. Attentive sunlight throws loving arms around Her Majesty's kingdom. A kindly embrace shrugs off layers of halfhearted cloud. Streaming affection on London's Thames, sunbeams bounce and play amongst gentle waves. Spring's welcoming kiss. My Queen chooses to stride into her morning, arm in arm with her courting Sun. She lifts her face skyward; inviting the warmth of his benevolent rays.

Hyssop hedges burst forth with tiny ivory buds. As though in preparation for the soon-to-be May Day celebrations, hawthorn bushes and laurel trees wave hale greetings with hints of vibrant foliage to come. Her Majesty strolls cobbled pathways below a promised canopy. The doting Sun follows his Queen, offering his divine caress, assisting her working up her morning heat.

Her Majesty, intent on her daily exercise, does not slow her pace in order to admire her magnificent sundial. The sparkling timepiece squats in her enchanted garden, surrounded by a fountain with multiple sprays. My Queen circles the dial, round and round, glancing toward it with proprietary satisfaction. And yet I cannot stop from pondering whether my Queen or her timepiece governs the other.

Here within the Privy Chamber, the Sun's confidence flags. A dimness hovers over me as I hold the troubling letter to the window's light. The letter arrives from Leicester House, from the Earl himself. A foreboding surrounds his tiresome note. It is uncommon for her Gypsy to write. Only when the words strike him as unpalatable does he lift his little used pen. I am sorely tempted to keep the objectionable message from my unsuspecting sovereign. But loyalty prevents such interference. On her return, I place the unopened letter into Her Majesty's outstretched palm.

My Queen receives the sealed correspondence in one hand, while with her other she dabs at her forehead with a silky towel. Her Majesty glances into my eye, admonishing me for my disapproval, but does not utter a word as she seats herself to read. Surely she too comprehends her Gypsy well enough to know he delivers unwelcome news?

Her Majesty's gaze travels with a fitful, energetic haste, the entire width of the page. She scans the first few lines of penned text.

Her hand, towel still clenched within it, wanders to her collar bone. My Queen's grey eyes, aware I watch every motion, close for the briefest moment. When they reopen, all is changed.

A wintry determination chills her initial panic. She acknowledges a notion formed long ago. Yet a reddening blemish appears high on her breast. Her Majesty's life's blood forces its way to the surface of her porcelain complexion. The spot, daring Her Grace with its contradiction, grows and spreads, belying her outward calm. I cast my eyes into my lap. I pretend not to notice my Queen's inward struggle to conquer her body's revolt. With a composed elegance, ever so precise, Her Majesty reverses her plodding direction. She rereads. A second perusal might convince her uncomprehending heart that all is well. With another reading she may find the contents more to her liking.

If only the sentences would rearrange themselves. Reform into something other. If only Her Majesty could interpret his words differently and respond with a gay bit of laughter and a saucy shake of her curls. Surely Her Grace misunderstands her Gypsy's message. But the sinister insistence of the ink, so black it tints a blue hue, refuses to yield to her wishes.

Her Gypsy's signature seals the note with authenticity. His seal swamps Her Majesty's slimmest hope. The spreading crimson spot on her chest blazes hotter. My Queen's heart hovers, opened, on her breast. A mottled bruise for all to witness.

Her Grace abandons her charade. She allows the note to drop from her hand, fluttering with a delicacy it surely does not contain, into my seated lap. My Queen studies the scrap of paper as it lies there. It rests, as though wholly innocent, within the folds of my skirts. She catches my eye and nods, directing me to share in her dismay.

I think it likely her Earl's message requires a reply. I wonder if Her Majesty's answer will be a welcome one to her Gypsy. Her response forms itself already, behind her frantic eye. My Queen issues curt orders to her ladies-in-waiting to prepare for a clandestine journey. I retrieve the letter from its resting place on my knee. I, too, draw in a sharp breath as its contents spill into my understanding. The Gypsy disappoints once more.

***

"Your Majesty?" Lord Robert Dudley, Earl of Leicester startles at his Queen's sudden appearance before him. He struggles, with difficulty, to raise himself up from his settee. He attempts to offer the required deference, but her Gypsy squints at the toll the effort takes on his sore frame.

Her Grace, unmoved by his predicament, gestures with an impatient flick of her wrist for Leicester to remain where he is. And so he does, ensconced within his layers of woolen robes. Her Earl makes as though to dismiss me, but Her Majesty stays his request. She indicates a chaise in the corner of the room for me to rest on. I rush over to my waiting couch, eager to evacuate the hostile terrain my Queen and her Gypsy occupy. They stare across the expanse of the carpeted chamber as if awaiting a cue to engage one another.

"Robin, I understand you have been ill. I come to inquire after your health, and to offer what comfort I may. Though, from what my own eye discerns, you appear remarkably well." Her Majesty's voice betrays little of her pained disposition. She raises both eyebrows together. Disbelief hoists them just beneath her hairline. Her eye lingers on her Gypsy, daring him to contradict her suspicion.

"Thank you, Your Grace. I improve by the day.... Have you received my letter, Your Majesty?" Leicester attempts to raise himself up.

His Queen flashes him a scornful warning. Her lips purse with contempt. A Gypsy's belated respect for her throne will not erase the blow he lands on her person.

Still he lounges in his upholstered chaise, his lap covered in layers of woolen comfort. But Leicester's demeanour does not match his restful position. A threatening aura overtakes the room. Misgiving spills from his worried expression. The Earl's countenance prickles with unease. He searches his Queen's blank features for a hint of her affection.

Her Majesty, in no hurry to ease his anxiety, leaves off her unnerving inspection of her Gypsy and casts her eye about, avoiding my questioning stare. She crosses the length of the chamber, and approaches the doorway.

Does Her Grace prepare for our departure so soon? Her Majesty glances up and down the hallways of Leicester House. It is as though she searches for an article dearly valued, lost due to inattention or neglect. The Gypsy's gaze, growing ever more wide-eyed, follows her every movement.

"Robin, do you love your Queen, as you have professed these many years?"

"Your Majesty, but of course. I will forever be your trusted advisor, your closest and most faithful brother…"

"Faithful brother? …but not, as you have decided, a husband?" Her Majesty ends her search of Leicester's premises, and returns to her Gypsy. She stands over his reclining form, staring down on her source of discontent.

The Earl reaches upward for his Queen's hand, and she draws back. Her Majesty ensures she remains wholly out of reach. Leicester sighs, but does not give up his pursuit.

"I beg of you, Majesty. Hear my explanation. For twenty years and more I have courted my darling Bess, and always I am declined. The realm did not wish it. Baron Burghley did not wish it. All Europe did not wish it. I was at last forced to acknowledge my own Elizabeth did not wish it. Your Majesty, I am but a man..."

"This is your case then? You are but a man? Do you not comprehend; I am not *but a woman*? A hefty crown I balance between us. These many years I hoist its weight, while holding you always in my warmest regard, Robin. How can you deny knowing of my fondness for you?"

Her Majesty bites hard on her bottom lip, puncturing the tender flesh. A circular bead of crimson emerges, and my Queen presses her lips together one on the other. Her own blood, as though in sympathy with Her Majesty's plight, becomes a cosmetic shimmer on her trembling lip. *Any show of weakness must avoid detection.* Yes, Father.

"But I do not deny your affection, Your Majesty. Always, I..."

"Have I not shown you every consideration? In childhood, and when we shared horrendous months together in the Tower, I doted on my Bonny Sweet Robin. I have provided you with land and title and all you require to live as a respected courtier. I have turned my eye away from your disgraced family, and from a multitude of dalliances. And I have forever invited you to share my confidence."

The Gypsy attempts to reply but Her Majesty's hand silences him. Her eyes fill. I fear her tears will soon flow despite all her brave attempts to stay them.

Once more, Leicester reaches up to comfort Her Majesty. Again, and without hesitation, she rebuffs his unwanted touch.

My Queen's voice, all tremors, threatens to contradict any semblance of serenity she pretends. As her accusations mount one on another, as her Gypsy's transgressions multiply, so does her volume escalate. A sovereign's façade shatters, giving way to the shrillest of hysterical complaint.

"With loyalty I showed my tenderness to you. And you have disowned it. Did you not know if I were ever to marry... you and you alone, were the only husband I considered? How can you not know this? All these years..."

"With the deepest of respect Your Majesty, though pressed with much affection by myself and others, you have not wed me. Or anyone."

"You dwell on the obvious Robin, but you cannot begin to consider what a Queen ponders. How do you presume to understand the complexity of my decision? My own cousin...Lettice. I shall hate her as the she-wolf she is, ever after this."

"Your Majesty..."

"You dare to reprimand me? You *will* not understand the compromises a Queen must submit to. Always I must consider the people's wishes. It is imprudent.... it is dangerous for a Queen to marry an Englishman of the Protestant faith when Catholic thrones roar all about us. In all things I must consider the security of the realm."

"I did stand by while you enjoyed much courtship from others, Your Grace."

"I told you myself, and many times, those popish princes held no sway. To whom did I forever return? Always to you. But the realm requires I negotiate. Will you not comprehend? Did I once agree to marry any of them? Yet you throw yourself away on Lettice Knowles."

"She carries my child, Your Majesty..."

"She has entrapped you then? Where does this evil-doer hide?" Her Majesty rushes toward the Chamber doorway again, scouring about. I realize, since we arrived at Leicester House, my Queen has wondered about the whereabouts of her chief rival.

"My dearest Majesty…"

"Do not dare to address me with this familiarity, Sir…" My Queen bristles.

"I apologize, Your Majesty. My bride does not reside here at Leicester House. Lettice is housed at Wanstead in Essex. I attend to her when my duties at Court allow it."

"But she ensnares you with the threat of a bastard…"

"An heir, Your Majesty. Something I have desired for many years. I must, in good faith admit it…I have willingly, and without hesitation become husband to Lettice. The wedded state compliments my temperament. I am sorry, Your Majesty. I waited until your intentions were clear."

"You are sorry, Robin? That is all? And I? I too regret you commit this violence against your devoted Majesty. What is your discarded Queen to do now?…"

"Your Grace, if you wish it…"

The Gypsy knows no end to his galling self-interest. Bound in law to another, he tempts Her Majesty. He opens his arms to his Queen. He offers to her an embrace the likes of which makes bile rise to my throat. I contemplate this wondrous morning. The skies bestowed their spirited attentions on Her Grace. Nature's holiness magnifies in my regard next to this profane suitor and his corrupt intent.

From my shaded corner of the room I whisper earnest warnings to my Queen. And as so often before, she ignores my urgent plea.

Her Majesty, bereft of the proud force of her lineage, accepts her Gypsy into her world-worn embrace. I turn from the shameful display, my own cheeks burning with my monarch's indignity.

As she rises from his appalling hold on her, my Queen pauses. She draws his hand to her wounded lip and places a tender kiss on each finger. When she reaches the fifth and final digit Her Majesty remains there. My head hangs low, eyes averted. I fear she will refuse to release the gentleman.

But finally, with her characteristic grace, my Queen withdraws. Beckoning to me, she announces to the hushed chamber our imminent departure. Linking her trembling arm through mine, Her Majesty sheds Elizabeth's girlish infatuations.

"Marriage reeks of the destruction of genuine feeling. I consider it an abominable institution. Its very existence, with harmful repetition, thwarts all happiness, and drains true sentiment from familial kinship. All that remains after the dreaded ceremony is an empty cask of unreachable expectation. Wretched remnants of an idea, fading more with each new betrothal I am forced to witness."

Her Gypsy, moved by Her Majesty's distress, adopts a semblance of decorum. He bows his dark head low, and accepts his reprimand.

"My Bonny Sweet Robin, hear this. Your hateful wife will not attend at Court. She will remain at Wanstead, where I will not have to look at her. Do not provoke me in this, I warn you. For neither you nor she will like the outcome."

Her Majesty gathers her dignity. My woeful Queen and I, linked arm in arm, bound by our mutual distrust of a roaming Gypsy, march through the chamber doorway.

Though a healthy resolve sustains my dislike for the gentleman, I wonder at how enduring my Queen's aversion will be.

***

What a dismal return to Whitehall. A murky drizzle sets in on our departure from Leicester House. It persists for the entire length of the carriage ride to the palace.

It is very late, near midnight when we enter Her Majesty's chamber. I pause to study my Queen, marveling how droplets of rain perched on her curls imitate the glitter of jewels around her forlorn expression.

With gratitude I survey Her Majesty's demeanour, and discover her grey eyes dry. A hardened glint. So different from the tearful waters filling them only a few hours before.

I pray her Gypsy's marriage does not burden Her Majesty with too great an affliction. Perhaps the Earl of Leicester's betrayal will serve to support my Queen's extreme dislike of the married state. Perhaps her spirit will rise up with this new vindication of her long-held belief.

But my Queen's disposition does not support my hope. Her Majesty wanders without intent into her chamber. With no flicker of recognition does she greet her favoured place.

Raindrops seep to her scalp, causing her curls to droop in dampened mourning. My Queen takes no notice of her disheveled appearance. A single drop of rain - the tear she dare not cry - meanders from a place above her brow, and steals along her otherwise dry cheek.

Where before, in moments of turmoil, Her Majesty sought King Henry's portrait on the wall, tonight she remains alone within her chamber. What woman turns to her father to register a complaint against the man who replaces him in her affection? What can the much-wed King Henry offer his Elizabeth that might comfort her about a Gypsy's faithlessness? I think it best the daughter retire to her own counsel.

Her Majesty slumps on her bedstead. She cradles and rocks her face between two pressed palms. Will the rhythmic motion transform her grief into a fitful slumber? If only she could return to the happy time before she read the awful letter. I cannot judge Her Majesty for wishing to relive that blessed moment of ignorance. When a Gypsy's heart belonged to her alone.

I will help. I will remind Her Majesty of everything a Queen must overcome to hoist a crown with graceful ease. I will remind Her Grace of a certain story which will banish a faithless Gypsy from her heart.

Her Majesty's disdain for the married state persists. And yet, I recall one circumstance where Her Majesty would acknowledge a marriage did benefit a Queen. Or should I say, in truth, the marriage itself did not cause the benefit. But its dissolution provided the happiest conclusion. My Queen will approve of this tale. I am certain of it.

***

A full two decades ago at least, when Her Majesty was but a youthful maid and her sister Mary ascended the throne... I believe it was on Queen Mary's Coronation day, the 30th of September, the year 1553, our Lady Elizabeth rode in the procession next to one of her beloved stepmothers, Anne of Cleves.

At two o'clock in the afternoon, the procession began its winding through London's populous lanes of Fenchurch, Gracechurch, Cornhill; by the fancy shops of Cheapside, and the dignified shadows of St. Paul's Churchyard; on through Ludgate and Fleet Streets, all the way to Whitehall Palace. As the older lady and the young maid rode with graceful ease on their mounts, they spoke of matters very near Lady Elizabeth's heart.

Elizabeth, a twenty year old English Lady, and the Lady Anne of Cleves, a matronly, cast-off dowager Queen who no longer qualified for the favoured title, spoke with candid, though lowered, voices.

"I fear Lady Elizabeth, for your security under our new popish Queen. I am sure your sister does not prefer a Protestant Queen-in-waiting."

"Fear not, Lady Anne. I know, with an instinctive certainty, our Protestant God will prevail. With patience we shall one day witness this blessing. Until then we will behave as faithful subjects to my sister, Queen Mary. The very first but not perhaps the last, Queen of England." Elizabeth turns from her conversation to nod and wave at the nobles, merchants, servants and their dust-streaked children lining the streets, row upon row. All strain forward, arms reaching, in hopes of some little acknowledgement from the royals. In answer to Lady Elizabeth's exuberant wave, an energetic hoorah sends the women along their way.

"You were but a girl of six years when I occupied the throne beside your father. You were perhaps too innocent to understand my departure from your family. I have known the ease with which a Queen may lose her title when her King does not prefer her company. Step with caution Lady Elizabeth. England's first Queen loves her Catholic God above all. Queen Mary will not endure competition for her throne."

"Do you forget, Lady Anne, my father reclaimed my own title just as he did yours? From Princess to Lady in the blink of an eye. I am too aware of a crown's fickle nature. I will not provide any antagonism for Mary to answer to. How I tire of religious bickering. I will not offend the Catholic sensibility of my beloved sister." The Arabians' hooves land with magnificent claps on the cobbled ground, as though they applaud Lady Elizabeth's circumspection.

"Well said, my Lady Elizabeth. I trust you will stay in your sister's good graces."

"Forgive me, Lady Anne, for intruding on what may cause you painful memories..."

"By all means, speak freely my dear."

"I do not wish to dwell on the squabbles stemming from pious fanatics but I do yearn to know of something else..."

"Speak, young one." The Lady Anne draws back on her reins and eases her majestic animal into a steady walk beside Lady Elizabeth's mount.

"Very well. I do not understand what caused my father to decide as he did, to go forward without your pleasant companionship? I find you always to be of the most considerate and friendly disposition."

"My darling Elizabeth." The dowager Queen casts an indulgent eye on her stepdaughter. She grins and shakes her head at Elizabeth's innocence. An innocence she herself once possessed. "You are not far from the age I was when I wed your father. Though I doubt you are quite as unknowing as I was then. Put simply, while your father's passion for his Anne of Cleves arose from his need for an alliance with my brother the Duke, his personal inclinations did not align with his political needs."

"But you possess a most agreeable nature. You are well-educated in all things domestic. If memory serves me well, you doted on my father in a generous way, and with faithful reverence."

The elder lady's eyes alight hearing Lady Elizabeth's girlish reconstruction of the events of her childhood. Lady Anne's lips widen in an open smile. One hand maintains a firm grip on her reins, while the other she waves at a raucous gathering of English citizens lining the route for their new Queen's Coronation.

"Dear Elizabeth. I do enjoy your charming candour. But my domestic abilities paled when your father hearkened back to your energetic mother's intellect, or forward to Catherine Howard's teasing manner. My poor English frustrated him, I think. When he requested I play for him a melody, or read to him a simple sonnet, well, in all these things I did disappoint..."

"I am sorry to inquire and to pain you my respected mother. I meant no offense." The Lady Elizabeth draws herself up on her mount, and makes as though to trot ahead.

But the elder lady maintains Elizabeth's speed in the saddle. Lady Anne stays by Elizabeth's side, reassuring her stepdaughter. "No offence is taken, Lady Elizabeth. Lean closer to me, my child. It is immodest of me to tell it, but the procession lightens my mood. I will share an anecdote with you that you will be sure to enjoy."

"Do not feel an obligation to explain that which is not my concern, Lady Anne. Your memories of my father belong to you alone.

"Obligation?" Lady Anne stifles a giggle. Good-natured amusement greets the Lady Elizabeth's somber tone. "I suffer under no obligation, whatever. I experience only pleasure in our amiable conversation. I will continue, if you desire it."

"As you wish, my Lady."

"Thank you, my dear…Now where to begin?…When my English ladies-in-waiting approached me after my first night as your father's wife, they inquired as to my liking for the King. I, but a maid, and yet still a maid, told them of your father's courteous conduct." Anne glances toward Elizabeth, who leans closer with expert balance in her side-saddle position.

"I informed my ladies, 'When our King comes to bed, he kisses me and taketh me by the hand, and biddeth me 'Goodnight, Sweetheart', and in the morning, kisses me, and biddeth me, 'Farewell, darling'. Is this not enough?'" Lady Anne pauses and glances at Elizabeth. Lady Elizabeth's grey eyes crinkle slightly. Forever aware of England's watch on her, her lips hide knowing smiles.

"To my inquiry, 'Is this not enough?' my poor ladies gasped at my innocence, and shook their heads. In unison, I believe three, or maybe four of them replied, 'No, Your Majesty. No. It most certainly is not!'"

Lady Anne glances over at Elizabeth. Elizabeth does not meet her eye. Her lips twitch with a merriment that would not befit her sister's coronation procession. Lady Elizabeth, sensing she might soon give way to a disastrous outburst, ceases her inquiry. She stares ahead at the backs of those preceding her mount. Elizabeth studies with especial concentration, their flowing robes and golden epaulets.

Lady Anne, ignoring Elizabeth's effort to maintain a dignified detachment, carries on. "When I looked wide-eyed back at them, for I did not know what they spoke of, they gaped at each other as though to say, '*You* must draw the shades from this ignorant young woman's blindness and let in the light of carnal knowledge. Not I.'"

Elizabeth and her stepmother quiver with laughter at Anne's lusty tale. Elizabeth hastens her mount into a halting trot with hopes of disguising her gathering mirth. Still, the older lady's horse keeps pace beside her.

"Lady Anne, I do apologize for causing you to recall unfavourable memories of your ill-fated marriage to my father. I vow never to raise the topic with you again..." Elizabeth forces the corners of her mouth to flatten. Everything depends on her respectful adherence to tradition.

"But I do not suffer knowing I was not a wife in the truest sense, my dear. I rather celebrate my circumstance."

"I do not understand. Did my father not humiliate you with his callous rejection? Did he not abandon his youthful wife in a strange country? And without friends or family to comfort her? I would lack your ability to forgive with this wholehearted ease. If a husband found me so easy to resist, I would detest him always after that."

Lady Anne smiles at Elizabeth's lofty pride, and refrains from admonishing the youngster's ignorance. How can the young understand what they know nothing of? A husband and his wife are not explained with ease. So much passes between them, yet remains unacknowledged. Even to the cherished pair themselves. How might a bystander unlock that which remains so closely guarded within two sheltered hearts? And when a husband is a King, the wife a Queen, even more will be left unspoken.

"I dare say your father's generosity to his *sister*, Anne of Cleves, as he ever after referred to me, was much appreciated. In return for granting him his desired annulment King Henry bestowed on me several manors and estates which earn my household an income of three thousand pounds per year."

"Three thousand?" Elizabeth's expert balance on the well-oiled saddle almost fails her. She teeters with a perilous rocking motion, until the Lady Anne draws up close beside her, grabs hold of her elbow and steadies our young Lady.

Elizabeth nods her thanks, straightens her torso, and breathes deeply.

Still, the Lady Anne speaks, as though her newfound freedom of expression winds round London with the same energetic flow as the procession itself. "Yes, my dear. I, in all my independence, enjoy an income considered enviable to any Lady in my lonely position as outcast wife."

"It is true then. You have little reason to detest my father for his inadvertent kindness to you." Lady Elizabeth pauses and regards her stepmother.

"Little indeed. I enjoy my tankard of ale. I take many a turn at the gaming table. On this, your sister's momentous occasion, I don this lovely gown. I store various glorious dresses in my personal closet. And of course, for companionship I have my beloved step-children..." At this, Anne grasps Elizabeth's small hand in her solid one, and rides close beside her young companion.

"...All of these privileges I have enjoyed without the cumbersome duty of the devoted wife, ever hankering after her husband's favour. Or of the harried mother, bowed with concern for the well-being of her innocent offspring when another ruinous plague strikes. I cannot but feel gratitude to your father for ensuring I live an unimpeded life. I am honoured as a part of the royal family, yet unencumbered by a King's authority. I am content with my position. And most grateful for my unfettered existence."

Lady Elizabeth squeezes her companion's hand with gratitude of her own. "I am indebted to you, Lady Anne, for improving my awareness. With little knowledge I declared you pitiable. In truth, you provide an inspiring example. I offer to you my thanks, and my boundless respect."

"And I to you, my young Lady Elizabeth. Your beauty is only transcended by an understanding which exceeds your tender years." The two women straighten in their saddles. Chins pointed forward, they ride.

***

Though Her Majesty expresses gratitude for my tale, a fortnight passes before her tears dry. I dare not mention the topic of her Gypsy's marriage to Lettice Knowles. Few comprehend the real cause of her quarrelsome attitude. Her Majesty guards her injured heart with a bow fully taut; pointed arrows at the ready.

Emerging at last from her locked Privy Chamber, Her Majesty addresses her ladies in a querulous manner befitting her foul mood. Her Grace complains of everything. From the cloying air within Richmond's walls, to the lack of salt in her clear broth. I dare not reveal my scribbled-upon pages to her envious eye for fear Her Majesty will snatch them up, tear them to pieces, and scatter them on the tiled floor in a flourish of majestic rage.

Though I dread Her Majesty's well-reputed temper, still I pity my Queen. I would not care to shoulder such a burden on my own delicate frame: A crown and a kingdom's future; a fully drawn crossbow to guard her womanish heart; and a blacksmith's spade, so Her Majesty may bury her unrequited desire for a Gypsy.

When Her Grace finally throws open her dark chamber, her world remains fraught with danger. Spain eyes England, greeting our Queen with his insatiable leer. France casts lascivious attentions toward the weakened Netherlands. And as Catholic France challenges the independence of England's lone Protestant ally, Philip of Spain's design on the coquettish England intensifies.

And so our Queen accepts, with a reluctance she hides, the attentions of a French Duke. I fear her disloyal Gypsy makes Her Majesty vulnerable to a popish Prince's charms. I hope capricious Fate will dote favourably on England. I hope our Queen remembers a mother's duty to her brood must prevail over a woman's desire for a faithless rogue. Or worse, an ambitious Frog.

With luck, Her Majesty will meet this Duke of Anjou as Queen of England. Hopefully, the heartbroken Elizabeth will stay within her chamber. All hidden away, pining for a false Gypsy. Perhaps a spirited dalliance with Her Majesty will prove enough to keep a French Duke's fingers away from the Netherlands' exposed neck. England's Dutch ally beckons with naked weakness. France's lust for European pre-eminence answers the distressed call. I only pray a sample of our English Queen's fine intellect, like a full-bodied claret, satisfies a French Duke's slavering appetite. And loosens France's grip on our weakened ally's pulsing throat.

***

Within one short month of the faithless Earl of Leicester's nuptials, the French Duke of Anjou graces Her Majesty's shores. His Court invades Richmond Palace's dignified corridors. Out of my Queen's hearing I sigh, disdainful at the sight of French canvas pavilions strewn all over Her Majesty's lawns. How would our Queen's beloved grandfather, Henry VII, respond to his palace's air filled with the stink of *les Francais*? A Duke all decked with clinging Parisian silk? And silken-mouthed, with wooing words of courtship for our grieving Queen?

Her Majesty, chastened by the loss of a genuine love, reaches for a pretty replica.

Will Anjou's youthful glow brighten her lusterless eye? Will this pollywog replace the hurt in my Queen's heart with a spark of that cheer she once genuinely felt?

"You may write this to the King of France: the Duke of Anjou shall be my husband." Her Majesty addresses the French Ambassador and issues her proclamation. Turning to the smiling Duke, she presses her mouth hard on his thin lips. All taut, Anjou forces his mouth into a monstrous grin with the shock of Her Majesty's declaration. His girlish locks, as astonished as he, dance a jig about his face as though to aid in the celebratory mood.

My Queen tugs an emerald ring from her finger. Round and bright as the French Duke's wandering eye, and circled with twenty cut diamonds, Her Majesty slides it on her suitor's hand. The Duke of Anjou, knowing his moment arrives, does not hesitate to bestow his own symbol of official betrothal. He places on Her Majesty's finger a square-cut diamond, surrounded by fine gold filigree. The couple embraces as though their passion for one another was genuine.

In fairness to my Queen, perhaps the loss of a Gypsy makes room within her heart for her Prince Frog. I never envisioned my Queen considering any betrothal, but only yesterday, I heard the flattering Duke declare:

"Je vous aimerai jusqu'a ce que la Mort lui-meme m'enleve de votre presence." *I shall love you until Death himself would remove me from your presence.* Her Majesty, with pride in her mastery of her French, replied: "Je vous aimerai jusqu'a ce que ma petite grenouille traverse vraiment l'etang et reste par mon cote pour toujours." *I shall love you until my little Frog crosses the great pond and stays by my doting side forever."*

Each speaks this nonsensical gibberish, the likes of which I never heard pass Her Majesty's careful lips. Yet my Queen and her "Little Moor" fawn over one another. Their delicate fingers intertwined, their lips ever seeking a cheek or a nape to press against. As though they mean it. Either each performs with consummate skill, or genuine feeling invades their willful politicking.

Knowing my Queen as I do, the heartbreak she has endured, I believe it to be some of both. Perhaps, this betrothal game began as a ploy to keep Catholics from her shores and tweak a Gypsy's unfaithful nose at the same time. Yet, Her Majesty appears to have fallen under the spell of Anjou's accomplished courtship. My Queen persists in baffling. As for her Prince Frog, I do not pretend to know his heart.

Gasps of shock, mine included, greet Her Majesty's declaration. A low rumbling of hushed whispers fills the Presence Chamber at Richmond. Her Earl of Leicester hovers in the back of the chamber. The Gypsy stares long into his Queen's eye, contemplating her purpose. With a deliberate nod, he acknowledges her triumphant moment of revenge upon him. And in this one gesture, Leicester accomplishes more of an exchange with Her Majesty than all the exemplary French phrasing she utters to her Prince Frog these past months. The Gypsy, his lips whispering beneath a sheltering beard, congratulates Her Majesty's ingenuity.

My Queen finds the courage to meet her Robin's gaze for a glancing instant, her expression neutral. She stares past her Gypsy, through his greeting. Her Majesty swallows hard, lifts her chin, and returns to her French Duke. Lord Robert's gesture remains unacknowledged. My Queen smiles at the impact of her announcement on the Court with her eternal, enigmatic poise.

But hold. Her Majesty's eye will defy even her own strict command. Ignoring the shouts of congratulation mingled with gasps of horror at the prospect of a French King for England, her gaze returns. In search of her Gypsy's discontent. My Queen scans the far reaches of the Presence Chamber, at last falling on Leicester's straight back.

Her Gypsy walks with a new purpose from his Queen's chamber. He leaves Richmond Palace with no backward look. Her Majesty may benefit Lettice Knowles in her grand triumph. Surely after this late, and fiercest of duels, the Earl of Leicester will find Wanstead at Essex a place of restful ease.

I fear Her Majesty treds her onerous path more alone than even she might imagine. Her councilors claim to offer their steadfast loyalty. Yet her Earl of Leicester withdraws in outrage. Baron Burghley, her good Sir William Cecil, declares: "Blessed be the Lord!" and "God help England and send it a King!" For the English people, Baron Burghley sighs with relief at the prospect of his Queen, now approaching the elderly age of forty-eight, agreeing to lie within her marriage bed. But I hear it said, within specially gathered meetings of the Privy Council, our Lord Burghley speaks from the other side of his bearded mouth, declaring *"Monsieur is a Frenchman and the people of this realm naturally hate that nation."*

Lord Burghley, as ever, reads the will of the people with consummate skill. As tongues persist in their relentless wagging, whispers erupt into cries of disdain. I fear Her Majesty fails to hear their rising voices of complaint. Usually she sways in rhythmic tune with her people. Has weathering a relentless battle with her Gypsy deafened her heart? A French King for England. Surely Her Majesty's senses take their leave.

It is left to Her Majesty's ladies to gain our Queen's ear in private discourse. We must address the consequences of Her Majesty's rash declaration. And surely enough, after closeting herself within her Privy Chamber, Her Majesty erupts in a panic-stricken tirade. All of the fingers of her left hand clutch at those of her right, forming one tight fist. Letting go, Her Majesty rubs her knuckles to and fro with such force; I fear she will knock her French filigree engagement ring to the floor under her foot.

"God's Death. What have I done with this declaration? I cannot marry. Subordinate my will to a silly Frog's. I would rather die first. Perhaps like my own dear mother, I will die for my witless infatuation."

All her ladies step backward. Cowering shoulders pressed to papered walls, we stare, one at the other, uncertain how to comfort our Queen.

"Your Majesty I beg of you, try to stay calm ..." I step forward, and am waved back to the outskirts of the room. My Queen has not completed her pique-filled fit.

"I declared it before the entire Court. What ghoulish phantom overtook my senses, causing me to utter such folly? And if my betrothed does not kill me, surely his offspring will. I will join my mothers, Jane and Catherine, in an early grave. My babe murdering me from within my womb..."

I move toward my Queen once more. "Please, Your Majesty. We cannot bear to watch you suffer..."

Her Grace startles. She hesitates in her rampage. Her Majesty looks wide-eyed at her ladies. We must appear to her like parchment images of our true selves. We stand all pressed up against the walls of her chamber like so many one-dimensional paper dolls. The sight of us causes Her Majesty to adopt a conciliatory posture. Our Queen smothers the force of her own emotion.

"Never before have I set my heart on, nor wished to marry anyone in the world. I have, on occasion, pondered a change of mind. I am human and not insensible to human emotions and impulses. Yet, more than once I have declared I would rather live as a single beggar woman than as a married Queen. Does this not say much?"

Our Queen stares at her ladies, looking for a declaration of wisdom from us. Surely Her Majesty does not look to her Keeper of the Books for an answer so critical to the realm? Yet my Queen's distress obliges me to offer some hint of comfort.

"Your Majesty, perhaps your people do not wish for a King from France. A Catholic at that..." I need not fret about overstepping my humble position, for Her Majesty fails to register my reply. She stalks the room, reckless in her despair.

"Sir Cecil, our Baron Burghley, favours my marriage always. He seeks an heir to the throne. While I, your loving Majesty, seek to prevent my own downfall. Is this not what a sovereign ought to do for her devoted citizens? Shall I live for my beloved people and reign as Queen? Or do they seek their sovereign's death on a holy marriage bed? God's wounds, I do not know how to appease them any longer."

Her Majesty stops her frantic pacing. She lingers alone within the centre of the chamber. Her arms hang limp by her sides. Her form, customarily straight, hunches over. Her Majesty shuts her eyes tight, concealing her panic.

Her Grace's ladies sense less imminent danger. We shuffle out from our uncomfortable position against the chamber wall. With hesitant steps we approach Her Majesty as though our Queen is a volatile child, having earlier stomped and raged in an unmanaged tantrum.

Sensing a new friendliness in her passive demeanour, I attempt to appeal to Her Majesty's intellect. "Your Grace, the Duke might prefer another Queen. One more devoted to his popish ways. Perhaps you should alter your terms so the French will refuse them? Certain obstacles could be placed with strategic design...a request he break with the Church of Rome perhaps?" Again, I go unheard.

"I have wedded myself to my people. They are where my loyalty lies. I have nothing to offer a princely frog... But a part of my being favours Anjou. That part of Elizabeth I swore to abandon presses me with her overwhelming want... Well, she will not prevail. If she does, I forfeit a crown. If I prefer the crown, the affection I must forfeit..."

Her Majesty's voice fades to a whisper. Acceptance of her loss shocks my Queen into silence. A tear escapes the unwavering grey of her stare. As though with an eerie understanding of its only route, it hurries along her cheek. The fugitive tear drops with dutiful ease. It disappears into the lace fabric of Her Majesty's collar. My Queen does not concern herself with wiping away the evidence of its sly retreat.

"Your Majesty, though the Duke of Anjou possesses considerable charm, your people do not seek a French speaking, Catholic King for England. You have the citizenry's support to reign as you always have..."

"So I may not wed. And if I seek to love? To mother a brood, as any natural woman might?" My Majesty pretends to covet everything she disdains. I fear her wits take leave of our Queen.

"Your people think of England's interests, as do you, Your Majesty."

"God save them all. Surely they comprehend. They may have many step dames after my death, but they will never have a more natural mother than I mean to be. Leave me. Before I celebrate my betrothal to England, I will mourn love's passing."

Heads bowed, Her Majesty's ladies file from her bedchamber. As I attempt to pass, my Queen places a tentative touch on my shoulder, beckoning me to stay. Throughout the sleepless night, I watch over Her Majesty. Uninvited sighs escape her lips. An entire league of fugitive tears steals their way along her cheeks, joining their earlier comrade in a joyless procession.

***

The rising of the sun threatens to greet us with its perpetual cheer. I make every effort to remain wakeful into the dawn, but sleep overtakes me. I place my head on a silken pillow, and leave my Queen to her pressing cares.

An hour passes in what seems like minutes. I rise up, stretch my arms, and clear the haze from my tired eye. Her Majesty takes no notice of me. She stares out her chamber window on Richmond's gleaming timepieces, thinking differently about their friendly glimmer. Her proprietorial certainty all shaken.

I rouse myself and rummage on my littered desktop for some makeshift toiletry items: tooth cloth and picks, hairbrush, a small comb. And then I discover the project that has kept Her Majesty wakeful through the night. The parchment, written on in a hasty, blotted manner lies neglected on top of my papers. Through smudges made by her plentiful tears, I read my Queen's contemplation. I press it to my own fond heart. And before Her Majesty discovers my rummaging, I place her poem back within the scattered papers on her own untidy desk.

Her Majesty composes the tender verse for a French Duke. Though she might speak with equal poignancy to a fleeing Gypsy.

On Monsieur's Departure, Circa 1582

I grieve and dare not show my discontent;
I love, and yet am forced to seem to hate;
I do, yet dare not say I ever meant;
I seem start mute, but inwardly do prate.
I am, and not; I freeze and yet am burned,
Since from myself my other self I turned.

My care is like my shadow in the sun –
Follows me flying, flies when I pursue it,
Stands, and lies by me, doth what I have done;
His too familiar care doth make me rue it.
No means I find to rid him from my breast,
Till by the end of things it be suppressed.

Some gentler passions slide into my mind,
For I am soft, and made of melting snow;
Or be more cruel, Love, and so be kind.
Let me or float or sink, be high or low;
Or let me live with some more sweet content,
Or die, and so forget what love e'er meant.

Elizabeth Regina

Autumn II – Escaping the Dungeon of the Body

And from vain pleasures past I fly, and fain would
know
The happy life at last whereto I hope to go.
For words or wise reports ne yet examples gone
'Gan bridle youthful sports, till age came stealing on
The pleasant courtly games that I do pleasure in
My elder years now shames such folly to begin.

-- *Elizabeth Regina*

7th February, 1582

I hunch over my little desk and drag my hand across the page. A boisterous gaiety issues from within Her Majesty's bedchamber. The diversion cheers me and I smile at the unusual noise. It has been months since the unmistakable sound of my Queen's laughter has greeted my ear. I lay down my favourite mother-of-pearl quill and rise with only a little stiffness. I tiptoe to Her Majesty's doorway.

Various ladies-in-waiting circle my Queen. Keeping time, they encourage her as she whirls. Her Majesty, her spine as straight as the lines of script on my page, leaps into the air. She dances a glorious galliard. She lifts her skirts above her knee, exposing a wine-coloured garter. Her laughter, like Sunday morning's bell-ringing, elevates our leaden spirits.

What does Her Majesty celebrate? Only days ago she erupted in a fever after making a pledge to a French Duke. And today, the departure of that French Duke causes her to dance. Accompanied by a retinue of Her Majesty's trusted nobles, Anjou set sail from Sandwich this morning. The Gypsy Earl of Leicester returned to his courtly duties to escort Anjou across the Channel. I am certain the Gypsy, though hesitant to face his monarch, relishes this particular commission.

"Blanche, join us. I dance well for a matronly lady of forty-eight years. Wouldn't you say so?"

As I part my lips to offer my Queen a reply, she spins away. Her shoulders rise and fall, both with the exertion of the dance, and with the exuberance of her mood. Her Majesty behaves like a joyful child. And the reason for her high spirits? The departure of a favoured suitor. Yet my Queen resembles a school girl at her first May Day celebration. She looks more like a girl who has just met a handsome youth who prepares to plunder her heart. The more I bear witness to Her Majesty's frolics, the more contradiction settles on my page.

I raise my voice, attempting to gain my Queen's ear over the swishing of satins and the tittering of ladies all gathered round. "Your Majesty, your graceful leaps resemble an antelope's poise."

"Blanche, you flatter your elderly Queen with descriptions of an agility I no longer possess. But today I'll allow it. Today is a magnificent day."

"What do you celebrate, Your Majesty?"

"Have you not heard, Letters? France throws open her arms and welcomes to her bosom a Frog Duke who would be King. He swims away from England's shores without a Queen to croak at on his crowded lily pad. I will finally enjoy a night's sleep without the annoyance of a regretted promise prying open my lids and battering my poor conscience." With her declaration, Her Majesty kicks at the air, as though Anjou still inhabits her kingdom and is in need of an extra nudge to send him on his way.

"I am pleased the Duke's recent departure does not trouble you, Your Majesty. You did appear to grow quite fond of him while he attended you."

"I did appear fond, didn't I? Excellent. Fondness I will offer, like a scrumptious banquet. For Philip of Spain and all Europe to devour. And within my chamber, I will twirl with fond recollection, as Anjou sails away on the Channel for the final time."

Her Majesty links her left arm through mine. She poses, face to face in front of me. Her Grace beckons me into her dance. She invites me along on a mood-enhancing reel. As we twirl round the chamber, we study one another as though we stare into a mirrored looking-glass. Each of us marvels at the strangeness lurking beneath the other's laughing mask.

Our linked arms carry us round and round in dizzying circles. I give up searching for my Monarch's evasive spirit. It requires all my concentration to remain on my feet as I skip next to my Queen. When Chance offers the opportunity, when our whirling motion subsides, I stare again, into her profound depth. Can my wishful probe unearth a sovereign's secret identity?

Returning to my desk and its scattered papers, I rifle through stacked diary pages. I contemplate the tablets filled with rambling observations of Her Majesty. Do I commit an injustice against my Queen? The purest of intention directs my errant pen, but the result would say otherwise.

My Queen strolls among her people with majestic self-possession; a proud mother surveying her offspring. She performs her duty with dignity befitting a prince.

Yet, when portrayed by my pen, she appears all too human. Her accomplishments reach pinnacles of achievement well beyond those I write of. My Queen's nurturing arms encircle our kingdom and its people. Yet I fail to capture the essence of her embrace on my page. Her Majesty's energetic spirit flees from me, as though the reining in of it with pen and ink threatens its very substance.

The commonness of a blank canvas cannot reflect the measure of Her Majesty's grace. And so my Queen's merits go unnoticed, while trifling flaws emerge. Her few undignified moments stand out like pockmarks on the finest porcelain complexion. I balk at my disloyalty. So easily I fill my page with what does not illustrate Her Majesty's favourable traits. If I were to fully reveal my beloved sovereign's worth, the pages would multiply tenfold.

Mine is a reticent Queen. She chooses to maintain her silent dignity before her public. She shelters her people from harmful truths that rain down on her throne in an everlasting deluge. Yet *I* betray all. I, her Keeper of the Queen's Books, custodian of her most intimate secrets, do not earn the trust she grants me. Instead I hover in Her Majesty's presence. I depict a temper that frays too readily. I wonder about an eye that strays too frequently to a Gypsy's lifted jaw. I write of a clenched hand that closes with jealous ownership on her favourites' future happiness.

I shuffle through my stacks of papers, only to discover a Queen I do not recognize. For she is not one lady, but many. And each I misconstrue. I blame my words. My inadequate words cannot decipher my complicated monarch.

Her Majesty, an oft-mothered, yet motherless child wanders, searching, through my pages. As does a girl who poses with pride next to her powerful father, while she scorns his brutal methods. A cast-off princess cavorts with her childhood sweetheart, as though her life does not depend on it. A mature Queen offers her heart to an unworthy Gypsy, while she rejects his pursuit of her. A gracious monarch, decades on her throne, trusted by her people, issues vows she does not honour to relentless suitors she will never consider.

She both weeps and dances at love's departure.

Artful pretender? Unhinged matriarch? I bend over my desk. I press my pen to paper. I write and write, and still I do not know.

***

Her Majesty's frolicking with her ladies, like all happiness, will not endure. Her gentlemen, all stern in appearance, stride toward their Queen's chamber. A monarch's cares, unaware of a woman's need to dance, interrupt the play. The weight of her gentlemen's news lands with an odious force on our celebratory mood.

My Queen's Secretary of State, her "Moor", leads the approaching group. Sir Francis Walsingham steps forward, his neck all straightened by the enormous and pleated white lace collar he favours. Such a contrast the frill provides to his ebony robes, and the tight black skullcap clinging to his graying curls.

Such a precise Protestant gentleman Sir Francis is. One would be forgiven for failing to guess at his odious profession.

He protects our Queen with no less than fifty paid spies, spread among a variety of European courts. Why, it is said Lord Walsingham's greatest skill resides in his ability to tempt errant Catholics to infiltrate the popish courts. And all on England's behalf. I am inclined to thank our Protestant God Sir Francis remains resolute by our Queen's side.

Her faithful Moor addresses Her Majesty, surrounded by his cache of lusty gentlemen. One of his companions stands above the others in stature, and in attraction also. Her Majesty has missed the constant company of her Gypsy Earl of Leicester, though she will not speak of him. My Queen studies the stranger from the corner of her eye, while she pretends to offer Walsingham her undivided attention.

Walsingham approaches, and with respect, bows low before Her Majesty. "Your Grace, please forgive me for intruding on your festivities."

Our Queen offers her hand, all decorated with the emeralds and pearls she prefers. Tiny beads of perspiration stand on her temples due to her vigorous exertion. The gentlemen, all but one, remain too intent on their mission to notice Her Majesty's disarray. From his position in the rear of the room the alluring stranger studies my Queen's countenance with a particular intensity. He considers every shimmering bead on Her Majesty's flushed skin.

Walsingham's gentlemen remain posed behind their leader. Hands at their sides, or laced in a loose hold behind their backs, they survey her Moor with some unease. Walsingham bows low before his Queen. The gathering transforms our late merry-making, oppressing our happy mood. Only Her Majesty's countenance, the stubborn droplets clinging to her brow, shows any sign of remembering we danced at all.

"You are forgiven, Sir Francis. I do not doubt your intentions are sincere. Surely you would not intrude on your sovereign with trifling matters. Rise up and proceed."

Walsingham lifts his knee from the floor. He stands before our Queen, and matches her inquiring eye with his own unshakable confidence. "Your Grace, I have vowed to break the neck of all dangerous practices in England."

"For your efforts, we are ever grateful Sir. Now please, tell us."

"I have discovered evidence of grievous treason against the realm, Your Majesty. I apologize for the unwelcome nature of this, my latest intelligence. However as I have more than once stated Your Grace, it is not my role but my destiny to preserve your place on England's throne."

Her Majesty's eyebrow, imbued with an energy of its own, lifts in reply. "Such dramatic flair you perform for us, Sir Francis. I will listen with care to my intrepid Moor. However, do not forget *all* the niceties in the interests of political pursuits. I trust you will introduce me to your entourage before speaking further?"

As she makes her inquiry of Walsingham, my Queen raises her other brow, and stares with pointed interest at the handsome stranger. Try as she might to rein in her curiosity, Her Majesty's appreciative eye returns to that of the unknown courtier. The stranger welcomes her appraising gaze. He nods with an almost imperceptible, wholly mischievous acknowledgement. In a moment, an understanding is reached between the two.

"Please excuse my incivility, Your Majesty. My intelligence is of such import, I forgot myself. This is Lord Raleigh. Lord Walter Raleigh, of Devonshire. He is the great-nephew of your beloved governess, Kat Ashley. Today he carries correspondence from the Lord Deputy in Ireland."

Lord Raleigh advances to my Queen's throne. He bends low at Her Majesty's jeweled slipper, proffering his letters of introduction as he stoops. I attempt to purge my eye of its suspicion, but I swear as he rises up, he and my Queen exchange a look I have seen before.

Does Her Majesty not recognize Lord Raleigh's vigorous youth? Why, my Queen lays claim to two decades more of life than this striking upstart. If a Gypsy once worried my pen, forcing it to transcribe what my eyes would not see, this swarthy Devonshire gentleman flusters it beyond all knowing.

Still Her Grace stares at Lord Raleigh. Walsingham's unwished for news all forgotten, she studies Raleigh. She memorizes each whisker darkening his coarse beard. His eye, large and laden with intelligence, or perhaps with only a knowing boldness, stirs my Queen's fascination. If Walsingham does not regain Her Majesty's attention soon my Queen will dismiss her Moor and his gentlemen to entertain her newfound Raleigh in private discourse.

"Your Majesty, I apologize but I must inform you, there is news of Queen Mary of Scotland." The Moor plays his trump card, confident of the result.

As expected, this name of all names pricks at Her Majesty's attention, robbing Raleigh of the warmth of a Queen's scrutiny. She returns her attention to Walsingham.

"Mary of Scotland is detained by us at Sheffield Castle, South Yorkshire. Our Earl of Shrewsbury guards her there with loyal diligence. He has done so without incident these several years. What possible news can there be of my intractable cousin?"

"Your Majesty, the Queen of Scots hatches another Catholic plot to alight herself on your throne. We have discovered and decoded a cipher, written in her hand, implicating her involvement with several of your Catholic enemies. The Guises of France, the Italian Pope and his relentless Jesuits, and Philip of Spain all join hands in an effort to replace you with the Scottish Queen Mary."

"Sir Francis, the intelligence you bring is always trustworthy and accurate in its nature. Yet I wonder at such a wealth of Catholic energies colluding together on my behalf. Do they not have enough tapers to light? Or idols to polish? Surely their bead counting occupies much of their enthusiasm?"

Her Majesty's telltale fidgeting begins, as her fingertips run along the arm of her throne. Her dainty fingernails begin an impatient tapping. Walsingham's gaze follows her involuntary drumming for a brief moment.

"They plot against your throne, Your Majesty. Each tentacle protruding from this unholy alliance threatens you. We must act to rid England of this dangerous Catholic assembly. If we do not, like cockroaches in the pantry, the popish presence will swarm over England's unprotected table." As though his report does not contain enough devastation, Walsingham, his arms outstretched, portrays the realm in popish swarms.

"We appreciate the vivid scene your poetic discourse evokes, my Moor..." Her Majesty hesitates, nodding at Walsingham. She turns her attention back toward Raleigh so they might share another smile. "...however, we hesitate to take punitive action against our innocent Catholic subjects. Most support our reign. It does not serve England to set our own people against each other. And all due to petty religious differences. Surely, the Queen of Scots cannot gather an uprising from her prison cell at Sheffield?"

"Your Majesty, do not dismiss your wily cousin. With every scheme we uncover, she invents another tactic to smuggle correspondence from the Earl of Shrewsbury's watchful presence. The dreadful Scots woman will not cease until she perches on your throne, Your Grace."

"What of this cipher, then? Does it contain details of our cousin's plot?" Though Her Majesty's fingers cease their nervous tapping, now they clutch at her throne's arm, white with the effort.

"No, Your Grace. We have obtained only preliminary letters of introduction. The parties share their sympathies. They agree on the furtherance of the popish faith, and on their mutual loathing of the present state of affairs in England. But I promise you…."

Her Majesty's tight hold on her throne's arm releases in an instant. Her hands now resting in her lap, our Queen interrupts. "You have uncovered no actual plot against our throne?"

Her Grace's patience drains from her already half-emptied cup. Usually, Her Majesty allows Walsingham more latitude than any of her faithful counselors. However, today, both his timing, and his judgment in providing an alluring diversion, is ill-conceived.

"Not precisely. But Your Majesty…the preliminary evidence points toward the Scots Queen's guilt."

"Sir Francis…" A lengthy sigh issues from her lips. "…your Queen cannot issue execution orders for treason based on suggestions and letters of introduction. As our honoured Secretary of State, you would not have us act with rash impunity on mere inklings? No matter how sincere and well-founded they might prove to be. Nor would our people desire it, I assure you, Sir."

"Yes, Your Grace. However…"

"It is our cousin's life we ponder. Though we love the lady little, Mary Stuart is an anointed Queen. We have removed her from her throne, and held her captive these many years. And for what cause? A murder concerning her own reckless heart. Not our throne's imperilment."

Her Majesty rolls an impatient eye. "Would you have us seek her head for merely corresponding with those who share her popish faith?"

"Your Majesty, I must insist, the Queen of Scots constitutes a deadly threat to your throne." Still the heedless Moor meets Her Majesty's eye full on.

"I comprehend the threat, Sir Francis. Better than you might imagine. And I have done so for a decade and more." With this assertion, Her Majesty only stares. The chamber goes still, leeched of all air. We cease to draw breath. Stricken we are, with how fully Her Majesty grasps the relentlessness of her enemies. *To perceive is to suffer.*

Walsingham persists in his dramatic performance, but Her Majesty displays her resolve with equal zeal. True to her nature, my Queen raises the stakes ever-higher in this contest of wills. "I cannot play the tyrant. Nor can I claim heads to which I have no right. Though a king and a potent monarch, still I must answer to God's greater command. Do not request it of your sovereign to place her own soul in peril so you may close your eyes with greater ease in the night our hasty Moor." Her Majesty, rising, swaddles her rebuke in an indulgent smile.

Walsingham bends low, forced to resign himself to his failure. But the gentleman cannot resist his nature. "As you wish, Your Majesty. For the present, with my little evidence, I cannot proceed against your faithless enemies. However, I will return to you." It is a wonder her Moor enjoys my Queen's esteem. Such insolence he flaunts.

"I am certain you will, my Moor." Her Majesty's patience returns to her as she bestows another whimsical smile on Walsingham's bent head.

"...I *will* bring indisputable evidence with which to condemn the conniving Scots woman. I anticipate attending you with information to appease the conscience of a meticulous Queen, and to sharpen the blade of Her Executioner, all at once." Walsingham's prostrate form belies the determination issuing from his oath.

"My Moor, your resolve is only outdone by your loyalty to your grateful monarch. I almost pity our Queen of Scots and her devoted allies. In grasping for my throne they awaken the ire of Cerberus himself. Farewell, Francis. May God follow you in all your hazardous pursuits."

The gentlemen bow, Walsingham lowest of all to the tiled floor, as Her Majesty's skirts rustle by them. Only Raleigh's eye remains on our Queen's straight back. Its studied darkness absorbs all Her Majesty's shrewd stewardship.

***

Her Majesty concludes her audience with Walsingham and his followers. She seeks out Lord Raleigh's company instead. For weeks and months following, I act as chaperone while my Queen entertains her dashing gentleman caller.

I will not demean Her Majesty by suggesting her attraction to Raleigh stems only from his comely appearance, though the gentleman possesses much to recommend him. His is a lofty, elegant carriage. I cast my eye down as Raleigh approaches, the bulky muscle of his thigh ample with athletic poise. His entire form exudes a robust energy. My Queen admires his masculine acts of courtliness.

When Raleigh bounds through her Presence Chamber's doorway, Her Majesty's gaze does not falter. Unlike my modest bowed head, Her Majesty's scrutiny follows each stride he takes toward her. She looks on him with pleasure, and she will have him know that this is so.

His complexion is of an olive hue, as though he sprung from an Arab desert rather than a Devonshire plain. All is dark about him. His brown eyes, wide with youthful extravagance, suggest a depth of wisdom my Queen wonders at. His pointed beard covers his mouth so that his face never fully reveals itself to her. Whether Raleigh smiles with derision or with genuine warmth, she can only guess. All his attention he directs with a fixed intensity on Her Majesty. But this Raleigh speaks without filter, apparently devoid of fear. His tactless declarations, made in the company of his many enemies, trouble my Queen. Her Majesty often shouts at him for it. She attempts to muzzle his insensitive insults, his careless laughter at those who resent his favourable position at Court. In truth though, his brash disregard earns him her smile as frequently as it does her wrath.

I cannot claim the same courage as Raleigh. I fear for Her Majesty's inexperienced heart. And I know it beats with an accelerated eagerness each time the gentleman's name is uttered.

Unlike the naughty Gypsy, Raleigh does not presume to lay his hand on his Queen. Yet, I fear his methods succeed with Her Majesty where even the Gypsy's do not. Raleigh's Reason, trained as it is on Her Grace's, wanders where her Earl of Leicester's hands did not go. "Your Majesty, with respect, you do not claim Boethius's Almighty God to be his primary concern in *The Consolation*? If that is true, why does he converse with the lovely Philosophy instead?"

"It would seem you have already answered your own query, Lord Raleigh. Do tell me, my young friend. Why, as his execution looms, does the brilliant Boethius consult Mother Philosophy, when his Almighty God might offer him greater comfort?"

Her Majesty meets Raleigh's challenge with genuine pleasure. Not since her youthful studies with Master Ascham has my Queen enjoyed the opportunity to exercise her rhetorical skill. Her Majesty meets Raleigh's eye, bending forward to him at her waist. Her Grace offers her new companion a startling opportunity to view her exposed décolletage. She smiles and turns away, as though wholly unaware of her naughty gift.

And her young man's response to her provocation? Though Raleigh's dark eye does not follow where Her Majesty leads, his argument suffers from Her Majesty's attempt to distract him. "Mother Philosophy's beauty fascinates Boethius. He is a man of some eminence, but he is still a man, Your Majesty."

"Do you refer to our trusted philosopher, or to yourself, Warter? Do you suggest a sordid motive for Boethius' choice of Consoler? Does he attempt to rouse an elicit passion in his reader, rather than instruct him? Surely not, my Lord." Her Majesty, whirling back toward Raleigh, feigns shock. She seeks to confuse her new friend in playful twists and turns. Her copy of *The Consolation* she willfully abandons, as she pursues the admiring eye of Raleigh.

"Boethius speaks of Philosophy's fairness with a sensual wonder, Your Grace. As She so deserves. He drapes Lady Philosophy in finely woven silks. Yet Her layers of gossamer fabric are torn asunder by all those seeking to plunder Her knowledge."

I must credit Raleigh. Not for his poor understanding of the text, but for his robust effort to deny Her Majesty's provocation. His eye remains steady, resting on hers.

"You misunderstand the metaphor, young Sir. Boethius condemns the *partial* grasp of Philosophy's priceless gift. Those who do not comprehend Her argument in its entirety, claim small swatches of Philosophy's gown. The selected scraps represent bits of Her knowledge that the ignorant apply at will. Their shame lies in their failure to piece Philosophy's argument together. Rather than attending to Her whole treatise, they pick and choose the parts that justify their own wrongdoing."

"You see, we agree, Your Majesty. Dishonor exists in partial application of Her teachings, but still there is no indignity in appreciating Philosophy's feminine attractions."

"Beauty of all kinds inspires high regard, my dear. But I fear, in this argument you miss the point altogether."

"There is another point?"

"Do not tease, Sir. We know you always offer your studied opinion eventually."

"Very well. I will indulge my Queen's intellect, rather than dragging it through murky disputes. I will concede, Boethius responds with some warmth to Philosophy's argument for the soul's redemption through belief in a God."

"There." Her Majesty honours the upstart with an indulgent smile. "You say it yourself, Warter, though in your customary manner. Why do you imbue Philosophy's gift of wisdom with such base concerns? Are Her physical attributes really of more concern to you?"

Her Grace rouses her favourite today. While she scolds him for dwelling too much on his carnal appetite, she runs her fingers along the silhouette of her tiny bosom. The heel of her hand dips inward to her tapering waist. Even now she takes much pride in her feminine form. Her Majesty tempts young Raleigh to consider the very thing she pretends to disdain.

"Your Grace, I do not seek to dwell on man's base nature. But if you desire it, we may address the problem. What harm can arise from dressing a brilliant intellect in appealing feminine charms? You would agree no mischief need come of it. You, Your Majesty, combine the two, and have done so since you stepped onto your throne to lead us."

"Hah! Now you praise your Queen's charms in order to win your point? Do not think I will surrender so readily, Sir. In truth, it is my aim to escape this dungeon of a body." Her Majesty flings her hands away from where they rest on the layered fabric at her hip.

"I would not refer to your elegant form in such an unflattering manner, Your Grace." Raleigh stares at his Queen in a way that makes me squirm. She, with feline ease, stretches before him as his dark eye surveys her length.

Raleigh's studious eye wanders from the red-blonde curls as her temple to the rim of Her Majesty's cheekbone. After studying the light freckles on the bridge of her nose, he moves to her throat, which betrays a vigorous pulse I am sure my Queen would conceal if she could.

With instinctive awareness, her fingers rise to her jaw line in search of her telling pulse. Raleigh ignores the self-conscious gesture.

His curious eye lingers on the lace trim circling the neckline of Her Majesty's gown. In his typical contrary fashion he avoids what she offers there, skipping from the decoration on her bosom to the opalescent pearls sewn into the fabric on the bell of her hip.

Aware of his close inspection, Her Majesty's hands return there, smoothing the fabric against her outer thigh with the flats of her palms.

Raleigh, a young man who understands better than many, the importance of an instant in time, returns to Her Majesty's steady gaze. They stare at one another in silence.

Soon my Queen cannot endure the arrangement she herself commands. A mere look, though warmed by Raleigh's dark eye, provides the poorest of substitutes for an illicit touch.

The hands ruling all of England rise up in protest. Her Majesty replies. "Your Queen seeks to escape vile nature and dwell in the company of your exceptional understanding, Warter. *I count him braver who overcomes his desires than him who overcomes his enemies.* It is your monarch's wish that we flee at once. On a route charted with the sole purpose of the exchange of fanciful ideas. Let us hasten to a charmed fortress, where together we will resolve all the ancient questions. Petty Scots Queens dare not accompany us. Popish Princes will not know our whereabouts."

Her Majesty returns to herself in due haste. She and Raleigh teeter on this brink often over the weeks and months she entertains him.

But Her Majesty does not forget a Gypsy's lesson. Master Ascham, with the assistance of Plato, Aristotle and Cicero, instructed her in virtue. But Her Majesty learns well from all her teachers.

The education my Queen depends on while jousting with Raleigh? Those happy moments gathered in the loving arms of a faithless Gypsy, and the piercing bite of their cost. The lesson stays engraved on her careful wisdom.

"I am honoured I serve my Queen's need for diversion. However, I do not praise Your Grace without reason. I will not underestimate your ingenuity, for many times I have found myself on the wrong side of it."

"Enough of this banter." Her Majesty flutters her hands in protest. "We stray so far from Boethius' argument, my ill-used wits cannot begin to take flight. The lovely Philosophy offers her *Consolation* in the only manner She has. The intellect's deliberation. And still She leads the tormented soul back to his God. It is not a complex problem. You have no argument."

"I beg your pardon, Your Grace, but I have a legitimate reason to debate Boethius' intent. I return to my original query. Why does your *tormented soul,* on the very eve of his execution, not appeal to his all-powerful God? He prefers to consult his Queen of the Intellect, our beautiful Philosophy. Given his short time remaining on this earth, why does our exceptional gentleman not call God to his side? You must admit, Your Grace, like yourself, Boethius prefers a life of study and contemplation to that of religious fervour."

"God's death Warter, you test me. You plead the very argument affecting every decision I make within my realm. This accursed religious turmoil haunts all of my decrees like a hovering spirit. Bloody Scots Queens and their lust for popish idolatry. And yet, I am answerable to none for my actions but to Almighty God alone. God shall guide His Queen Bess forward. The imprisoned Boethius did ultimately accept His will."

"Your Majesty argues that Boethius accepts an all-powerful deity. But is Plato not his primary source of inspiration? Is it not within the *Republic* that Boethius reads of the ascent of the soul? Plato argues for the *Idea of the Good*, an inward light casting itself on goodness, as opposed to a Christian God floating about in the heavens." Raleigh gestures with arms raised above his head, toward arched ceilings.

Her Majesty, her chin resting within one hand, vacillates between smiling on his boundless energy, and frowning on his boldness. "Take care, Raleigh. Do not underestimate your Queen's grasp of the argument. Our Christian faith serves us well. Especially in the preservation of that societal order a sovereign requires to lead her State. I am certain our God has enough human misery to contend with, without concerning Himself with the inconsequential details of a Queen's reign."

"Your Majesty declines to consider your Archbishop's position then? How do you reply when your Church's leader shares with you his opinion on State matters?" The audacity of the upstart. He questions Her Majesty's very rule.

"Warter, must we caution you once more? Your Queen extends due respect to her Archbishop, and fully appreciates his contribution when delivered at Sunday altars. However, a monarch expects her Clergy to return her consideration. When we issue a decree from the throne, a Queen's Archbishop must comply with the scepter."

"So your cherished God oversees all, leaving more worldly matters to His judiciously chosen sovereign?" As though Raleigh's disdain for our Lord God is not enough, the gentleman addresses Her Majesty as though she does not occupy a throne. I am amazed the young man still draws breath.

"Warter, your tone reverberates with something resembling insolence. I warn you. Do not step where others have tread their last. Much is whispered of your poor belief. Do you deny your God's presence?"

"No, Your Grace. I would not go so far. I only suggest our truth-seeking Boethius and my Queen prefer to call on Reason for their guidance. You do not adopt that blinkered faith which prevails in Christian thought."

Her Majesty remains entranced by Raleigh. She smiles with parental lenience on his unholy cheek. Though I doubt she considers herself a mother to this beautiful boy.

I admire my Queen's composure as she avoids his baited argument. *It is the mark of an educated mind to be able to entertain a thought without accepting it.*

"Warter, does Boethius not conclude that Reason itself is a gift of God's grace? Does he not say: '.. *God the Creator watches over His creation. The day will never come that sees me abandon the truth of this belief*'?"

"Your Majesty, you choose to misconstrue my intent. I do not suggest the philosopher feels disenchanted with his God. I only say Boethius, in his time of greatest need, seeks solace from his intellectual masters rather than his theological ones. Philosophy asks: *"Why then do you mortal men seek after happiness outside yourselves, when it lies within you?"* She infers Her belief in the power of the intellect."

"Hold, Sir. You distort the text to your advantage." Her Majesty's patience wanes. A heightened colour pinkens her cheek. She bites on her lip as she listens to Raleigh's outrageous claims. And yet Her Majesty persists in the juvenile debate.

"God provides that happy state lying within. As you well know. Philosophy agrees to this. As for your Queen, Warter, when I peer within my judicious soul, it is with the wholesome intent of offering gratitude to God. I always attempt to measure my happiness not by popularity, but by the voice of my own conscience." Her Majesty stares down at her hands. She grips the arms of her throne, and in so doing she reminds the careless Raleigh whom he addresses.

"Your Majesty, we argue the same point, while failing to seek agreement. As your loyal subject I remain devoted to my sovereign's wisdom. I do not place my faith in a system of wondrous belief. Such resoluteness must remain in the ordained laps of monarchs. It is beyond my reach."

"Tread carefully with your indulgent talk, Warter. Flattering discourse does not erase the sting of heresy. I like you too much to have to put your charming head on the block." Another beatific smile for her favourite. Another lighthearted reminder.

"A monarch with your prudence values virtue and justice more than your beloved people's hysterical systems of belief. With all respect, Your Grace, your threats deflect off my breast. It is as though I attend you in full armour. You can do no harm to your Raleigh." Another insolent reply from her companion, all wrapped in flattery as it is. Surely only the youngster's beauty saves him from a Queen's displeasure.

"You will soon require that armour, Warter, if you continue to prod your loving Queen with the tip of your pointy lance. I might return you to Ireland to face the barbarians."

"I cannot believe that, Your Majesty. I am too convinced of your loving nature to imagine you capable of any treachery against your beloved Raleigh."

'You speak the truth, my dear. No longer can I bear to part with my belligerent Warter. Even after your saucy disrespect, my dry mouth burns with thirst when my Water wanders too far from my throne's side." As Raleigh rises, bowing, Her Majesty feigns to choke in parched need of him, until both collapse in laughter at her outlandish display.

***

15th December, 1583

No fool, Sir Francis Walsingham. Her Majesty's Moor does not err a second time. He will not approach our Queen's throne ill-prepared.

Sir William Cecil, our Lord Burghley and the Gypsy, Earl of Leicester stand by Walsingham's black-robed side. It is Walsingham's belief Her Majesty's favourite councilors will shepherd her conscience. Better that they do. Walsingham leaves the charming Raleigh off his list of invitees. Her Moor appeals more to the astute politician, than to the lively intellectual. As for the Gypsy's presence, the Moor can only aim to please Her Grace.

Her Majesty smiles on them all. She relaxes on her throne, reclining with an ease I have not witnessed in some time. My Queen looks with pleasure on her favourites gathered together. She has felt the Earl of Leicester's absence with a sore heart, even with having Raleigh to divert her. The reunion of her faithful gentlemen returns a blush to her cheek and a luster to her grey eye. Until Walsingham speaks.

Walsingham's verbal assault, prepared over many months, includes not only the presence of my Queen's trusted advisors, but also a thick dossier tucked under his arm. The log book bulges, as Walsingham has stuffed it full of documented evidence Her Majesty can no longer ignore. At least in Walsingham's estimation.

The gentleman bristles with his hatred of the Scots Queen. His chest expands with confidence in his work of the last eighteen months.

Walsingham removes his folder from its sheltered place. With a deliberate air of solemnity he lifts its leather cover and addresses his first document. He speaks in a barely audible tone just above a whisper. All strain to hear his startling declaration.

"Your Majesty, I have gathered the evidence you seek in order to confirm the guilt of your faithless cousin, Mary of Scots. Our network espied Lords Howard and Throckmorton for a full six months. They paid call to the French Embassy in London on behalf of your traitorous cousin."

Walsingham's mention of Mary Stuart lifts Her Majesty's torso. She sits perfectly upright within her throne. Her smile retreats, so as Her Majesty's body straightens upward, the expression on her face falls in reply. "Tell me of these clandestine visits to the French Ambassador, Sir Francis."

"When stretched on the rack, Throckmorton remained silent." Walsingham, the consummate performer, glances up from his page and pauses. Baron Burghley casts a hurried glance at the Gypsy by his side, then back to Walsingham. Sir Cecil, aware of his Queen's short store of patience shakes his head at the Moor, warning him against his theatrics.

"It sounds as though you still do not have the evidence we require. Why did you request this attendance?" Her Majesty frowns at Walsingham, Sir Cecil, and even at her Earl of Leicester. None meet her eye. All stare at the leaves within her Moor's folder as though her reply resides there.

Walsingham persists. He continues reading in his muted tone. "...until his second day on the rack. Lord Throckmorton spoke before his torturer could grasp onto the handle of the vise."

Her Majesty winces. "My Lord, you know I do not care for brutal methods of torture, yet you will not spare your Queen the awful details of their practice. I did not sign an order of permission for you to proceed in this manner."

"The gentlemen are traitors, Your Majesty. I took it on myself, in the name of protecting Your Grace, to discover the treachery they plot against you."

Another searching glance around the chamber and Her Majesty realizes her Moor has perhaps out-witted his Queen. Her cherished moments alone with Raleigh, while providing much exhilaration, have left her vulnerable to Walsingham's complaint. Her Majesty casts a look of exasperation toward Leicester, and receives in return a doleful shake of his head. He studies the cobbled stones at his feet. Her Majesty relents. "What then, have you discovered my diligent Moor?"

Walsingham thumbs his overflowing volume. The pages, all fluttering, stack up one on the other. Each leaf, as promised, provides more sharpening of the Executioner's blade. Flipping from one sheet to the next, Walsingham strips the traitors' disguises away.

With his evidence firm in hand, Lord Walsingham raises his voice to announce his accusation. "No less than four separate sieges against England, Your Grace. Soldiers and mercenaries gathered in Scotland, Ireland, Arundel in Sussex, and in Norfolk too. Your murder and Mary Stuart on your throne. All of this agreed to between the Scots Queen, King Philip of Spain, and their popish allies in France, Scotland, and here within the realm itself."

As though Walsingham, with his unwished for message becomes less trustworthy, Her Majesty turns to Baron Burghley. "Are we to understand you have written evidence of this deceit, Sir Spirit?"

Burghley hesitates. He has promised Walsingham his support. He does not care to usurp the Moor's authority by answering on his behalf. But Walsingham nods his assent. He closes his dossier. With that, he transfers Her Majesty's anxious plea into Baron Burghley's fatherly embrace.

Sir Cecil, ever the diplomat, replies with subdued regret. "We do, Your Grace."

Walsingham, though unasked, offers Her Majesty the indisputable details of Mary Stuart's betrayal. "We have intercepted communications between the Court of Philip of Spain and the wicked Mary of Scotland, Your Majesty. She also corresponds with the Archbishop of Scotland. Our agents in the French Embassy in London led us to Howard and Throckmorton. The third gentleman involved is the Earl of Northumberland. On Throckmorton's person we discovered numerous papers, maps, and pamphlets detailing your murder. All is contained within. As are Mary's notes and letters, in her own hand, Your Majesty." Walsingham offers the file to his Queen should she wish to peruse it.

Her Majesty waves it off. Her lids close over aching eyes. If only they could protect their Queen from all the plots hatched against her. No wringing of hands follows. Her Majesty no longer fiddles with the voluminous fabric in her skirts. Nor does she shout.

Instead, Her Majesty quietens. "We will respond to these conspiracies. We must defend the realm. Go to Spain's Ambassador Mendoza, my Moor. Inform him he is to leave England. He need not return."

The gentlemen stare at one another, confused. Who is this Queen? How does she rule on these grave issues with this newfound detachment?

Walsingham is the first to gather himself together. "With pleasure, Your Grace."

"I suppose we must execute the traitors you detain. God help me." Again Her Majesty shuts her eyes as though to hide from herself the execution order.

"Only Throckmorton and Howard, Your Grace. The Earl of Northumberland has already seen fit to end his wretched existence while he waited in the Tower." Walsingham cannot restrain himself. The question leaves his mouth before he realizes the thought hangs there. "What of Mary of Scotland, Your Majesty?"

"She is a sitting Queen, Walsingham. *All virtue is summed up in dealing justly.* Though she does not behave as one. She tests my patience at every turn, yet I cannot tolerate becoming the instrument of her death. *We are what we repeatedly do. Excellence then, is not an act, but a habit.* Remove my cousin to Wingfield in Staffordshire immediately. We will write to Sir Paulet, and request he accept charge of the troublesome woman at Tutbury. This should quiet the clucking of the traitors."

"Your Majesty, I must protest. Certainly Sir Paulet will apply his strict Puritan sensibility to the Scots woman's depraved soul. And the fortress at Tutbury will contain her physical presence. But the wretched woman represents victory to the Catholics. She declares, and with insistence, her singular purpose to sit on your throne. I demand, for your own sake Your Majesty, and for all England's, you must execute the villainess."

As Walsingham's exchange with Her Majesty grows ever-heated, Burghley and Leicester glance at each other. They shift their positions with unease. But neither intercedes. Each realizes the Moor might best succeed in bending a Queen's will to their own.

Again the gentlemen hear the unexpected from my changeable Queen. The once-pink skin of Her Majesty's cheek pales. It slackens and grays. Her brow, screwed into a tight frown, matches well her downturned mouth.

Our monarch ends the meeting with her dispassionate plea. "You demand too much of your old Queen, Sir Francis. More than you realize. I am grateful for your tireless efforts. They shall not go unrewarded. You have dispatches to carry out. Go now, all of you. Leave your Queen to ponder her dreadful options."

They should rule who are able to rule best.

Walsingham, with whispered encouragement from Baron Burghley, leaves his Queen's Presence Chamber. The gentlemen leave as they arrived. Shoulders joined in solidarity, he and Sir Cecil hasten from Her Majesty's company before another melee can erupt.

Only the Gypsy hesitates. Her Earl of Leicester turns his head to cast a parting glance as he passes out of Her Majesty's chamber.

Her Grace's Bonny Sweet Robin looks on what he has not witnessed before. His troubled eye rests on a weary Queen. I could tell him the sight, with too common regularity, greets my eye. Only her Gypsy's intrusion makes this occasion different.

Her Grace, shoulders stooped, leaves her chamber. Unlike her gentlemen, she does not pass through the accepted entryway.

Her Majesty withdraws far into herself. My Queen still occupies her throne, even though her Gypsy would swear the imposing chair stands empty. Her Majesty looks into a hovering absence. A stillness invades her demeanour. An aching distance separates my Queen from her companions.

Her Gypsy, believing his unreliable eye taunts him, approaches closest to the truth. Her Majesty does fly from the gentlemen's presence. And though the Earl of Leicester believes his downcast Majesty reduced by Walsingham's news of a traitorous Scots Queen, it is here his understanding fails him.

She cloaks herself in her robe of isolation. My Queen journeys to where a trusted companion awaits. Somewhere, away, she confides all to a cherished second self.

Autumn III - A Final Course

*I would rather go to any extreme than
suffer anything that is unworthy of
my reputation or of that of my crown.*

--Elizabeth I

18th August, 1586

I fear Her Majesty's memoir becomes a dated descent. An interminable progress toward a Queen's premature death. While *my* Queen remains too much the politician to suffer this fate, Mary of Scotland does not possess the same judgment. Unfortunate woman.

The Queen of Scots' malicious intentions toward Her Majesty persist. It is said Queen Mary Stuart's appearance is much altered since imprisoned by us these eighteen long years. We can only imagine the lady's transformation. My Queen and her rival consider themselves kin, yet neither has ever looked at the other, face to face. Each relies solely on her artist's miniature portraits.

We are told the Queen of Scots' hair, once a rich auburn hue, streaks with bars of grey. Her elegant form, once distinguished by her six foot height and graceful carriage, bears added weight.

My Majesty, too, alters her outward appearance. Time hurries Her Majesty's decline with an inexorable rhythm. Once filled with a forgetful kindness for our Queen, Father Time reminds Her Majesty of her mortality with an implacable cruelty. Her Majesty, once a woman of robust health, struggles with the anxiety a throne demands. The unease a Scots Queen provokes, adds to my Majesty's travails.

"Blanche. I sleep so little." Her Majesty breathes deeply and exhales.

In all the years I have faithfully served my Queen, I have marveled at how little sleep she requires. Frequently Her Majesty does not lay her head on her pillow until the early hours of the morning. Long after midnight I awaken to the whispers of Her Majesty and her Lord Treasurer Burghley together in her Presence Chamber. Their voices rise barely above a distant murmur, but I decipher their topics: Her Majesty misses her Earl of Leicester. The Gypsy attempts to govern in faraway Netherlands. Or the state of the Treasury. Her financial concerns frequently haunt my Majesty's late hours. And then a roundabout return to the Earl of Leicester's extravagant spending in the Netherlands. On and on my Queen and her Sir Spirit whisper.

I grasp at my nightcap. I tug the lace trim down over my own meddling ears. I clutch at my feather duvet, pulling the weight of it up and over my head. Its downy weight provides some insulation, but still tense whispers creep into my awakened ear.

Her Majesty once rose refreshed in the early hours. She wakened before dawn, when the sky hadn't yet blinked its sleep-addled eye. But a rival Queen's plotting claims more of Her Majesty's vigour than she cares to disclose. "I tire Blanche. While my Privy Councilors harp on this matter of the Queen of Scots, I fear their sleepy Majesty will abandon them. I will have drifted off in a happy slumber. And now I understand Babington confesses to a plot to poison me. Do all the stars align to have me govern as my unyielding father did?" Her Majesty puts to me this impossible question. Her demeanour tells me she expects no reply. My Queen turns away from me, fidgeting with the emerald on her pointer finger. She glances down with dissatisfaction at the weighty gold cross around her neck. She pats at the pocket of her gown, ensuring her worn copy of Seneca remains there.

"I suffer to hear of your distress, Your Majesty. I have heard the brutish calls from Parliament to treat the Catholic traitors with a heavy hand."

"How my tooth throbs." Her Majesty raises both hands to cradle her sore cheeks. She closes her eyes on her affliction. Blinded, my beloved Queen may also cease to feel.

"Bring me a poultice for my aching jaw. I abhor complaint, Letters. But my mouth causes so much hurt. Sometimes I wish Babington's poison would remove me from my throne. It might be better than suffering the indignity of a tooth's reckoning." Her Majesty rubs at her face, raising a flushed hue to her prominent cheekbone.

"Perhaps the aniseed sweets you prefer do not favour your ailing mouth, Your Grace." Given the choice, I speak of candy rather than the dreaded prospect of Her Majesty's murder by poison. To my delight, Her Majesty follows my evasive lead.

"For two full hours each day my ladies wash and dress me. Yet with all their careful ministrations, this wretched tooth pains me so." Her Majesty cradles her cheeks, massaging in a circular round and round motion, but no relief ensues.

"Should I fetch a lady-in-waiting to bring a tooth cloth and picks, Your Majesty? Another cleaning, perhaps?"

"If only a cleansing were the remedy, Blanche. Another dousing with marjoram will not alter my mouth's wretched insistence." My Queen roots within her gown's pocket, plunging her hand deep into the pleated fabric. "I will call on Seneca instead. Perhaps his wisdom will dilute the throbbing of a Queen's jaw. Maybe his soothing words will provide a warming balm for my poor conscience."

***

18th September, 1586

This morning Her Majesty wakens with a throbbing headache. My Queen struggles with great difficulty to rise from her bed. I leave her to fetch her chief physician, Dr. George Baker. Her Majesty berates me and the beleaguered gentleman too. When he attempts to minister to Her Majesty's ailing head, she sends him away. She grips her tight curls as though by tugging on them she can rid herself of the pounding at her temples.

"Have I lost my senses, along with my physical health, Sir? I do not recall summoning you to my chamber. It is nothing but a small headache. Nothing for a chief physician to fuss about. Be gone, Sir. And do not return until you are called on."

Dr. Baker scurries from Her Majesty's bedchamber. Since I summoned him on her behalf, I fear I will be next.

"Blanche. Do not presume to know what heals your ailing Queen. I do not require my physician when Gerard gives me my herbs to brew a cordial broth. This you well know."

"Yes, Your Majesty."

"Remember it. Now call my ladies to me. I must prepare to see Walsingham."

When at the appointed hour Her Majesty's Moor hurries in, no evidence of my Queen's malady lingers. Only once do I catch Her Grace reaching up to massage her left temple. But when Her Majesty notices Walsingham studying her with a puzzled expression, her fingers fly from her aching head. As she often does, she deploys her sharpened tongue to distract her Moor from her own distress.

"I need to know your mind, Francis. The execution of Babington and his conspirators takes place today at St. Giles's Fields. Due to the wretched nature of the crime, I have ordered particular attention be paid to the conditions surrounding their deaths. These traitors should suffer as none before them for plotting the murder of their Queen."

I do not understand my Majesty. In most of my experience she exhibits only sympathy to those condemned to an untimely death. Her Grace harbours a genuine loathing for ruthless punishment. Yet today she requests her Executioner carry out the most deplorable acts in their entirety. Surely Walsingham will not honour Her Majesty's cruel request?

"Baron Burghley informs me of your disquiet, Your Majesty. He suggests the full extent of the law, including the quick hanging by the neck of each of the prisoners, followed by removal of their bowels and members, the burning of these organs under their own living nostrils and finally, their beheading. This will suffice."

"Is no further action to be taken then? Can we not exhibit to our people our supreme displeasure with these attempts on the throne?"

How can a fine gentleman such as Sir Francis and my cordial Queen make civil conversation about such horrors? How can this endless list of punishments not satisfy a Queen's vengeance? I do not comprehend Her Majesty's changeable temperament.

"Your Majesty, with respect, Baron Burghley and I consider the executions as described to be sufficient. In what other manner might we bring Babington and his co-conspirators to their deserved ends?" Walsingham lifts and opens his large palms to show his Queen he does not deny her request. Her Majesty's enemies receive all he has. Walsingham's capable hands express the frustration his words cannot.

"Do not trouble me with the sordid details of men's deaths, Francis. I only impress on you the necessity of sending our meaning to our people. Our loyal subjects will have their lust for blood duly sated. They have borne witness to their Queen threatened with her own murder."

"Your Majesty, though you do not wish to hear it, it must be said. The traitors will die ingloriously as they deserve, but what of their wicked temptress? You punish the followers with undue force while leaving the depraved Queen of Scots, their leader, to further threaten England's throne."

"She is a *Queen*, Walsingham." Her Majesty lifts a wrist to caress her sore temple. She hesitates. She glances toward her Moor, before lowering her hand into its mate within her lap.

"The wicked Scots woman thirsts for your blood, Your Grace. She will not stop until she drinks it. She must be tried. The Privy Council demands it."

"Enough, Sir. Ensure the traitors are hanged, drawn, quartered. The full extent of the law must be duly meted. Now leave me."

***

6th October, 1586

Madam,

We are given to understand, to our great and inestimable grief, you are indeed void of all remorse. You pretend with great protest to be uninvolved in any attempt against our throne. We find, by most clear and evident proof, the contrary will be maintained against you. We have therefore found it expedient to send to you our most respected noblemen of the realm, together with members of our Privy Council and some of our principal judges. They shall charge you with the most horrible and unnatural crime of plotting your own cousin's demise.

Given at our castle of Windsor the 6th day of October.

Elizabeth R

12th October, 1586

At last my Queen's own hand demands Mary of Scots face her accusers. Yet, never have I feared more for Her Majesty's waning stamina. Each turn Her Grace takes on her specially-built walking terrace at Windsor strengthens her lithe form. Each hunt my Queen rides out on in the Great Park persuades Her Majesty of her resilient constitution. And yet. Lying in wait, a lurking predator in the form of a Scots woman, tests my Queen's emotional hardiness. Her Majesty's dark Moor and I share one mind on the topic. The Scots Queen represents the most particular threat. But the menace I fear most is not Walsingham's talk of foul poison, or an assassin's honed dagger.

As I write, Her Majesty prepares to rise. I pray happier news will greet her ear. Perhaps the sun's prodding rays will cheer her spirit. My desires prove in vain. Metallic bars of the densest cloud confine the Sun's warmth, shutting it away from Her Majesty. And the Queen of Scots stands trial at Fotheringhay in Northamptonshire.

My mighty Majesty, when confronted with the entire Privy Council's demands and her good people's too, at last concedes defeat. England will try her royal cousin for treason. Her Majesty has attempted with all her clever wit to elude this moment. Yet my gifted monarch fails to harness Parliament.

I now understand my Majesty's ferocity. The mercilessness with which she dispatches Babington and his companions. Her Majesty seeks to prevent the execution of a fellow Queen. But she errs in her strategizing. Her citizens' outrage is not appeased by the gruesome executions of Babington and his fellow traitors for one reason alone: A Queen of Scots' head remains perched on her faithless shoulders.

As I write, Burghley, Walsingham, Hatton, Paulet, and the Catholics, Montague and Lumley - the majority of Her Majesty's noblemen - sit at Fotheringhay in judgment of a Queen of Scots. Her Majesty remains at Windsor, alone with her Keeper of the Books, and a smattering of ladies in waiting.

"Blanche, are you within?" My Queen summons me from my little desk.

"Yes, My Grace, I am here."

"Come to my bedside. I must see you at once."

I approach Her Majesty's canopied bed, my head bowed, but my eye still on my Queen. I study her worn countenance. Once, my Queen's pink-hued skin stretched taut, highlighting her aristocratic nose and her statuesque cheekbone. I stare into my Queen's grey eyes. They appear all sunken within their sockets. Beneath her thinning lower lashes, grey half moons match the steely grey eye that returns my scrutiny. I fear Her Majesty's bloom has abandoned her. These last few weeks have claimed our Queen's youth. I glance away from my discovery, for fear my Queen might read my thoughts.

"Of course, Your Majesty."

"I cannot sleep, Blanche. I dare not. When I try, my mother seeks me out. My ladies tell me she suffered from the same lack of sleep plaguing me."

"Yes, she did, Your Grace."

"My mother seeks me for that company only a daughter can offer." Her Majesty's eyes open wide with juvenile awe. Dream-like visions of her departed mother send my Queen hurtling backward into long ago childhood. Still Her Majesty's hand rests on one cheek, rubbing at her throbbing tooth.

"Your Majesty, should I fetch your physician? Or John Gerard for an herbal remedy? A sleeping elixir to give you ease?" I turn to go but my Queen reaches out and grabs onto my bare forearm.

"No. I haven't time for wasteful slumber. My poor mother beckons to me from beyond the grave." Her Majesty's sleepy eyes, wide with childish wonder, erase for a moment, Father Time's wilting pull.

"Your Majesty, surely…"

"Blanche. Hear me." Her desperate hand releases me, but Her Majesty's command takes a tighter hold.

"Yes, Your Grace." I stand before Her Majesty as she wishes. My stillness belies the dread my heart races with.

"Mother begs me to put an end to Mary of Scots' trial. I must undo the evil deeds of my father. I cannot allow the Executioner's axe to swing down on the neck of a God-anointed Queen."

I consider contradicting my Queen, but I cannot find the courage or the will. Her Majesty speaks as though to herself alone. My presence, my voice, evaporates in the company of her awful anxiety.

"Mother whispers to me as I sleep. I awaken, my bleary eyes open to the darkness. I attempt to remain awake to erase the frightening vision, but heavy lids return me to her. When I slumber again, she speaks her message once more. *Do not err as your father did.*" Her Majesty lifts her pretty hand to her cheek, cupping it as she repeats Anne Boleyn's insistent message.

"The Council may pronounce the Queen of Scots' guilt, but I alone declare the sentence. I will bestow clemency on the hated Mary of Scots. Hear me."

I do not wish to stand with Walsingham, in precarious contradiction of my Queen. Yet I do it. "Your Majesty, the Queen of Scots seeks an end to your life. Your Council only desires to protect their Queen. And all England."

"Blanche, I am too aware of Walsingham's godforsaken collection of facts. But I must first consider my conscience. My beloved Mother calls on me to enact what is right, in the eyes of God alone. I will stay the Executioner's sword. I must put an end to this gross misdeed. I cannot put to death a God-anointed sovereign."

"If I were to stay by your side, would this ease your restless mind, Your Grace? Some breakfast perhaps? Should I summon the kitchen to prepare tea with honey or some leavened bread... softened with warm milk to soothe your sore mouth?" Once more I rise. Once more Her Majesty's voice holds me in my place.

"Blanche, your tone remains deferential, but your eyes betray your wanting faith in my wits." Now Her Majesty studies my countenance.

"No, Your Grace..."

"Your Queen does not approach madness just yet." Her Majesty's smile replaces the anxious expression she wears these last few days. The chamber brightens, as though we pull aside a curtain from the window and expose the room to its natural elements.

I would like to take pleasure in Her Majesty's small jest, but I cannot when she believes I lose confidence in her soundness. "Your Majesty I do not doubt you..."

"I do not wish to sleep longer. Nor do I wish to eat." Her Majesty thrusts herself up and swings her legs over the edge of the canopied bed. She stands over me in flowing white robes. If I were to join Her Majesty's fancy, resist all that is sensible, I would swear my Queen was a redeeming angel. Hovering above, she whispers disordered messages of wisdom into my waiting ear.

"Blanche, I fully understand my Mother's demand. She insists I show measured but loving consideration to my cousin, Mary of Scots." My Queen stalks around the chamber. Her renewed energy invigorates her argument.

"Your Majesty, I accept without reservation your blessed mother's presence in your conscience. But the Queen of Scots does not behave as a cousin to you. Will your mother not comprehend this?"

"But she does, Blanche. She contemplates all of it. She beckons to me from beyond, where she surveys all our world's machinations. She bears witness to our cousin's long imprisonment and sheds tears for a fellow Queen who faces her same fate. I can put an end to the duplication of this evil-doing."

"Your Majesty..."

"Blanche, if pity were not shown me when my Catholic sister Mary sat on *her* throne, all England may not have enjoyed the peaceful reign it has seen these three decades with their Elizabeth. I too may have marched to the Tower to rest my head on a block. And at my own sister's bequest."

"Surely your mother does not remind you of this hurtful truth?"

"Mother speaks only of her love. She encourages forgiveness for my wayward cousin, the Scots Queen. She considers Mary another pitiable, imprisoned wretch, as Mother once was herself."

"But Your Majesty, the Queen of Scots, in her own written hand, plots against your throne. The situation differs from that of your mother."

"That does not bear consideration. You *will* not understand. I am foolish to expect you would." I fear Her Majesty loses patience with me. "Princes transact business in a certain way, with a princely intelligence such as private persons cannot imitate. I am your absolute and sovereign mistress. Now move from the bedside. I must rise immediately. Fetch my quill and paper. I will send to Sir Cecil to prorogue the court and rescue a Queen."

"Yes, Your Grace."

"...And I will stake my very soul on it." My harried angel rushes from her bedchamber, her white robes trailing behind in frothy disarray.

***

12th October, 1586
To William Cecil, Lord Treasurer Burghley, Fotheringay
By the queen.

Our well-beloved councilor, we greet you well. We understand from your late correspondence, the Scottish Queen does refuse to stand trial. As she also refuses to submit to our noblemen's questioning, you have no choice but to sentence her on our behalf. Though you shall undoubtedly find her guilty of the crimes she is charged with, it is our wish you do not pronounce sentence upon her until you have returned to us. We would require a full report on all the proceedings before we can act upon the sentence applied.

Elizabeth R.

***

14th November, 1586

To elude Her Majesty's gentlemen, who persist in claiming the severed head of the Scottish Queen, my Majesty and her Court remove to Richmond Palace. When we leave Windsor, Anne Boleyn thankfully flees to her quiet grave in St. Peter Vincula at the Tower. Well away from Her Majesty's poor embattled conscience. I pray a special thanks to our Lord God for His small mercies.

Her Majesty finds strange consolation at Richmond, her grandfather Henry VII's, palace. I cannot criticize my Queen's desire for the conveniences of Richmond. Perhaps when a Queen feels poorly in her mortal body, she is inclined to dwell more on creature comforts. Richmond offers more comfort than any of Her Majesty's great estates. Unlike my Queen, I do not dwell on physical ease so much as I fret about Her Majesty's chastened temperament. I pray another unwelcome, royal specter does not haunt my besieged Queen's slumber.

Her Majesty spends her waking hours in her favourite turret at Richmond. Crowned by a glittering dome, then crowned once more with a wind vane made of genuine gold and gleaming silver, the turret houses our Queen and her troubles in impeccable grandeur. Where errant winds whistle through the chamber ways of Windsor and Hampton Court, Richmond's sturdy walls contain no such noisy draughts. Her Majesty's rotunda warms with a pleasing snugness in the mid-day sun.

I watch Her Majesty seated so still within. She stares out arching windows. I worry she may acquaint herself with more deceased relations. So eerily the weather vanes make chiming music of the gusts. But to my delight, a needed ease greets my Queen at her favourite palace. And for this, I offer my gratitude.

Her Majesty stoops under her latest burden. Her aching teeth deny her sleep, causing my Queen to cry out with muted whimpers she believes I do not hear. Persistent pain shifts from her shoulder blade, up the base of her elegant neck and into her temples. Her head throbs with worry over the Scots Queen's destiny. Each image of the falling axe on Mary Stuart's neck means a new assault on my gracious Lady's health.

And now another ill-timed interruption intrudes on my Queen's meditation. The lady who delivers an unwanted summons remains just outside the entry to my Queen's chamber. She bends at her waist, leaning into the room. She speaks in hushed tones.

"I beg forgiveness for disturbing you, Your Grace. A large retinue of gentlemen rides from Westminster to attend you. They wait in the Withdrawing Chamber."

Her Majesty's low grumble issues from within. "We have only just left Windsor to escape these gentlemen. I do not wish to hear their foul talk of treason. Can they not find company amongst themselves and leave me to my own disheartening thoughts?" My dejected Queen does not turn to address her lady. She speaks as if to herself alone while studying the tiny panes of glass. She appears determined to ignore all else.

"Should I dismiss them, Your Grace?" Her Majesty's lady leans further into the chamber. The curved bell of her silken gown is all that remains outside in the hallway.

No reply. Her Majesty stares below to Richmond's gardens as her lady bends in growing discomfort.

"They number near sixty gentlemen, Your Grace. I recognize some of the members of your Parliament and some of your Council." Her Majesty's young lady attempts encouragement. The quiver in her voice speaks only of unease.

No reply.

"Your Grace, they carry with them a verdict on the Scots Queen. They are requesting you sign their petition for her Execution." The young lady, having delivered her unwanted message, teeters in the chamber doorway.

Her Majesty at last takes pity on the frightened girl. "Your Queen will not disappoint this determined gathering." Surrender invades Her Majesty's response. "I do not see how to evade the insistent rogues. Tell them I will attend them presently." Her Grace does not stir from her upholstered bench.

***

Her Majesty claims a brief moment to compose herself. She remains seated, staring out her little tower window, before rousing her aching form. She rubs, with heartrending habit, at the base of her neck. She sighs, and finally rises to join her gentlemen.

We ladies gather outside the closed door of the Withdrawing Chamber. I jostle, pen and paper in hand, for my position in the chamber doorway. On the other side of the door, my Queen's voice reverberates. At first, I hear only the odd word of Her Majesty's entreaty to her trusted courtiers.

The entourage imagines itself possessing the upper hand with its formal petition for the Scots Queen's traitorous head. It should rethink its premise. Her Majesty's voice, now clear and dominant, rises above the rabble. My Queen's meaning, with abundance, issues forth.

"I thank God my disloyal subjects are few. I am sure I have the hearts and goodwill of most of my beloved subjects. When I am told of these horrible treasons, to tell you truthfully, I am not grieved for myself or for mine own life. My own life, in itself, I value little, as I know that less life means less sin. And I

assure you, little do I desire to live. I rather think that the happiest person is that person who is already dead..."

Her Majesty, my educated lady, quotes from Sophocles' tragic *Oedipus*. I cannot help but worry. My Queen speaks of a tragic hero's desire for death as though it were her own dear hope. I stifle tears for my monarch. She holds so precious her reputation and the love of her people too. She remains certain all will dissolve should her gentlemen force her to succumb to their demands for the Scots Queen's life.

Lace-covered elbows attempt to shove me from my place outside Her Majesty's chamber door. I do not respond to their pointed demands. Instead I hunker down, straining to hear Her Grace. With repeated assertions of her innocence, Her Majesty appeals to the gentlemen to understand their Queen's heart.

"I take God to witness, I bear her no malice, nor do I seek revenge. I only wish, with all my heart that she may repent her crimes...I wrote to her, advising her that if she would confess the truth and name the conspirators in this action, I would cover her shame and save her from this end. I assured her I did not deceive her in any way or form. My offer she refused utterly, and persisted in denying her guilt."

I myself transcribed this pleading letter of Her Majesty's to her faithless cousin. All the while I suppressed my own grief. How can the Fates demand that a blameless Queen should have to plead with her own tormentor so that the very tormentor should live?

"You have laid a hard and heavy burden upon me in this case. All is to be done by the direction of the queen, an uncommon course to take in such cases. But, to answer your plea, you shall understand the case is rare and of great weight. I must consider all advice, for the matter is grave. And yet I know delays are dangerous."

Her Majesty gets to it. She makes known her desire to refuse them.

"To your petition I must pause before I give an answer. Princes stand upon stages. Their actions are viewed and beheld more than any man. I am sure my decisions will be considered by many fine intellects, within the realm, and in foreign countries. We must look to persons abroad, and at home. Be assured of this: I will be most careful to do that which shall be best for the safety of my people. And best for the good of the realm."

Her Majesty finishes. Silence greets her final word. Her gentlemen's dismay slows their usually ready complaint. The distinctive click of my Queen's heels hurries toward the chamber doorway. Her gentlemen's shuffling feet reach our group's furtive ear. Our curious gathering outside the Withdrawing Chamber disperses, much as wandering Spirits return to their mysterious realm. When the disgruntled group emerges from the Withdrawing Chamber led by my victorious Queen, it is met by a hush. The recently emptied war room echoes in silence.

***

24th November, 1586

Less than a fortnight elapses before the gentlemen return. Like a pack of slavering wolves gathered round my Queen, her noblemen circle. They approach from all corners of the Withdrawing Chamber. Do they mean to pounce on their prey until she displays her exposed throat? Her Majesty, as the poised gazelle leaps to safety, leads the chase all round the room. She dodges their vicious demands with the alacrity of her intellect.

The petition for the Queen of Scot's head lies open on the table between them. Her Majesty's noblemen unfurl it immediately on gaining their Queen's presence. Lord Hatton slams the chamber door against our curious eyes, but not before we too dare a glance at its wicked contents.

The document's bright white background suggests a purity of thought. But the grasping signatures, marked in the blackest ink – so representative of the Lords' dark hearts – cause it to resemble a chess board. Our Queen leaps with ease about the board, commanding an early position of strength. She delivers a torrent of words, in a voice honeyed with indulgence. Can she silence the noisy calls for an execution of a fellow Queen?

Her gentlemen argue. They claim Her Majesty exhibits confusion. They accuse her of an ignorance of the rules of the game they play. In their opinion, their Queen forfeits her advantage each time she moves in for her own idea of a victory.

"I hope you have considered with care my last message. For it does hearken from an earnest desire and a hungry will in me. Cannot some way be found by you to ensure my safety without the execution of a Queen? I have pardoned many traitors and rebels. I remember very well half a score treasons which have been either dismissed or examined only slightly. In doing so, mine actions have saved me from being named a tyrant. My people's regard does matter most of all..."

My poor Majesty. Forever she struggles with the desire to wrench her name from that of her father's. My Queen remains steadfast, and determined to stand alone as protector of her realm. Willingly she accepts the role of saviour to an undeserving Scots woman.

I, jaded by years spent in the presence of her Lords, anticipate rude interruption of Her Majesty's speech. Several nobles, those standing closest to their Queen, exchange murmurs of dissent. Leaning, with my ear pressed against the chamber's closed door, I swear I hear Lord Walsingham sigh. He whispers words of callous complaint: *I wish to God her Majesty would be content to refer these things to them that can best judge of them, as other princes do.* Yet her gentlemen know better than to argue noisily against Her Majesty while she speaks her mind.

"It seems most strange to me that everyone: my lords, my councilors and the rest, should all find it impossible for me to live in safety without execution of your demand for a Queen's head."

Flawless rhetoric. Master Ascham, be proud. Her Majesty escapes the snare yet again. Twisting and turning the matter, she writhes free. How, my Queen inquires of her counselors, have *they* not alighted on a better solution? An answer that might preserve their Queen's cherished reputation for peaceful civility. Why cannot her trusted advisors temper the mortal danger Her Majesty faces from her formidable opponent?

I must agree. Is it not these Lords' duty to protect our Queen? Mustn't they guard her physical health, her bodily comfort, and also her envied place of respect within the European realm? My gracious Lady places the black-hearts in Check.

"But now for answer unto you, you must take an answer without answer at my hands. For if I should say I would not do it, I might say that which I did not think. If I should say I would do it, it is not fit in this place and at this time. Therefore, I must advise you to remain satisfied with this answer answerless."

And Checkmate. For a time. Her Majesty, with words devoid of meaning or promise, adjourns Parliament once more. Not until February will her nobles reconvene. We hasten to Her Majesty's birthplace. Greenwich for Christmas. Her Majesty, eager to escape a trap laid by one opponent, flees to another. Her Gypsy Earl returns from the Netherlands. Leicester awaits Her Majesty and her Court at Greenwich. God help us all.

***

1st February, 1587

A Gypsy's gentle attentions do not threaten Her Majesty with the same dishonour they once did. With a grudging acquiescence I admit her Earl of Leicester provides the ease my Queen needs at her Christmas holiday. Since the Lady Lettice Knowles occupies his bed, her Gypsy does not leer at Her Majesty in his predatory manner. No longer does he, with boldness unimaginable, put his swarthy hand on the contours of my Queen's fine cheek. A Gypsy's desires appear doused by cherished wedlock. For this I am grateful.

The pair wanders Her Majesty's gardens beneath verdant awnings. Their shoulders, innocent of past transgressions, no longer brush against the other in pursuit of illicit warmth. Instead they lean in, one on the other. A cherished support. The Gypsy becomes a trusted advisor to Her Majesty. A friend. For this too, I am grateful.

Forgive my inconsistency. Not only will a Queen vacillate. So too will a Keeper of the Queen's Books. Her Majesty's best interests are my own. And so I turn, and find myself in favour of a Gypsy's devout affection. My Queen needs a companion.

Those closest to Her Majesty harp about her indecision. Her Council complains of Her Majesty's tendency to ponder a resolution unceasingly, until none gets made. But who of them would put to death their own cousin without some consideration of their own soul's fate? With too much ease, a man casts judgment on his friend's weakness. When judging his Queen, he forages all the deeper, unearthing a multitude of sins to justify his complaint.

I love my Queen. And so I defend her pitiable position. Her Majesty earns my devotion. She holds off the vicious pack for as long as she can. But Parliament insists. Vigorous demands leave my Queen with few alternatives. Her Majesty must face the reality of her plight. The pawns are so numerous. Their numbers make up for what they lack in political strength. They swarm my Majesty's tolerant stance.

"Letters, I use all in my inadequate woman's power to hold them off, yet I fail. I have had to authorize their wicked formal proclamation on my cousin. It made me so wretched I was hardly able to transcribe it in my quivering hand. And now I must sign a warrant for her death. How can I do that?"

"Your Majesty, we know you do not lack boldness. You only hesitate to inflict suffering on a fellow Queen. But the Lords of the Court will say otherwise. Fear governs their tongues, Your Majesty. Their dread causes them to utter slanders against their monarch..."

Her Majesty draws herself up, taken aback. I hope in my candour I have not made an impossible situation more unbearable for my Queen. "Blanche, I take great pride in my reputation for tolerance. Surely my people love their Queen?"

"They do, Your Majesty."

"I have shown them my devotion. I have offered them a prudent, peaceable kingdom. What slander do they utter against me?"

"Your Majesty, forgive me." I know my Queen too well to consider couching my harsh words. Most of all, she values my honesty. So I offer it, with my own security weighing in the balance.

"Your Grace, the Council questions your authority on the throne. Parliament complains bitterly of your tendency to mislead them. They claim a woman's judgment is clouded by the weakness of her sex. They grumble about your advancing years." The raw accusations tumble from my mouth. I speak them with as much haste as I can offer Her Majesty. Perhaps if delivered with a certain velocity, their impact may be less. A glancing blow instead of a cruel slap.

My Queen's shocking reply threatens to end our awkward exchange. "Perhaps they are right. I do not see how I can give them my cousin. I simply cannot, without destruction to myself. Though she seeks my mortal life, must I also forfeit for her my soul? The committing of this dreadful deed will remove all God's grace..."

Her Majesty answers me not with the rage I feared, but with a surrender I fear more. Pitiless, I proceed. "Your Grace, even as we speak of it, London floods with rumours of the Queen of Scots' escape. They say she plots with the French and Scottish Ambassadors to hide mixtures in your diluted wine to put you into an endless slumber. It is true that good men's anxieties lead to their doubting you. It is their fear that beckons you to hasten this Execution. Ghastly though the deed may be."

"So if I am to live, Mary of Scots must die?" Her Majesty refuses to look at me. Instead, she stares into her soul's future.

"Your Majesty, I fear it is true..."

With a predictable ease, Her Grace transforms. She discards her anxiety. She lets go her impossible desire for the securing of a Queen's soul. Just a single fleeting consideration among so many. Her Majesty meets my eye. An ironical smile denies all the horrors of the last months.

"It is fitting Walsingham would take ill at this time. And my good Sir Cecil lost his seat on his horse and fell to the ground? Their Queen requires their presence more than at any time before. If I did not understand these gentlemen, I might question their resolve in this deplorable business. Call Sir William Davison to me. I will sign their wretched document. They have won."

A different Queen greets her stand-in Secretary. When Sir William Davison enters, Her Majesty storms through the Presence Chamber. Silken layers of her gown separate and rustle with the same panic their mistress wears. Her Majesty speaks in Latin, under her breath. *"Suffer or strike!...In order not to be struck, strike! Suffer or strike!...* Would you agree, Lord Davison?"

"I would, Your Majesty." He offers the detestable document to his Queen.

"You would do well alongside my beloved father. Give to me your godforsaken papers. God's Death. You ask everything of me. My peace of mind. My bodily health. My very soul I must forfeit. What else should a Queen relinquish to ensure her beloved people's satisfaction?"

Her Majesty snatches the Execution Order from Davison's hand. She tosses it on her desk, and with no hint of hesitation, scrawls her long awaited signature. Davison does not comprehend his Queen's sacrifice. Her Majesty proves herself a princely master, willing to forfeit all for her people. Only my Queen and I know the true cost. Her Majesty's trembling hand seeks her temple. She massages it with a deliberate pressure. Her last attempt to erase any knowledge of her despotic act.

***

7th February, 1587

"Lord Davison, return the Order of Execution to your Queen at once." Her Majesty rises from her throne. She stands over the bowed Davison, her hand outstretched.

"Your Majesty?"

"We must delay for a time. With careful deliberation, means may be found to avoid this monstrous miscarriage of a sovereign's duty. Consensus might be reached with further consideration." My Queen's hand stays outstretched. The certainty of her demand calms her tremors.

A confused Davison lifts his head and engages Her Majesty's frantic eye. On looking there, he winces, not liking her expression. To his credit, his reply is an honest, if not welcome one. "Your Majesty… the Order of Execution has been delivered. It is too far gone."

"It cannot be." Her Majesty's form stiffens. She braces for a blow she has already received. Her fingers collapse in on themselves, balling into futile fists. "Damn you. I did not mean it to go forth. I only meant to sign the document and put it away for a time. Until I could come to a better solution for addressing my cousin's machinations."

"I beg pardon, Your Majesty? I do not comprehend…"

Her Grace steps away from Davison, toward the window. She stares into its diffused light, then strides the length of the room, turning at the far end. She returns to Davison with her new proposal. "What if, between now and the dreadful beheading of a Queen, an accidental death was to befall the Scots woman? I will speak to Lord Paulet. Perhaps the Oath of Association would allow for it…I do not see why my gentlemen cannot make the arrangements…"

Her Majesty whispers her murderous intentions as though to herself. As though she believes her chamber empties. She considers the matter as though alone with her thoughts. Her fingers fly about, all animated. She does not direct their motion to Davison, or to her ladies, but to an invisible companion. I fear my Queen is lost.

"I am sorry, Your Grace. The Execution Order went to Fotheringhay to Lords Paulet, Walsingham and Burghley. It is too late for delay." Davison makes no attempt to mask his horror at my Queen's suggestion. An accidental death for Mary of Scots? The foul murder of a Queen? His mouth gapes in an unbecoming manner. The gentleman quite resembles my own cousin's slobbering hound.

Her Majesty casts aside her desperate plot, in answer to Davison's startling assertion. "Too late? That cannot be. We squander one Queen's life and another's soul, Sir. Do as I say, and immediately. Fetch that document. On pain of death, do it man."

Her Majesty returns from her perilous reverie. Her presence breeds a menace in the Withdrawing Chamber. A chill invades our company, and we all hunch over a little. I grasp hold of my elbows. My arms wrap round myself as though my own embrace might protect me from my Queen's threat.

But the steel of her eye lands on Davison alone. Petrified by the sheer engagement of her will, he hesitates. The pair's concentration on each other results in an awkward quiet. I fear his distraught monarch outmatches Davison.

"Your Majesty, I do all in my power to serve you, but I cannot retrieve the document. The Great Seal is appended. The warrant has already gone to Fotheringay..." This truthful man provokes. Her Majesty, consumed with anxious worry, does not seek plain speaking.

"Go then. To the Tower." Spoken low, so guttural with rage, the guards do not immediately step forth. "My Lord you have murdered one Queen, and plunged a steely blade through the beating heart of another." Her Majesty's lips tighten as she hisses her accusation at the befuddled Davison.

"Remove him now." Her Majesty's command curdles the air we breathe, making it painful to inhale.

Several gasps meet her command. Her Majesty casts her glance about the room. All of us hover in mid-movement. Her Majesty's outrage gathers momentum.

A vibration, like the undetectable force lifting a lioness's hairs on her arched back, springs forth from Her Majesty's person. "Get him out!"

A flinch spreads, like a contagion, from one to all within the chamber. Eventually, it frees us to answer our Queen's command. Her Majesty's bristling energy wakens our uncooperative limbs, moving us around the room in a chaotic dance of fright. Her Majesty's guards leap at Davison. A blameless messenger bears the brunt of a monarch's disfavour.

***

8th February, 1587 2:00 p.m.

I scribble in my journal, pretending an easy fluency. Tucked away at my desk, I conceal myself in silence. My Queen's ladies-in-waiting gossip as though Her Majesty's diarist does not dwell amongst them.

Weighty consequences will follow my covert vigil. I pay a high toll for my eavesdropping. In return for my lurking among them, they bestow on the Queen's Keeper of the Books, unwelcome news. The Council ignores my Queen's longed for wish. My faithful quill shudders for Her Majesty.

"It came to pass at Fotheringhay Castle, this morning. And all within doors, I am told." Lady Charlotte's cousin, Lord Thomas, witnessed the momentous event this morning. Lady Charlotte claims for herself all the status her painstaking details bestow.

"Within doors?"

"Why yes. The scaffold took up much of the chamber. It measured a full twelve foot square, and stood two foot high. All covered in creamy linen. The Scots woman required assistance climbing up to it." Lady Charlotte's lids flutter as she shuts her eyes and lifts one knee, attempting to ascend an imaginary flight of stairs.

Her arms, fingers pointed outward, rest on invisible attendants' shoulders. Lady Charlotte enjoys her limited celebrity too much, I dare say.

"And what of the beastly woman's demeanour? Did she dare to lash out at our Queen?" Lady Beatrice, the youngest in the small cluster of women, interrupts the folding of Her Majesty's hose in order to whisper her flurry of inquiries.

Lady Charlotte basks in the younger woman's curiosity. Beatrice's rapt attention acts as an insistent nudge on Lady Charlotte's bent head.

"Not at all, according to Thomas. The conniving woman thanked her accusers for ending all her troubles. Her greatest concern was for her polished crucifix, her pomander beads and all her idols she carted along with her to meet her popish God. The Earl of Kent advised her she ought to carry the cross of Christ in her heart rather than in her hand. You know how the devout Catholics cling to their superstitions. Woe upon any who attempt to take back their precious idols." Charlotte, her eyes open wide, places one pointer finger on top of the other, forming a cross. She rotates her fingers until they form a forbidding X. Lady Beatrice rewards her friend with a helpless giggle, hidden not at all behind her cupped hand.

"I am told the brazen woman rejected our Protestant Dean's prayers." Lady Margaret, the eldest in the group, interjects. As the most devout Protestant lady, she possesses an abiding distaste for the Catholic Scottish Queen.

"Not only that. The Stuart woman spoke her Catholic devotions with a loud voice over top our Dean's, even as he attempted to bless her."

"The boorishness of the woman."

"...and she prayed on the scaffold for the conversion of England and Scotland to her popish faith."

Lady Charlotte and Lady Margaret tip their brows downward and shake their heads in mutual disapproval.

"I heard of weeping and carrying on." Lady Beatrice, tiring of the Scots Queen's devotional habits, leads Charlotte back to the site of the execution. Her ladies follow with little encouragement.

"Yes. But not of the Scots woman's making. Gathered round her were an abundance of servants who carried on with great lamentation for the Catholic whore."

"Do not speak in such a coarse manner. Not of the dead." A brief silence ensues, all the ladies respecting Lady Margaret's fulsome sense of propriety.

Lady Charlotte grimaces with only a little chagrin, before acknowledging her error. "I beg pardon. But I cannot pledge a whit of sympathy for the Catholic Scots Queen. She might have ruled over all England. What if our fearless Queen had not stayed the murderous woman's plot?"

"It is said the Executioner laid his hand on her." Lady Beatrice, with her interruption, leads the ladies in her direction once more. Her youthful curiosity dwells in the most vile regions.

"On a Queen?" The elderly Lady Margaret sits up to attention, so shocked is she by the younger's revelation.

"Yes. Apparently he pulled off her doublet. Her neck and throat shone like craggy alabaster for all to see. There were hundreds there, you know. So Thomas says." Another allusion to her faithful witness. Lady Charlotte returns to her comfortable role as crier of sordid details. On and on she tells it.

"...A ghastly business. Fortunate for her, her women were there. Though she mightn't have deserved it. One of her ladies tied a handkerchief over her eyes, and still she kept up her pitiful praying to her Catholic God."

"What of her death? Was it an easy one then?" The youthful Lady Beatrice knows no shame. She ceases her folding altogether as the meat of the conversation emerges.

"Thomas tells me it took three full strokes to sever a Scots Queen's head. And still the lips fluttered for a full quarter of an hour after. The horrid woman prayed to her popish idols even after her own death." Lady Charlotte shuts her mischievous eyes. She tilts her head to one side as though it hangs by a thread, and mimics a devout whispering. The others reward her with their laughter.

"More proof yet she was a demon." Lady Margaret states her case with fulsome purpose. According to our Lady Margaret, The Queen of Scots cavorted with Satan himself.

"The Executioner pronounced, *God save Queen Elizabeth! May all the enemies of the true Evangel thus perish!*" Then he removed the dead Queen's dress of lawn..." Gasps from her small audience place a wide grin on Lady Charlotte's countenance.

"Removed it?"

"Do you know what he discovered beneath? Her hair shorn like a prized ewe. What remained on her head...pasty as an unbaked English tart shell. White as can be."

"So much for the auburn beauty..." Lady Beatrice trails off as Charlotte casts a warning glance her way. She will brook no impudent interruption.

"Thomas says her expression changed with such drastic measure, she became unrecognizable to all the gathering."

"A demon, as I said..." Lady Margaret's sage pronouncement once more. Her ladies dare not question her wisdom in matters of such spiritual significance.

***

9th February, 1587, 9:00 a.m.

If toothache and nagging pain at her temple troubled Her Majesty before, my faithful pen can hardly transcribe the affliction plaguing my Grace now the Scots Queen has breathed her last.

The message arrives on the morning of February 8th. Her Majesty looks down at it and cries out. It is an agonizing, plaintive call, as though my Queen's own neck feels the blade descend there.

Surely her remorseful wails echo round to all England's borders. Her inconsolable pain could awaken Her Majesty's subjects well past London's harried streets and laneways. Beyond, into pastoral lands in the counties, my Queen's agony registers.

Her Grace writhes in her distress. Beneath ill-fitting layers of taffeta and silk, her skin crawls with guilt's gnawing bites.

Her Majesty scratches at her limbs. She tears at her head's pretty curls until handfuls of silken hair lie within her clenched up fists. I fear she tries to scrape away with her fingernails, an act that brings damnation on her soul.

We attempt to comfort our Queen with whispers of condolence. Those of us more brazen, offer an errant touch. She refuses all our care. She sends us from her. She demands only solitude. Her Majesty sets alight, with a glowing rage, any who cast their shadow in her chamber's doorway. The entire Court scampers for shelter when mournful cries issue forth from her bedchamber.

Her Majesty's fury feeds, while her slender body starves itself of sustenance. While my Queen's rage fuels itself on an unknown source, not a crumb passes her parched lips. My Majesty will not eat. Nor does a hint of needed sleep offer her the respite she so needs. My Queen dares not sleep. She fears our Lord will claim her in return for the terrible sin she has committed.

Her Grace paces her chamber's floor hour after blessed hour. Her frenzy radiates. It heats Her Majesty's rooms until we no longer feel as though we dwell within our Northern Island's climate. Her fury emits a brilliant glow. Her Majesty's chamber at nightfall almost glimmers as though fully lit. I fear that Her Majesty's touch, once so comforting to those fortunate enough to receive it, would scorch any who venture near her.

Across England, rejoicing echoes through the streets. Her Majesty's cries of mourning respond. She shrouds her pounding head in blackened veils. Her mouth, all bent in an unhappy grimace, hides beneath the sheaths of mourning. We watch her with frustrated loyalty. Her Majesty does not trust any of her ladies enough to accept a condoling word.

I remain Her Majesty's obedient subject. But I wonder at my Lady's grief. I do not know what she mourns. A Scots Queen's life? An English Queen's reputation? Or an Elizabeth's condemned soul?

***

Baron Burghley must possess either an overabundance of courage or in his elderly foolhardiness, he forgets himself. The gentleman requests an attendance with Her Majesty in her Withdrawing Chamber. Surely her Sir Spirit will be the next to wince at the sting of Her Majesty's ire.

"Baron Burghley wishes to attend his Queen?" Beneath Her Majesty's veils I detect movement of an eyebrow upward. "Does he wander so far from his wits? Have I not made my wishes known? Hatton, Walsingham, Leicester and Burghley are forbidden from my presence. I fear what I would do with them, were I to behold their traitorous faces. Given leave, I might hang each by the neck, and before my own ravenous eye." Her attendant receives Her Majesty's reply, bowing low. As the servant prepares to take his leave, his message to convey, the chamber door opens.

"Your Majesty." The gentleman appears.

God's Death. I cannot comprehend his boldness. None other than Baron Burghley bows before Her Majesty. Today, of all days, he chooses to defy his Queen. I fear for all our necks.

Her Majesty, betraying little of her distress, addresses her Lord Treasurer. "Ah, our courageous leader. The same one who snatches away his Queen's hope for a little of God's grace. I return his letters unopened and unread. But this is not refusal enough. He would, for some peculiar reason, dare to believe I desire to look on him. In this, my Lord, you are unhappily mistaken." Her Majesty, buried in layers of blackened silks, retreats further into the confines of her throne. She cannot escape far enough from Baron Burghley's presence.

"Your Grace, if only for a moment..." The elderly Burghley pleads with his Queen, as does a father, whose errant child wanders far from her family's loving fold. But Her Majesty's wrath gathers. It shows no hint of abating for her Lord Treasurer. I fear our Queen falls under the spell of a vengeful conjurer.

"Though commanded to steer far from your Queen's chamber door, still with reckless limp, you approach. Does your advanced age not lend you more sense, Sir?" A glimmer beneath the veils. Her Majesty's eye, glaring at Sir Cecil, fills with tears. Tiny jewels glisten on her cheek.

Burghley, his head bowed in obedience, takes no notice. "Your Grace. I ask only for an opportunity to plead before you our wholesome intent..."

"Very well. Your persistence, and let us not neglect your purity of motive, betters your Queen's yet again. Let us have at it. How does it feel, My Lord, to rupture, with the purest purpose, your Queen's heart while still it beats within her tender chest?" All goes deathly quiet in the Withdrawing Chamber. I swear I hear the broken heartbeat Her Majesty alludes to.

"Your Majesty, I beg you to hear me… For the first time in many years, you reign safe on your throne…"

"Ah, I understand my Sir Spirit. It is your Queen who is remiss in this affair." Her Majesty gazes about the chamber, addressing an absent audience. She pretends to declare her fault in the matter. I fear my Queen's sincerity falters.

"So I should offer gratitude to my Sir Spirit? And to my Lords Walsingham and Hatton? And I cannot neglect our dutiful Lord Davison. How should I signify my pleasure? Patents for all? Land grants perhaps? Or an increased allowance? I am afraid I do not fully agree with your assessment, my Lord Treasurer. I might suggest your Queen is owed some heads for all her trouble."

Her Majesty peruses the Chamber, seeking fellow-feeling. Her ladies hunker down. Tilted chins erase their necks as they press hard on quivering chests. The ladies resemble a flock of pigeons, huddling within the confines of St. Paul's churchyard. Their tiny hearts race against blustery gusts.

"Your Grace, your loyal servants carried out our duty. It was always with the aim of preventing harm from befalling Your Majesty. Your protection remains our chief concern. The Scots woman would not demur. She did, with constant evil-doing, seek to occupy your throne…"

Her Majesty carries on as though Baron Burghley does not speak. "How did Davison enter into it? Perhaps Walsingham's illness and your unfortunate fall from your saddle were of a convenient nature? Meant to excuse your direct involvement so you could arrange a Queen's downfall behind the scene? Well, you have succeeded. Davison remains the sole conspirator occupying the Tower..."

"Your Majesty, your faithful counselors serve you with loyalty, as we always have..." I pray Baron Burghley does not lose patience now. He sighs with irritation just as his neck depends on his tempering his emotion.

"Loyalty and faith. Is this how you portray your little plot? Your Queen names it something else. Your Queen might, on her own tongue, try the taste of..."

Her Majesty hesitates. She searches for a vivid description of her gentlemen's betrayal. She lulls us all into a disconcerting quiet. Until in the next moment, she springs from her throne. My Queen rushes to Burghley, her skirts slapping the cobbled floor, her complexion tinged with rage. The old gentleman falters, rocking backward on his heels. He raises his elbow up, should she strike.

But my Queen's tongue delivers the only blow. "Traitor. False dissembler. Wicked wretch. How do you like my rendering, Sir? How could you, of all my counselors, betray me thus?"

Beneath Her Majesty's veil, jewels rain down. They dampen the bodice of my Majesty's gown. My Queen ignores the deluge. She stands before her Lord Treasurer. Her malice causes the pleated veil on her head and face to quiver as she speaks.

Baron Burghley draws backward, away from Her Majesty's attack. But he asserts his position once more. "We did not plot against you, Your Grace. We only sought your security on England's throne..."

"Ah, but you did, Sir. I expressly warned Davison to keep hold of the signed Order. Those too eager to wait on a Queen's conscience seized it in their own hands. They took it to Fotheringay for their own purposes. You committed this atrocity in your Queen's name. Do you know what they label your Queen all over Europe?"

"No, Your Majesty." Sir Cecil's head bends. Compliant, he awaits Her Majesty's next volley.

"I am the Heretic. The Jezebel. France speaks of your monarch as a bastard, and a shameless harlot. I have murdered a Queen."

"Your Majesty..."

"And I have my trusted counselors to thank. I do not know which to fear more. My people's hatred or my God's shunning. What have you done to your Queen, Sir Cecil?" Her Majesty no longer embodies the raging monarch. She turns from her Sir Spirit, retreating into her throne where she weeps openly.

"With respect Your Grace, we have secured your throne. Forgive me, but I cannot repent. I feel only pride in our protection of our beloved sovereign." Burghley kneels before Her Majesty in obedience, but his words belie it. They cut.

"Get out, Sir. You go too far with your boastful declaration. Your Queen mourns her cousin, whom you and I myself have killed. If you cannot respect your Queen's command, you will honour her desire to grieve in private. Without the eyes of a traitor on her. Leave us." Her Majesty looks away from her Lord Treasurer, signaling his departure.

Burghley's brow twitches. He flinches with the sting of his Queen's redress. With some difficulty, he rises up before her. Sir Cecil studies his sovereign's profile for a long moment before limping toward the chamber door. He entered an elderly gentleman, but I fear he leaves an older one yet.

***

22nd February, 1587

A fortnight passes and little alters. Her Majesty wanders Richmond Palace. The rustling of her mourning weeds remain as muted as their wearer. My Queen waves away all our company. She sniffs at then pushes her tiny meals back to her waiting servants. She drifts through palace corridors, an apparition, while we sleep. She persists in haunting her favourite chamber within her warm tower, accompanied only by her little books, all full of enormous ideas. Seneca, Aristotle and Plato distract her from her suffering. *Evil brings men together*. My Majesty grieves in solitude.

Her Majesty believes her beloved people abandon her. I hear word from all about Court, and ache to tell her otherwise. If my Queen would only listen to my assurances. Her people rejoice at a Scots Queen's beheading. Freedom from popish insurrection lifts the daily cares of her people. All England makes merry with feasting and revelries the likes of which I have not seen in many years. The dusty streets become impassable, so filled are they with happy citizens lifting tankards to toast my Queen. My countrymen find themselves waking to the crow of the cock, out of doors. They so enjoy their cups night and day, their empty glass of ale sits by them, their only companion to the dawn.

Yet, while her citizens toast Queen Elizabeth, their monarch grieves. So small she becomes. Slouched within her throne. Hidden beneath mourning layers. Her head throbs with a humiliation only she comprehends.

"Why?" Her Majesty inquires of her little books, "...why does there exist this gaping gulf between the goodness we know to be right, and the darkness hovering all round our hearts?" Though she thumbs the pages of her favoured philosophers, the ancient masters ignore her pleas. Cruel silence their only reply.

Winter I - Death of a Dream

But who to love can give a law, Love
unto love itself is law.

-- Boethius

6th March, 1588

Her Majesty banishes me for weeks. This separation causes me a great deal of sorrow. Then at last she invites me back into her daily presence. I am grateful to bask in my Queen's favour again, even if it is only to hear Her Majesty argue her point on the traitorous Scots woman.

"I know I am not a lion like my father, Blanche. But England *will* pay for the murder of a Catholic Scots Queen." Her Majesty taps her fingers on the arm of her throne. It has been many weeks since I have observed my Majesty's anxious habit. I celebrate its unhappy drum.

"Your Majesty, with respect, the Council only sought to secure your life…"

"We have heard this before." A dismissive wave of her hand. A hint of a rancorous tone invades Her Majesty's voice. Does she lose patience with me so soon?

"Listen to me, my dear. We run round and round this argument until we pant with our efforts. But in the end, our words fare no better than leaves in autumn. They flutter down and collect with abundance. Then they cover the honest earth in their brilliant subterfuge. Only truth remains steadfast, Blanche. All plain. And buried deep beneath the showy dance of colour. Where most of us keep our awful truths…"

"Forgive me, Your Grace. I do not wish to cause you distress…"

"You are forgiven." The tender smile I have missed brightens Her Majesty's features. "I understand my cousin plotted against my throne. I know she represented Philip's and the Catholics' goals. Popish control of England."

"Your Majesty, if you comprehend so well the threat of the Scots woman, why do you suffer like this with her death?"

The lengthy pause that follows my query makes me fear a slap might reward my impertinence. I balk a little, turning my cheek aside. I behave more like a skittish mare, awaiting the inevitable lash of the tail o' nines. But Her Majesty remains awash in a magnanimity I have not witnessed for many months.

"Blanche, a Queen's conscience may be known only to herself." Her Majesty glances away from me, toward the chamber doorway. Does she expect the approaching footsteps of her gentlemen? None arrives to disturb us, but the brief interruption in her train of thought provides a respite. Her Majesty hides her genuine feeling. *Video, Taceo - I see all and say nothing.* Though I sense my Queen wishes to unburden herself, she daren't do it. Her crown's metallic stoicism repels her faithful servant's concern.

"…I learn each day to accept the horrific deed as mine. My lack of resolve did it. I am certain."

Strangely, Her Majesty's confession does not weigh on her delicate shoulder. Instead, her acceptance seems to improve her confidence. Unlike her former self, she sits tall within her coveted throne. She surveys all England with a mother owl's unruffled stateliness. Time, though it cannot fully repair all life's injuries, offers Her Majesty a soothing salve. And yet, a dormant festering continues to plague her.

"My conscience twists and turns with a great unease, Blanche. My gentlemen sought to protect their monarch from an enemy within our kingdom, but they have managed to prod a sleeping foe outside the realm. The death of a Catholic Queen has awakened a lurking enemy." Her Majesty's skittish fingers, at rest for some time, resume their searching for her throne's arm. I hear the clicking of Her Majesty's fingernails as they signal the distress she attempts to hide.

"You speak of King Philip, Your Majesty?"

"Indeed. While Mary Stuart lived, Spain clung to their hope that a French-Catholic Scots woman would soon replace England's Protestant mistress."

"A silly dream at best…"

"…Nevertheless, Philip's spirited aspirations worked in our best interest. He imagined our people welcoming the Pope to England, arms all open in greeting. My faithless enemy served me well while she lived. Mary Stuart fostered a King of Spain's childish hope: A Catholic England; and his own galleons all safe in a Spanish port." Her Majesty scoffs. "And now? We have murdered both a sitting Queen of Scotland, and a King's waking dream, I estimate."

While Her Majesty converses with me as though I occupy her entirely, I do not claim all her attention. Behind her conciliatory eye many thoughts collide. But what does she withhold? It does not trouble me that I represent little more than a diversion. A fraction of Her Majesty's consideration feels better than none at all. I have suffered such lonesomeness these several days as my Queen, alone in her Privy Chamber, mourned Queen Mary Stuart.

"Your Grace, what *will* King Philip do? Now we have rid England of the Scottish Queen? Is it possible the Spanish might hazard a strike?"

Her Majesty glances again toward the chamber doorway. "We have succeeded in sheltering our realm for a considerable time. For eighteen years we declawed a Catholic Queen. And Drake unmanned her dark mate, the Spanish King Philip. On the open seas, Sir Francis plagued Spain's fleets. He ensured the Spanish cargoes from the Americas did not arrive in Madrid. But my Council and my Parliament seek other methods for thwarting the Spanish. I hope my gentlemen have not triumphed too well in their cunning ways. They now possess a Scots Queen's head. I only pray their own Queen's head remains firmly planted on her dainty shoulders."

Her Majesty leans forward on her throne, emphasizing her point with an upward thrust of her torso. Her Grace brings almost three decades of peace to England. Though an uneasy peace for our monarch.

"I pray every night for your long and prosperous life, Your Grace." I curtsey, bow my head, and lace my hands together in prayer. When did Her Majesty and I become so formal in our banter? As our propriety increases, our ease slips away. Each orchestrated gesture drives a greater wedge between us.

Her Majesty reads my thought. "Why all this somber talk? Why not celebrate with our good citizens the newfound security we enjoy? The terrible deed is committed. It cannot be undone. Your Queen cannot repent a thing forever. My conscience must occasionally slumber." Her Majesty leans toward me, her slim torso tipping forward. Smiling her encouragement, she takes hold of my hand and squeezes.

"Let us congratulate ourselves. We have snatched from Philip his most satisfying wish. I have stayed past my welcome, though a mighty Spanish King desires me gone. This victory offers your Queen tremendous pleasure."

Another benign smile. Her Majesty parts the curtain and illuminates the chamber with her pleasure. I am blessed.

***

9th November, 1587

King Philip offers his reply with his weaponry. Walsingham's spies tell us the Armada prepares at Lisbon. We do not know when the Spanish galleons are set to sail, but one hundred and thirty ships sit ready, and thirty thousand sailors man them. All of Spain's disappointment faces toward England's shores.

Her Majesty's gentlemen, like eager hounds baying at their elegant, red-coated master, call on their Queen. Their one wish? A taste of the fox's blood. Philip's lurking at England's shores taunts their keen sense of the enemy's scent.

When Her Majesty's Home Defense Council arrives at Whitehall, my Queen, with her typical grace, poses before the Tudor family portrait in her Presence Chamber. Though Her Majesty does not admit it, she exploits the powerful impact her father's image provides. She takes comfort in knowing he hovers just over her dainty shoulder.

Her Grace's grandfather, Henry VII, on the left, balances his wife, Elizabeth of York on the right; and a favourite stepmother of my Queen, Jane Seymour, makes a pair with our King Henry VIII. Holbein, the wily artist, provides for Her Majesty an effective backdrop. The life-sized mural depicts a host of Tudor relations, though one, as always, dominates the tableau.

I survey the gentlemen as they charge into the room. Their eyes do not focus immediately on their living Queen, nor do they study the royal grouping. Always, they turn, with an irresistible pull, to King Henry VIII's fulsome figure. The collective gaze travels directly to his belligerent stance. From his magnificent jeweled and padded shoulders to the clenched fists on his sturdy hips. The dagger on his thigh receives a brief, anxious bit of attention from everyone.

The Earl of Leicester, Lord Robert Dudley, looks away from the knife, toward King Henry's prominent codpiece. The lusty detail proves difficult to avoid. I have witnessed some ambassadors - the French in particular - sneaking a glance at its largesse, before ending on His Majesty's wide spread thighs. Just as our King would have it. The belligerent pose of a hero standing his ground, prepared to strike forth in battle.

Those of us who knew King Henry best also know that by the age of two score and five, his stature was not what it had been in his youth. But Holbein, in his artful rendering, makes it appear otherwise. The royal portrait maker well understood his monarch's wishes. France and all Europe will be made to acknowledge Henry VIII's commanding virility.

And now, Her Majesty borrows Holbein's message. She speaks to her gentlemen as they enter. And without uttering a single word: *Do not forget who you meet. Before you stands a Tudor Queen. Daughter of a mighty lion. And though a woman only, still an imposing huntress.*

Her Majesty goes further yet. She mimics her ancestors' regal stance. My Queen places her fine hands, one on the other, on top of the velvet bell of her gown. Her knees remain, with required modesty, pressed together. Her gaze too, is Henry's. One eyebrow raised, her intense grey eye focused on theirs, Her Majesty stares on the rabble entering her Presence Chamber. Not one, but three monarchs greet the gentlemen. The Henrys, captured for always, offer their perpetual support for a granddaughter, a daughter, a live Tudor Queen.

Walsingham, Burghley, Leicester, Hatton and Wooley might expect to hear their long departed King's booming salutation. Here, Her Majesty diverges. She welcomes them instead with a motherly concern. She lulls them into finding similarity where substantial difference exists.

"Please enter, gentlemen. Does Sir Francis Drake not join your party? I have summoned him to us here." Her hands flutter from their resting place on her gown. She opens them in a gesture of warmth. While likenesses of family members emphasize the might of her throne, Her Majesty enjoys a more indulgent approach.

It has taken several months, but my Queen offers forgiveness to her counselors. Her Sir Spirit, Baron Burghley, appears humbled by Her Majesty's grace. This past June she visited with Sir Cecil at Theobalds for a full three weeks, at which time she reinstated the Lord Treasurer in his fatherly role. Sir Cecil says little of his Queen's visit, other than to note *Charity is nowhere more becoming than in a prince.* Both Her Majesty and Sir Cecil find Reason trumps fickle passion. Both benefit from the harsh lesson they have learned.

"He follows close behind, Your Majesty." Sir Cecil's head swings round at the clang of the chamber door shutting. The diminutive Sir Francis Drake bustles in, lighting the chamber with his charming grin. The arc of his smile divides the ruddy bush of his mustache from the coarse beard at his chin.

"Your Majesty." A sweeping bow. The glorified pirate, who my Queen still calls her *merchant adventurer,* lifts his plumed hat and with an ease belonging to the favoured, returns it close to his breast.

"Sir Francis Drake. We cannot begin to express our pleasure in your return." Her Majesty offers her hand to the ruffian, smiles as he bends to it with an awkward grace, and continues her gushing praise. "We have heard Cadiz was a great success. We look forward to hearing more of your adventures at sea."

The remaining gentlemen, all gathered round to witness, react with various expressions. Walsingham and Leicester, great supporters of Drake and happy recipients of their share of the pirate's booty, celebrate with their Queen. The others, particularly Sir Cecil, appear constrained. They watch the little drama unfold with diplomatic quiet.

"We must express our immeasurable gratitude for your exploits at Cadiz, Sir. Philip's losses are England's gains. I understand from Walsingham your successes postpone Philip's looming Armada for six months at least. We thank you, sincerely. We will embark, as I have always aimed, on further negotiations with the King of Spain to make his violent plans for England's overthrow wholly unnecessary. This is as your Queen wishes it."

"Your Majesty, negotiations have been years in the making, and still King Philip plots England's demise. Philip calls on Sixtus V to forward him funds so Spain and her doting Pope can kneel on England's exposed throat. Though Master Drake provides us with months at best, he does not turn Spain's interest away from England altogether." Walsingham's willingness to share his espionage splashes an unwelcome chill on Her Majesty's reception of Sir Francis Drake. To my surprise, the pirate joins forces with her plain-speaking Moor.

"I agree with Lord Walsingham, Your Majesty. Though I heartily enjoyed singeing the King of Spain's beard yet again..."

The jubilant Earl of Leicester interrupts Drake's celebratory mood. "I have heard King Philip was incensed about your recent looting. He became so warm about the collar, his golden crucifix reddened with heat, and branded his puffed up chest. Santa Cruz's own flagship destroyed? Thirty-seven more sunk, burned or sailed straight into England's ports?" The Gypsy chuckles, and rests his hand on Drake's shoulder.

The Gypsy celebrates more than just a pirate's successful exploits. Her Majesty has fetched him back from the Netherlands especially to confront her growing Spanish problem. Like Sir Cecil, her Bonny Sweet Robin appreciates his own return to favour. Contentment becomes him. But as he slaps the compact shoulder of Drake with his left hand, his right goes with unconscious haste to his abdomen. A negligible wince tightens his features before his gracious smile relights. Still he encourages his Queen with the warmth of his enduring fondness.

Drake returns the Earl of Leicester's good humour, but in measured tones. He smiles on the Earl before regaining his Queen's attention. "….I advise we prepare in England immediately. And most by sea. Stop him now, Your Grace, and stop him forever." Sir Francis Drake, at first shoulder to shoulder with Leicester, saunters nearer to Her Majesty's throne. He bends before her, all solicitude. But his eye holds my Queen's with unbridled confidence. The kind my Queen prefers.

Not a Moor, a Gypsy, nor a Pirate can convince their Monarch. Her Majesty's desire to avoid her father's style of rule eclipses her fear of Philip's looming galleons.

I wonder at the sweetness of this quirk of fate. The paradoxical nature of my Queen's decision. In her enduring quest for a peaceful England, Her Majesty runs contrary to her Council, her Parliament, and her beloved subjects. Yet Her Grace remains unafraid. In my humble estimation, my Queen reveals more courage in her quest for harmony than all her surrounding counselors who in their pack, yearn for an enemy's running blood.

"Remember, Sirs, with whom you speak. Has not your Queen always sought to keep England from engaging in these dreadful acts of war? Less careful Kings give in to such temptation. Not I. Why should I send my sons to war, when I might settle Philip's forbidding temper with some cordial talk?"

Walsingham, losing patience with his Queen, rushes toward her throne. "Cordial talk, Your Majesty? Is King Philip one of your ladies who pays visit? You do not suggest Spain will engage in such play? I cannot comprehend your hesitation. Perhaps you continue to suffer the effects of the Scots Queen's death?"

The chamber, previously animated with the to and fro of amicable discussion, goes still as my Queen rises up before them. Walsingham's candour, often tolerated by Her Majesty, receives a blunt rebuke. "Do not mention that, Sir. That is done. Mary Stuart no longer troubles us. Davison is released from the Tower, as you all wished. I have forgiven those who betrayed me..." Her Majesty cannot resist a glance toward Sir Cecil, who lowers his head in response. "My decision has nothing to do with the Scots woman."

Her Majesty's tone, tempered in its volume, holds a crisp precision demanding caution. While most of my Queen's counselors take heed, mimicking Sir Cecil's passive stance with bent heads, Walsingham chooses to disregard her warning.

"Your Majesty, England must prepare for war. It is inevitable. King Philip only negotiates with us while his navy in Cadiz licks its wounds." Walsingham casts a terse nod of appreciation to Drake, who grins in reply. "Spain will attack our shores. We must prepare."

"We sympathize with your apprehension, Lord Walsingham. England should prepare for the worst." Her counselors lift their bowed heads. They shuffle with a tentative hope their Queen might relent. Her Grace takes the opportunity to press her point. "Your Queen chooses to negotiate with Spain so long as the chance of a peaceful outcome remains."

Her Majesty stares hard at Walsingham. To stress her point, she returns to her throne. Three sharp taps ring out on her throne's arm. Her Majesty strikes it with the emerald ring on her pointer finger.

"As to your advice Lord Walsingham, though we place great value on plain speaking, we counsel you to restrain yourself in your manner. We appreciate honest words, but there is a point at which your Queen must place the period. My beloved subjects deserve their Queen's protection, and they will have it."

Sensing Walsingham's difficulty, Drake re-enters the fray. Perhaps the pirate in him cannot resist the unwinnable battle.

"Your Majesty, the advantage of time and place in all martial actions is half the victory. You must prepare for war, even if you do not intend to embark on it. I would not speak with such boldness if I hadn't the success to back my hard words."

"Gentlemen, Baron Burghley will enlighten you with our Treasury's pitiable state. England cannot muster the resources of Spain. Master Drake succeeds beyond all expectation..." A glance of recognition toward the pirate, who preens in his Queen's attention. "...and still King Philip loads his monstrous galleons with tons of metals from the Americas. And do not forget Spain's friends in Rome, who place a hefty price on your Queen's head. If we engage King Philip, our David meets a mighty Goliath. One we cannot topple with England's little slingshot." My Queen looks away from those who contradict her, toward her Lord Treasurer.

Sir Cecil struggles with the effort of straightening his bent form. His gout troubles him today. "I am of the same mind as Her Majesty, gentlemen. England's resources are limited. Our armies wanting." At last he utters a conviction conducive to Her Majesty's waiting ear. She rewards her Sir Spirit's efforts with a triumphant nod and a warm smile.

"What of *Drake's* recent contributions?" The Earl of Leicester, his sore side forgotten, breaks in. "What of Cadiz? Can we not muster a fleet with these funds?"

Sir Cecil sighs at the Earl's recklessness. He wonders how little the man changes, though the years add weight to the Gypsy's girth, and several chins to his countenance. Her Majesty answers for him.

"Gentlemen, still you do not care to hear your Queen when she speaks. The infamous Italian says it best. *War is a gamble.* Your Queen will do all she can to prevent wagering her own sons in the game. Attempt another way."

"Your Majesty, there is no other option. Philip's ships will come whether you wish it or not. When they do, England must be prepared." Walsingham persists. Relentless Moor.

Her Majesty sighs. Like her Gypsy, her Moor does not mellow with age. Walsingham cannot contain his opinions, even following his Queen's caution.

"I will enlighten you, gentlemen. Before you dash off to commit another crime in your Queen's name." Her reference to the Scots woman adds a sharpness to Her Majesty's formerly lenient tone. She hesitates as she studies her Moor. Her Majesty grows irritated with his brazenness, but she cannot deny his loyal service.

"Make yourselves comfortable gentlemen, while I explain to you my mind on this matter." Her Majesty gestures toward a table constructed of heavy walnut timbers around which are gathered her counselors' broad chairs. "Be seated. Though your Queen may squander her breath in telling it, at least I will comfort myself with the knowledge I attempted it."

Her Majesty rises from her throne. She stands in front of her favourite portrait once more, returning to the fold of her waiting family. She poses so close to her beloved relatives the gentlemen blink once or twice to clear their faltering vision. Henry VII looks down on her with the delight of a doting grandfather. But his is not the support my Queen seeks. Her Majesty shifts her position, until it appears she stands posed within the portrait itself. My Queen glides across it, edging nearer to her father. Having gained her place next to King Henry VIII, Her Majesty poises herself to summon her gentlemen's collective ear.

"I have endeavoured throughout my reign to earn my English subjects' love above all else. In my heart, I consider myself Mother to my people, and nothing means more to your Queen than to preserve a peaceful realm for all. The security of my people is everything to me."

Her Majesty stands so near her father, she could reach for his jeweled hand and cradle it within her own. The gentlemen, all silent at their long table, appear transfixed by this image of their Queen. One moment she appears to pose within the portrait, and then she sidles alongside it, reminding them of her continued presence.

One persistent voice interrupts her performance.

"Your Majesty, we understand all of this. You speak of it often ..." The heedless Moor interrupts for a third time.

As the Earl of Leicester, Sir Cecil, and Francis Drake gape at Walsingham's unrelenting audacity, Her Majesty at last puts an end to it. Her Grace's voice rises above the gentlemen's quiet murmurs. All heads snap to attention as their Queen's command issues forth. "Be silent, my Lord. Your Queen speaks." The lash of her voice on the stillness resembles Her Majesty's riding crop, slapping hard on her favourite mare's haunch.

Her Moor finally joins the hush in the chamber. He slouches, quiet in his black robes, a sullen expression hovers on his countenance. It is rare anyone silences Walsingham.

"I loathe your request for war, Sirs. Every whisper of it scrapes at your Queen's conscience. The people of England are my own sons and daughters. The young soldier, who takes up his sword to march with a noble naiveté from his family home, causes my poor heart to ache within my breast. He abandons *me,* his own mother. I weep as he goes..."

Walsingham makes as if to rise in complaint, but Sir Cecil presses a hand on his forearm. Her Majesty's gaze, previously on her Council, looks inward. Unaware of Walsingham's and Burghley's exchange, she carries on.

"...every mother who shrieks and falls to her knees on learning of the slaughter of her beloved son makes her Queen a grieving grandmother. I shed tears for my daughters' cruel loss. How do you not understand? Where do your hearts reside, if not with your Queen?" Her Majesty glares hard at her gentlemen but her form trembles. Her family, posed behind her, remains unmoved in its infinite stance. Deaf to Her Majesty's plea, the portrait's figures stare out in the comfort of their dynastic supremacy. King Henry's imposing form lingers next to his breathing daughter, but he offers no sympathy or guidance.

Her gentlemen's heads bow low. The proud Walsingham will not meet Her Majesty's accusing eye. All cower as their fretful Queen defends her insupportable position. As the gentlemen remain seated, heads bent, they resemble a wayward gathering of rebellious children, made to atone for some mischievous wrongdoing. Shamed by a Mother's pitiable indictment.

***

I confess Sir Francis Walsingham is not the only loyal servant to burden his Queen's conscience. I too add to Her Majesty's weighty concerns.

Her Grace changes as the months pass. I know she often envisions herself an actor on her own prestigious stage. How she loves to don resplendent costumes and feathery masks. My Queen portrays a variety of characters at her whim. But now Her Majesty changes with ever greater frequency. My distress mounts as I wonder which of my Queens will appear when I awaken each day.

Entering Her Majesty's chamber in the early hours, I curtsey before her. Her Majesty returns my greeting with a gracious smile. Energized with her daily exercise, her cheek pink with the heat of all her strenuous movement, Her Majesty resembles our Lady Elizabeth of years past.

But following thirty minutes of reading her correspondence, or after conferring with Council on the approach of the Spanish galleons, Her Majesty retreats so far into her own constant worry, I do not recognize her. Her lovely complexion, all aglow with rosy warmth, turns sallow. The grey shadows under her eyes match the deadened tone of her iris. A preoccupied scowl pulls her lips downward. And what of her gentle tone? It turns sharp, filled with a suspicion I do not recognize as my Queen's.

"Blanche?"

Her Majesty calls out to me. Which Majesty will I meet? I cannot be certain. I lift my pen from its paper. I whisper my prayer that a friendly Queen will summon me.

"...Do you recall many years ago, when my sister Mary summoned me to the Tower? The day our carriage transported us into a putrid London, all littered with the remains of innocent Protestant souls?" This subject does not bode well. I cannot imagine it will ease my Queen's tortured conscience.

"Your Majesty, I beg you. Do not trouble yourself with awful memories..." I answer with pretended calm, but my dismay lingers.

"But I must, dear Blanche..." All honey at the moment. Still I sense the hovering malevolence of another Queen. "...I cannot send from my mind the sorrowful image of that family..."

"I am sorry, Your Majesty. I do not recall the citizens you refer to. It was so long ago. We encountered such horrors on entering London that day, and I responded with cowardice.... I squeezed tight my eyes to avoid all the dreadful suffering." With a reflex I cannot control, my eyes close. My face screws itself into a terrifying mask as I imitate my former weak-willed self.

"You must recall it, Blanche. How can you not? The family my sister Mary destroyed with her indomitable faith. Their limbs, all bent and broken. Their poor children's sad misshapen forms, all strewn about the avenue, like the wooden dolls your own little Elizabeth once played with..."

"...Your Majesty, I beg you..." My distress annoys my Queen. She silences me with an impatient to and fro wave of her hand.

"...I vowed at that time, should God grant his Elizabeth the wherewithal to command it, I would not allow any Clergy the authority to snatch my subjects' lives from them. Yet... an Armada, its Catholic flags wagging, descends on us for that very reason..." Her Majesty's grey eye takes her far from the comfortable chamber we inhabit to that day long ago. Our carriage rattling into London's dampened stench.

.... *a lifeless mother's torn and soiled petticoat; the shades of blue on a father's bruised and broken neck; each caked-up sore on the blackened flesh of their tiny son's cracked skull, his knees miraculously free of the usual childhood bruising...*

Her Majesty ponders England's future: Spanish galleons littering the Channel with Catholic ambition. Her Majesty's much loved sons floating face-down nearby.

Seated behind her desk, Her Majesty stares across the chamber at my scribbling fingers. She wonders at the swiftness with which the heel of my hand glides across the page. She inquires how to avoid smudging all the pretty script above where she now writes.

I answer from where I perch at my little table. I demonstrate my technique, lifting the heel of my hand so that only my sharpened quill touches the blank paper. Between our snatches of conversation, we persist in our writing. A matched pair of toiling scribes, my Queen and I scratch our symbols on the page.

Her Majesty's fine script directs an entire kingdom's activities. Her pages will someday fill the shelves of the world's finest libraries with a monarch's wisdom. And mine? What does my futile scribbling produce? I only mirror a Queen's talent. I produce a poor imitation of Her Majesty's fine wit. Perhaps my little diary serves no purpose but to amplify Her Majesty's anguish. Do I provide a service to my Queen, or commit an offence? I do not know. And yet, without my scandalous recording of the details Her Majesty leaves out, no one will bear witness to her story. If the smallest part of Her Majesty's humanity – even a wisp of breath on a looking glass - slips with timid grace from what I scribble here, it is reason enough to do it. And so I persist in my thankless task.

"God help me. I cannot remove the poor wretches from my stubborn memory." Her Majesty places her palms on her throbbing temples. She pulls at her tight curls. My Queen attempts to pluck each member of the unfortunate family from her conscience. One by one she will remove them, even if it means pulling all the fine hair from her head.

Her Majesty looks me in the eye, insisting I share in her heartrending retelling. "...Every detail remains. The lady's pale hair, all newly arranged. Her gown all pressed and cleaned with such attention and yet..." *...a lifeless mother's torn and soiled petticoat...*

"Your Majesty, let us go to the garden. Your favourite damask rose bushes will bloom very soon, I think..."

In my flurry to distract my Queen, I hasten from behind my desk and approach hers. I approach; attempting to take Her Majesty's jeweled hand in mine. Her Grace rejects my impropriety with a familiar curdling tone.

"Do not attempt to divert your Queen. I require your respectful companionship, not your condescension." So we remain, huddled bookends. Quarreling, scribbling, and seeking with desperation to write on the page words we dare not speak.

By mid-afternoon, even the gentle scratching of my pen on paper grates on her nerves. My Queen dismisses me from her chamber. Rising from her desk, Her Majesty chases me from her presence. ...*the shades of blue on a father's bruised and broken neck.*

I gather my papers, quills and ink, and rush from the room. My skirts almost catch in my slipper as I pass through her chamber door. I must leave her to face her wanton demons alone.

***

It is the next day before I test Her Majesty's patience again. I shrink from intruding on my Queen, but I must approach her. If I do not provide some needed solace, her gentlemen may notice her fragility. Then who can tell what might befall my beloved monarch? I choose my moment with care, approaching her after she has stalked her favoured terrace for her morning exercise. My Queen blots her towel against her shiny forehead. It is Her Majesty's very best time of day.

"Your Grace, please pardon my intrusion. I must express my concern with your well-being. Though you will find me impertinent, I feel it is my duty to address a sensitive topic with you."

Her Majesty peeks from behind her towel, amused by my seriousness. "I am certain I will find you most impertinent, Letters. It is one of the best qualities you possess, and one of my favourite reasons for spending endless hours in your company. What is it that troubles you? Tell your loving Queen of your anxiety."

"It is a delicate matter, Your Majesty…"

"Well, say it quickly then, Blanche. I haven't all day to mollycoddle, while you choose comfortable words with which to unburden yourself. Speak, my dear. Your Queen will attempt to receive your honest counsel with grace. As a loving monarch should."

My heart strikes hard against my rib cage. I fear it will pop from my mouth when I part my lips to speak. Yet I must do it. "Your Majesty, your frame of mind seems to shift to and fro. At times you possess only patience, while at others you find everyone utterly objectionable. It perplexes me…"

"Is this all then? Blanche, a Queen's cares are many." …*each caked-up sore on the blackened flesh of their tiny son's cracked skull*… Her Majesty sighs. My Queen cares for me with a mother's affection, though I am her elder by several years. "…in the midst of all my worries, my various moods will shift. As the winds do, heaving clouds this way and that." Her Majesty grips her towel at opposite corners and waves it as though breezes send it fluttering. I sought lightness in my Queen's mood, and yet I fear her lack of gravity does not serve my purpose either.

"Lady Fate offers and then withdraws her sympathy. She can disturb one's calm, and debilitate one's spirit. But you mustn't concern yourself, Blanche. Your Queen, in her advancing years, has learned to comply with the mysterious forces governing us. I harness the blustery energy, though it whisks me in one direction and then another."

Her Grace does not wish to hear my careful warning. But she shall. I will make sure of it. "Your Majesty, may I address the advancing years you speak of?" I approach a treacherous edifice with my Queen.

"Be careful Blanche, where you tread. Your Queen admits to a maturing beauty, but is not prepared to become an elderly crone just yet." Her Majesty knows full well no such insult will pass my lips. She winks at my expense.

"Your Majesty, I promised myself I would speak to you of my concern. At peril of my neck, I must." I pause, breathe deep. "Is it possible your climacteric causes your anxiety? It occurs to me you have reached a milestone where this might be so..." I have said it. I exhale. Tiny droplets glisten above my upper lip. My tongue reaches up to catch their salty sting. The chamber spins, while my ears echo with the pounding of a pulse inside my temples.

I duck my head, preparing for the inevitable blows to fall on it. Her Majesty's bell-ringing laughter cascades down on me instead. "My climacteric? This is what you trouble your Queen with?" More laughter. Her Majesty can barely speak, so heartily does her mirth ring out.

"Blanche, if I did not know better, I would guess you were Sir Cecil in matronly disguise. You sound just like my insolent Council. My gentlemen forever claim that all my faults lie within my womanhood. Now you suggest my middling age robs me of my intellect?" She smiles on me, but Her Majesty's pleasure at my discomfort alarms me just the same.

"Your Majesty, I do not, with any such insolence suggest such a thing. Just that the strain of reaching this momentous maturation...the realization that marriage and children may not follow..." I cannot continue. My humiliation is complete. I am interrupted by my jovial Queen.

Her Majesty wraps her arms around her slim, corseted sides. Still her laughter rains down. "Dearest Blanche." She sighs, searching the floor at her slipper. I do not know if frustration or hilarity overwhelms my Queen more.

"Your monarch has long passed the stage of requiring attention from European Princes. I do enjoy motherhood. All of England is my wayward child." Her Majesty sweeps her arms before her, opening them toward her beloved realm. A gesture I have witnessed so often when her gentlemen stand before her.

"All my subjects, even my ill-mannered Walsingham, suckle at my loving breast in one manner or another. And I receive much fulfillment from all this nurturing." I blush at my Queen's graphic illustration. This image unsettles me immensely. My discomfort only serves to renew Her Majesty's giggling.

"My climacteric? Dearest Blanche. You do underestimate your Queen. Consider yourself blessed I value your steadfast loyalty as dearly as I do. If I did not, I might wonder at you broaching this absurd subject with your monarch." Her Majesty lets off the waving of her towel, crumples it into a ball, and tosses it aside.

"I am sorry, Your Grace. But you vacillate so, from day to day. I understand the strains you endure, however I fear your Council expects more constant guidance...."

"...Blanche, your Queen manages her Council. And you will cease to trouble me with this nonsense. I am a Prince. With princely cares you cannot comprehend. My subjects, like needful babes, squeal for their Queen's attention. I respond to *their* beseeching cries. Not to my own trifling miseries. Your Queen thanks you for your concern. But it is misplaced." Her Majesty pauses, grins. "And most impertinent. Now, leave me, dearest Lady. Your monarch has far-reaching concerns to occupy her.

Her climacteric will have to wait." Her Majesty cannot resist another smile at my expense.

My Queen turns from me. Hardly a moment passes before I glimpse her brows turned downward again. All crimped with the cares Her Majesty conceals beneath her beguiling smile. ...*each caked-up sore upon the blackened flesh of their tiny son's cracked skull...his knees miraculously free of the usual childhood bruising...*

***

4th August, 1588

Fate's lumbering wheel persists. It grinds and lists in an upward ascent for my Queen. On the surface of it, Providence does not favour Her Majesty. My Queen fails to convince her Council to adopt a peaceful approach to Spain's threat. England prepares for Spain's approaching Armada. The Port of Plymouth readies itself for war.

I am not certain my Queen fully intends to lose the ongoing argument with her gentlemen. Her Majesty, though she abhors bloody conflict with the entirety of her passionate nature – and will publicly argue against war - cannot deny her practical temperament. The Queen's navy prepares to face Spain's massive fleet of galleons. She offers her gentlemen this win. Her navy responds.

England's seamen, my Queen's beloved sons, take to the waters off the Port of Plymouth. Her Majesty's Council insists on this preparation, and to their enduring relief, their willful Queen complies.

England prevails with an ease causing pleasant surprise for Her Majesty's seasoned naval commanders, Drake and Raleigh included. Indeed, Her Majesty and her Court barely get settled in at St. James Palace, deep in London, when reports of the English victory arrive.

My Queen scoffed at her Council's insistence we move the entire Court from Windsor Castle to the interior of London. Her Majesty did not appreciate the temporary loss of her covered terrace for daily strolling. But never a fool, Her Grace complied with her gentlemen's concern for her safe-keeping. St. James resides in a sheltered portion of London, where omnipresent guards can protect a monarch at this harrowing time of unwished for war with Spain.

Upon my arrival in my chamber, I see to my best loved possessions first. As I empty out my cumbersome box of paper, my collection of ink-stained quills and half-used pots of ink, the news arrives. Spain's dreaded Armada has already retreated in a chaotic flurry of listing sails, and half-sunk, smoking death holds. Her Majesty's messengers report King Philip's humiliating defeat. Our sprightlier *hell-burners*, sent out from Plymouth's raging ports, take the day. Her Majesty considers her fiery vessels to be aptly named. I believe if my Queen had the wherewithal, she would send all her vessels of war directly to the bowels of the earth where they belong.

What finally moves Her Majesty to act after many months of prevarication? After all the dreadful standoffs with her trusted counselors? A letter arrives from Lord Howard of Effingham, Her Majesty's High Admiral of the English Navy. I believe this missive precipitates Her Majesty's hasty change of heart, or at least weighs heavily in its favour.

For the love of Jesus Christ, Madam...awake thoroughly and see the villainous treasons around you, against Your Majesty and your realm, and draw your forces round about you like a mighty prince to defend you. Truly, Madam, if you do so, there is no cause to fear. If you do not, there will be danger.

Your most humble servant,
Lord Howard of Effingham,

Her Majesty's small fist – her right hand in which the letter resided – trembled. No one in the Presence Chamber took notice, other than myself. And I? I drifted toward Her Majesty, who remained motionless, curiously dwarfed within the overwhelming presence of her throne. Kneeling before my Queen, I positioned myself between her and her gentlemen. I became her protective shield for just a moment.

Pity threatened to overwhelm me when I witnessed Her Majesty's uncomplicated trust in me. I withdrew the offensive paper from Her Majesty's grasp. Folding it in my hand, I curtsied. And then I glided away, vanishing from the chamber. My Queen and I achieve all this before her Council can take notice of a woman's faltering hand.

Still, Her Majesty remained faithful to her stalwart nature. English sailors amassed in Plymouth, but Her Majesty's ambassadors, following their monarch's order, continued to hammer away at peace negotiations throughout. Diplomatic envoys continued to sit at the table together, even as King Philip's galleons attacked her cherished sons.

***

8th August, 1588

Her Majesty bickers with Walsingham and Sir Cecil in her Presence Chamber. Within her Privy Chamber, her ladies prepare our Queen's belongings for the journey to Tilbury. The Earl of Leicester, her reckless Gypsy, plans a spectacle of sorts there.

Though a Gypsy's digestion falters recently, his wits serve him well. The Earl of Leicester distracts Her Majesty. Only days ago, when blackened skies still reeked of the remains of Spanish galleons, my Queen announced she would ride with her soldiers toward Plymouth's shores to view the scene for herself. Sir Cecil and Walsingham responded with slack-jawed astonishment.

"Ready yourselves, my Lords. Your Queen travels in her barge to England's south shores to witness the final destruction of Medina-Sidonia and his ships. My ladies prepare as we speak. Your Queen joins her loyal servants in their brave undertaking at Plymouth." Her Majesty rises. Her gentlemen hesitate, bow low. Nothing about their bent forms speaks of submission.

"Your Majesty, with all due reverence..." How I admire Cecil's forbearance. "... you cannot consider putting yourself in the way of such dangers. You represent our sole monarch. You possess no issue to replace you should you not return to us. Nor have you named an heir. We cannot recommend it." Cecil's shock is only outdone by Walsingham's horror. While her Sir Spirit appeals to his Queen's ear, Her Majesty's Moor lunges across the room. His ebony robes swirl about him, further accentuating his forceful opposition to Her Majesty's plan. Walsingham hovers over Her Majesty, as though to bar her movement. Another dispute will erupt. I am certain.

"Gentlemen. This is how you speak to your Monarch? No one utters the words 'must not' to their Prince." Her Majesty maintains an unnerving equilibrium. "England rears up to defeat King Philip. Your grateful sovereign will ride out to inform our soldiers of our pride and consideration for their sacrifice. It is the very least a Prince can offer. Would you not agree, gentlemen?" Her Majesty, now smiling at her Moor's disapproval, brushes past Walsingham without interference. His form, towering over her, offers little in the way of obstruction.

"Yes, Your Majesty..." Sir Cecil, speaking to his Queen's retreating back, stares at Walsingham. Neither gentleman attempts to mask his growing frustration with his Queen.

And Her Majesty? She goes to her ladies. She inspects our preparations for her progress. Whether Her Majesty notices her gentlemen's distress is of little consequence. Her Majesty believes Sir Cecil and Walsingham should master their own fearsome demons. Just as their Queen manages her own.

Fortunate for Walsingham, Cecil, and all England too, Her Majesty's Gypsy rides to her rescue, in the form of a happier letter he sends. My Queen receives his message with a subdued expression. She scans its contents and presses the fine paper to her cheek before placing it in my palm. She allows its feathery weight to brush past her lip for the briefest of moments. Her Majesty holds the Gypsy's letter only slightly longer than she has to, warming herself in its writer's hand before letting it go. A slip of paper delivers her to its writer's side.

In his flattering manner, the Earl of Leicester suggests her Majesty ride instead to Tilbury, where she may impress her army with her magnetic presence. With his own well-being at stake, her Earl offers an oath to protect Her Majesty at all costs. And as is always the case, the Gypsy has his way. Her Majesty rides to him. The sole man who harbours her favour above all others. And to her gentlemen's qualified relief, away from Plymouth's harrowing shores.

***

9th August, 1588

My loving people,

I have been persuaded by some that are careful of my safety to take heed how I present myself before armed multitudes, for fear of treachery. But I tell you that I would not desire to live to distrust my faithful and loving people. Let tyrants fear. I have so behaved myself that under God I have placed my chiefest strength and safeguard in the loyal hearts and goodwill of my subjects.

I am come among you at this time for my recreation and pleasure. I have resolved in the midst and heat of the battle, to live and die amongst you all. To lay down for my God and for my kingdom and for my people mine honor and my blood, even in the dust.

I know I have the body of a weak and feeble woman, but I have the heart and stomach of a king, and of a king of England too – and take great offence that Parma or any prince of Europe should dare to invade the borders of my realm.

I myself will venture my royal blood. I myself will be your general, judge, and rewarder of your virtue in the field. I know that already you deserve rewards and I assure you in the word of a prince they shall be duly paid you. In the meantime, my lieutenant general, the Earl of Leicester, shall act in my stead...

***

5th September, 1588

I ponder, with only a little prejudice, the pleasures Her Majesty has enjoyed in a Gypsy's company these last thirty years and more: illicit caresses – the stolen intimacies of youth; shared months in the Tower – all separated by walls of stone; whispered oaths - both honoured and unkept. And the inevitable progress to old age. My Majesty and her Gypsy have been altered by Father Time: Now loving companions, they stroll through palace rose gardens. Whispers, once holding mischievous suggestion, turn reflective, comforting. A stroke of a hand offers warmth, chaste kindness rather than teasing want.

But all is undone. And in only a moment. Word arrived this morning of the Earl of Leicester's death. Where there is abiding love, exquisite loss must follow.

Taken ill with stomach disorders shortly after Her Majesty's dramatic victory against Spain, her Gypsy travelled to Buxton to drink the healing waters. I have before me a letter he scrawled to Her Majesty while he voyaged there. His ailing health did not allow him the luxury of the entire progress. Only to Rycote did he ride, before he wrote:

29th August, 1588

I most humbly beseech Your Majesty to pardon your old servant to be so bold in sending to know how my gracious lady does. And what ease of your late pain you find. For you are the chiefest thing in the world I do pray for. Your good health and long life. For my own poor case, I continue with your medicine, and it amends much better than any other thing that hath been given me. I hope to find a perfect cure at the bath, with the continuance of my sincere prayer for Your Majesty's most happy preservation, I humbly kiss your foot. From your old lodgings at Rycote this Thursday morning, by Your Majesty's most faithful and obedient servant,

R. Leicester

Six days after Her Majesty receives her Gypsy's hopeful message, another arrives. News of the Earl of Leicester's death reaches us at Whitehall Palace. How does Her Majesty receive the news? I, alone, may report on her pitiable state. My Queen confines us in her chamber, refusing all others.

On learning of her favorite's death, Her Majesty wilts before my eye. Her sacrifice is now complete.

She stares at the indecipherable meaning on the page for some time. How does the heart, having loved for three full decades, comprehend such news? How does my Queen accept an end to all she cherishes in the time it takes for her eye to travel a single line of penned characters?

Her Majesty summons the courage to reread the unspeakable news. Her disbelief alters her features. Shock wipes all expression from her eye as she absorbs the awful message. And then worse. Comprehension takes her over. It batters her poor temples. Her Majesty's fingertips press on her brow. Her thumbs massage her jaw line. She stares out from a cage of her own making. And then she tosses the hateful note, rejecting its truths. The blasted letter wafts to the floor at our feet. The bleached paper lies there, suggestive of innocence. But its contents crush a mighty lioness.

An other-worldly howl lashes the tapestried walls in her Presence Chamber. My senses must surely desert me. I swear Her Grace's family portrait, hanging in its constant place, shudders at Her Majesty's anguish.

The completeness of her Gypsy's abandonment finds its way to Her Majesty's understanding. Like a bell, broken at the handle, my Queen collapses to her knees. Her torso sways inside frothy layers of silken robes. Her Majesty, like a poor babe separated from her doting mother, weeps with abandon. Her ladies, I regret to admit, myself included, stand stupefied in our shattered Queen's midst.

After what feels like hours of uninhibited sorrow, though I am told afterward, it was only minutes, Her Majesty scrambles to her feet. We rush to lend our assistance, but Her Grace, with one look, communicates to her ladies our aid is not required.

Her Majesty stalks across the chamber, her eye fixed on me alone. My eyes open wide with fear and ignorance for at this time, only Her Majesty herself has read the ominous message. I do not know what distresses her so.

Her Majesty seizes me on my upper arm. Five reddened masses erupt. She drags me into her Privy Chamber and slams the door on everyone else. My last glimpse before I disappear within is of the familiar Tudor mural, slightly askance on the wall after all the flurry it beholds.

Here within her Privy Chamber, my Queen and I remain. The chamber door closed tight. A realm waits as a Queen grieves. If plentiful tears were to drop on Her Majesty's soiled gown, I might feel an ease in their release. I might encourage Her Majesty to find such a balm for her suffering. But my Queen does not respond with further weeping. Instead, with a frightening calm, a boundless energy, Her Majesty recites for me all her Gypsy's finest qualities. My Queen seems to understand that in all the Court only I might fully appreciate her pleading case.

"After our great victory over King Philip at Plymouth, I ordered my Council to make the Earl of Leicester, Lieutenant Governor of all England and Ireland. Did you know this, Blanche?"

"I did not, Your Grace."

"I trusted my Robin more than any other. I wanted more for him than for any other. My gentlemen, without due consideration, denied their Queen. They denied my faithful Robin his honour. Now he is dead, and he will never know of his Queen's gratitude..." Her Majesty, seated at her desk, stares as she has done these last days, into the far reaches of the chamber.

"Your Majesty, I understand the Earl had numerous detractors. But the Council only sought to protect your throne. Perhaps your Lords doubted the prudence in extending such far-reaching power to one gentleman alone..."

Unlike my Queen of old, who might have pounced on me for the mere suggestion of the Earl of Leicester's unworthiness, Her Majesty glances away as though I have not spoken. "I loved him, Blanche. As Elizabeth, and as your Queen. I loved my Bonny Sweet Robin as I shall love no other. And for this pitiable reason I could not have him near me. I could not have him as a husband to Elizabeth, for Elizabeth dared not risk the weakness of a heart's attachment. And I could not have him as my King because I listened too earnestly to Robert's enemies. Their distrust always reached far beyond the heights my affection ever could..." Her Majesty stares into the chamber's far reaches.

I attempt to move my Queen's attention away from her crippling grief. And back to my side. "Your Grace..."

"Do not interrupt your Queen." My Majesty of old re-emerges. I cover my satisfaction with bowed head. "How does hatred thrive so well? They all despised Robin, you know...my Council, Parliament..." Her Majesty looks to me for agreement. I dare not respond.

"How does the bitterness of my enemies flourish like Philip's limitless fleet of hulking galleons? Why is there always another cruelty to take the place of the last? How can their loathing survive in such abundance? When my Robert... my love... A brother and a best friend, is gone. And not to be replaced."

I fear for my Queen's reason. "Your Grace, I do not know your heart, but..."

"No, you do not."

"I appeal to you... you must seek solace..."

"What solace? Your Queen is alone, Blanche. Her only friend departed, she is but one." *A friend is a second self.*

Her Majesty rushes to my table. She rummages in all the stacked papers until she unearths what she is seeking. The Earl of Leicester's message in hand, my Queen returns to her desk. Holding it like an ancient document that could crumble in her fingers should she mishandle it, she folds her treasured letter. Taking up her pen, Her Grace writes in her own script beside her beloved Gypsy's: *His last letter.* Her Majesty returns to her bedside table and lifts the lid of her carved wooden jewel box. Shutting her eyes, she presses the letter to her dry cheek before placing it in the box.

"Let us go, Blanche." A tired sigh. "A realm, all thick with plotting, wonders at our whereabouts."

Her Grace approaches the Privy Chamber door. She studies it for a moment, as though wondering at its ability to contain her, and with no further hesitation, throws it open to meet her waiting gentlemen.

Winter II - A Virgin Queen Unveiled

The gods, too, are fond of a joke.

--Aristotle

5th October, 1591

Do not doubt me, Reader. It does seem like your Queen, at the advanced age of sixty years, begins her story all over again with the date of my Christening. This is not true. Your spinner of tales – Yes, it is I, not Blanche - must begin to atone somewhere.

Everyone who attended at Court that Sunday, September 7th, in the year 1533, when I was delivered by more poor Anne Boleyn, observed their King Henry's chagrin. In his wrenching regret at my birth, my beloved father chose not to attend my Christening ceremony the following Wednesday evening. I sympathize with his disappointment. What father, what king, will favour a squawking, red-curled Miss, when he desperately requires an heir to inhabit his throne? A tiny girl-child will not satisfy his need. Will it, Father?

My big sister Mary, England's first Queen proved you correct, Father. Surely a woman lacks the necessary qualities to become a successful Prince. Mary was a serious lady, and a devout follower of her faith, but my sister did not seek her loyal subjects' love. Our Mary divided her people, where more prudent monarchs seek to strengthen their position with community. Yes Father, Mary was a woman driven by her emotions rather than her intellect. My sister murdered all who summoned the courage to disagree with her strict Popish sensibility. Shameful, really. Perhaps you are to be forgiven in your assumption I would persist in this same way, equally bereft of princely virtue. Perhaps I too would be full of the irrationality that must accompany womanhood.

Though I understand your harsh judgment of me, still your deliberate absence from my baptism pains me. Here I stoop, an old woman of fifty-eight years, a Queen of England for more than three full decades. And still bruised by a long-dead father's willful neglect of his poor babe.

I am a ridiculous old woman.

***

And so we meet at last, faithful Reader. Or, should I say, I discard my cumbersome *nom de plume* in the interest of full disclosure? I hope you will consent to forgive a monarch gone astray. Perhaps Blanche, God bless her departed soul, would have shown patience for my cruel deception, given the opportunity. With time, and with the reasons for my wicked subterfuge Dear Reader, your acceptance will certainly prevail.

Already I presume to speak on your behalf. Without any knowledge how you might balk in the face of my trickery. I fear soon you will request Blanche resume the storytelling. Though this, of course, cannot be. Only your Queen remains. Her Keeper of the Books a faithful memory.

I must address Blanche Parry, whose name I have abused throughout our entire journey. What can be more dishonourable than placing within an unsuspecting lady's mouth, words she did not speak? Does it matter that these words of truth might never have discovered their home on a page, were it not for a willful Queen and her reckless letter-writing to herself?

My crime seems especially unpardonable considering Lady Blanche kept her secrets to herself, always considering her Queen's interests. Yet unbeknownst to Blanche, her Monarch whom she sought to protect spills all. Blanche honoured the throne's privacy, as I demanded. And I, her beloved Queen, known well for my discretion, spare no detail in telling everything.

If only I could claim, with some honesty, Blanche and I communed together on our ambitious project. The stories of my early childhood were scribbled by Blanche, and the later events were written by your Queen. If only my Keeper of the Queen's Books and I had produced a glossa – a compendium of experience. If some passages had sprung from a loyal subject's eye, while others originated from a Queen's meticulous inner search, the diary could represent a shared adventure. If this were the case, I could acknowledge a real friendship. A shared endeavour. But this is not the case.

Given my beloved Lady Blanche's recent parting, your Queen's transgression seems even more objectionable. Like so many of my beloved friends and councilors – my Lord Robert Dudley with a stomach ailment, our Christopher Hatton with failed kidneys, and our ever-saucy Walsingham of his wasting disease - Blanche has left my service to attend a higher power than a Queen. God bless, Bonny Sweet Robin. Christopher. My faithful Moor. And my dearest Blanche. Rest you in peace, always.

Faithful friends, with God's grace, take their leave of this world. Your Queen remains the sole witness of her awful truths. I am bereft. Words cannot illustrate my grief with any adequacy as those I shared a lifetime with leave my side forever.

Do not pity your Queen. I do not ask it. I only require you know it. All of it.

And so my reputation for *seeing all and saying nothing* appears unearned. A role I did adopt. Many roles I played. Indecision did not trouble me, as slanderous writers of pamphlets would say. Nor was it feminine instability, as others suggest in whispered reports about the Court. Only well-considered prudence. A mere woman could not ignite my people's imaginations. How was I to give them a plausible example of a mighty monarch?

A mere woman? God's wounds. My faithful Sir Cecil shouted it himself, and many times....*God help England, and send it a King!* In the very presence of his own Queen my Sir Spirit pled for an heir to oust the mere woman from England's throne. How many times have I pretended not to hear this traitorous request? How often have I pretended my loyal subject's treasonous whispers did not reach my ear? Were it not for my ambitious masquerades, and my extravagant pantomimes, my people might agree with Sir Cecil.

What is a mere woman to do?

Well, I offered my people what they yearned for. With loving protection, I mothered them. But from a careful distance. No mother's child cares to find himself all tethered to a suffocating breast.

And when I wandered near their searching eye? I paraded before them a Goddess! On one occasion, in the summer of 1563 – a lovely, temperate summer - while I went on my yearly progress, I strutted about as Astraea, Goddess of Justice. My gown fairly glistened. All embroidered in golden threads with the weighted scales of fair play, I promised to provide for my people an impartial monarch. Robin teased me unmercifully about my glittering robes and their loud message, until I had to silence him with a stern pinch on his belligerent cheek.

On another occasion? I portrayed Diana, the Huntress. Amusing, that one. But truthfully, I was happiest while seated in my saddle on my spirited *Pool* or my patient *Black Wilford*. I loved to canter alongside Robin. Hunting deer on the grounds of Nonsuch, in Surrey. My father's favourite palace. So I rode among them in full Huntress regalia. Diana's golden bow slung over my shoulder. Her pointed arrows gathered in a leather pouch at my thigh. My subjects need to know their Queen safeguards their interests. If I must wear an immortal's costume to gain their confidence, I will do it.

Did I see all, and say nothing? My people believed so. I grew adept at my portrayal of the stately, silent monarch. But in my own humble opinion? I said more than '*God save you all.*' I said '*Fear not, my beloved people. Your Queen, possessing the powers of courageous Heroines and Goddesses alike, will shelter her realm as no mortal monarch ever has.*'

A mere woman? God's Death, no. On behalf of my people, with willful sorcery I transformed my very soul. The unwanted daughter of Henry VIII remains their doting Prince for three decades now. And a loving monarch she will be. Mother to all England.

Their Virgin Queen. This is what they name me. Their flattery forces a wink and an unbidden smile to my thinning lips. Their words lift my chin with sinful pride. An old woman of near sixty years, yet they look on me as though I dance the ribbons of the Maypole with young ladies of the Court. Perhaps my people believe my purity preserves them. Keeps them endowed with God's grace. How can harm befall those who worship such a virtuous monarch?

My mystical personas convince my people. My subjects find reassurance in elevating their Queen, and I dare not take away their ease.

Let them hasten home with confidence. May they fasten their latches on plain plank doors and lay their beleaguered heads on waiting cots. They enjoy their security because their Queen, in her charmed capacity, oversees all their worries, real and imagined, waking and conjured.

Sleep well, my dutiful people. Your loving Majesty watches over you all. You may well have a greater prince, but you shall never have a more loving prince. Though your devoted Queen cannot hope to reign forever, her faith in you shall endure always.

***

I denied it for many years. I will not any longer. A Queen suffers the sting of loneliness. I have endured it for an entire lifetime. And with this shouldering of isolation, something gives way. Hairline cracks, bonded together by a monarch's silent governing, will open. A torrent of words flow forth. Will you receive your Queen's gift? With a determined hand, I grasp hold and twist the fissures until they crack wide. I admit to you all my harsh solitude, once and for all. It rests within your understanding now.

Can you not imagine I might have craved, for the whole of my solitary life – I near sixty years - a companion like I have written? A woman such as Blanche to hover by my side? Someone to squeeze my hand for each monstrous act perpetrated against me. Someone to squeeze harder still for every monstrous act I did myself commit? A friend. A companion to grant her devotion, no matter how loud my tirades rang in her patient ear. If my desire for this sort of kinship remains impossible to imagine, my own humanity must remain equally in question.

Do not suppose Blanche Parry was incapable of such an attachment. Nor should you doubt Lady Parry's constancy. She granted all of this to me and more. It is not the quality of the Lady, but the quality of the daily correspondence I alter in my telling. Blanche served me with a fine Lady's decorum. She kept her own opinions all locked up within. Where they belong. You see, she was unlike me in that way. Unlike your forthcoming Queen who claims all the unearned discretion for myself.

Were I offered such a companion – the Blanche I portray - much might have differed. But it was not possible. I am Queen first. Elizabeth second. Or perhaps, Elizabeth not at all. Nothing surpasses the demands of a throne. And so Blanche's friendship I failed to notice. If I am to remain wholly plainspoken, I in fact disdained it.

My Bonny Sweet Robin, for the longest period, filled that space in me. The need for companionship. He was the sincere friend, the devoted brother a woman desires. And I desired my Robin. All of him. It is true. For my Gypsy, as he was named, of all my trusted advisors, found his Elizabeth to be *enough*.

Yes, he wedded, and bred with others. Lettice Knowles. Damn you to hell. I hate those unwanted syllables on my tongue. But Robin? He was only a man, and a comely one at that. In his Elizabeth, Robin recognized himself. I inhabited his soul, and he mine. We were separate, and of one essence. It was more than enough. My beloved Robin and he alone, did not persist in the odious search for more decisiveness, less ire in his Queen. Robin found satisfaction in the Elizabeth who stood before him. He was the only one to do so. There was a time when I loved Robin. I have made myself forget when that may have been.

For three long years I have endured without my darling brother. I contemplate his generous smile each day. Perhaps I am blessed with Robin's absence; for no one remains to remind me I once loved. As a woman does. Still, I miss the comfort of his melodious voice. The unique warmth of his waiting palm beneath my elbow. His tender affection, hovering close by my side. This was Robin's presence. He was the only one to offer it. His uncalled for reassurance was ever there, like the glass I stare into each morning. He and it reminding me of my presence. *I am enough. I am enough, Father.*

Now I have only myself to whisper to. So this I do. Quiet breaths leave my lips, filling an empty chamber. I pretend Robin hears and nods in agreement. He approaches me and lays his hand on mine. My sole support remains close at his Queen's side, conjured by the force of a lonely woman's unanswerable desire.

Desire? I stumble on that unholy topic. I find it a tiresome consideration, for do we not all share the same loathsome appetites? Once, all of continental Europe found the topic of an English Queen's purity more important than her ability to reign. Why on earth, when curiosity can roam like a pilgrim on his spiritual progress through all the wonders of this glorious world, does it insist on creeping about in the darkest crevices? Very well. A Queen, too, can shed her fine robes and crawl there. Do not ever accuse your Majesty of claiming a superiority she does not justly earn.

In the perpetual contest between my close-guarded maidenhead and my sweet Robert Dudley, only one victor could emerge. I promise candour, but on this subject I will claim reserve. A Queen's purity is a matter of State, entitled to be treated with discretion. Though I will disclose this: With the ardent assertion of a monarch's chastity, I gained the privilege to reign a nation. Who of you would not choose as I did? In my solitude I remain blameless. And though not always alone, respectable seclusion remains my customary way of life.

That is all I will say on the matter. Let us escort one another from our hideous corner, and return to where warmer rays might expand our spirits.

My Council forever derided my choice of companion. My loyal gentlemen proclaimed my regard for Robin a weakness of mine. I submit an argument against such hardheartedness. It is this. May a Queen not possess some combination of attributes? May she not feel both an eternal passion for a gentleman, and yet manage to exercise her healthy God-given intellect? I argue your Queen may indeed. And I did, with more courage than most. Even after his death, I continue to care for my beloved Robin more than my own life. And still, I choose to reign. And I will do so as though my yearning does not govern me. Does this not require a fearlessness? I denied the one love offered me, and gave all my fondness to my people instead.

Audacity. Not emotional folly. This I lay claim to.

When Almighty God proffered His plentiful blessing, crowning Elizabeth your Queen; when Lady Fate bestowed all Her gracious endowments, I chose you. My people. I disdain my own happiness. For this, perhaps you will agree, I deserve some little inkling of esteem.

***

5th July, 1593

It is peculiar. And a little poignant. Having disclosed my rightful identity in plainspoken fashion, I become reticent. While Blanche spoke in my stead, my words poured forth, unceasing in their chatter.

Yet now that I claim my place on the page as your spiller of Courtly secrets, I dare not scribble with the same ease. When Blanche tells it, all remains permissible. But your Queen's unveiling of herself? Another thing altogether. I recoil. I feel timidity strikes me. I am frightened by my own act of disclosure. And so my quill, once busy in its mischief, dries up. My implement, once so willing to forfeit its bounty, ceases to speak when clutched in the age-spotted hand of the exposed monarch.

All too human is this pen. So contrary in its willful dance of spite.

I shake it into submission with my bold will. We cannot turn from our task, my fickle instrument. Having journeyed this far, we must uncover our earlier deceptions. We must grant the honest disclosure a Queen owes her beloved people.

***

5th November, 1593

I mark this day with a pride that in some devout circles might be frowned upon as sinful. I have translated Boethius's entire *Consolatio* from Latin into my native English.

My bent form falters on occasion now that I turn sixty ancient years, but my mind functions as it always has, with an efficient energy. Aristotle says: *Education is the best provision for the journey to old age.* I take heed from my Master, and accept his suggestion. Your Queen applies her elderly intellect to her translation exercise with a twofold destination in mind. I will challenge my aging faculties, and in mastering the text, instruct my beloved people. Just as Boethius's Latin translations preserved Aristotle's Greek ideas for us all, so too Elizabeth preserves Boethius's Latin for her beloved English men and women.

Why the *Consolatio* you might ask? In Boethius I intuit another kind of brother. He and I share a kinship of sorts, if it is only our mutual regard for knowledge. My esteemed Boethius found himself forced into an unasked for political role, when a life of quiet contemplation might have served his temperament better. And like Boethius, a book fits into your Queen's hand easier than a scepter. But Boethius and I both agreed to lead while our studies waited. We made our way ever outward into a world of chaotic confusion, when an inner world of lucid questioning beckoned to us infinitely more.

Most fail to see it as we do. My brother of ideas and I. This binds us tighter in our view of the world. I know, and my Boethius knew it too. Our singular power, our political influence over so many, is an illusion. It is but a sacrifice we make. Our sacred duty. Those concerned with directing others' lives find ourselves left with the fewest moments to marvel at our own.

My books lie neglected, unopened on my desk, or buried deep within the pocket of my gown, as I thumb the pages of a monarch's duty.

I grip my quill and peruse the documents my gentlemen consider more appropriate for a Queen's attention than her volume of fanciful poems. Declarations, sermons, patents, occupy my eye more often than not. Plutarch, Sydney and young Master Shakespeare stand by, impatient to be heard by their loving Queen.

My brother, Boethius, might argue against your Queen on this one point. Our philosopher suggests it is to the State's advantage it be led by we who don the philosopher's cap. And so, while I whinge at pushing aside my literary pursuits in the interests of governing, I improve my governing with the steadfastness of a studious mind. I shift aside that which I enjoy – a life overshadowed only by the limits of its own imagination - to advance my people's well-being. The surrender of a spirited mind's frolic, for what? I spend that same mind governing the masses. A sacrifice? Perhaps. Yet, in the end, a willing one.

Do not dare to pity your Queen. I do not need your sympathy. A mother feels the greatest joy when ministering to those she dotes on. So too, your Queen.

While Robin, my Earl of Leicester provided me with an earth-bound brother, my long-deceased Boethius ensnares me in a bond which joins two sympathetic minds. And so a philosopher known only on the page, and a departed companion whose gentle touch I pushed aside, occupy a Queen's inner life. My cherished gentlemen force me to comprehend the sacrifice so necessary for princely virtue.

I beg pardon. Your Queen prattles on when she desperately needs to map her direction. My pen follows after my wandering spirit with little regard for its destination. I do request your forbearance. I must claim some deference. Is that not owed a monarch?

Your ancient woman, seated alone within my chamber, my hand quivering with the effort of dipping this quill into a pot, cringes at my own cumbersome tale. I speak of *my* Robin, *my* Boethius as though they hover by my side. One my friend in matters of the physical world. The other my intellectual ease. In this depiction your Queen errs yet again. Solitude remains my ever-present companion. Perhaps your courageous Queen does not wager as high as she claims. I rejected Robin's touch for the uncomplicated reason he inhabited the flesh of a man. Only after his death do I proclaim my wanton hunger for him. Can my regret pose as a Queen's sacrifice? Or was I simply afraid? I dare to embrace Boethius only because the centuries and the written page keep him from me. Boethius's irresistible ideals are mere abstractions. Theories. No friend sits by my side to hear my musings.

Once, a while ago, I found all that I admired in one gentleman. His comely appearance was matched only by his fine intellect. The allure of Sir Walter Raleigh's many charms frightened me. So, did I invite Raleigh to become his Queen's constant companion? I did not.

Perhaps in the end I was proven right about him and all his kind. *Forgive me, for I am but a man.* Is this every man's answer? How is a Queen to respond? All the Court knows Elizabeth Throckmorton has borne the knave a child. But a Queen? How does a Queen drink the Water she thirsts for, when she knows that drink will drown her as she sips? This was my Sir Walter Raleigh.

Little choice offered itself to me. Your Queen, on learning of Raleigh's faithlessness, poured her Water and his Lady Throckmorton into the Tower, with just one tiny tip of my goblet. But this did not suffice for one so full of wanderlust as my Sir Walter. Always he must sail on the beckoning oceans. Away to distant lands. Perhaps he needed to join together with his own fluid element and sail to a foreign shore. Away from his loving Monarch.

Away from his consort and her bastard child. Always away. Farewell, Warter. Your Queen will not despair over that which she oughtn't crave.

And so your Monarch, seated at her desk, bends inward. I am an old woman. My shoulders all curved, I sit alone. Even the holding of my head upright on my shoulders, crownless, becomes too great a burden. My neck tilts toward where my sagging cheek rests. Weary in the palm of my withered hand.

Within my Privy Chamber, Solitude governs. So absolute its quiet power. Your Queen comprehends that separation afflicts every man. Can a devoted Prince really *know* his subjects? Though arms link together in an outward show of constancy, inward thoughts march, one after another, toes treading on the heel in front. In perfect single file. Unaccompanied. No matter how well-intentioned the social order would have it. Only God and my own persistent musing accompany your Queen through these days of listless brooding.

***

2nd August, 1598

The stingiest cracks of sunlight steal through tapestry draperies. Yet the room's odour defines it more than its somber appearance. The murky chamber stinks of death. A sour aroma reaches my nostrils, as though Death himself taunts me with that smell I find most difficult to endure. I wish to offer my Sir Spirit, our Lord Burghley the esteem he has earned these fifty years. It requires all my decades of practice hiding honest feeling to deny the bile rising in my throat. I mustn't retch, no matter how my body directs me otherwise. I lift my gloved hand to protect my nose and mouth from the rising stench. Traces of lavender, wafting from my freshly laundered glove, mix with the scent of sweat-soaked bedding.

Sir Cecil lies propped on several down pillows. His eyes, all closed when I entered, strain open for a moment to glimpse who approaches, and then return to rest on waiting lids.

My beloved councilor gathers all his remaining vigour and tilts the corners of his mouth upward. His dutiful courage causes me to feel a pang of regret. My battered conscience silences my body's desire to escape.

Even in the face of wily Death, Sir Spirit considers his Queen first. He saves, for me alone, his faithful smile. In that moment, my shameful repugnance vanishes, swept away by an onslaught of gratitude.

Where last I wrote of readying myself for my own waiting tomb, my perspective alters with Lord Burghley's single devoted gesture. In this brief exchange I come to appreciate what has escaped me these many years. Huddled under layers of feather down, and almost separated from me behind Death's sheltering gaze, lies my father.

I recall my girlhood self. The child of fifteen years, who welcomed Sir Cecil not only as a trusted advisor, but as the gentleman who for five long decades tended me in my genuine father's absence.

"Your Majesty..." My Lord Burghley attempts to raise himself to offer a proper greeting.

My chest tightens as I witness his valiant effort. I lean across his poor form to embrace his shoulders, all shrunken now. Playing the nurse, I return my patient to his waiting bed. "Do not try to speak, my dear Sir Spirit. Allow your indebted Queen to whisper instead. Let me wipe away the anguish from your brow."

Beads of moisture gather on Sir Cecil's forehead. Still he tries to respond to a Queen's unlikely visit. With my own liver-spotted hand – the elderly daughter ministers to her ancient father - I reach for the cloth on his bedside table and dab at the water on his brow, at his temples, and finally on his upper lip.

Always the obedient minister, Lord Burghley remains motionless as I cater to him. My faithful servant's eyes rest shut as I go about my duty.

As I complete my task, he forces his lids open. He lifts a palsied hand from beneath his duvet, and places it on mine. Sir Spirit stares with an expression I have not seen before on his countenance. So intense and haunting is his determination to address his Queen.

"I wish to share with you, Your Grace, the infinite pleasure I have felt in serving you these many years..." His voice remains vital, yet patient – a unique combination known especially to Burghley – but his faltering breath will not comply. Before he can finish his tribute to our shared endeavour, a harrowing cough escapes his lips.

I hold to his shoulders, hastening my palms up and down his sleeves, urging the hacking fit to subside. When he is quiet again, I respond. "My dear Sir. We all know what pleasure you have endured. Your Queen best of all, perhaps." I smile and place my hand on his with only a little irony.

A lifetime of loyalty makes it impossible for my Sir Cecil to diverge from his only known road. And so he supports his Queen in the time of his own greatest want. Might he remain with his chosen daughter just a little longer? My selfish thought remains unsaid. I resist the temptation to urge Sir Spirit to battle his failing health for his Queen.

Sir Spirit's man-servant enters, wooden tray in hand. On it rests my Lord's steamy cordial broth and a sterling spoon for ladling. As the servant places his platter on a side table and prepares to feed Lord Burghley, I wave him off. Cupping the bowl in my hand, I dip the spoon in the tepid liquid and offer it to my Spirit's parted lips.

Startled, Sir Cecil, in his accommodating manner, accepts his broth from his Queen. And so we proceed. The warmth envelops us as we slip into our repetitive roles. My offering, his receiving – almost spiritual in its ritual aspect. I dip into the clear soup, tipping the spoon to my Sir Spirit's uninterested lips. I interrupt his feeding only to blot errant drops from my Lord's snowy beard.

While I convince myself my Sir Spirit improves with this nourishment, he only satisfies his Queen's wishes. In truth, he awaits my departure and his return to his welcome deathbed. Something in his determined eye tells me he has decided. Yet he knows his Queen does not wish to hear of his surrender. And so Sir Cecil complies. He accepts each spoon of broth I offer.

"Your Queen has not made your task a simple one, Sir. And yet you, with constant and unerring discipline, ensure we remain on a path of righteousness. Sir Spirit, how will I continue without you?" I said it. Without remorse, the daughter calls on the weakened father to save her from a world of ills. I should feel shame at my selfish dependence on him. But I do not. I elevate my Sir Spirit with a Queen's boundless trust. Hear me Reader. I will not have it interpreted any other way.

"My dearest Majesty, you will continue to thrive. And with the same grace you have always displayed. You prove yourself a mighty lioness in your care of England's people. But it is time for others to take their place by your side. My son Robert will serve you well in my stead."

Another fit of coughing interferes with Sir Cecil's attempts to reassure. I do not wish to contemplate Robert Cecil or the Earl of Essex or any of the others left to me. Young blusterers, who whisper and roll their eye at their Queen's rulings. Every one of them displays a lack of esteem for their elderly monarch. No such son will fill the father's empty place at my side. Sir Spirit's reassurances only serve to make clear the depth of my loss.

"My Lord Burghley. If you do not know it now, perhaps you will never understand. You have been more a father to your Queen than a councilor. I do not desire to continue as Queen or as Elizabeth without my Sir Spirit by my side..."

My hand shudders in an unruly manner. I return the leaden spoon to its half full bowl and set it down on the waiting tray. My moment of weakness seems to invigorate Sir Cecil. The invalid turns nursemaid. He takes hold of my trembling wrist. His hands have a texture to them. A man of letters, I imagined my Spirit's touch would glide smooth across my wrist, but Father Time carves Sir Cecil's bent fingers with little troughs. Coarse grooves, filled with the sand of the river's edge.

"Your Majesty, I am honoured by your devotion. But your servant has reached a desperate age. It is more a relief than an ordeal to face my last breath. Death brings an end to all woes. With regret, I must request you release your Sir Spirit from his duty. It is time, Your Grace." Sir Cecil withdraws from me, sinking backward into his waiting pillows.

Your Monarch – shameless am I – cannot accept his leaving so soon. Still I tug at my councilor's sense of duty. I will him forward, even when misery greets his every breath. While a Queen pretends perpetual strength for her people, she wavers before her father.

"But my Earl of Leicester has already gone. And now my Lord Burghley goes from me too...Who will stand by my side? All my reign I have acted the gracious monarch. Though not compliant in all things, I listened to every suggestion. Where will I turn now?"

"You must look within, Your Grace, as you always have. You did not choose motherhood, yet you nurtured all England like a mighty lioness. You nurse your ailing Burghley with a compassion equaling any honest mother. I am honoured to have served you, for you repay me tenfold in your princely understanding. Be well, my Majesty..."

Sir Cecil shuts his eye to my relentless need and turns his head from my cringing want. He dismisses from his presence his demanding Queen. His rejection burns deep. Never before have I had to face his refusal.

Is none compelled to linger by his Monarch's side? Always this perpetual return to solitude. The cost a Monarch pays for a place on the throne of England.

The historical record will accuse me. Unnatural woman, it will say. Yet I will embrace my fate. Though a crown weighs heavy on my sinking shoulder, I do not regret my decision. My throne and its people. Always. If my adopted father bequeaths to me his son, Robert Cecil, I accept his gift. I will make of him my creature. Sir Spirit, your Queen will respect your wisdom. A lioness must endure.

***

15th September, 1598

"Your Majesty, I beg you, open the chamber door. There is news from Spain, and it is of the greatest importance."

The wretched gentleman, his fist balled, raps on my barred door until my poor head vibrates. My lower jaw throbs, pulsing with each blow. My teeth are a perpetual ache. The jabs of wrenching discomfort wend their way along my cheek to my hairline. I support my head between my trembling palms. I massage my temples, and pray the clattering will subside, and the interloper will leave my door. But he does not. His pounding enters my chest. My heart keeps time with the knocking on the door.

When I crave company, I find none. Yet, when I desire solitude in which to mourn, no solace is granted.

"What is the matter? God's Wounds. Stop that incessant noise." The rapping ceases. I lean against the door. The very cause of all my suffering. Bending my neck into its rough hewn boards, I massage my head on its hard surface. I speak through its thickness. "You have seized your Queen's attention. Who dies this time? Who do I hold dear to me in Spain? Tell me. What is the new loss?"

"Your Majesty…"

The breathless voice wishes to reply, but I interrupt. "…Surely no one must remain there, or anywhere. All my friends fly from me like swallows lifting their wings in the gathering winds. I do not need your announcement, Sir. Leave your Queen to her own company." I turn away from the chamber doorway and shuffle to my bed. The only place where peace resides.

"But Your Majesty, it is the King of Spain. Philip II is dead. England's brutal enemy no longer breathes. The news is all over the Court. Sores and pustules consumed his entire form. He was hardly recognizable in the end, for all the ooze that engulfed him. As though the Devil himself had come to claim his due…"

The disconnected voice, all proud revelation, penetrates the grooves of the massive door. It reaches for its Queen. It tempts me from my refuge with its boastful song of hope for England. True to my character, I succumb.

"That will be quite enough, Sir!" The man's insolence requires his Queen's reproof. I swing the door open. The fool does not forget all propriety. He drops to one knee, head bowed low. "To whom do you speak, Sir? Your Queen does not approve of your disparaging of the dead. You speak of a King. Your superior in all ways."

"Forgive me, Your Majesty. I aimed to please Your Grace. I did forget myself.."

"This is God's reply to his Queen?" I do not invite the gentleman to return to his feet. He remains head bowed, before me. The plume on his beret sweeps the stones beneath us with a gentility its master does not possess.

"Your Majesty? Forgive me. I do not comprehend your meaning..."

"God's Death. This is your Queen's compensation, in exchange for her insufferable loss? Our Sir Spirit is gone from us one month, and the vile Spanish King's death comes in the next? This contract does not please your Queen. I would happily squirm under the heel of the Spanish Catholic despot if it meant my Sir Spirit would return to me."

Despite my intention of remaining the indifferent monarch, at the mention of Sir Cecil, the hot tears of a woman escape my eye. My curses and tears both tumble down on his bared head. My decrepit age betrays me more each day.

"I beg your forgiveness, Your Grace. I only thought you would be pleased to hear of King Philip's death. I will leave you...." He motions as if to rise. How did this Cretan find his way to our Court? Sorely I miss my Sir Spirit.

"Stop Sir. Your Queen has not finished." Reaching downward, I press on the man's brow. I detain him. The feather of his hat waves in reply to the rustling of my skirts.

"Little pleases your Queen today, Sir." Does Death alone await my attention? Do all the living flee my presence? Even my enemies succumb.

The gentleman, huddled below, hesitates. I confuse the wretch. I detain him, and at the same time speak of my craving for his absence.

"Go from here, Sir. Do not place your wretched foot at this doorway any more until you have acquired a courtly manner. Do you understand your Queen?"

"I do, Your Majesty." Still he hesitates, awaiting his dismissal.

"You improve, Sir. Your Queen appreciates your obedience. Leave me."

He rises ever so slowly. And then imagining he has escaped his Queen's eye, he scurries from my chamber's hallway. Be gone, Sir.

***

There is an advantage to losing all one cherishes. Less remains to be cast away. My faithful companions join our Holy Father in their place of rest. Fewer to mourn, I assure myself.

Perhaps that unwanted time has arrived. Perhaps I should set aside my monstrous pride and request a hint of the pity I once disdained. The telling of all this weighs on me. This loathsome disclosure and its inevitable conclusion bends even the will of a lioness. Let me rest on my spent haunch. Let me hide among wind-blown reeds, and leave the bloody hunt to those who still relish the scent of the gathered herd.

Your lioness tires.

Winter III - A Queen's Golden Hour

Time crumbles things; everything grows old under the power of Time and is forgotten through the lapse of Time.

- Aristotle

27th January, 1603

We arrive at Richmond Palace. I call Richmond my warm winter box. The journey from Whitehall, plagued as it was by sleet and driving rain, troubled the horses and our coachmen. I remained within my carriage, protected from the elements and their raging. I held this little diary in my lap through our entire voyage. More and more I find myself escaping into the downy comfort of memory. The conditions outside? A mere diversion.

I mourn my country before I part from her. Like all of one's children, she escaped my hearth before I pushed her from it. Healthy offspring will venture forth. I parented well. I know I succeeded in nurturing my people to a newfound maturity. Soon this Queen's children will smile on their devoted mother's memory, even as they skip away, secure in the company of their European brothers and sisters.

And now, my mothering done, I stand with my arms wrapped round my waist, holding fast to rough elbows. I stare out my many paned window. Not at the endless stretches of manicured gardens. Nor at the marble figures resembling my favourite deities. I look closer. Peltering drops of rain beat against the beveled glass. Hours creep away. Still I linger, surveying the limitless grey. Has it been days or only hours since we arrived at Richmond? I do not know. Nor do I care. It no longer matters.

In company, I pretend an awareness of trivial details: contractual agreements, speeches, prayers, dates, times, signatures. Mundane events remain so crucial to the gentlemen of the Court. But here, I linger alone. I contemplate each drop of rain on my window – how each shimmers with its own unique brilliance. I struggle to find the particular distinctions now my eyesight wanes. And then I drift to where meaning rests.

I draw back from the glass, bringing into focus the portrait before me. The pane of the window, at first all bathed in one lurid splash, reveals each raindrop in its lovely originality. Like the faces of my countless subjects. When looked on from my balcony above, they join together. A roiling wave of abject want. Yet when I ride amongst my people, jostling through the ecstatic crowd, brushing the flesh of a waving arm, each expression offers me a new reason to carry on.

My gentlemen warn against it. They urge caution against the assassin's waiting blade. Their vigilance proves no match for a Queen's will. A mother's sacred duty to hover near her children eclipses prudent counsel. If it is only a cloudless day or a flock of swallows taking wing above London's soot-stained roofs, I will share something of their lives. A gasp of astonishment filling a girl's eye as her monarch passes. A young woman's chafed hand, fingering the ragged patch sewn to the waistline of her muslin dress. Decades of want weighing hard on an old man's curved back. To each, their ancient Queen offers a smile and a comprehending nod.

My eye retreats from the watery pane. The spattered window loosens its hypnotic draw. My throbbing jaw asserts itself. An ache erupts under my gum, and advances. The angry presence of it burns my cheek, forcing its way to my temple.

I place my index finger inside my lip and feel the give of the tender flesh. I push on the raging tooth. Perhaps a different sensation will lessen the throbbing. But when I remove the pressure, the agony reasserts itself. So I run my fingertip first along my bottom gum, then along the top. But none of my massaging detracts from the mutiny my mouth wages against me.

I will block one sort of pain by introducing another. I hasten to my jewel casket, lift the hinged lid and retrieve what remains of Robin. *His last letter.* My own handwriting announces it with a brutal scrawl across the width of the page. I brush the crisp parchment against my aching cheek. Its cool surface releases me, but only for the briefest moment. I tear open the seal.

How many times have I read and reread my Bonny Sweet Robin's assurances he would travel to the healing waters at Buxton? He would soon fare better and return to me with haste? One tear, unasked for, finds its way along my sore cheek. It drops, and spreads itself in a tiny pool on my precious page. The misery of Robin's abandonment overtakes me, offering a perverse pleasure. It provides a welcome release from the pounding at my temples, the insistence of my jaw.

I read once more: *...pardon your old servant to be thus bold in sending to know how my gracious lady doth, and what ease of her late pain she finds, being the chiefest thing in the world I do pray for, for her to have good health and long life...*

I smile at this quirk of fate. Robin writes of his devotion to Bess. While his person he squandered on my enemy, Lettice Knowles. Reading to the end of Robin's letter, my eye lands on his final salutation. The one I so often addressed to him, he returns to his Queen: "Semper Eadem". *Always the same.* Another broken promise from Robin. Nothing remains the same. All is different. He has gone from me.

Perhaps, in the perverse way God has of humbling even His highest placed daughter, I am taught a lesson. *Always the same.* Robin's oath rings true. His absence does remain constant. No hope of relenting.

How morose I become. Long ago, this barefaced self-pity would have earned a sharp slap on the cheek of she who whispered such nonsense in my ear. What calamities do I complain of? An aching joint? A tooth that whinges? A lover gone astray and renouncing me forever? It seems like only days ago I poked and teased at my own ladies for these trifling complaints.

Enough blustering and drawn-out sighs. Only one thing answers all this abysmal sadness. I fold away childish papers, return my trusted quill to its unhappy pot, and stop. Though I have not laid eyes on Thomas Tallis in a long while, his treasured music stays within me. His melodious notes wander about in my head, intruding at their leisure. I welcome them to my lips. I hum the melody, lifting my ample skirts. My chamber fills with imagined revelers, swaying to the song with their Queen. We dance.

***

16th February, 1603

"Is there no alternative, Sir?" I struggle with the plain band of gold on my ring finger. It ceases to exist as its own object, merging with a Queen's soul.

"I believe there is not, Your Grace." Robert Cecil, inspiring little of his father's confidence, backs away from the swollen mass that was once my slender hand. It is all the Pigmy can do not to turn his nose upward and sniff at his Queen's dilemma. I do not like him. But the elfin creature remains my only companion. And so we persist in our feigned esteem for one another. An affinity born of necessity alone.

"I have worn my coronation ring on my marriage finger since I was crowned." I hold my puffy fingers out to him, daring him to recoil. On this occasion, he stands his ground. "Not once have I had it off these forty-five long years. It serves as a symbol of your Queen's devotion to her throne. It deflected suitors from all corners of Europe with the fierceness of its metal."

The Pigmy looks on, uncomprehending. Why do I attempt it? I grip the band, attempt to turn it, urging it upward. The once beloved piece of jewelry bites harder into the tender flesh around it.

"Your Majesty, if any other recourse were to be had I would suggest it. Forgive me, but your flesh grows until the swelling almost hides your sacred ring. If we do not cut it off at once it will embed itself wholeheartedly into your finger and we will need a surgeon."

I search for anything that might endear me to Sir Spirit's son. His countenance pleases me well enough, but his bent form repels. All hunched and mangled, Robert Cecil stoops by my side. The creature cannot help that he was dropped on his head as a small babe and made deformed, but is it too much for a Queen to be surrounded by a more sightly example of humanity? Nor does the Pigmy's conscience equal my Lord Burghley's. I cannot say in what way he is lacking exactly. I sense it is more in what he does *not* say, than in what he does.

Yet this time something in his intense expression, his dedication to my comfort, the simplicity of his continued presence, tells me I might trust him. Well, I must trust him. And so I will. Affinity born of necessity. I stifle a sigh. I must smother my disappointment if I am to accept Sir Cecil's gift of his son with appropriate grace. I owe my Sir Spirit at least this much for his lifetime of paternal service.

"Your father contradicted me much the same as you do, Robert. My Sir Spirit, with his gentle prodding, scolded me now and again, though he did not order me about with quite the heavy hand you wield..." Old age mortifies. The mention of Sir Cecil's name leaves his son's eye dry, while mine spills over. How can one Cecil differ so much from another? What natural cause denies the son the father's enduring kindness?

"Very well. If it must be so, cut off the ring at once. Let it be quick, so parting with it does not turn your Queen into a sentimental half-wit." I let go of my obstinate resistance. I have learned, late though it may be, to choose with care my moments for revolt. I extend my hand, and give permission for their desecration of my throne.

"Robert, your Monarch bears witness to another piece of her beloved kingdom slipping from her grasp. Yet another parting for England's doting Queen."

The younger Cecil lifts his bowed head and with an admirable directness stares into my eye. I match his gaze. In that moment my pulse quickens a little. My Sir Spirit stands before me. Lord Burghley returns to his Queen's side. He nods his reassurance. Once again he offers his beloved son in his stead. I accept with gratitude.

Two of my ladies brace my aching hand, swollen and reddened, on the table. A smith drags his file to and fro across my wedding band - the golden ring with which I gave my oath to sit as England's Queen so long as I live.

He saws through the sturdy metal. The battered jewelry makes an onerous squeal, and an unpleasant odour emanates from where he works. All my intuition warns me against this moment.

Despite myself – what have I become? – I bawl like a heartbroken babe. My tears fall so plentifully, they drench my ruined hand. One of my ladies lets go, reaches for her silk handkerchief, and dries my tear-strewn cheek. The other presses her palm into my opposite hand. Protocol forbids she touch me like this but her compassion overrules.

What a sight we make. Ladies and gentlemen all gathered round their Queen. The smith, his file sharpened, sawing with every bit of strength he possesses so his ordeal might end sooner. The drops of perspiration on his face cause him to resemble his Majesty's weeping twin. His glistening temple gives the lie to his confident stroke. While his arm, all poised, scrapes at my ring, his brows knit themselves together. So terrified is the poor man of slipping and scraping his elderly Queen's papery skin.

I release my free hand and tap him lightly on the forearm. I wink at him with my tearful eye so another drop squeezes out and lands on his work. The poor tradesman will have some little reassurance from his Queen. I fear he is more in need of comforting than I am.

He works his way through the remaining thread of gold. Two golden half moons fall to the table. I lower my lids on downcast eyes and transport myself far from this chamber. To the shadows of a tower, where my mother once knelt down and laid her head for severing. When I conjure up my mother, I always try to envision her vibrant with life. She strides, determined, into the jeering crowd. Anticipating her awful fate, she thrusts her chin forward. Anne Boleyn smiles on them all. Her hair, dark as a raven's wing, compliments her unnatural pallor. She has never before appeared so lovely. When she lays her cheek on the block, I stop, ending my daydream. I refuse to allow my father his bloodlust.

I have throughout my reign, considered it advisable to refrain from mentioning my mother. I see her pretty face often in my mind's eye, but her beloved Boleyn name does not pass her daughter's lips. Who would want to hear of her? And so I choose to remember her in my own way. Preserving little glimpses here and there. Fragments of memories wrung from the banks of a three-year-old's tiny storehouse. I've held those memories close in an old woman's heart by covert means.

Often, of late, she returns to me while I sleep. Her spirit whispers to me of the abundance of fear lurking in men's troubled hearts. I do not divulge these visitations. Enough infamy already accompanies your Queen through her reign. I cannot afford any suggestions that my fragile mind wanders to outrageous locales. But I do have visions. And I receive my mother's haunting words with a willing heart.

She whispers to me of a Queen's short duration on her throne. She complains about a King's doubt. *I loved your father. But my love for him was insufficient. Only a son's birth, a son's love, might have spared me.*

Does my mother condemn our illustrious King Henry VIII? He who cut short the lives of those he claimed to cherish? In death, as in life, she forgives his tortured search for a male heir. *We cannot know how your father suffered. He believed with his soul that God punished him for marrying his brother's wife, our Catherine of Aragon. I endeavoured to help him cleanse his conscience. Instead, I became the reason for its taint.*

Then, without a morsel of irony in her prayer, her hands folded with reverence, my mother thanks our Lord that her Henry spared her Elizabeth. *Thank you God for your infinite mercy.* For that, she and I choose to remain ever grateful.

***

16th March, 1603

Your elderly Queen was unwise to travel from Whitehall to Richmond, exposing myself to the unforgiving elements. My throat joins my aching teeth in a painful duet. Barely can I swallow my cordial broth without the piercing reminder of its sting.

My ladies encourage me to sip my broth. First one and then another enters my Presence Chamber with fingers wrapped tightly around a new steaming bowl. I have no appetite. It hurts to speak of my displeasure at their intrusions, so my eyes take over. I raise my bent head from where I stare at my desktop and meet their inquiring looks with a hard refusal. I shake my sore head to and fro, and point to the chamber door where they may let themselves out.

This trusted diary remains within my reach, but it too I will neglect, in favour of floating free with my memories.

Still, I question the correctness of it. The writing of all my thoughts. Should my personal journey remain my own? Instead, I expose my memories, consigning them to a page where they will be trapped forever. Where strangers may visit them like caged beasts at a travelling carnival.

Do I want the world perusing my life at their leisure? Am I not a fool to consider offering myself up? But then, I already have.

For a moment I forget the wrenching claims of my jaw. My head burns hot with fever. I reach for a handkerchief and pat at the perspiration on my brow. Then I return to my beloved work.

My gentlemen insist their Queen submit herself to her physicians for bleeding. I refuse. The idiots offer tinctures of gold and other useless medicines. They insist on their concoctions for purging. These too, I refuse.

Have I not given enough of myself? In life I had little use for such treatments. Why on earth as Death greets me, should I accept their legitimacy?

They all insist I should take to my bed. I deny this request also. Though Death beckons to me, like all my suitors, I resist his outstretched hand. I do not fear him.

I have given all of myself to my people. And willingly so. It is only my death they await. I sense it in their impatient hovering. They shall have that too. But only when I have readied myself. This I have not yet done. Something remains.

I have my Ladies arrange an assortment of pillows on the floor next to my bed. Large, overstuffed horsehair cushions to lounge on. Daintier feather ones to prop my aching head on. Square and rectangular and round. Velvets and satins, woolens and silks. They crowd together so my chamber takes on the look of a splendid sultan's tent.

I stretch out on the downy pillows, raise my wasted arms above my head and imagine myself all veiled in gauzy mauve. A favoured wife, I bask in my sheik's harem.

Only my sheik enjoys the sacred privilege of removing the whispery veil. He approaches, and lies next to me, propped on one elbow. He releases the fabric, so it slips free from the bridge of my nose. He strokes my bare cheek with his smooth fingertips.

I cannot enjoy my simple daydream for any length of time. Always interruptions serve to steal a Queen's fancy. Robert Cecil drives my swarthy companion from my side.

So we embark, the younger Cecil and I, on our predictable journey. All round the world we chase one another. The son receives from his father a stick with which to prod his loving monarch. Throughout my youth, my Sir Spirit tortured me with his pleas that I marry and provide an heir for England. Now that old age claims me, the son takes hold of the pointy device. He harangues me about my choice of successor.

"Your Majesty, pardon my intrusion. We think it best you should rise from the floor and take to your bed with haste. Only in the warmth of your bedclothes will you find comfort." The Pigmy stands over me. He urges me to rise so I can fall back into my bed.

"Be gone, Robert. Your Queen will restore herself in her own way, just as she has governed. Only one thing is certain. Your intrusions do not assist in your Queen's healing." We discuss my improvement as though it remains a genuine likelihood. If only Sir Spirit were here to attend me. I might avoid such charades. How I long for Sir Cecil's honest companionship. Instead, his elfin son and I must persist in our contest of wills.

"Your Grace, if you will not be persuaded to rest... I beg for your patience Your Grace, but I must ask of you..."

"God's wounds, Pigmy. Out with it. Your Queen shall not live forever while her Secretary stutters. Speak your mind, Man." The throbbing in my mouth loosens my tongue. My impatience wins out.

"Though you do not choose to discuss it, I feel it my duty to inquire..."

"Robert...."

"Very well. Your Majesty, in the unlikely event your recovery does not take place, would your nephew, King James of Scotland, ascend the throne?" The Pigmy exhales. Having delivered his unwanted query – the same one he asks of me daily - he braces himself for my robust reply.

Does the younger Lord Cecil believe I forget he asks this question of me every day? He laces his trembling fingers behind his back, bringing to mind his father's old habit. His torso he rocks to and fro before me. He cannot help himself, the simpleton. He cannot pretend he does not await his next sovereign with an eagerness that can only be described as unseemly. Very well. He leaves me no choice but to bat him about the chamber a little while longer.

"Always the same concern, my young Cecil. Your Queen's reply remains the same also. I will not name an heir to my throne. When I leave this world, the people of England will decide on their monarch. The dead have no voice, Robert. Let our people decide. Now leave me."

With reluctance, the little man turns away. Bowing and scraping he finds his way backward through the chamber door. I exhale. Relief washes over me. And then, in the stillness of my chamber, my breath echoes with a rattle I detest. I attempt to inhale again and the clattering sound fills the room. I cough, attempting to dislodge the suffocating mucus from my throat. But a heaviness descends. It is as though my Bonny Sweet Robin himself lies down on my heart. Of course he does reside there. Always.

But this new burden feels different than that which I have carried since Robin left me. This load forces itself on my chest with a harder will. As though Robin's entire weight abides there. He presses on the bony plate between my small breasts, interfering with all my attempts to catch my breath. Bonny Sweet Robin searches for his Elizabeth.

***

22nd March, 1603

I lie prone on my bed, giving in to Robert Cecil's wishes at last. Though I will not say it, I find comfort here beneath the weighty bedclothes. The first day in my bed I rallied somewhat, requesting a little warm broth. I sipped at it from the hands of Lady Warwick herself. Today, when Nottingham, Egerton and the Pigmy Cecil hover by my bedside, staring on me as though my last breath represents their first, I give my disloyal gentlemen what they desire. I lie back on my pillows, close my eyes, and exhale an unearthly gurgle from deep within my chest.

They startle. Even Dr. Parry, my favoured chaplain, trembles at the outbursts my failing lungs utter. I cannot with my own eye, witness their anxious starts, for my lids refuse to lift. But I hear the gentlemen shudder to attention at the horrible sounds emanating from their Queen. In another time, in the past, I may have smirked at my little joke, or laughed outright at their cowering. But no longer will my disobedient lips obey the thoughts I harbour within. My teasing smile lurks somewhere inside, unseen.

The younger Cecil will have his dead monarch. And a new King also. My Scottish cousin will not nurture my people as their loving Queen did. But I cannot muster the caring any longer. It is beyond my power.

I see all and say nothing. This once was true. But no more. An elderly Queen sees little, and has much to say. And nothing to fear losing in the saying of it. I proved to my people my fitness as their Prince. I buried all that womanish sensibility that would make me unfit to rule a nation. All my love I poured into one cup. England was my one and only consideration. A truth, and yet an untruth.

Only months ago, or was it a year? It was November. The last Parliament your Queen attended. How my gentlemen railed at me about the unfairness of the monopolies. I responded with much speed to their concerns. I reviewed all of the unpopular measures. I revoked all of the unfair privilege. And in addition to my righting of the wrongs, I charmed them. I invited the entire Parliament to Whitehall, and within my Council Chamber spoke to them of things I had never spoken of before, or have since...

I do assure you there is no prince that loveth his subjects better, or whose love can outdo our love. There is no jewel, be it of ever so rich a price, which I set before this jewel – I mean your loves. For I do more esteem it than any treasure or riches we know how to prize. Your love and thanks I count invaluable, and though God hath raised me high, yet this I count the glory of my crown: that I have reigned with your loves... For above all earthly treasures I esteem my people's love, more than which I might care to admit...

It seems a whole lifetime has passed since I entertained my gentlemen, wooing them with a Prince's allure. Yet, only a few months have passed. The looks of pride I witnessed on bearded faces that day in November are now sighs of pity.

I am certain this sympathy lurks in their expressions now, though my eyes all clouded, can no longer see it. Thank God I cannot.

To be a king and wear a crown is a thing more glorious to them that see it than it is pleasant to them that bear it. For myself, I was never so much enticed with the glorious name of a king or royal authority of a queen as delighted that God hath made me His instrument to maintain His truth and glory, and to defend this kingdom from peril, dishonor, tyranny, and oppression…

That day in November, a respectful hush greeted my speech at Whitehall. So unlike this day. Today, my gentlemen whisper amongst themselves at the foot of my bed. Because my lids remain closed, they imagine so too do my ears. But I hear. Will they not, even at the very end, find a way to appreciate their Queen's keen sensibility?

While Lady Warwick and Lady Scrope perch by my bedside casting anxious glances between them, the gentlemen, Lords Nottingham, Egerton and Cecil, shuffle at the foot, whispering about matters of State. Will they not comprehend their Queen is beyond caring for it?

"Cecil, you must persuade Her Majesty to name a successor. The time draws near, and England's future depends sorely on it."

"I have made the attempt on every occasion. Her Majesty will not comply. I cannot suggest it without her lashing out at me." The Pigmy fears his Queen, and yet he whispers his insolence, thinking I cannot hear it. Then he peeks from the corner of his eye at his world-worn Majesty, as though I might rise from my restful bed and box him about the ears. A Queen's failing will can only accomplish so much, Pigmy.

"Little does Her Majesty rail now, Lord Robert."

Silence. They all desist, casting more pitying glances my way. They believe, in error, I will speak to them on this matter of my successor. I will not. I will not speak to them again on any matter.

"Her Majesty does not awaken. Our Queen has not uttered a word for many hours. How will we retrieve from her the name of her successor?" Both Egerton and Nottingham turn to Robert Cecil for guidance.

"There is no need. I have formed an idea as we huddle here together." I presaged my Pigmy and his silences. He contemplates much. And in his irksome quiet, he forms his wily plot.

"You play with treasonous thoughts, Sir. Be wise with your counsel." Always the most cautious, Nottingham remains truest to character.

Robert Cecil, the junior Cecil in more ways than one, demonstrates to his Queen how unlike his father he chooses to conduct himself. "I do not commit treason. I think only of England's well-being. Her Majesty will leave us soon, and without an heir or successor to the throne." Though I cannot lay my wasted eye on them, I imagine the other two leaning into Cecil, their hot breaths fanning his ambitious flame. Very well then. Let them to it. I am done.

"We will not claim our Queen spoke words she did not. This would expose us to the charge of treason." The other two rustle about. I do not see, but sense their anticipation. There is something in the greater nearness of their whispering voices to Robert Cecil's plotting tongue.

"...we explain that we suggested King James of Scotland for England's throne, and then..." They receive Cecil's careful plan with an agonizing mix of alarm and relief. Nottingham draws back and gasps. Egerton leans closer still.

"But Lord Cecil..."

"Allow me to finish...we will report that Her Majesty raises her arms above her head, using her fingers to shape a crown upon it, like this." I sense, rather than see Robert Cecil enact his little drama. "Then we say that Her Grace nods her assent, and drifts away in a comfortable slumber once more." I imagine Robert smiling. Satisfaction bathes his expression so an unnatural calm settles over their little clutch.

"But Her Majesty does no such thing." Nottingham again. Always the man to demand every detail. Details be damned. Go forward, Cecil. Find your new monarch. The realm requires your scheming in the absence of her loving Queen.

"We do not have a successor, Lord Nottingham. Do we let our Queen die without one? What chaos will England plunge into without a monarch named?"

Excellent, Cecil. Have at it. Your Queen approves at long last.

"Lord Cecil speaks correctly, if not absolutely honourably. England must have a King. If Her Majesty refuses to offer one, we will find him ourselves." Egerton has the final word. With more urgent whispers he convinces Cecil of the necessity of his plan, and closes down Nottingham's reservations all at once.

While they whisper, fearful I might hear their words of dissent and deposit them in the Tower for their troubles; I lie still, buried in layers of down-filled bedclothes. I wait. Not for my gentlemen, nor for their disheartening slurs. Their concerns fail to land with any force on their Queen's conscience. I have done my all. I am finished raising my beloved children. A Gypsy waits.

***

For the duration of an entire lifetime, I postponed an encounter with my second self. And as I declined him, I denied my own self. *A friend is a second self.* But a crown is both a beckoning world and a barred cell.

My masquerade produced a worthy monarch. And distorted the woman beneath the crown. A Goddess's robe inflated a Queen's authority. But the costume smothered Elizabeth inside it. While a Queen cared with tenderness for all of England, Elizabeth, the little girl-child cowered in a corner, friendless. Gratitude replaces the animosity I feel toward my gentlemen. In naming their Queen's replacement they unlock the cell. Finally, they release Elizabeth from her darkened corner.

As Robin greets me, my princely robes – made of my own fashioning – give way. Loosening their rigid hold, they release a Queen's mighty spirit. From behind a cracked-open mask, Elizabeth peers forth.

As I emerge from my fractured disguise, all my mothers gather round. My own Anne Boleyn reaches out, drawing me toward her breast. As I rest my cheek there, she whispers longed-for endearments her infant daughter heard for such a short time.

And then she guides her Elizabeth to her beloved stepmothers – Jane and Anne and my two adored Catherines, all standing next to one another. Straining forth with fluttering hands they offer their affection. All kindly embraces.

Elizabeth emerges from the centre of the group of women. Another elderly Queen, once overly familiar, now a stranger to my recall, awaits me. She stands before me, arms outstretched. She embraces me. Only one article divides our resilient hearts. A string of clattering pearls, wound round the other's neck and bosom. They form a barrier of sorts. A knowing smile, and the old Queen turns away from me at last.

Nottingham, Egerton and Cecil, my Ladies too, with all their mortal concerns, gaze on me and perceive a dying Queen. Why with my death should anything change? In life they acknowledged a fraction of their monarch. A woman, weakened by fits of uncertainty. The wavering daughter of a great king. *God help England, and send it a King.* My Sir Spirit, you shall have your wish.

***

Robin stretches his length next to me. We ease our silken robes off, revealing bared shoulders. All pure in their untouched quality. As needed coverings fall away, we stare on each other, hungry in our careful scrutiny. Robin does not appear like the last time I saw him. All ruddy-faced, and heavy in his gait. Now he is the beautiful youth I watched from my tiny window when I wandered the yards of the Tower all those decades ago. He moves toward me, empty of those tensions we once harboured. Mild in his approach. I open my arms to him so he will know I welcome his embrace.

My sweet Robin and I dance. Together, we perform an intricate succession of steps. A fine galliard. We move together with an uncertainty. As untried partners do when meeting another's cadence for the very first time.

***

There will never queen sit in my seat with more zeal to my country, care to my subjects, and that will sooner with willingness venture her life for your good and safety, than myself. For it is not my desire to live nor reign longer than my life and reign shall be for your good. And though you have had and may have many princes more mighty and wise sitting in this seat, yet you never had or shall have any that will be more careful and loving...

Now bring them all to kiss my hand...

Acknowledgements

Many thanks to all my generous friends and family who spent many hours reading and re-reading various drafts of *A Second Self*. I am so grateful for your time. Special thanks and much love to my family who patiently wait behind the door, while their partner, their mother writes. Your love and patience mean everything.

The following books were used in my research: for Tudor history: Trea Martyn's *Elizabeth in the Garden*; Garrett Mattingly's *Catherine of Aragon*; Paul Johnson's *Elizabeth I: A Biography*; Susan Ronald's *The Pirate Queen*; Alison Weir's *The Life of Elizabeth*. Some of Elizabeth I's own words (italicized in my text) were taken from Leah S. Marcus, Janel Mueller and Mary Beth Rose's (Eds.) *Elizabeth I: Collected Works*.

All of the characters in my novel lived. Their particular feelings, motivations and conversations have been fictionalized in an effort to understand and appreciate Elizabeth I's truly remarkable life.

About the Author

This is Lori Callan's first book of fiction. Her short fiction has appeared in *The Dalhousie Review*. Her poetry has appeared in *Queen's Quarterly* and *Pan del Muerto,* U.of T. Graduate English Assoc. In addition to creative writing, Lori Callan has written for *Maclean's Magazine*. She has written a number of book reviews and conducted interviews for *Surface and Symbol*, The Scarborough Arts Council publication. In addition to English literature, Lori Callan studied psychology at the University of Toronto and creative writing at the Toronto Writing Workshop with Libby Scheier and Cary Fagan. She currently lives with her family in Toronto.

Printed in Great Britain
by Amazon